SHADOW HUNTER

OTHER BOOKS AND AUDIO BOOKS
BY GUY M. GALLI:

Lifted Up

SHADOW HUNTER

A NOVEL

GUY M. GALLI
JEFFREY R. GALLI

Covenant Communications, Inc.

Cover images: Nuclear Bomb Test, Nevada, August 18, 1957 © Masterfile. Business Travel by JSmith©
iStockphoto.com

Cover design copyrighted 2009 by Covenant Communications, Inc.

Published by Covenant Communications, Inc.
American Fork, Utah

Printed in Canada
First Printing: April 2009

16 15 14 13 12 11 10 09   10 9 8 7 6 5 4 3 2 1

ISBN-10 1-59811-770-X
ISBN-13 978-1-59811-770-7

He who fights with monsters should be careful lest he thereby become a monster. And if thou gaze into an abyss, the abyss will also gaze into thee.
—Friedrich Nietzsche, *Beyond Good and Evil*

ONE

SAM RYKER HAD THE SHOT. His trigger finger tightened almost automatically in anticipation of the kill, but he restrained himself. He needed the man in his crosshairs alive, at least for now. The target's name was Yousef Al-Mina, and he was wanted for the death of twenty-six tourists killed in a roadside bombing in the Sinai a month earlier. Eleven had been American, hence Ryker's interest and personal attention to bring this criminal and coward to justice.

Ryker had taken his position atop a small, two-star hotel that catered to the more undesirable population that frequented the run-down corner of Cairo. Lying flat on the roof, a duffel bag under his chest for support, he looked down the barrel and telescopic sight of his U.S. Marine Corps M40 sniper rifle. Ryker was practically invisible, hidden behind the glare of the hotel neon sign, and it was there, clad from head to toe in matte black, that Ryker first spotted Al-Mina step from the flashing and deafening nightclub across the street.

"Target acquired," Ryker said over the police radio.

A second later he was answered. "Confirmed. Teams Two and Three move to follow." The voice on the radio belonged to Hasan al-Mohammed, chief inspector of Egypt's National Police, and one of Ryker's most trusted associates and friends. They had worked together on many assignments over the years, though most of them outside the official liaison channels put in place by their respective governments. Egypt and the United States were on friendly terms—allies, some would say—but each insisted on maintaining some secrets and working alone to further their national security. Ryker and Hasan, however, understood that more could be accomplished working together than covering the same ground twice, giving their targets double the chances to elude capture and swift justice. They had each been warned and reprimanded by their superiors for their dangerous and rogue behavior, but in the world of international counterterrorism, the ends often justified the means.

"Team Three?" Hasan's calm but authoritative voice broke the brief silence. "Status?"

The radio crackled with static. "In position."

"Team Two?"

"Ready."

"Sam," Hasan said, switching to English, "you still on?" Hasan used English, not for Ryker's benefit—Ryker spoke Arabic better than most natives—but to keep their personal exchange and comments from his men.

Ryker moved his earpiece mic down his face. "Are you kidding? Wouldn't miss this for the world."

"You did it again, my friend," Hasan said. "Are you certain I cannot persuade you to share your source for Al-Mina's whereabouts? I'm sure I could arrange a sizeable retainer."

Ryker smiled beneath his dark ski mask. Hasan was nothing if not persistent. "Put the two of you in touch with each and miss all this? Not a chance."

Hasan chuckled. "Then if you will not transmit my government's generous offer, perhaps you will at least convey my thanks and gratitude."

Ryker had no doubt that Hasan had a good idea what his source was, but he knew better than to communicate it over the air. Ryker's undeviating moral compass had earned him the respect of everyone he had ever worked with, allowing him to forge strong and lasting friendships. One such friendship with an Israeli Mossad agent had evolved into a brotherhood of sorts. It was strange, Ryker had thought many times over the years, that a Christian, a Muslim, and a Jew could work so well together despite their government's continually strained relationships. It was a funny thing, the politics of man.

"Trust me; he was all too happy to help."

"Perhaps when we finally admit that we are no longer young men and decide to leave this work in the hands of men half our age, you could arrange a chance for me to thank him in person."

"He would like that very much."

The leader of Team Two cut in. "Target on the move."

Ryker immediately refocused his attention on the street below. Flanked by half a dozen bodyguards, Al-Mina stepped out from beneath the night-club's awning and toward the street, drunk and laughing, women of the night on each arm. From the line of cars parked along the street, a four-door black Mercedes-Benz pulled out and stopped at the curb in front of him.

Even at this late hour, other club patrons arrived and departed in symbols of Western wealth and affluence, no one paying particular attention to the killer who stood among them.

"Team Three?"

"We see him."

Ryker looked further up the street, noting that Hasan's principal surveillance team sat ready, disguised in their dull, nondescript French Citroën.

"Team Two?"

Out of sight, Ryker knew they were there to pick up the secondary tail. "Ready," they answered.

The sound of a loud engine grinding its gears commanded Ryker's attention, and he watched as a large delivery truck jerked and sputtered as it rounded the corner and headed his way. A twinge of panic seeped into his stomach. It was an irrational fear, losing sight of a target moments before apprehension, but there were so many elements in the field that he couldn't control. A good agent could only do his best, prepare for the worst, and roll with whatever came his way. Controlling the flow of traffic was one of those elements.

"Hasan," Ryker said. "Blackout approaching. Confirm target."

"Team Two?"

"Confirmed."

"Are you sure?" Ryker interrupted. "Don't lose sight of him."

"Don't worry," a member of Team Two replied. "He's not going anywhere."

"Famous last words," Ryker said under his breath.

"There is nothing to fear," Hasan assured him. "Once he is clear of civilians, we will have him."

The truck passed in front of Ryker's line of sight, and immediately Team Two reported in.

"Target on the move." Up the street the French Citroën pulled out into traffic. "We're on him."

Al-Mina's entire entourage was gone, women and all, as the Mercedes pulled away.

"Team Three?"

Further up the street the reply came. "We see him."

"Keep it tight," Hasan instructed, "but don't spook him until he's in the open. No mistakes, men. We need him alive."

"Relax," came the confident voice of Team Two's leader. "You are almost as bad as the American."

"That's enough!" Hasan barked over the radio. "Move to frequency beta. Say again, beta."

Both teams confirmed the radio frequency change and then the line went dead.

"Sam?" Hasan asked once they were gone.

"Still here."

"I apologize for my men. For some of them, national pride sometimes overshadows their better judgment."

"No worries. Besides, you *were* starting to sound like me."

Both men chuckled but quickly resorted to an uncomfortable silence.

"I wish you could come with us," Hasan finally said.

Ryker didn't answer right away. "Like the old days."

"I could make room in the backseat. What's one more?"

Ryker shook his head. "I think we've broken enough rules for one night."

Hasan chuckled softly again. "Always the voice of reason."

"You will get him, won't you?"

"If the Koran permitted it, I would swear to you I would."

"I know you will. Now, go. You have a terrorist to catch."

"I will call you the minute we have him."

"Thank you, my friend. Out," Ryker said.

Ryker watched as a second car, this time a four-door BMW, pulled into the street. Ryker raised his hand in acknowledgment as Hasan drove past and in pursuit. An anxious regret washed over him. If his own CIA had been half as quick to act as the Egyptian National Police, it would be him following Al-Mina and Hasan relegated to the role of consultant.

Ryker sighed and started cleaning up his eagle's nest, stripping his sniper rifle and packing away his tripod. Even before the attack in the Sinai, Ryker had followed the bloody career of Yousef Al-Mina. But until the attack, he and his "Will of God" had been a pathetic footnote in the volumes of international terrorism. Born in Syria, Al-Mina had joined the Lebanese-based Hezbollah, or Party of God, but didn't distinguish himself in any way. After a few years of mediocre service, he quit Hezbollah and joined the Islamic Resistance Movement, or Hamas, and served a few years fighting the Palestinian fight, again just blending in with the rank and file, until he denounced all other militant Islamic groups and founded the Will of God. A two-bit, hack organization, the Will of God was slow to make any real noise in the world of Islamic terrorism but was quick to claim responsibility for acts the world over, whether they had committed them or not, making eloquent and angry speeches for the press to clip on the evening news.

Until two weeks ago. Intelligence confirmed that Al-Mina had planned and executed the tour bus bombing, which just didn't fit his profile and modus operandi. Which naturally started Ryker thinking that perhaps—

A loud and unruly laugh from the street below sent a shock of alarm through his entire system. Ryker dropped to his stomach again and crawled to the edge of the rooftop. He looked just in time to see Al-Mina step into the backseat of another black Mercedes, calling for a giggling woman who was stumbling out of the club entrance.

Hasan is following the wrong car!

Ryker fumbled with the radio, trying to reach Hasan, but all he got was the static of dead air. He ripped the earpiece out and grabbed the cell phone on his belt, dialing Hasan's office number as he ran for the building's back fire escape. Halfway down, the dispatch operator answered his call. He knew it would be useless trying to explain who he was and why he needed to reach the chief inspector, so he counted on urgency and brevity to carry the message quickly to Hasan's attention.

"This is an urgent message for Hasan. He is following the wrong car! Repeat, he is following the wrong car. Target made the switch. Have him call me at . . ." Ryker left his local cell number before hanging up. If the dispatch operator followed protocol, she would reach Hasan via the radio and play back Ryker's message.

Ryker rounded the hotel just as the Mercedes pulled away from the curb.

His own car was parked almost three blocks away. There wasn't time to get it. Ryker looked up and down the street. Parked five or six cars up from the club was a taxi. Sprinting across the street, Ryker watched as the taxi began to pull away. Unwilling to let it go, he lunged in front of the car and slammed his hands on the hood. The taxi stopped suddenly, the driver's face wide with fear. Ryker quickly slipped in the back door.

"Follow that car!" he ordered, pointing to Al-Mina's Mercedes.

Ryker reached into his jacket and removed his Glock nine-millimeter semiautomatic and checked the clip. Full. Fifteen rounds. But it was a false sense of security. This was not American soil; he had no authority to carry— let alone fire—a weapon. Diplomatic immunity only went so far, and Egypt had strong and harsh gun laws. Any shot would have to be seriously considered, and every shot would have to count.

He holstered his gun, leaned forward, and tapped the driver on the shoulder.

"Follow the Mercedes at all costs," Ryker said in flawless Arabic. "I am working with the National Police. You will be greatly rewarded for your help tonight."

The driver looked back at Ryker and sized him up.

"You are American?" he asked in broken English.

"Just drive," Ryker said, this time with an edge of authority in his voice.

The driver held Ryker's stare for a beat and then turned his attention back to the road. He stayed about four car lengths behind the Mercedes, matching its speed and even running a stoplight to keep up with it. They were headed northeast, out of the city, toward one of two airports servicing Cairo. He figured he had, at most, fifteen minutes to stop him. Without the help of Hasan or his men it was going to be difficult. Even if he could call in CIA reinforcements, it would take longer than that to cut through the red tape and explain why he was working with the Egyptian National Police without the proper authorization.

Sam Ryker was on his own.

Without any warning, Al-Mina approached the next intersection, drove halfway into it, and then made a hard left. Ryker's heart began to race. They had been spotted! Ryker reached up and touched the taxi driver's shoulder and gestured to stay with them. The driver was the big unknown in this whole impromptu operation. The thought had crossed his mind back at the club to eject the taxi driver and just take his car to follow Al-Mina, but he never expected to do anything but follow him and let Hasan apprehend him.

The taxi driver reached the intersection and made a hard right.

"Hey!" Ryker shouted. "What . . . ?"

The taxi pulled to the side of the street and came to a sudden stop, throwing Ryker into the back of the front seats. When Ryker bounced back, he found himself looking down the barrel of snubbed-nose Smith & Wesson. The driver was shaking and had a wild, nervous look in his eyes.

How could he have been so careless! He should have seen it, but he had underestimated the enemy. The taxi—pulling away at the same time as Al-Mina. The cab driver was a watchman, falling in behind to watch for any sign of a tail, and Ryker had just burst in and handed them the whole oper-ation. *Sloppy,* he thought to himself. *Just plain sloppy.*

"Get out!" the driver blurted. He waved the gun again. "Get out!"

The taxi's back door opened, and two hands reached in and jerked Ryker out of the cab and onto the ground. Rolling with the momentum of his assailant, he got to his feet and quickly assessed his situation, dire as it was. His back to a wall, he stood facing three large men, each armed with a club of one kind or another. As intimidating as they each tried to be, smiling with anticipation of the attack and gently thumping their weapons in their hands, Ryker knew that none of them were professional or even experienced fighters. These were what he called "heavies"—enforcers, bullies, posing as bodyguards to scare and intimidate. Under the right set of circumstances, and with a frightened victim, they could be deadly, but their actions, for the most part, were driven by a need to *show* strength instead of actually *use* it. True to form, the men circled around, forcing Ryker to move from the wall and back up against the cab, cursing him and the entire Western world as they did.

Ryker didn't have time for this. Al-Mina was getting away, and every second he spent there, waiting for Al-Mina's lackeys to make their move, was just going to make his apprehension that much harder. It was time to take control of the situation.

Ryker faked a lunge to his right, drawing one the heavies' attack. The assailant swung his club—a weathered baseball bat—striking the side of the cab. But instead of pulling back as an experienced street fighter would have done, he let it remain pressed against the dent he had made in the car door. The show of force was enough for Ryker to grab the wooden bat, pushing and pulling quickly to dislodge it from his attacker's grip. Stunned at the sudden loss of his symbol of power, Ryker pulled back and delivered a heel kick into his abdomen. Ryker winced at the pain associated with executing a kick like that without stretching first but dismissed it and took up a ready fighting stance.

It had been years since he had faced real attackers, and he was a little surprised to watch as his body took over, instinctively moving from attacker to attacker, quickly and efficiently, blocking and striking with enough force to disable the gang of heavies, taking each of them in turn to the ground.

Ryker turned back to the cab driver in time to see him bring the gun to bear, shaking, and pull the trigger. The shot went wide, missing him and hitting the far wall behind him. Not wanting to give him the time to steady his shot and fire again, Ryker shoved the wooden Louisville Slugger in the passenger-side window, connecting with the driver's chin. The driver dropped the gun as his hands reached for his broken jaw. Ryker jumped and slid across the hood of the car, threw open the driver's door, and pulled him to the ground. The driver did little but plead for his life in the name of Allah as he fell to the ground, spitting out teeth and wailing in dramatic pain.

"Maybe you should consider a new line of work," Ryker said to the driver, stepping over him and behind the wheel, flooring the accelerator. The cab fishtailed on the sandy road, turning around and speeding through the intersection in the direction he had last seen Al-Mina's BMW. He glanced at his watch. Nearly three minutes had passed. It would take a miracle to pick up the trail and stop him now.

Ryker settled into the calm he experienced as the hunter. Well, then, he thought, he'd just have to *make* the miracle.

Ryker quickly laid out the grid of Cairo in his mind, only half aware of the blur of city streets racing past him as he sped to make up for lost time. Al-Mina was supposed to have already left the country, no doubt headed for Syria until the next attack. If it were not for Ryker's Israeli contact and his willingness to share Al-Mina's change in plans, they would have missed the chance to apprehend him before he disappeared. But now, due to a colossal error of judgment, Ryker was going to miss that opportunity again. But if Al-Mina's extended stay in Cairo for one more night of pleasure and sin was just a delay in his overall escape plans, then he would still need a quick way out of the country. Cairo International Airport offered too much exposure—his name and face were still making the evening news. Which left a smaller airport with a private jet.

Ryker mentally worked his way through the city and then found it.

Almaza.

Situated just south of Cairo International, Almaza airfield serviced many of the smaller charter aircraft that swept the world's tourists to the many cities of antiquity that lined the Nile. Where Cairo International brought them in from afar, Almaza moved them around while they were there.

Al-Mina's hard left back at the intersection must have been a diversion. Ryker stomped on the brakes and took the next right, backtracking until he hit Elthawra Street and a straight shot to Almaza.

As he made the last turn in the road, he caught a set of taillights turning into one of the many private entrances to the airfield.

I have him!

Ryker floored the accelerator, pushing the taxi cab to new speeds.

As he drove along the south side of Almaza, Ryker took notice of the many private entrances to the airfield. Each were secured with fences or gates, and running the length of the road was a roll of razor wire to deter any unauthorized, over-the-top access. He tried to push the cab even faster, but greater speed was just not possible. As he approached the entrance he had seen Al-Mina's BMW use, Ryker saw a thick metal gate closing. He didn't have much time, and his options were limited. In a split second, Ryker reasoned that his best option was the direct approach, using the car's speed and momentum to ram through the barrier. *Besides,* he thought with a cynical smile, *it always works in the movies.*

Ryker kept the accelerator pressed as far as possible and braced for impact. With a scream of crashing and twisting metal, the taxi sailed through the gate with seemingly little effort, tearing the doors from their hinges and throwing them to either side and up and over the roof of the car.

Ryker's triumphant yell, however, caught in his throat as he spotted the line of jagged metal claws protruding from the ground just inside the airfield entrance. A fraction of a second later, the tire shredder caught hold of the cab and ripped the rubber from the rims, sending the car skidding across the asphalt. The thought only briefly lit on his mind that the remote for the gate must have also lowered the tire shredder as the exposed wheel rims protested and gave up their forward momentum.

Two hundred meters ahead of him, Al-Mina's car slowed and stopped next to a twin-engine, twelve-passenger Learjet, ready for takeoff. Knowing the cab's obvious limitations, and not seeing any other options before him, Ryker threw open the car door and started off after them on foot, removing his Glock and chambering a round. It was bad enough to discharge his weapon in the city, but to start shooting on airport property spelled almost certain arrest, detainment, and deportation if he was lucky. But Al-Mina was not going to get away—not on his watch.

About fifty meters into his sprint, the BMW's driver spotted him, yelling into the car for Al-Mina to hurry and then producing a handgun and opening fire on him. Ryker could tell that the driver was a chauffer first and bodyguard second as his shots went wide.

Ryker's, however, did not.

Never one to take a life unless it was absolutely necessary, Ryker aimed for and hit the man's shoulder, throwing him backward over the hood of the car. The woman Al-Mina had picked up outside the nightclub dove out of the car, falling to the ground before standing up, off balance in her studded high heels, screaming and running away from the exchange of gunfire.

Another man emerged from the car, drawing his gun and leaning on the roof of the car to steady his aim. By his calm and deliberate movements, this bodyguard proved to be the first professional he had encountered that night. Ryker had just enough time to dive behind a luggage taxi as three slugs with his name on them whistled by his head and became embedded in the metal trailers behind him.

Ryker could hear the jet engines begin to whine to life. He peeked around the corner. True to his training, Al-Mina's genuine bodyguard had refused to move, waiting for a clear shot to take Ryker out. Al-Mina hadn't yet left the safety of the BMW, but Ryker knew that wouldn't last for long. The sooner he got on board, the sooner he would be in the air and free. It was now or never. For both of them.

But the solution to Ryker's problem wasn't just a few steps away, as it was for Al-Mina. He was pinned down with no backup and no bigger plan to implement. He checked his gun. A full clip, for what it was worth.

Ryker checked his situation. He was still over a hundred meters away, with nothing between him and Al-Mina but the empty tarmac and the many floodlights that dispelled the cover of night—CIA training at Langley couldn't have come up with a more difficult field agent testing scenario. He had to come up with something. And fast.

Ryker stole another glance but pulled back almost automatically as another bullet sailed dangerously close to his head. In that brief moment, however, he did see that the jet's stairs had been lowered to the ground. He had to act! Now!

Ryker laid his own cover fire, squeezing off about a round each second. He sprinted toward the car and jet, zigzagging to keep out of the brightest lights. After he had expelled ten rounds, Ryker stopped shooting and running, took a deep breath, and waited. As he had expected, Al-Mina's man had taken cover behind the car, waiting out Ryker's volley and the chance to finish off the job. As soon as the shots ceased, the bodyguard popped up to return fire, only to be met with Ryker's dead-on aim. The bullet glanced off the bodyguard's weapon and traveled into his arm. He dropped his gun and screamed in pain.

Keeping his Glock at the ready, Ryker ran cautiously the rest of the way, looking for any sign of movement behind the tinted glass. There wasn't any, and that worried him. He had been careful not to shoot the car and risk hitting Al-Mina, so where was he? Ryker made his way around the back of the car, keeping himself low and out of view of the back window. Ryker knew that it wouldn't fit Al-Mina's profile for him to attack an armed lawman, but then again, the attack in the Sinai didn't fit his profile either.

The back passenger door was ajar. Ryker thrust his gun inside.

"Don't move!" he yelled in Arabic. But there was no one there to obey his command.

The pitch of the jet engine whine changed as the plane behind him began to move. Ryker turned around to see the jet's retractable stairway folding up as it turned away.

Al-Mina was already on the plane!

A shot rang out from the jet's closing door as it continued to turn away from him, but Ryker didn't even flinch. It wasn't meant to hit him, and at that angle it was all but impossible. No, Al-Mina was just giving Ryker something to remember him by as he made his escape, a little memento to ring in his ears and haunt him long after he was gone.

But Ryker wasn't about to let that happen. He had run out of patience with this chase and decided to end it before things got out of hand. Standing and leaning over the roof of the car, Ryker took careful aim and shot out the plane's front tire. The nose of the plane dropped sharply a few inches as the pressurized gas escaped in a small explosion of air. The pilot, however, panicking and thinking somehow that he could still get his aircraft in the air, throttled the engine higher. Without the smooth front tire to carry the plane forward, the small metal wheel hub caught on the asphalt, collapsing the front landing gear, bringing the front of the plane smashing to the ground.

The engine whine died down, and Ryker sprinted after the downed plane. Afraid that Al-Mina might feel trapped enough to take drastic measures, Ryker knew he had to get inside and secure the plane as quickly as possible. As he neared it, he could see that the door had not yet completely shut and sealed itself. Wedging his fingers in the small gap, he braced himself with one foot on the fuselage and pulled with what little strength he had left. The door refused to move much at first, but then the hydraulic system gave way and the door folded open enough for Ryker to squeeze his way inside.

"Police!" Ryker yelled in Arabic, not so much for Al-Mina's benefit but for the pilot. Quick movement from the cockpit caught his eye, and he trained his weapon on the cowering pilot. He had dropped to his knees, hands interlocked behind his head, clearly having been through this routine before. Not wanting to turn his back on him, Ryker motioned with his Glock toward the door.

"Get out!" he ordered, and the pilot was only too willing to comply.

Ryker turned his full attention to the cabin. There were three rows of seats—six seats on each side of the aisle, all of them empty. Broken glass littered the floor near Ryker, a wide assortment of alcohol having been jolted to the floor from the mini-bar at the front of the plane during its sudden stop. At the rear of the cabin was the lavatory, but there was no trace of Al-Mina.

"Yousef," Ryker called out in flawless Arabic, "there is nowhere else for you to run." He listened for the sounds of his elusive prey, but only silence prevailed. In that silence, though, Ryker heard the first signs of relief approaching with sirens wailing in the distance. He only hoped it was Hasan and his men, otherwise he'd have a great deal of explaining to do.

"Do you hear that? It will be better for you if you are already in custody by the time they get here. The police will only need the smallest excuse to skip the trial and carry out your execution. Let me bring you in safely."

No response.

"Don't do this, Al-Mina," Ryker said, creeping his way down the aisle. "This is not like you. You don't—"

A sudden sound from the lavatory gave Ryker all the direction he needed as he leapt to his feet, lunged for the door, and yanked it open hard enough to tear it off its top hinge. Al-Mina's back was pressed up against the lavatory wall, his arms extended, his gun aimed and ready to fire. Without time to think about his next move, Ryker instinctively ducked and shot his left hand up, deflecting the gun the moment Al-Mina pulled the trigger. Knowing from years of training that the quickest way to control an opponent's weapon was to control the opponent, Ryker put his weight behind his right fist and connected squarely with the man's midsection. Al-Mina dropped to the floor the same time the gun did, and almost before it had started, the fight was over.

Ryker dragged the beaten terrorist out of the bathroom and pushed him toward the front of the plane. Al-Mina stumbled to the ground, coughing and wheezing, trying to get his breath back. Outside, red-and-yellow lights flashed and cut through what was left of the darkness as the Egyptian cavalry arrived. Ryker twisted his arm and applied pointed pressure to the web of flesh between his thumb and finger. Al-Mina winced in pain.

"Now we're going to walk out of here with no problems," Ryker said with more than a hint of threat in his tone. "Don't give them any excuse to open fire, and you just might live to see another sunrise." He applied more pressure for emphasis. "Are we clear?"

Yousef Al-Mina, self-appointed head of the Will of God, and coward down to his core, just nodded helplessly and cursed under his breath.

"Let's go."

Ryker grabbed the back of Al-Mina's shirt and pushed him through the open door. In an unexpected display of courage, Al-Mina reached around and grabbed Ryker's arm, using the momentum to pull Ryker off balance. They tumbled out of the plane together. Ryker released his grip for only a second, but it was enough for Al-Mina to break free and make a run for it. Ryker scrambled to get to his feet, but a heavy boot to his back pushed him back down to the pavement.

Al-Mina didn't get more than three steps away before he was assaulted by two National Police officers and roughly and unceremoniously thrown to the ground. Both men were surrounded by ten men, guns drawn and aimed. Three more officers approached them, guns trained and unflinching. Ryker looked up but didn't recognize any of the faces as belonging to Hasan's men.

"My name is Sam Ryker," he said. "I am an American citizen working with Chief Inspector Hasan al-Mohammed of the National Police. If you will—"

"Arrest that man!" a voice called out from beyond the perimeter of the police car headlights. Ryker looked up but couldn't see past the glare. Then a figure stepped into view. "Help him up and bring him to me."

Ryker smiled. He recognized the voice now. He was helped to his feet by Hasan's lieutenant. "What took you so long?"

"It would seem our dispatch security protocols may be in need of revision to better handle . . . certain emergencies." Hasan smiled. "Hey, I tried calling you. Twice. But you didn't pick up."

Ryker pulled the cell phone out of his pocket. The cover was cracked and the LED display dark. He tapped it a few times then shrugged. "They don't build them like they used to."

Hasan nudged his arm. "You or the phone?"

Ryker stretched his arms and neck, feeling the pain of pushing his arguably aging body to young man limits. Both friends laughed, though Ryker's was underscored with stiffness and soreness coursing through his body. "Both, it would seem."

TWO

SAM RYKER PAUSED OUTSIDE HIS office door at the U.S. embassy in Cairo and took a deep breath. His ribs still hurt from the night before. He checked his watch. Nearly 10 AM. Coming in late and leaving early, he thought. Unusual behavior, to be sure, but it wasn't every day that he took two weeks off to spend some time with Susan and the girls.

In a rare display of self-reflection, Ryker took a moment and looked up and down the embassy hallway, taking particular notice of where he stood. *Where he stood.* Lao Tzu once said that the journey of the thousand leagues begins from where one stands, and not with the first step, as the saying was generally thought to go. A four-inch-thick, steel-reinforced door that bore no signage separated his kingdom from the camera trained on the second floor corridor. Admittance was via assigned security codes punched into an alpha-numeric keypad recessed in the metal jamb. This maze of cubicles and windowless rooms beyond it constituted the Central Intelligence Agency station in Cairo, and Ryker was its head.

He wondered if Lao Tzu's insight applied to the end of the journey, too. But, he thought, wasn't one journey's ending just the beginning of another?

Ryker shook his head as if to clear his mind, not quite sure where this philosophical nonsense had come from. He put forth his hand, entered the day's entry code, and pushed on through. He was greeted by a hushed office staff, not by the buzz of excitement usually generated by working for the world's premier intelligence gathering organization in the hotbed of Middle Eastern relations. All eyes were on him, somber and serious. Ryker couldn't imagine the news he had missed that had caused them to react with such gravity. Just as he was about to ask what was wrong, a young agent standing along the far wall reached beneath his desk, produced a weathered CD player, and pushed play. Immediately the orchestral sounds of John Barry performing the theme to James Bond filled the office. Smiles and laughter broke out, and a few people applauded.

"What the . . ." Ryker started to ask, pleased that it wasn't bad news but embarrassed by all the attention. He had only submitted his report four hours earlier, but it would seem that news, good news in this case, traveled fast. He would be lucky to still have a job once it was reviewed by his section chief in Rome, and he had planned to keep the whole fiasco under wraps until then. What he wanted and what his staff wanted, however, appeared to be two different things.

Ryker held up his hands in mock surrender and looked around. "I don't know what you're talking about," he protested, trying to keep a smile from showing. "And turn that music off—this is not MI6."

The senior logistics agent, a young man by the name of Herschi, reached over to press stop. "Anything you say, Mum." More laughter from the staff.

"I don't know what you all heard," Ryker said, quieting the room, "but officially the Egyptian National Police were the apprehending agency. In fact, I had very little to do with it. I was a consultant, that's all." Ryker was sticking to his official story, but he knew it was futile, and he gave in to the accolades and pats on the back. A moment later, Herschi tapped a small shot glass and held it up.

Ryker looked up with even more embarrassment across his face than he'd had when he walked in. "No . . ."

Herschi smiled. "Oh, yes. It wouldn't be right not to."

Ryker's office had adopted their own recognition and reward ceremony for valor in the line of duty. And it was fine when the attention was on someone else, but it was an entirely different feel when all eyes were on him.

"If I could have your attention!" Herschi called out, tapping his shot glass again.

"Brad . . ." Ryker protested weakly.

"Everyone?"

Ryker looked around as everyone in his office produced a similar shot glass with the CIA seal imprinted on it. Ordering a case of them from a gift shop in D.C. seemed like a good idea at the time. He wasn't so sure now. Someone had opened a bottle of champagne and had begun moving around the room filling many of the tiny glasses with "a bit of the bubbly," while others, his included, were filled with Sprite. Herschi held his up to toast his boss.

"To our fearless leader," he said while the others responded with a round of here-heres as they raised their glasses also.

"To life, liberty, and the pursuit of happiness," they all chanted in unison and then threw back their shots. It was a simple ceremony, some might say silly, but it was a small reminder that what they did every day served to further the inalienable rights envisioned by their forefathers.

Last of all, Ryker held up his glass before drinking it in one gulp. "Now get back to work, you slackers." There was a sound of laughter, and then the fanfare was over. Ryker had a lot of work to do before two when he was scheduled to leave on his long-time-coming and much-needed vacation.

He'd attempted to block out the noise by closing his interior office door a number of times that morning, but every few minutes, without fail, there'd be a knock and he'd be confronted with something "urgent" requiring his personal attention.

No sooner had he reshuffled the papers on his desk than another knock rattled the opaque window glass.

"Come in," he groaned.

The door opened slowly.

"Sorry, Sam."

Deborah Reid, Ryker's right hand, slipped into his office, softly closing the door behind her and walking across the room to his desk.

"These should be the last of them." She set the papers down.

He looked at the unruly pile and then up at her.

"I don't understand it," he said. "Is there a reason Dave can't handle this?"

Of course Dave *could* handle this last batch of paperwork, but the real question was if he *would*. Dave Matheson, Ryker's deputy, was as capable as any agent produced by the CIA, but lately Ryker had been having second thoughts about Matheson's suitability as his second-in-command. He'd become less than enthusiastic—*lazy* would be a better word—about pursuing his responsibilities.

"He is here today, isn't he?" Ryker asked. "I didn't see him earlier during the . . . you know."

Deborah did her best to hide the look of disdain on her face. "He's here. He just . . . well, you know Dave."

"I know, I know," he said, starting in on the pile of paperwork. One form concerned him.

"Can't I appoint you, instead?" Ryker asked lightly.

Deborah smiled. "I'm flattered, Sam. Now sign it and get it over with. Besides, it's not like it's permanent or anything. Just until you return."

The security form, prepared by Deborah's careful hand, transferred full authority to Dave Matheson, who would become acting station head in Ryker's absence. As much as Ryker—and the entire office, for that matter—would have preferred Deborah to run the office while he was gone, they both knew that wasn't possible. The responsibility fell squarely on Matheson's shoulders.

Ryker breathed in deeply and signed the authority transfer.

"There, it's done." Ryker handed the stack of unsigned paperwork back to Deborah. "The way I see it, the rest of this is now Dave's problem."

"Yes, sir."

The telephone on Ryker's desk rang. The read-out appearing on the miniature LED screen across the bottom of the phone identified the call as coming from home.

"Hi, honey." It was Ryker's wife and better half, Susan. Deborah quickly gathered the rest of the paperwork. He mouthed a thank-you as she sneaked out, closing the door gently behind her.

"No . . . what? Obviously, I haven't left yet . . . Yes, I know what time it is . . . Yes, yes, I'm trying and I'll be leaving in a few minutes . . . All right, I'll pick it up . . . I love you, too. Bye."

As much as Ryker disliked confronting Matheson on *any* subject right then, given the man's attitude, he had one more assignment to delegate. He pressed the intercom button for Matheson's office.

"Yes?" Matheson replied.

"Dave, I'd like to see you in my office. I've got something to discuss with you before I leave."

"Right away, Sam." Matheson was good at masking his true feelings and intents, a necessary skill developed by every good field agent, but Ryker was too good not to pick up the subtle voice inflections which told him that his deputy was anything *but* anxious to meet with him.

Ryker gestured to a chair opposite his desk and tossed Matheson a file folder he had picked up on the way to work.

"What's this?" Matheson asked.

"I need you to follow up on this while I'm away."

"What is it?"

"Egyptian National Police report of the interrogation of Yousef Al-Mina—"

"Head of the Will of God?"

Ryker couldn't help but smile. "Not anymore."

"Why wasn't I informed?"

"Officially, no one knows," Ryker said. "Not yet, anyway. If you had joined us earlier, though, you might have been brought up to speed with the rest of the office."

"How did you get this?" Matheson was not one to leave well enough alone.

Ryker chose to ignore his deputy's concern. "I need you to check our databases, tap into MI6's, and cross-reference any connection that the Will of God, or Yousef personally, may have had with any terrorist acts over the past eighteen months. Every arrest, every suspicion, everything."

Matheson, also fluent in Arabic, remained silent, thumbing through the mostly handwritten report.

Ryker was sure he was listening, though, and continued. "Then get with the Office of Economic Development at Langley and match up any connections and correlations between these events and domestic and international economic fallout. Again, I don't care how small or insignificant."

Matheson failed to respond and continued reading the interrogation report.

"Dave?" Ryker finally asked. "Did you hear me?"

Matheson looked up from the file. "This didn't come through official channels, did it?"

Ryker didn't like where this was going. "Call it an occupational necessity."

"Does Chandler know about this?" The ambassador was not one for rogue operations or doing anything except by the book.

Ryker was never one to take chastisement from anyone, especially by the likes of Matheson, but he held his tongue and tried the route of reason first.

"You know as well as I do how often breaks like this come around, and there isn't time enough to sit on this until I get back."

"Why not get your golden girl to do it?"

Ryker didn't have many shortcuts to his temper, but Matheson seemed to find this one well enough, and his smirk just added fuel to Ryker's fire.

"Deborah is every bit as capable as you, and this whole office knows it. If it weren't for your father's connections at Langley, you'd still be filing expense reports in some basement office somewhere."

Matheson just sat there, a white hot flame of hatred seething through his narrowed eyes. It was true that his father had pulled some strings in the intelligence community to get him recruited right out of college, despite his faltering GPA, and that he'd been assigned cushy stations the world over. When your father sat on the United States Senate Select Committee on Intelligence, returning favors was just part of the game—and Matheson had become quite adept at milking it for all it was worth. He may have been a lot of things, but stupid wasn't one of them.

Ryker regretted the words the instant they left his lips.

"Dave, we can't let this one slip by. That report would have been made available to us eventually—you know that. But by then the information will be useless to us. The time to act is now."

Matheson closed the file. "And what *exactly* am I looking for?"

Ryker hesitated. He had known the question would eventually come up.

Matheson tossed the file back onto Ryker's desk. "Wait, don't tell me. This is about your *Chameleon* theory, isn't it?"

Ryker took a deep breath and put his head in his hands. It had been almost two years now, and to date, no intelligence agency supported him in his belief that now bordered on conviction that there was someone behind much of the world's acts of terror. A phantom terrorist he had dubbed the "Chameleon."

"It's all there," Ryker said, lifting the interrogation report. "Al-Mina mentions being paid for what his men did in the Sinai. *Paid,* Dave. Those buses weren't randomly blown up for political or religious reasons like they claimed. This was staged and then ideological buzzwords shouted to the press to throw us off the trail, and I want to know why."

Matheson shrugged his shoulders. "Assassination? I don't know. Someone on those buses worth knocking off?"

"That's just it. No political leaders, no one with any governmental influence. Just a bunch of rich tourists. That's what I want you to start looking into while I'm gone."

Matheson scoffed. "C'mon, we've been over this before. There's nothing to it. It's a waste of time."

Ryker held out the report until Matheson reluctantly took it.

Matheson stood. "Is there anything else? 'Cause Deborah dumped a whole mess-load of paperwork for me to start plowing through now that I'm in charge, so if you don't mind . . ." And he turned his back on his boss and left.

Ryker was stunned for a moment at Matheson's utter contempt for Ryker and his position. Then he threw open his desk drawer, tossed down a couple Tylenol, and finished readying his desk for a two-week hibernation when a soft tap on his door announced Deborah again.

"Sorry. One last memo for you to approve."

Ryker scanned it and then initialed by his name.

"Didn't go well?" she offered.

He just shook his head.

Deborah said, "A transfer of power is never easy. I know it's only for a couple of weeks, but Dave's testing the water with this and counting down the days until your retirement."

"No, it's not that," he said, motioning for her to sit if she'd like. She did. "I asked him to follow up on what Hasan learned from Al-Mina."

"About his being compensated for his work in the Sinai?"

Ryker wasn't surprised she knew exactly what he meant. Deborah possessed a skill that was both a blessing and a curse, but for different reasons. She held the ability to see, hear, or read something once and have total recall with little effort. This frightened many of her coworkers and associates, but not Ryker. This was a gift he had used for the good of the Company time and time again. It was, however, not very helpful in those times he needed her to conveniently forget protocol or bend rules or regulations to get the job done. She had scanned the file before passing it on to Ryker and, hence, recalled every detail of the terrorist's confession.

"This is my first real lead on this," Ryker said. "I've been so close for so long, but proof—real and hard evidence—has always just been out of my reach. Until now. And I have to leave it behind and let the trail go cold."

Deborah was about to offer a comforting response when the intercom buzzed through.

"Mr. Ryker," sounded the office operator, "I have Hasan from the Egyptian National Police on the line for you. He says it's urgent."

Deborah made to get up, but he motioned for her to stay. "Put him through."

Ryker put him on speaker. "Hasan."

"Sam . . . I am afraid I have bad news."

"There's nothing like getting right to the point, now is there?"

Hasan ignored the attempt at levity. "He is dead. Al-Mina is dead."

A pit in Ryker's stomach opened wide, and he could feel his hands begin to tremble.

"What? How?" were the only words he could find.

"About an hour ago. Prison riot. Shortly after he was returned to his cell. A dozen injured, two dead—Al-Mina and the instigator." Hasan continued quickly, answering the question he knew was on Ryker's mind. "I've seen the tapes. His death was an accident. The prisoner wrestled a gun away from one of the guards, tried to shoot him, but missed. They were standing in front of Al-Mina's cell."

Ryker began to break free of the fog that had descended upon him with Hasan's sudden news.

"Did they know each other?"

"No. The shooter had been in a full six months. No ties to Al-Mina or his organization. He was in on robbery, his third offense, and was looking at a lifetime behind bars if he didn't escape." Hasan paused to let it sink in. "I know what you must be thinking, but by all accounts, by my own account, Al-Mina's death was a terrible accident, nothing more."

By now, Ryker was back and thinking again like a CIA station head. "His death must be kept under wraps. Al-Mina's men must continue to think that we have him for as long as possible. They'll be scared, they'll make mistakes. We must make them think that he is still feeding us information."

"Agreed. My men will keep their tongues. Al-Mina's death was only witnessed by a few inmates, and they have all been put in isolation until we can sort this thing out."

Ryker took a deep breath and let it out slowly. There was nothing more he could do. Not right then, anyway.

"You'll keep me updated?"

"You will know everything the moment I know it."

"Thank you, my friend," and he hung up the call.

After a beat, Deborah said, "I'm so sorry, Sam."

Ryker was scarcely aware of her. "It doesn't make sense. I don't believe for a minute that it was an accident."

"But Hasan—"

"I know, I know, but we're missing something. I just can't seem to . . ." Ryker sat back and drifted off into thought.

"Hasan's the best investigator outside this office," Deborah offered after a moment or two. "If there's a connection, he'll find it."

Sam Ryker started to nod, distracted and not really paying attention when he muttered, "Generosity . . ."

"What?"

"Deb," Ryker said, sitting up straight and fumbling for a notepad and pen on his desk. He began making frantic notes as he spoke. "I need your help."

"Anything, Sam."

Ryker checked his watch. He should have left almost an hour ago. "Call Hasan. Tell him to look into the shooter's family, particularly their financial situation, bank accounts, purchases, debts, anything he can find."

Deborah became visibly uneasy. "This sounds like something Dave should handle; it's not proper—"

"The shooter may not have known Al-Mina from Adam, but he had proximity to him, and I'm betting that's all he needed."

Deborah seemed to see where Ryker was going with all this. "Who? It's all *who* needed?"

Ryker was unapologetic. "The Chameleon. I'm close, and he knows it."

Deborah held his serious stare for a moment.

"Of course," she said, taking the notepad from him and jotting a few of her own thoughts to follow up on. "You sound sure about this."

"It's what I'd do." Ryker winked and stood up, briefcase in hand. "Call me the minute you hear back from Hasan."

"But you're on vacation. Susan would shoot me if I called and interrupted your time together."

"Deb—"

"No. Whatever comes of this, Hasan will handle it, or it'll wait until you get back. Now go enjoy yourself."

Ryker wasn't one to take no for an answer that easily. "But that's just it. I won't be *able* to enjoy myself until I know one way or the other. It's this not knowing that kills me."

"Sam—"

"Deb, please. Page me. I'll find a minute to break away and call you back."

Deborah sighed. "All right, but if Susan gets wind of this—"

"Leave Susan to me."

"My telling you from a woman's point of view that this is a huge mistake won't change your mind, will it?"

"I can't let this one go, Deb."

Deborah smiled. "If this goes badly, 'the secretary will disavow any knowledge,'" she said, quoting the familiar *Mission Impossible* phrase with her country-girl charm.

Ryker smiled for the first time that afternoon. "Whatever they're paying you, it's not enough."

"You could fix that, you know." She smiled back.

"When I get back." He laughed.

"Sure you will, and I'll have that grade advancement request on your desk when you do."

***

A notice chimed through on the computer. His search criteria had found a match. Swiveling in his leather chair, he turned his attention to the new message. Hitting enter, he opened the electronic file and read through its contents.

A smile crept across his face.

He checked his watch—a Tag Heuer Chronograph—and then checked his computer screen again. His timing would be tight but possible.

He deleted the incoming message and then picked up his desk phone and dialed a local number.

"Yes, good morning," he responded in English. "I need to book a flight. Last minute business, you know."

"Of course," the pleasant voice answered. "Destination?"

"Jerusalem," he answered. "I need to leave immediately."

THREE

IT WAS MIDAFTERNOON WHEN Ryker and his wife checked into their hotel suite in the heart of Jerusalem and unpacked. The trip had been blessedly uneventful. However, Ryker had not been able to sleep on the way over, his mind working overtime on the whole Al-Mina development. But finally, as they made their final approach into Ben Gurion International Airport, Ryker could see that Susan had noticed his distant thoughts, and he made an effort to dismiss them and focus on the here and now. Traffic was congested all the way from the airport, and the cleanliness and smell of the cab they had hailed left much to be desired. Authentic Israeli cuisine and a quick shower to wash away the miles were just what they needed to settle in and start their family time off right. They still had almost six hours before the girls arrived.

Before heading out, Susan ran a comb through her blond—though graying—hair and attended to her makeup. She leaned in toward the mirror and took stock of the few wrinkles around her eyes. *It could be worse*, she thought. She stepped back, turned to the left, then to the right. She may have crossed over the half-century mark, but she'd still been able to hold on to most of her girlish figure. She wondered if her husband appreciated how tough that really was.

She glanced over at her husband brushing his teeth. *Why do men age so much better than women?* It was unfair. No one would even guess that he was in *his* fifties, too. His olive complexion gave the semblance of a perpetual tan, and when coupled with his muscled upper body and sun-bleached hair, he might have been mistaken for a rather handsome lifeguard.

In fact, Susan had frequently wished that her husband *had* been a lifeguard or stock broker or shoe salesman or anything other than what he was. They'd had a good life together—some might even say romantic, given the faraway and exotic places they'd lived—but she'd put her own interests on hold, every bit as married to the Company as her husband was.

When they first arrived in Cairo in the mid seventies, with twin nine-month-old girls in tow, he'd be gone for days at a time, but the rules precluded her from asking where or why. If it hadn't been for the fact that the girls were the darlings of the embassy with whom everyone begged to play, Susan would've passed the days and evenings alone. Nonetheless, with the future of their children to care about, his safety had always been on her mind. And rightfully so.

In those days, her husband had been the best covert agent that the CIA had in place. His specialty was Middle Eastern terrorism, and no one alive had a better grasp of the particulars. *That* she'd been able to piece together from the comments of other embassy employees or from the wives of fellow agents. Beyond that, his comings and goings had pretty much been a mystery to her. The last few years he'd been stuck at a desk job as head of Cairo Station. He didn't like being confined to an office, but Susan loved his hours and the fact that he was no longer a field agent.

Ryker had just finished brushing his teeth and was wiping his mouth with a hand towel when Susan moved next to him and put her head on his shoulder.

"I really love you," she said.

The gesture caught him by surprise, and he looked at her reflection in the mirror.

"What's *this* all about?" he asked, smiling.

"It's not *about* anything. I just thought I'd tell you that I love you. I know how hard it is for you to drag yourself away from the job, but this will be a special time for us all. You'll see."

"Of course it will," he agreed. "I realize that I've been too much of a work horse—a guy who hasn't taken the time to smell the roses. But come next year, we'll start to take those trips we've always talked about. No sitting around a living room for us, watching the paint fade. I want retirement to be an adventure. We'll go places and see things—London, Paris, Rome, but especially Paris. I'll show you a side of the City of Love that tourists seldom experience." He raised and lowered his eyebrows twice like Groucho Marx and grinned.

"I can hardly wait," she said, straightening herself. "Now let's go get something to eat; I'm famished."

* * *

Susan asked what time it was for the tenth time in as many minutes while searching the sky for the first glimmer of metal to identify the approach of the El Al Boeing 727. Ryker knew she'd be a total wreck until the plane and her daughters were safely on the ground. But before he had time to respond again, she spotted a distant flash in the early evening twilight. She grabbed his hand and squeezed tightly, never taking her eyes off the approaching plane. As it descended, a million worries raced through her mind, but she dismissed them all with her excitement. She began to giggle, mumbling, "It's them! It's them!" causing her husband to smile. He was happy, too, but nervous. He hadn't seen his daughters for so long.

The passengers exited as soon as the plane stopped next to its assigned terminal. The Rykers waited anxiously for the first glimpse of the girls. He wondered if he'd even recognize them. Despite his wife's restless scanning of the unloading crowd, it was he who spotted them first—Natalie with her long, strawberry-blond hair pulled back in a ponytail, and Niccole, wearing a blue-and-white BYU baseball cap. His eyes filled with tears at the sight of them. As soon as the girls and their luggage had cleared customs, Susan pushed through the crowd and threw her arms around them both. Ryker noticed that they were now young *women*, nothing girlish about them. The three of them made their way over to him, the two sprinting away from their mother, smothering their father with kisses and embraces. He imagined heaven felt a lot like this and hugged them back tightly.

"How was your trip, girls?" he asked, holding their hands and walking between them to the terminal exit.

"It was . . ." they both said in stereo, then stopped. They looked at each other and laughed. Niccole started again. "It was exciting. We hit some rough air over the Atlantic . . ."

Natalie jumped in. "It was pretty bumpy. And the landing in London was scary. It had to have been the pilot's first landing."

They both exclaimed, "Yeah!"

The evening sun was about to set when they arrived back at the Sheraton, across a two-lane highway from the Great Synagogue. The hotel was luxurious by Middle Eastern standards and was costing Ryker a pretty penny, but he figured his family was worth it. Natalie and Niccole didn't even unpack before brushing their teeth and crashing on the two clean and cool double beds in their room.

They slept until roused for breakfast. Still tired and a bit disorientated by jetlag, Susan said they would meet them in the hotel restaurant in half an hour. They were wasting no time and had planned a guided tour of historic Jerusalem that would be leaving at nine.

The bus was full. The girls found adjoining seats, but Ryker and his wife were forced to sit across the aisle from one another until the man seated next to him offered to exchange his seat for Susan's. He was a handsome Arab in a navy blazer and fashion sunglasses.

Ryker offered his thanks in Arabic and wasn't surprised when the man responded in British-accented English. Susan took his seat and then her husband's hand and listened as Ryker narrated much of Israel's conflicted history and struggle to establish a nation again after being forced from their homeland almost a thousand years earlier.

Their first stop would be the Western Wall, dating back to the Jewish Great Temple that had stood in New Testament times.

"The Wall is one of the most sacred places in the world for Jews," Ryker explained to his wife and daughters. "This whole area is part of what is called *Har ha-Beyit,* or Temple Mount."

"Like in the Bible?" Natalie asked.

"The very same."

As the bus pulled up across the way from the Wall, Ryker could see the awe in the faces of his family. Studying about religious sites, looking at pictures, and reading volumes about them was no substitute for visiting them in person and having your heart filled with the reverence that comes by standing in holy places. Ryker had once thought that perhaps Mohammed understood this truth when he made it the requirement of every faithful Muslim to make the pilgrimage to Mecca and pray at the Kaaba at least once in their lifetime. Ryker had been to Jerusalem on business several times over the years, but never had he taken the time to experience his own religious origins before then. Which made it all the more special now, hand in hand with his small family.

The first temple, Ryker explained, was built by Solomon and housed the sacred ark of the covenant, an elaborate wooden and gold box that held the tablets of law given to Moses by God on Mount Sinai, and the temple was the center of Israel's religious and political power. It was later destroyed, and a new temple was eventually built atop its ruins. It was this second temple, stained with the name of King Herod the Great, that was all but destroyed, leaving only this small section of wall as a testament that it once stood.

The Wall was lined with stands displaying copies of the Torah while the gentle and almost melodic prayers of the faithful filled the morning air. Some supplicants stood, others sat, and all prayed aloud for God to remember and bless His chosen people and to restore the temple and Jerusalem to their former glory. Even to an unbeliever, the sight was awe inspiring, and the Rykers appreciated it even more since they were a religious family with the deep convictions of their own Mormon faith.

"What are those?" Niccole asked, pointing to pieces of paper jutting out from the stone wall joints.

"Prayers," her father explained. "It is tradition to write your prayer and then wedge it into the crevices of the Wall."

"Can we do it?" Natalie asked. "Or do you have to be Jewish?"

Ryker didn't know the religious rules or etiquette of worship at the Wall, but he didn't think it would do any harm. "Go ahead, but don't make a scene about it."

Just then his pager trilled. Susan looked at him with a mix of surprise and disappointment. He had forgotten to put it on vibration mode. He offered his wife an "I'm sorry" look and then checked the number. It was Deborah.

"Sue," he started, "I need to take this."

Susan's defenses began to rise. "Sam, you promised. No work. You promised us."

"I know, I know, but this won't take long." He reached out and took her hands, bringing them up to his lips. "Two minutes, I promise. Then you can watch me turn it off. I'll even give it to you for safekeeping."

Susan looked around. "But there's no phone here."

Ryker removed his cell phone from his inside jacket pocket and again appealed to his wife with all the boyish charm he possessed.

"You were expecting this call." It wasn't a question. "Can't Dave handle whatever it is?"

Ryker shook his head. "I gotta take this. Please."

Susan wasn't sure she wanted to consent, but in the end she could do little against his sincere charm. She checked her watch. "You'd better hurry."

And Ryker did. Walking back toward the buses and out of earshot of everyone, he made the call.

"You were right," Deborah said with unmasked but serious excitement. "At first, Al-Mina's shooter appeared to have absolutely no connection to him whatsoever, but when we started looking into his family, Hasan found that ten thousand Egyptian pounds had been deposited two days ago—the day of Al-Mina's arrest—into a trust set up in the shooter's family's name. The wife apparently knew nothing about it and could not explain it. Hasan doesn't believe that the wife had any part in the conspiracy."

Ryker could not have been happier. "And the money trail?"

"Cold, at least for now. The money was wired from an offshore bank in Bahrain, but Hasan's men—"

Suddenly, behind him and back toward the base of the Western Wall, Ryker's trained ears picked up on a police whistle followed closely by several shouts in Hebrew and French to evacuate the square. Panic flooded over him as a sixth sense told him that he and his family were in danger. He sprinted back, fighting the chaos of tourists and worshippers who were unsure what to do. The tightness in his chest relaxed, though, the minute he saw Susan and the girls safe, huddled close to each other and waiting right where he had left them.

Susan turned at that moment and met his eyes with her own and smiled, the relief shining through that he was all right, too.

The next instant his family was gone in a blinding light, and Ryker's world went dark.

* * *

Ryker awoke three days later in a hospital bed under the close watch and protection of two United States Marines. As soon as he was able, Ambassador Chandler was permitted to see him. He was followed by Dave Matheson. Uncomfortable silence took the place of small talk, then the ambassador broke the news of Ryker's family. They and seven others that morning had died in a bombing at the Western Wall. No one had yet stepped up and claimed responsibility, but both the Mossad and Shin-Beth, Israel's unmatched foreign and domestic intelligence agencies, were sparing no expense in tracking down the cowards who had committed the heinous crime.

"Sam, Dave has briefed me fully on your phantom terrorist, the Chameleon, as you call him, as well as your recent work with Hasan and Al-Mina. In light of your recent investigations and the unusual timing of it all, we feel it necessary to protect you further. If you *were* the intended target of the attack, then maybe it is best that they think they succeeded. I have spoken to the deputy director personally, and we have made arrangements to place you in the Agency's equivalent of the Witness Protection Program."

The two men looked at each other. "We've amended the initial reports. No one will know you survived."

Matheson kept his head low and had nothing to add.

The ambassador continued speaking, expressing his deepest sympathies and such things, but Ryker wasn't listening anymore. His family was dead, and with them his dreams, his hopes, his faith. He lay there silently wishing that he would wake from his nightmare.

They were going to declare him dead. Tears rolled down the side of his head, soaking his pillow. They didn't know just how right they were.

FOUR

No one took particular notice of the two men seated at a table at the rear of the seedy disco club in Khartoum, Sudan's capital, situated along the banks of the White Nile. Tobacco smoke filled the room, as red-and-yellow neon lights contorted into bizarre shapes, flickered, and pulsed in time to the beat of American rock and roll blaring on oversized speakers. A bevy of scantily clad women danced onstage to the music. Their performance was as amateurish as it was uninspiring.

"As agreed," one of the men said, "half now and the other half when they are brought to us." He nervously reached into his pocket, pulled out a small leather pouch, and pushed it across the table.

The other man, only his eyes visible from beneath a dark grey *kaffiyeh* wrapped around his head, opened the pouch and poured the contents into his cupped hand. The diamonds sparkled with the glitter of a half million dollars. Careful not to spill even the smallest one, he replaced the jewels, cinched the pouch closed, and slid them back to the quivering man.

"The terms have changed."

"Y-y-you can't—"

The masked man's tone hardened like steel. "You are in no position to tell me what I *can* or *cannot* do. But do not worry; the terms have swung into your favor."

"I-I don't understand."

"I would not expect you to." He produced a small piece of paper and forced it into the timid man's hand. "This is what I need."

"And the missionaries?"

"Relax, my friend. You will have them before the Hajj. I will complete my end of the bargain. By spring they will be yours." The voice then turned to malice. "So let it be written, so let it be done."

FIVE

Elder Jack Devereux was up earlier than usual this morning. The only sign of early morning was the digital 4:32 display on his nightstand clock. Outside, the night sky still refused to give way to the new day. He paused on the end of the bed, stretching his torso from side to side. Before getting to his feet, he glanced over at his beautiful wife of nearly thirty years. She stirred and mumbled something softly, smiled, and then turned over to return to the realm of dreams. Jack smiled, too, then pulled the covers up to cover her exposed shoulder. It was cool this morning in Aswan. Almost cold. He never would have thought that the Egyptian desert could get as cold as it did. Even with spring approaching, the night temperatures still hovered well below their comfort level. Having lived outside of Atlanta, Georgia, for most of his adult life, he didn't have much tolerance for cold weather. Sixty-five degrees was about as cold as he ever wanted to see the thermostat dip to.

Elder Devereux said something about how hard it was getting old as he rose to answer the call of nature. The two-room apartment shared a single bathroom which was luxurious by Egyptian standards. Internal plumbing with running hot and cold water was not common in the small city of Kom Ombo where he and his wife had been stationed since arriving almost four months earlier. Living just north of Aswan along the Nile River, they were perfectly situated between the supplies that would be flown in to the large city, and the poor farming villages that so desperately needed their help.

Jack and Abigail Devereux were the senior missionaries of the four-person medical team sent by The Church of Jesus Christ of Latter-day Saints. Jack and Abigail were both MDs, retired from the Center for Disease Control in Atlanta. Over their lifetimes they had worked closely with local, national, and international health organizations combating seemingly endless viral, bacterial, and parasitical threats, but nothing had prepared them for their latest assignment.

Since the construction of the Aswan High Dam during the 1950s, the annual high and low tides of the Nile were replaced with a constant supply of water. Though ideal for transforming seasonal irrigating and farming into a year-round business, one devastating and apparently unforeseen consequence of its construction was the immediate and exponential growth of a specific water-borne parasite. This parasite, or schistosome, incubated in the many freshwater snails (that now have an unending supply of wet, marshlands) before being released into the water. This parasite is unlike others in that it creates its own way into the body, excreting an enzyme to break down the outer layers of skin until it can enter the bloodstream. Going right for the host's liver, it feeds on red blood cells as it matures, later making its way to the kidneys and bladder, where it lives largely unaffected by the body's immune system. Once it fully matures, reaching lengths of about ten millimeters, the parasites can lay anywhere from three hundred to three thousand eggs per day, which are excreted from the body in the urine and feces, only to search out their snail hosts and start the process all over again. Though not usually fatal, the infection is extremely painful and difficult to treat. Once infected, human hosts are doomed to share their lives with the parasite unless it can be treated with either of the drugs, Praziquantel or Oxamniquine, both expensive and both being donated by the relief efforts of the Church.

Elder Devereux had been prepared to treat the many adult farmers infected with the parasite, but he was quite unprepared to see the number of children who were infected. Theirs was truly a mission of mercy, and he thanked God daily for the chance to serve and help relieve the pain and suffering.

But the Devereux were not sent out alone. They were joined by two young nurse practitioners, Elders Robert Evans and Thomas Anderson. Any doctor would consider him or herself extremely fortunate to have either young man working with them, and they were blessed to have the full support of both.

As Jack turned off the bathroom light and started back toward his room, he noticed a light on in the front living area. He shuffled out to make sure everything was all right. Elder Evans looked up from *al-Kitab Mormon*, his Arabic Book of Mormon.

"I didn't mean to wake you," he said apologetically.

"Are you okay?" Elder Devereux asked.

Elder Evans nodded, holding up his Book of Mormon. "Just studying up."

Elder Devereux smiled and sat across from the young elder. "Nervous?"

"You know I didn't serve a regular mission when I turned nineteen. What if I say the wrong things? What if this is their only chance to hear the gospel and I mess it up? I tell you what, I don't know how all those other missionaries do it."

Elder Devereux just smiled. He knew Elder Evans's history well. Elder Evans had grown up in a quiet suburban neighborhood twenty miles east of Los Angeles. His mother had died of breast cancer when he was ten years old. His father had taken an additional job at night to pay the staggering medical bills and had entrusted him with the care of his little sister, Jennifer, who had Down syndrome.

When he turned nineteen and it came time for him to serve a proselytizing mission for the Church, he felt uncomfortable about burdening his father with the expense of supporting him as well as leaving Jenny in the care of others. Instead, he accepted a full academic scholarship to the School of Nursing at UCLA, living at home and seeing to the needs of his sister between the mountains of homework and midterms. After graduating with honors, he interned at the University of California Medical Center and hired on thereafter with its nursing staff before eventually getting called on this special medical mission based on the recommendation of his local leaders.

"Converting someone to the truth would be a daunting task, to be sure," Elder Devereux consoled, "if it were up to you and your abilities, but it's not."

"I know, I know," Elder Evans said. "But those words still come out of our mouths. What if I hesitate? What if I stutter trying to answer one of their questions? Where is the line between being bold and pushing someone away?"

He closed his book of scripture to give the conversation his full attention. "Do I start with the Articles of Faith or launch right into Joseph Smith and the First Vision? I know that Muslims have a prophecy of the return of the twelfth Imam, or prophet, in the last days, and I think I should start with Joseph Smith's account and story, but is that what I want to teach them or what the Lord wants to teach them?"

He fumbled with the book in his hand. "I mean, what if they ask questions I can't answer? What if I say the wrong things? This whole thing sounded like a better idea yesterday."

The day before, while riding back from a stretch of flooded farmland to the north, two of the three-man security detail expressed a curiosity about what Mormons *really* believed. They had approached Elder Evans with their question, which Elder Devereux thought odd, given the culture's importance and respect for age and experience. The guards knew that they were forbidden from active proselytizing but reasoned that they could unofficially answer some questions about their faith. Elder Evans was nervous but accepted the invitation to share what he knew was true. But as the morning quickly approached, Elder Evans was feeling more than a little anxious.

He let out an exhausted sigh. "I don't know about this, Doctor."

"It matters less *what* you say," Elder Devereux said with quiet strength, "and more *how* you say it. The most important thing a missionary can do is seek and keep the Spirit of the Lord with him at all times. If he can do that, he can then let the Lord work on their hearts. You may even stumble with every word, Elder, but to them, if their hearts are open, they may just hear the most eloquent sermon ever preached. That's the miracle we are all entitled to by accepting the call to serve."

"Thanks," Elder Evans said. "You always know the right thing to say."

Elder Devereux smiled that warm smile that came so naturally to him. "You'll do fine. Just remember to breathe."

He left the young man to his early morning studies and then retired to a small, enclosed courtyard off the front of the apartment. He had sat at the wrought-iron table every morning since arriving in Egypt, taking a few minutes to reflect on the day before and plan for the day ahead, writing in his journal. He and his wife, accompanied by two fine young elders, were pioneers in the truest sense of the word, "boldly going where no *Mor*man had gone before," as Elder Anderson had once joked.

They had all met for the first time at the Missionary Training Center in Provo, Utah, and their classes were anything but routine. Where most missionaries spent their time learning the gospel and how to effectively teach it, sometimes in their own tongue and other times in foreign ones, this special envoy to the land of the pharaohs spent their mornings immersed in crash courses in Islamic culture, Middle Eastern history, and Arabic. Afternoons were only somewhat less arduous, spent at the Brigham Young University medical library, researching the biological enemy they were about to battle. When their departure day—or "D-day," as all missionaries termed it—arrived, the prophet visited with them and personally gave each a special blessing to aid in the difficult work that lay ahead. Elder

Devereux recalled, embraced by the calm of the morning, part of Elder Evan's blessing at the hands of the prophet, special to his struggle with Arabic, as he assured him that if he would simply *love* God's children in the land of pharaohs, the barriers of language would be removed. And they had all been witness to this miracle the moment they deplaned. His command of Arabic and his ability to adapt to the many dialects was nothing short of miraculous.

Elder Devereux opened his leather-bound journal and began writing in anticipation of the big day that lay ahead of them all.

* * *

The stolen military transport scarcely slowed as it maneuvered the corner. Had it been going any faster, it might have rolled. The man behind the wheel wore an Egyptian army sergeant's uniform in case the truck was stopped for any reason, but his face was now masked by a tightly wrapped head cloth.

The truck swerved and came to an abrupt stop in front of the cheap, worn-down Ramses Hotel. Two men stood outside in the cold, a black duffel bag on the ground between them. The streets were empty and lit only by the moon above in the early morning.

The driver motioned for the unkempt duo to climb into the covered bed. With the men and their equipment aboard, the driver jerked the truck back onto the empty road. Soon they crossed over the old Aswan Dam and turned north along the highway that paralleled the river's east bank. In rehearsal, the driver had taken the route many times. They would enter the small canyon in exactly an hour and fifteen minutes.

* * *

The ride in the back of the truck was punishing, but the two passengers weren't accustomed to first-class accommodations. Imad, the smaller of the two men, yawned as the truck bounced relentlessly. He stared blankly across at his companion leaning against the sidewall with his eyes closed. Nasr was the bigger of the two, the muscle behind Imad's brains. Strong as an ox, Nasr had the IQ to match. He was good at following instructions and getting the job done. Imad had taken it upon himself to look after him. Born in Iraq, and shortly thereafter orphaned, they spent their childhood being shipped from one state-run institution to another, often victims of abuse at the hands of those they looked to for protection. They'd learned early on that trust was nothing without a weapon to back it up. A bond of love and fierce loyalty had developed between them, stronger than mere brotherhood. For Imad and Nasr, it was them versus the world—and may Allah help the world.

With trust in their fellow man all but nonexistent and after a short tour in the military, the brothers opted for a life of solitude, separate from the rest of the world. Imad and his brother went by the name *Ithnayn,* or "Two" in Arabic, as one was never far from the other.

They had worked for the man grinding the gears up front on two prior occasions, neither time seeing his face. The driver called himself *al-Saiif,* "the Sword," and that was good enough for them. They were content knowing only what was necessary to complete the job and collect their fee. In this instance, they were each being paid the Egyptian equivalent of twenty-five thousand dollars.

As the vehicle crossed the Nile, the temperature dropped, chilling Imad beneath his jacket. A couple of minutes later the truck turned sharply again, throwing them to one side of the bed. He leaned across the truck bed and jostled his brother.

"Hey, try to stay awake."

Nasr yawned, flexed his arms in a stretch, and then turned over, seemingly ignoring Imad, and tried to get comfortable.

The covered truck pulled off the dirt road and parked behind an outcropping of rock, hidden from view. The sun was still below the horizon, and the morning air was brisk. Saiif slid back the cab's rear window to the truck bed.

"Time to go to work," he said as he lifted a green knapsack from the front seat and handed it through the open window. A pair of rough, muscled hands firmly grasped the sack, lifted it gently into the truck bed, and placed it inside a black duffel bag. As the two men jumped from the truck, their feet sank an inch or two into the cool desert sand. The pair walked back down the road a hundred paces without a word. They knew exactly what to do and precisely how to do it.

This stretch of rough highway was flanked to the west by a wall of eroded sandstone. On the east, a steep incline paralleled the road. Vegetation was sparse on either side.

In due time, Imad opened the duffel bag, removed a folding shovel, handed it to his brother, and then mentally gauged the distance from the bend in the road. He pointed to a spot on the ground, and Nasr started digging. Returning to the duffel bag at his feet, Imad extracted the small knapsack handed to him only minutes before. Inside was a metallic, saucer-shaped item covered with writing he recognized as Cyrillic but couldn't read. He deftly slid open a small plate on the underside of the device. He flipped the switch beneath and repositioned the plate. Carefully, he placed the live explosive into the shallow hole and helped his brother cover it with dirt. The first part of their job done, they walked back to the truck, using the duffel bag to brush away any telltale footprints.

Saiif had a tight schedule to keep and would have preferred not to carry out this operation so close to his other plans—little more than a week away—but the missionaries' security had been so tight that it had taken him weeks to discover a pattern in their movement, carefully designed to prevent precisely what was about to happen.

The government had established a score of temporary Red Crescent clinics between Luxor and Aswan. Each day, the small American medical team would vary clinics, times of departure, and routes. It would have been much easier to simply eliminate them—a sniper at a hundred meters could have ended their mission of mercy nicely—but he was being paid to abduct them, not kill them. That decision was up to *Al-Jum'ah*.

Members of this Sudanese revolutionary group were a pompous bunch, and he looked forward to seeing exactly what they had in mind. But whatever it was, it was certain to be over the top. They may have been relatively unknown when compared to their Palestinian and Lebanese counterparts, but they meant business, as evidenced by the car bomb two years earlier that had devastated American living quarters in Riyadh. Reports of the bombing had brought back pleasant and exciting memories of his time spent in Beirut: the simplicity of plastic explosive; the puff of super-heated air from the blast, almost lovingly caressing his body; and then the chaos as rescue crews sifted through the rubble trying to identify charred American and French remains. It still brought a smile to his lips, even after all these years.

From the seat of the truck, he removed a small black box, extended its short antenna, and flipped a side switch. A green light glowed atop the box, indicating that the deadly device buried in the road was now armed.

* * *

The two government security jeeps bounced over the washboard road on their way to the day's site, but the four men in the lead vehicle seemed oblivious to the violent jarring. The driver had no intention of listening to the words of the American missionary, but something struck him as he spoke. The young man's Arabic was flawless. Foreigners could spend a lifetime speaking Arabic and still have an accent, but this missionary had none. *Their God must be powerful,* he thought, *to bestow this gift of tongues,* and he silently joined the others as they listened with real intent to the story of a boy prophet, an angel, and the words of God engraved on golden plates.

In a flash, it was all over. The buried explosive device detonated with enough force to turtle a tank. The lead vehicle shot fifteen feet into the air, its gas tank igniting as it caromed off the west wall. Engulfed in flame, it somersaulted across the road and down an incline.

Elder Jack Devereux, at the wheel of the second vehicle, swerved away from the explosion, careening down the embankment as well, crashing into a bolder and shattering the windshield. Fear and disorientation had only a moment's control over the seasoned doctor before giving way to years of medical and crisis training. Devereux quickly examined his wife for any visible injuries. She was badly shaken but otherwise okay. Elder Anderson's eyes were closed, but he was stirring to consciousness. Elder Devereux's attention then turned to the flaming mass of twisted metal just ahead of him, and a hole in the pit of his stomach opened wide.

"Dear God, no," were the only words that escaped his lips.

He fumbled at the door handle, unsure of exactly what he could do but knowing that he had to try to do *something*. In his peripheral vision he caught a glimpse of movement. He turned to his left and found himself looking down the snubbed barrel of an ominous-looking automatic weapon. On the opposite side of the vehicle, another assailant appeared, bigger than the first, thrusting his shoulder-slung weapon at the head of his wife. Head cloths obscured their faces. The first man, not taking his eyes off Devereux, directed his heavily accented words toward Anderson.

"Don't," he sneered in barely recognizable English.

The smell of burning gasoline and rubber nearly overwhelmed Devereux with nausea. He slumped in the driver's seat, defeated.

"The other one, where is he?" his assailant yelled, pressing the gun barrel against Devereux's temple.

Elder Devereux gestured with his head to the smoldering frame of the jeep. "He was riding up front today." His voice was little more than a whisper.

Abigail began to cry softly, the shock of the ordeal setting in.

As the two men dragged the three missionaries from the vehicle at gunpoint, Elder Devereux sensed another presence. With his hand shielding his eyes, he saw a figure standing atop the incline, silhouetted against the bright morning sun, his face shrouded except for his eyes. Their gazes locked for only a second, but in that instant, Elder Devereux knew that their terror had only just begun.

* * *

Four hundred miles south of the attack, in a dimly lit basement apartment in the Sudanese city of Abu Hamad, four men wearing dirty cotton pantaloons and loose, layered shirts stood around a small table littered with cigarette butts and empty coffee cups.

"It is done," one of the men announced, placing a bulky cellular phone on the corner table. "It is time."

A fifth man stepped to the light, nodded, and left without saying a word. The thin wooden door closed noisily again, shutting out the light to the shadowed room.

"Talib is an obedient servant," Mahmud said once he was sure they were alone, "but as you know, he was not my choice for this mission."

Jamal, self-appointed head of *Al-Jum'ah*, was not accustomed to being criticized by his little flock of pious cutthroats and thieves.

"Did he not obtain the services of the one man capable of seeing our plans to their glorious end?" Jamal asked. "This mysterious, *Al-Har'ba?*"

"Yes, but what if something unforeseen happens anywhere along the way? How will he react? Can he think on his feet? What makes you so sure he will not betray us if problems arise? You were a *fool*, Jamal, to have involved him in the first place and may very well have jeopardized the operation."

Jamal focused his gaze squarely on his accuser.

With speed acquired through years of kill-or-be-killed situations, Jamal shot his hands out, grabbing Mahmud by the shirt collar, pulling him off balance over the table. Then just as quick, he released his grip and shoved him backward. Shocked and humiliated, Mahmud fumbled for the knife at his belt. Blade in hand, he was met with a drawn nickel-plated pistol. No one moved.

"Mahmud, you fail to see the will of Allah," Jamal said down the barrel of his gun, "and your lack of faith will get you killed one day. You are weak, like the masses who oppose the Western Satan with their mouths but drive home in their Lincolns and Cadillacs, listening to their American rock and roll. What you need—what you all need—is proof that resistance is not futile, that the common Arab can make a stand against the West! The great ones have all gone before us: the Muslim Brotherhood; *Fatah*; *Hezbollah*. And now it is the hour of *Al-Jum'ah*! We are not asked to win the war, merely to wage battle. It is Allah who will triumph, with *Al-Jum'ah* at His right hand."

No one spoke for the longest time, and Jamal lowered his weapon. Mahmud sheathed his weapon as well.

"We do not doubt your vision. It is one we all share. It is this phantom you have employed . . ." Mahmud looked around for support from his peers but found little. "It is curious that one of such mystery would be so easily bought."

"A million in diamonds is no trifle amount."

"And with no guarantee that he will deliver them. And how did you find this *Saiif*?"

For the first time Jamal looked uncomfortable and did not answer his lieutenant.

Mahmud continued but with extreme caution. "It feels like *we* are the ones being used and not the other way around. Might he not just kill Talib and take the remainder of the diamonds?"

Jamal had regained his confidence and leadership. "May Allah show you mercy for speaking ill of His servant. The man we have contracted with is legendary in fighting for the causes of Islam."

"Even so, we have still pinned our success to Talib." Mahmud remained undaunted in his disapproval.

Jamal chuckled in a condescending way. "It is you who are the fool, my young friend. We have done no such thing. Can you not see? Our *success* is assured as long as our enemies are divided and concern themselves with petty ideological differences. We are united, and thus we are invincible."

Jamal clapped the backs of some his men. "It is Allah's will that the Americans be taken, and we will all be witness to His power and glory against the enemies of truth."

SIX

JAMES CANNON, THE PRESIDENT OF The Church of Jesus Christ of Latter-day Saints, was working late in his study, revising a draft of his general conference address, when the telephone rang.

"Jimmy?" the voice on the other end of the line said, "I am sorry to disturb you at this hour. I know it is late, but there has been some trouble here. It is your missionaries."

All fatigue was washed away by the ice water that now pumped through his veins. He suddenly felt sick. "What about them?"

"One has been murdered; the other three are missing."

"Oh, no," were the only two words that escaped his lips. The horrific news came from Faud al-Mohammed, retired Egyptian foreign minister and longtime friend of President Cannon. They had met decades before while President Cannon—then Ambassador Cannon—was serving throughout the Middle East. Faud had been instrumental in clearing the way for the small team of health missionaries to live and work in his country. It didn't seem possible that tonight he was calling to report that one of them was dead.

"It happened about two hours ago—"

"Two hours?"

"Yes, yes. I only learned of this minutes ago and felt it best to call you and tell you personally before you learned it from your television."

"What happened?"

"The details are . . . how you say? . . . sketchy. The stories are still coming in and are not clear. All I know is that they were on their way to a temporary medical facility in a village north of Aswan, traveling in a two-vehicle convoy. When they failed to arrive, the Red Crescent coordinator assumed that they had changed their plans and were visiting another site. A short while later the local police were called when smoldering wreckage was found along one of the desert roads. It seems that some of the locals remembered hearing an explosion and seeing smoke but had no way to contact the authorities any sooner."

President Cannon could not believe this was happening, and in this numbing state of disbelief, it was a struggle to block out his own thoughts and feelings and fears and to listen to the words of his long-time and trusted friend.

"Egypt, as you know, has strict national procedures when suspected terrorist attacks are committed within our borders," Faud continued. "Once local police determined who the victims of the attack were, they notified our offices. When our men arrived, they found the lead vehicle, or at least parts of it. The blast had killed the four men riding in it—three security detail and Elder Evans."

President Cannon still couldn't seem to wrap his tired mind around what he was hearing, and it felt like the walls and floor were swaying. This was not possible.

"The other vehicle was found off the road and down an embankment. It was empty. There was no sign of the others. We believe that your missionaries were targets of a kidnapping and are still alive, except, of course, for Elder Evans, who for whatever reason was riding up front with the security detail. Who did this and why are still unknown. My son, Hasan, a chief inspector for the National Police, is overseeing this personally. I wish I could relay his optimism, but I cannot."

The former ambassador and spiritual leader for millions leaned back in his chair and looked up at the ceiling. The news finally settled upon his mind, the shock wearing off, and he was able to start thinking clearly.

"Has the American embassy been alerted?" he asked.

"Of course. They were notified about an hour ago, before my son was informed. However, I am told that the response from authorities there did not appear as animated as I might have hoped."

"I see." That bit of news was disturbing to President Cannon too.

"My son tells me that he will keep me informed of all developments, and I of course will relay everything to you as it unfolds."

Neither friend said anything, letting the silence express the feelings that neither had words for.

"I am truly sorry, Jimmy, and I am embarrassed that this terrible thing has happened in my country."

"Yes, me too," was all he could muster to say before hanging up.

After a reflective moment, President Cannon stood up and walked to the window. Outside, the streets of downtown Salt Lake City were still busy, with cars and buses taking people to and from work, to and from home, and he was suddenly struck with the thought that it was the hope for tomorrow that drives and inspires men and women today. Take away that hope, and life becomes a dark and fearful place . . . meaningless. We have nothing if not hope.

And hanging onto that hope, he knew the next step he had to take. He stepped back to his desk, looked through his rolodex, and found the once-familiar Washington, DC, area-code phone number and checked his watch. It would be a little after one in the morning there. He dialed the number anyway.

The twenty-four-hour operator answered in monotone, "State Department. How may I direct your call?"

"This is former ambassador James Cannon. I need to be connected with Howard Stillman, undersecretary for Middle Eastern Affairs. It's urgent."

Howard Stillman had been the official channel that had secured the missionaries' Egyptian travel and work visas, though they had been expedited through personal calls made from Faud to certain Egyptian government authorities. Stillman had, however, taken all the credit and pledged his ongoing support of this "rare diplomatic opportunity," as he had called it. But President Cannon had doubted his sincerity.

Three categories of diplomats inhabit the State Department. There are the elite, whose tuxedos are always cleaned and pressed, ready at a moment's notice to attend an embassy or consul *soiree*. These individuals are concerned more with dinner etiquette than affairs of state. Then, there are "bureaucrats" in the worst sense of the word. They worship the god of document shuffling, date stamps, and time clocks. Their sole function is to keep the paperwork flowing. Lastly come those who realize that to make a difference in the world, one must actually *do* something more than just show up every day. They are the visionaries, the risk-takers, and those dissatisfied with the status quo. Stepping up to the plate and taking a swing is what they relish.

James Cannon had fallen into the last category. Those in the diplomatic corps who came to know him attributed his management style to his wartime experiences. He just couldn't have gotten the job done by digging a foxhole and hiding in it. He had to be on the move, analyzing as he went, calculating his chances and cutting his losses.

Sadly, Howard Stillman was a hybrid of the first two. He'd been an inept and fawning subordinate during Cannon's last few months as ambassador to Iran, but by some inexplicable twist of fate, he'd risen to prominence.

President Cannon was quickly frustrated by the resistance he encountered at every phone call and transfer on his way to speak to Stillman, having to raise his voice and assert his own authority to be connected at that hour of night. In the end, however, his call was put through to Stillman's home.

"Hello?" came a sleepy response.

"Howard? James Cannon here."

"Do you know what time it is?"

"Yes, I do. And that's the third time I've been asked in the last ten minutes," he replied evenly.

"Well, can't it wait until morning?"

"I'm afraid not. I want you to tell me what you know about the attack on my health missionaries in Egypt."

Stillman sounded more awake now. "What attack?"

"I figured as much. Doesn't your staff inform you when American citizens are victims of violence in the piece of the world that you're responsible for?"

"Maybe, but they know better than to bother me at home with anything other than a dire emergency."

The former ambassador was suddenly filled with righteous indignation. "Well, Howard, as long as you're up, let me give you my version of a *dire* emergency."

President Cannon repeated what he had learned from Faud's phone call. Stillman's relative silence might have given someone else the impression that he was taking copious notes and formulating an action agenda, but he knew better.

"Howard, it's a pretty sad state of affairs when a private Egyptian citizen has to break this news to me while my own government appears nonplussed. Look, I've got a boy over there who didn't bargain on his murder being part of the experience. I have an obligation to both him and his family to see that the right thing is done. And as far as the other three, well . . . What are your people going to do about it?"

"They'll do everything that *can* be done, but our track record on these things isn't very good. *If* we can get these missionaries back, it's likely to be a slow process. You must know that."

"What I know is that in the first hours or days of an abduction, these guys tend to make mistakes. That's when a rescue is best attempted. If this is allowed to drag on, the chance of three more *dead* missionaries becomes a real possibility."

"I know. I know! But I told you we'll get on it!" Stillman was on edge.

"You should *already* be on it! If the rest of those missionaries are killed because *you* didn't do all you could have, will you be able to live with it? Don't let the outcome of this incident become a stench in the nostrils of honest men."

"Now, I really think that kind of talk is . . . is . . ."

"Uncalled for? Is it? Don't forget, Howard, I've seen your work before."

There was only silence on Stillman's end. President Cannon knew that his assessment of the man was correct. Stillman would resist disturbing his own comfort zone and had to be motivated to action.

"I want you to *lean* on your people, Howard. No one rests until these missionaries are found and returned—and not in body bags, either. Don't make the same mistakes you did in Tehran. If I or the resources of the Church can be of assistance in any way, do not hesitate to call. You have my number." The former ambassador hung up. It had been uncharacteristic of him to vent his emotions that way, but Stillman's indifference had been hard to stomach.

Images of the 1979 Tehran hostage fiasco played through this head. He had been retired for a number of years by then and had just been called to the Quorum of the Twelve, unable to affect the events he saw played out on television for the world to witness. Swift action had not been taken, and instead an appeal to the humanity of the terrorists had been broadcast nightly. Even United States President Jimmy Carter had inadvertently given the kidnappers additional power and bargaining ability with his public prayers and pleas for their release. The debacle had lasted four hundred and forty-four days, during which time the hostages were physically and psychologically abused. In short, hesitation only made rescue or release that much more difficult. He only hoped that Faud's son was of the action type.

President Cannon noted the time again. There was much that needed to happen to help bring the missionaries back safely. The resources of the Church would need to be marshaled and coordinated with official efforts to find them and bring them home. Special meetings would need to be called, press releases prepared, and official channels of communication announced and opened to speed the recovery process.

But as he started to make a list, he stopped and put his pen down. Like a delayed reaction, a powerful urge to stop what he was doing overwhelmed him, and he slid from his chair to his knees, unable to contain the swell of emotion welling up inside him, sobbing and crying to the Lord for the loss of Elder Evans. Could all of this have been a mistake? Had his desire to expand the Church and the gospel to the far reaches of the world blinded him to the overwhelming dangers that awaited such actions?

These and a host of other thoughts raced through President Cannon's mind as he sat on the floor, leaning against the wall, mourning the loss of a missionary that he had personally selected from the hundreds of applications received from throughout the Church. Soon his thoughts turned to the other three, presumably still alive but missing. What fate awaited them? And with all the energy of his soul he prayed that God would watch over them, protect them, and comfort them until help could arrive.

Help. The word seemed inadequate. They needed more than just help. They needed a miracle.

President Cannon found the strength to get back to his knees and then pull himself up to his desk. There was another matter to attend to that he could not put off even one minute, despite the late hour. He stared at the phone as fear momentarily had a grip on him. It was never easy breaking bad news to family members. But they had a right to know before hearing about the fate of their family members from the likes of Stillman or worse, *Good Morning America.* Under other circumstances, the families of the kidnapped missionaries would be notified by others who worked for the Church, sometimes relaying information through local leaders to ensure that support was offered during their time of crisis. But this time the news was different and so would be the delivery.

Missionary names and home telephone numbers were not usually stored in the personal address book of the prophet, but these were no ordinary missionaries. He had met and interviewed them personally and had overseen their MTC and cultural training. He had gotten to know each member of the "Fantastic Four," as one member of the Twelve had called them; they had become like family. He had a special file with their family information in it. He had never imagined having to access it in order to break news of abduction—and in Elder Evans's case, his death.

He took a deep breath, and the fear subsided some. Part of him wished he could delegate this duty to one of the other Brethren, but he knew that the duty was his to bear. He found the first number, the one belonging to the eldest son of the Dervereux, dialed the Georgia 404 area code, and prayed that he would know what to say.

SEVEN

ELDER JACK DEVEREUX WAS BLINDFOLDED and had a course sack tied over his head. He assumed that his wife and Elder Anderson had been similarly treated. Under threat of death, none of them had spoken to each other as they were loaded roughly into the back of a truck of some sort and driven to destinations unknown. He quickly found his wife's hand and squeezed firmly, as if to assure her that somehow everything would be all right. She had called out his name softly, plaintively, but one of their captors heard her and sharply pushed the two of them apart. He fell over and hit his head on the metal truck bed—not hard enough to cut him or knock him unconscious but sufficient to give him a headache he would not soon forget. The next thing he knew, his hands were being forced behind his back and cinched with adjustable plastic ties that dug into his wrists.

The ride turned from bad to worse as they seemed to veer off the main road and traverse the rough and rocky back roads. Their bodies jarred mercilessly as the truck failed to slow down and hit innumerable peaks and valleys. Twice he heard Abigail cry out in a mix of fear and pain, and it angered him not to be able to attend to her. He had been a doctor all his life, committing his every waking hour to healing the sick and afflicted. Not once could he recall being so filled with rage as he was now that he wanted to kill another human being, but he'd never had to sit helpless as the one person he loved more than life itself was threatened and abused. He didn't like this foreign feeling. Not in the least.

The truck slowed and came to a stop.

"Get up!" one of their captors ordered. His English was heavily accented.

Although his command of the language was minimal, Elder Devereux had the impulse to tell them that they all spoke Arabic, but then resisted. If their captors believed that they only understood English, they might give up information that he could use to escape or otherwise help with their rescue.

"Move!" he ordered again, and they did.

Unable to see, and with their equilibrium off from the long, bumpy ride, they were dragged and pushed inside and down a flight of stone stairs into a damp and musty basement. A thick and solid-sounding door was closed and locked behind them.

In the silence, Elder Anderson's digital watch beeped. He had it set to go off at the top of each hour.

"Abby?" Elder Devereux called out quietly.

"Jack? Oh, Jack . . ."

"Are you hurt?" He heard some rustling next to him.

"Oh, Jack, is Elder Evans . . . ?" She couldn't finish, her words being replaced with cries.

"Elder Anderson?"

"I'm here, Doctor," he replied. "Tell me this isn't happening. Who are these guys? I mean . . . we're here to *help* them. Why would they—"

"Anderson," Elder Devereux cut him off. "I need you focused on what's happened to us right now. We'll figure out the reasons why later. Now, are you hurt? The big one hit you pretty hard back there."

Elder Anderson didn't answer right away. "I can move everything. My neck is sore, but other than that, I think I'm at a hundred percent."

"Good. Abby?" She was still sobbing quietly. "Abby, dear, I need you to stay with me. I need to know if they hurt you. Can you shrug your shoulders? I need you to make fists behind your back. Slowly turn your neck from side to side. Abby? Are you listening to me? Abby?"

The tears continued for another few moments. "I'm fine. But Robert . . ."

"I know, Dear." Elder Devereux inched closer to his wife. He felt her head rest on his chest. "I know. It'll be all right," he lied. "Everything's going to be all right."

EIGHT

PRESIDENT CANNON REPLACED THE PHONE receiver and buried his face in his hands. He was physically and emotionally drained. The calls to the missionaries' family members had taken most of the night and early morning, but he had refused to hurry along or cut short the time they needed to talk, vent, cry, and ask questions. The calls had all followed similar patterns. Once the initial shock of the news wore off, their anger toward Muslims and terrorists rose to the surface, and President Cannon took the opportunity to explain that the actions of a few men should not be used to judge all of Islam, though he couldn't blame them for their misconceptions and misinformation. For years the media had portrayed Middle Eastern terrorists as "fundamentalists" and continued to push on the world words and terms such as *jihad* and *shahids,* or martyrs, in the never-ending pursuit of shock spots, ratings, and sponsors. What the media perpetuated was a wide range of misconceptions and falsehoods that served only to generate suspicion, hatred, and anger toward Islam as a whole, justifying the criminal actions of the radical few. The cycle was insidious.

In fact, as President Cannon well knew from his many years spent serving his country in the Middle East, the very word *Islam* means "peace," and those evil men and women who committed heinous crimes in its name did so out of their own hatred and with their own agendas. Half truths, as he well knew, were more convincing and did more damage than straight-up lies. For example, the term *jihad* is used in Islamic teachings, but it largely has personal application, as Muslims everywhere are encouraged to fight the evil influences of the world, conquer sin, and emerge victorious at the judgment seat of God. It is true, however, that the Koran does speak of a holy war, or *jihad,* as an outward show of force, but it has strict rules to be followed. For instance, a *jihad* can only be called by a recognized and legitimate authority on the Koran. But even if a full-scale war were declared against Islam and the Muslim world, there would still be rules that must be followed without exception. It is forbidden to kill those who have done nothing to hurt you. It is forbidden to kill women and children. It is even forbidden to take hostages and to mistreat, torture, or kill prisoners taken in that holy war.

And what of their belief that if they were killed in this holy war as a martyr, they were immediately welcomed into paradise, or heaven? Here, again, the Koran is clear, but by the designs of evil and conspiring men, this truth has been lost to the world at large. If a rightful *jihad* has been declared, a warrior who gives his life fighting in the name of God is promised rest and relief in the world to come. It was similar to the teaching found in the gospels of Matthew, Mark, and Luke, where Jesus assured the early saints that if they lost their life in His service or through persecution of their faith, they should find peace and eternal life in the hereafter. And just as Jesus in no way encouraged or condoned planned suicide to reach paradise, a faithful warrior in a holy war is forbidden from planning or even knowing the time, place, or manner of his own death. The prophet Mohammed was clear on this teaching, declaring that those who take their own life during an attack, such as suicide bombers and the like, are destined for hell and not paradise. But here again, angry and evil men have corrupted the teachings of the Koran in such a way as to trick otherwise faithful men into committing these acts of terror.

Though President Cannon had only the opportunity to share a small portion of his knowledge of the Islam faith with the families of Elder and Sister Devereux, Elder Anderson, and Elder Evans, he knew he would have to explain this further to the Brethren and other members of Church leadership who would be helping those family members and who would be fielding questions from the press who would no doubt be hounding his office once the news was reported. He began gathering his thoughts and preparing an appropriate statement that he, and the Church at large, could stand by during this crisis.

A light knock tapped on his study door. "Jimmy?"

He looked up, eyes red from crying, and tried to smile. But he couldn't and started to weep again.

"It's my fault, Beth," he said. "It's my fault he's dead."

His wife approached softly and put her arms around her beloved husband of almost fifty-five years and just held him. She knew he didn't really believe what he was saying. He didn't need her to try and convince him otherwise. She knew that all he needed right now was someone to hold him. Someone to love him. Someone to support him in his dark hour of need.

After a long moment, Beth said, "Elder Crane called on the other line. He saw what happened on the news this morning. He's called a special meeting of the Twelve. I told him you were calling the families personally. He said they'd be ready when you arrived."

She put her finger under his chin and lifted his eyes to meet hers. "We cannot know God's will in all things. Sending those missionaries was the right thing to do—I've never been more sure of anything in my life. You are a good man, Jimmy."

President Cannon wondered how his wife could know the doubts and fears of his heart. She was an amazing woman. He tried again to smile and partially succeeded.

"Your suit is laid out on the bed," she said. "And I'll make you one of those breakfast tortilla things you like."

His smile deepened. "I love you."

Beth smiled and winked. "You'd better. Now go. There is too much work to be done to sit around here in your pajamas."

He took her hands and kissed them tenderly. "Thank you."

* * *

President Cannon placed another call to Howard Stillman once he reached his office.

"The attack and abduction is all over the news," he said to the under-secretary, "but the reports are silent as to efforts to find or rescue them."

"James, you've got to try to understand. These things take time."

"Time my missionaries don't have. I'm not expecting a miracle from you—I leave those to God—but I am expecting action on our part to make that miracle happen."

"But there is nothing you can do."

"And from what I hear there is *little* you and your people are doing."

"Listen, James! Things have changed since you left the service. We have to operate within certain clear and precise channels on these things these days. This is a sensitive topic to discuss with Middle Eastern countries. It has become more a dance of sorts—"

"One of my missionaries is dead and three more are missing and you're talking about dancing? Well, stop the music, step on a few toes if you have to, but get out there and get my missionaries back!"

It had been several years since James Cannon had felt the need to raise his voice to anyone, but this lack of action was unacceptable and could only lead to an unpleasant end. And as much as he hated to admit it, he knew, too, that the foreign service of today was much different than his old OSS days. Then, agents would be leaning on their sources, rounding up the usual suspects and squeezing information out of them they didn't even know they had. But today's world of intelligence gathering was hindered by myriad watchdog and civil rights organizations that were determined to protect the guilty at all costs, even at the expense of innocent lives. He knew that his old way of thinking was not popular in today's progressive world—and he did believe that men were innocent until proven guilty—but he could not understand letting valuable time slip away while innocent lives were at stake.

"Howard, I am sorry for accusing you of not doing your job. Please understand, though, that the fate of these missionaries weighs heavily on my heart. Our missionaries have been attacked, assaulted, and put in harm's way since our church's founding. But this is a first. Nothing like this has ever happened before. And I sent them out personally. I cannot just sit back and let the wheels of bureaucracy grind at a snail's pace."

Stillman paused. "James, you have to trust that we are doing all we can."

"I'm not accustomed to being out of the loop on such important matters."

Stillman paused again, this time longer.

"Howard?"

"This attack is a matter of national security. Please understand, you've been gone for a long time. Clearances are required for—"

"Clearances?"

"It's not like it was in the old days. We all appreciate what you did back in the day, but—"

"Spare me the retirement speech and just say it."

Stillman took a deep breath. "This is a highly sensitive situation, and in the interest of national security, information is being restricted to official channels only. I'm sorry, James, but you're not on that list."

"These are my missionaries we're talking about! You can't cut me off and leave me out in the cold. Surely the resources of the Church could be helpful."

"We appreciate the offer and support, but these things have to be handled carefully. 'Too many chefs,' and all that."

President Cannon could not have been more shocked and disheartened. This was not right. They couldn't do this to him, could they? With his service record and all he had accomplished during his career in the Foreign Service, how could they not use his years of experience?

"I promise to let you know what I can. I will do what I can to keep you in the loop, but don't spend your time just waiting by the phone. Again, this matter is being attended to in the best possible way. You have to trust me on this."

President Cannon had little trust for the man before this had happened, and this latest conversation did even less to inspire his confidence in the system.

"You have my office and personal numbers. Please keep me informed before I hear it on CNN."

"You have my word. Now, if there is nothing else . . ."

"Good-bye, Howard. And may God help you." *May God help us all.*

President Cannon carefully cradled the receiver. This latest news had come as a complete surprise. He knew that collaboration was the key to effective resolutions. The Church was not without global influence and could conceivably offer at least some assistance in getting the Devereux and Elder Anderson home. But he also knew from experience that outside meddling in foreign and diplomatic affairs often caused more trouble that it meant to solve. But surely there was something he could do. Some small work that would help rather than hinder.

A strong thought came to mind. "Of course," he muttered. He buzzed his secretary. "Grace?"

"Yes?"

"I need you to track down the membership records of a Samuel Ryker, that's spelled R-Y-K-E-R. If there is more than one with that name, his wife's name is Susan. He works for . . ."

He paused before continuing. *Old habits die hard,* he thought to himself. "Let's just say he worked for a certain government agency and has likely moved around a lot. He won't be the easiest member to find."

Grace laughed softly over the intercom. "Will I need a top-secret clearance?"

"It wouldn't hurt." He chuckled back, the weight of the morning beginning to lift. "Let me know the minute you have a number for him."

"Right away, President."

James Cannon first met Samuel Ryker when he was serving as the U.S. ambassador to Egypt nearly twenty-five years earlier. Then Ambassador Cannon had welcomed the sharp young man to the embassy's CIA office, but what struck him at the time was the fact that his young wife traveled with him. A career as CIA field agent was a solitary one, a career not usually conducive to a healthy, traditional family life, but somehow he managed to pull it off. Over the next few years, and until his retirement, Cannon had the pleasure of working closely with this Agency rockstar. Ryker's hard work and innovative approach to intelligence gathering aided him behind the scenes in matters of Arab–Israeli peace negotiations.

During their few years working together, they had immediately developed a special kinship between them, Cannon seeing in him some of the exuberance of his own youth, while Ryker looked to Cannon's experience and leadership with deep admiration. In all of Cannon's diplomatic assignments, he'd come across so very few members of the Church like Ryker. Ryker had enlisted in the military during the Vietnam era but had taken a leave of absence to serve a full-time mission to Belgium before returning to serve his country as a combat helicopter pilot. His faith alone could have formed the basis of the friendship, but Ryker was also the best covert agent that Cannon had ever known, and he'd known quite a few since his own exploits during the war as a member of the OSS and then later when he joined and ascended the ranks of the Foreign Service.

Their wives had grown especially close during that short time, leaning on each other when their husbands' work took them away for weeks on end. Even in the years just after his retirement and subsequent calling to the ranks of Church leadership, their wives continued to write and share with each other those special moments that made life truly worthwhile. After a while, however, the letters became less frequent. Susan had given birth to twins, which had overwhelmed her and had taken all of her time and efforts, and his own calling as an Apostle put both he and his wife on a busy schedule that would break couples half their age. True friendships were a rarity in life, and quite frankly, he was ashamed that he hadn't given the Rykers much thought over the years. Until now.

The name of Samuel Ryker had come to President Cannon's mind then. If there was anyone in this world who would know what could be done to help get his missionaries back, Sam Ryker would.

Grace returned twenty minutes later with a manila file folder in her hand and a confused look on her face.

"What is it?" he asked. "What's wrong?"

She hesitated to speak, starting and then stopping briefly before the first word had a chance to be released. "You were right. Brother Ryker has moved around a lot—overseas for the most part and in areas of the world where we don't exactly have a strong Church presence, if you know what I mean. But this is odd. His records end with him living in Cairo."

Her choice of words concerned him. "You mean he still lives in Egypt? Stationed at the embassy?"

Grace shook her head. "No, our records for him just end around the same time as the accident."

President Cannon couldn't find the words at first. "What accident?"

Grace stepped to his desk and laid the folder out in front of him. On the top were several photocopies of newspaper articles from London, Germany, and Israel from the previous July. They all reported the bombing at Jerusalem's Western Wall, each with black-and-white pictures of the aftermath of the attack. President Cannon began scanning through them one by one while Grace continued.

"Although the names of the victims were not reported, the date of the attack and Susan's death are the same. Our records also show that their twin daughters, Natalie and Niccole, died on the same day."

"And Sam?"

"That's just it. We have no records of his death. Just his family's."

"Could it be an oversight? A clerical mistake?"

"It's possible. I'll look into it. It's like he just vanished."

President Cannon's mind began trying to put together the pieces of this puzzle. It just didn't make sense. If Ryker had been on assignment, the specifics and circumstances of his death might be altered to protect national security, but then why was he with his family?

"President?" Grace asked. When he didn't respond she tried the next level of attention grabber, one that few dared to use in the vicinity of Temple Square. "James?"

President Cannon returned from his thoughts. "Sorry. What is it?"

"There is an odd note here," she said, referencing a small stack of papers she was still holding. "A financial contribution. A fast offering, registered four months after the attack."

"Where?"

"In a small branch outside Paris."

Ryker's mission. If he *had* survived the accident, it was plausible that he might have returned to Europe, to a time before his family—to a simpler time—to cope with his loss.

"Is there an address?"

"No, just a name."

President Cannon made some quick calculations in his head. "That would make it almost five there," he said to no one in particular. "Grace, I need you to find the branch president there and find out everything you can about this donation. We need to find him."

Once Grace had left his office, President Cannon picked up the phone and started flipping though his rolodex. Even after almost an hour of calling in favors and exerting all the influence a former ambassador possessed, he still did not get any of his questions answered. By every account, Sam had died in that attack in Jerusalem, although Israeli intelligence failed to include him in their initial reports. And that's where the trail stopped. No amount of pressure or pleading had revealed anything else. His only hope, now, was Grace.

A knock came at this door, followed by its opening.

"President," Grace started, "I think I have it," and she gave him a piece of lined paper with an international telephone number written on it. "It's almost six months old, but . . ."

President Cannon took it almost reverently. "Have you—"

"Called it? No. On the off-chance I'm right, I wouldn't know what to say. I figured that was between the two of you." She closed the door quietly behind her as she left him alone.

The slip of paper began to shake in President Cannon's hand. If Ryker *had* survived the attack, he was taking extreme measures not to be found. Maybe this was a mistake, too, like sending out the missionaries. He stared at the number, doubts running through his mind. With the tragedy so recent, how could he even ask for Sam's help?

President James Cannon dismissed all fears, picked up the phone, and dialed the number.

* * *

Seven time zones away, the late afternoon sun slipped through the drawn blinds, cutting the darkness with sharp blades of light, only just illuminating the dirty and disheveled one-room apartment. Sitting at the small wooden kitchen table, Sam Ryker held a crumpled snapshot of Susan and his girls in one hand, and his semiautomatic, nine-millimeter Glock in the other. He had run out of tears a long time ago and was left only with emptiness and pain and no way to express it.

A cheap ceiling fan circled overhead, softly clicking with every rotation. Outside, the sounds of traffic rumbled with the murmur of crowds that filtered up from the street, while the muffled sounds of the single mother and her two children next door pushed their way through the thin walls and added to the torment that was his life.

Clothes were strewn across the apartment, and the dishes piled in the sink and across the counter only added to his depression. He slept only in fits of exhaustion, and of late, the only food he had eaten was pâté smeared on stale bread bought when he'd left the four walls of his apartment and had ventured into the dark Parisian night days before. Where Paris at night is an inspiration to the thousands who visit the City of Love, to Ryker it reminded him of a promise once made but never fulfilled.

Ryker sat in the straight-backed chair and stroked the grip of the gun with his thumb, the rough texture the only thing his senses would register. In fact, he had been beyond feeling for months now. His life had grown beyond dark, a void that had swallowed up the last of his reserves.

Today's the day, he thought.

He had always thought of himself as a religious man. But in one fiery instant, those beliefs that had been so strong for so long had shattered like glass. He had been forbidden to attend the memorial service and instead had been forced to watch it on closed-circuit television from his hospital bed. The clergyman who'd presided at the service had said their deaths had been God's will—that God had called them home to a much more beautiful place—and that rather than grieve their passing, they should rejoice in the knowledge that they had lived exemplary lives and were now in the presence of the Lord. And with that absolute drivel still ringing in his ears, Ryker abandoned this God had that ripped from him everything he'd loved and held dear.

Ryker brought the picture up to his lips and pressed them gently to it. No longing to be together again. Just an end to the suffering.

Ryker thumbed off the safety and chambered a round.

The shrill ring of the rotary phone hanging on the wall jarred him, and he let out a sharp yell, his blood pumping. He couldn't remember the last time the phone had rung. It wasn't supposed to ring. All part of his "protection." He stared at the white box as it rang again. And again. And again.

Ryker threw the chair back and lunged for the receiver and shouted into it, *"What!?"*

Over the scratch of static, he heard a deep voice. "Sam? Sam, is that you? Sam, if you can hear me, this is James Cannon."

The mere mention of the name jolted him, and he dropped the gun. He leaned against the wall and slid his way down to the ground.

"James?"

"Sam," the strong voice on the other end continued, "it's good to hear your voice."

Ryker couldn't respond for a while as he sobbed. After a few minutes, an enormous weight lifted from his shoulders.

Ryker found his voice again. "James . . . I mean . . . President Cannon . . . I . . . how did you know?"

"Know what, Sam?"

And with that answer, Ryker started to cry again. He kicked the Glock across the room with his foot. How could he have been so foolish? So selfish?

"Sam, I just found out about Susan and the girls. You have my deepest sympathies. Susan was like a daughter to me."

Without being asked, Ryker recounted the whole story as best he could between bouts of crying. President Cannon, with years of experience hearing confessions and emotional narratives, just listened, acknowledged the pain, offered support, but never proposed solutions.

Once Ryker had finished bearing his soul, President Cannon offered what few words of support he could, took a deep breath, and then proceeded with the driving force behind the call.

"Sam, I need your help."

Ryker was not at all surprised. "My help?"

"We have a . . . situation in Egypt, and I believe that you are the only one that can help. You may have seen it on the news."

He hadn't even owned a radio since the attack, let alone a television, preferring to fortify his isolation from the outside world. "I . . . I'm sorry . . . I don't . . . I haven't heard."

President Cannon took the next few minutes recounting the events leading up to the call of the missionaries, their work along the Nile, and everything that Faud had shared with him earlier that morning.

"Faud has taken this attack personally and has asked his son to head up the investigation. He has pledged the full cooperation and resources of the Egyptian government in this effort, and I believe him."

Through the gauze that still wrapped his mind, Ryker was able to pick out Faud's son's name. If Hasan was on the case, then the case was all but solved already. Ryker took a minute to digest the situation fully. "But what can *I* do?"

Here, again, the former ambassador hesitated to speak. "I . . . I don't know. I need these missionaries brought back. Safely."

This *did* take Ryker by surprise. "I . . . I can't. You know that I . . . They won't let me just go off . . . rogue, like some mercenary, just like that."

"I know, I know. But I can't shake this feeling that you can help somehow."

"What about the embassy efforts?" Ryker countered, his mind becoming sharper as they talked. "Surely they're working on this—"

"Secretary Stillman heard the news from me this morning, *two hours after the attack*. I woke him out of bed. The authorities have dropped the ball on this one. Sam, nothing is being done to help them. It has all become too political, too hands-off to get the job done."

President Cannon took a moment to calm down and collect his thoughts. "You know as well as I do that those missionaries are as good as dead if they're not rescued soon. If I were a younger man, I'd go myself. But I can't."

Ryker knew exactly what he was *not* being asked to do. He thought about it for a moment. "James . . . President Cannon, I . . . are you sure I'm the one you want?"

There was a long moment of silence. "I'm sure you're the one the Lord wants."

Flashes from Susan's and the girls' memorial service lit in his mind, and those angry feelings toward God surfaced. "Let's leave the Lord out of this! Where was God when Susan and the girls died? Why didn't he save them?"

Ryker's hands began to shake again, but instead of anger, his whole being was filled with loss and a profound sadness.

When President Cannon spoke again, his voice cracked with emotion. "I don't know what to say, Sam. We're all called on to bear burdens—"

"No!" Ryker interrupted. "Please, don't. Until you know what it's like to lose your family . . . to watch as they . . ." He couldn't finish. He didn't have the strength left.

"I am truly sorry for what happened, and you're right—I can't even begin to imagine what you must be going through, but I know someone who does. We must not lose our faith. It is during times like these that our faith becomes our only source of strength. Don't give up on Him. He has certainly not given up on you."

Somewhere buried deep inside him, Ryker knew that President Cannon was right. "I'm sorry, James . . . I mean, President. I didn't mean—"

"No, you never have to apologize to me. Look, I know the timing of all this is not ideal, but the Lord needs you—*I* need you—and I want you to know that I will be praying with all the energy of my soul that He will not only help you find our missionaries, but help you find . . . whatever it is you're searching for."

Ryker braced for another round of powerful emotions, but they never came. "I'm not sure I even believe in that stuff anymore."

"Then I'll just have to do the believing for the both of us."

After yet more silence, President Cannon said, "Tell me what you need me to do."

A plan was already forming in the former intelligent officer's head. He checked the clock hanging askew on the wall and made a quick mental calculation. "For starters, call Faud. Have him tell his son I will be on the next direct flight out of de Gaulle. He and I go way back. He'll know what to do."

"Anything else?"

Ryker didn't answer right away. He looked at the gun in the corner of the room. "No. You've already done more than you'll ever know."

NINE

SAM RYKER HAD WASTED NO time making arrangements to fly to Egypt. He quickly packed a small overnight bag and hailed a taxi to Charles de Gaulle International Airport. He would worry about a ticket when he arrived. Ryker had a trick up his sleeve that would guarantee a seat on the next connecting flight to Cairo.

Once inside, he walked to a bank of pay phones opposite the baggage claim area, set his sole piece of luggage on the floor, took out his wallet, and fished through it until he found the small piece of paper he was looking for. A phone number with a Washington, DC, area code was written on the scrap. He'd called the number before but hadn't felt a need to commit it to memory. It was to a travel agency under contract to the CIA. Unlike other agencies, it was unlisted in the phone book, it asked very few questions of those who called, and it was open for business twenty-four hours a day. Other than that, it was a real travel business that even made money for the Agency. Callers would give their destination, a credit card number that was never questioned, and voila. The tickets, connecting flight arrangements, hotel reservations for any layover, car rental, and the like were instantly arranged. Even if flights were fully booked or hotels filled, room for one more was always found. Ryker made the call and was once again amazed at the efficiency of the service he'd used multiple times during his career.

He reasoned that, at worst, it was a sin of omission to use the service. True, he wasn't with the CIA anymore, but no one had asked, either. The American Express credit card number he'd given them was valid, and when he got the bill, he'd pay it.

He next made a quick mental calculation of time zones. It was nearly six now, making it almost eight in Israel. The Sabbath would have started by now, and he wondered if the call would be answered. He placed the call to Tel Aviv. This number he *had* memorized.

"*Shalom,*" the familiar male voice answered after the fifth ring.

"*Shalom.* May I speak with Rabbi Abraham Strauss, please," Ryker replied in Hebrew. He wasn't fluent in Hebrew, but he could get by in most social situations, albeit with a considerable foreign accent. These few words, however, had been practiced to perfection.

"You must have dialed a wrong number. There is no Rabbi Strauss here," the man said.

"Oh, I'm *terribly* sorry to have bothered you," he said, again in unaccented Hebrew. He hung up and looked at his watch.

The two close friends had only used the simple, prearranged code a handful of times over a twenty-year period. No one was apt to connect the dots when the dots were *that* far apart. The recipient of the wrong number in Tel Aviv was a Mossad agent by the name of Immanuel Lubin and was one of Ryker's longtime and only friends.

Despite what one reads about brotherly cooperation, the relationship between Mossad and the CIA over the years could best be described as "strained"—sometimes to the point of outright dysfunctional. For agents of these two organizations to conduct unauthorized communication would have subjected both to severe disciplinary action for breach of security.

That was then. This was now, but a direct contact between an *ex*-CIA operative and an agent of Mossad would've been even more suspicious to anyone monitoring the agent's phone, as was frequently the case. Mossad was absolutely paranoid about security; hence, the ruse.

Manni Lubin, a Polish Jew, had immigrated to Palestine after World War II. He was just a boy when he had arrived, accompanied by his aunt. His father, mother, and older sister had been unlucky enough not to get out of Warsaw before the Nazis began their systematic detention and subsequent annihilation of residents. Months before the ax fell, Lubin's parents had thought it best to have their infant son taken out of the country by the father's sister. The two refugees had lived like gypsies, relying on the good will of strangers to feed and hide them. Avoiding apprehension, they eventually reached Rome, where the Catholic Church gave them sanctuary in Vatican City. Even there they weren't free to walk the streets unmolested—Nazis were everywhere—but the Catholic clergy went to extraordinary lengths to protect the Jews who'd escaped their Nazi-planned fate.

With Germany's defeat and the imposition of the Iron Curtain, some refugees looked to brighter futures outside of Europe. Lubin's aunt was one of those and secured passage for herself and her nephew to British-controlled Palestine.

In many ways, life in Palestine was as hostile as what they'd experienced during the war; but in time, as the State of Israel emerged from gun smoke and ashes, life took on a positive direction. Years on a *kibbutz* strengthened Lubin in more ways than just physically. Work on collective farms developed a strong sense of self and community.

Israeli military service eventually lured Lubin away from the land. He was a disciplined spirit who excelled at protecting his adopted country. Though he had no formal education beyond what he'd been exposed to on the *kibbutz*, his analytical prowess became known to Israel's intelligence service, which recruited him once his enlistment was concluded.

Lubin was simply the best agent that Mossad had ever encountered. Israel's enemies were everywhere and constantly conspiring. He succeeded in every assignment—no matter the odds or how perilous. It was said that there wasn't an operation that couldn't be improved by adding Manni Lubin to the team.

The last twenty years or so, Lubin's forte had been counterterrorism—first as a field operative and more recently as a teacher of new recruits. He and his wife, Esther, spoke often about retirement, but the world of intelligence was in his blood, and his current assignment was such that he could generally set his own schedule. It was also much safer.

Ryker's use of the code signaled two things for Lubin. First, Ryker was trying to reach him. Second, he had twenty minutes to leave his apartment and go to a preselected pay phone two blocks away, where Ryker would call again. Such were the established rules of the trade, silly to an outsider but necessary for those within. He imagined, however, that this particular call would be met with no shortage of anticipation, given Ryker's sudden absence after the bombing.

Ryker crossed to another phone adjacent to one of the many snack bars. Again he glanced at his watch. It had been exactly twenty minutes since his last call. He dialed the second number from memory. He could only hope that the number hadn't been changed.

"*Shalom,*" a voice answered. It was Lubin.

"Hello, my friend," Ryker replied in English.

Lubin broke into English. "Sam, I can't believe it! So good to hear your voice. How are you? Where are you? You just disappeared after the . . . Are you all right?"

"I'm okay," he replied evenly. "I'm calling from a pay phone in Paris. And, no, I'm not with the Agency any longer, but I need help, and there were only a couple of people I could think of."

"This has to do with the missionary who was killed earlier this morning, doesn't it?" Lubin was nothing if not a true professional.

"I've been asked by James Cannon to find them and bring them back."

"Cannon? Ambassador Cannon?"

"He's taking their abduction personally," Ryker said. "It seems he doesn't have much faith in official efforts to secure their release."

"We've been following that incident closely. I took personal interest because I knew that these missionaries—medical personnel, if I'm not mistaken—were of your faith."

"I'm feeling better about this mission already."

Lubin paused to gather his thoughts. "Am I to assume that you're on your own, without the resources of your government?"

"You could say that. Technically, I don't even exist anymore."

"I don't envy your position, but I do understand Cannon's concern and request of you. As of this evening, we haven't been able to detect any real efforts to find your missionaries. Our evaluation of the situation is that embassy personnel in Cairo are sitting on their hands again, instead of beating the bush for those responsible. But alone . . . what can you hope to accomplish?"

"I know I'm asking a lot and that you could be prosecuted for consenting, but I need the most up-to-date intelligence you have on the incident."

This time it was Lubin who remained silent, undoubtedly weighing the consequences of assisting Ryker.

"You know, it's been quite popular of late for Israelis to visit the antiquities of Egypt. I've been thinking about a little excursion myself. What a coincidence it would be if two old friends should happen to run into each other there. By the way, what time did you say your plane was due to arrive?"

Ryker hastily outlined his itinerary and cradled the phone receiver. It felt good to speak with his old friend. They were both taking grave risks to have this conversation, but there was no one else from whom Ryker would rather receive help.

Ryker checked his watch. He had just fifteen minutes to pick up a boarding pass for the first leg of his journey. And with a lighter step than he'd had since leaving his apartment, he set off to do what he did best.

TEN

ELDER DEVEREUX COULDN'T BELIEVE HE was having this conversation. Not now, and not with Elder Anderson.

"Keep your voice down," he said. "They'll hear you for sure."

"I don't care," Elder Anderson whispered loudly. "Let them hear me. I've always preferred a straight-up fight as opposed to all this plotting and planning."

Elder Devereux's reasons for keeping the young elder's voice down were twofold. Of course, there was the likely consideration that a guard was posted just on the other side of the door—although he had not heard any movement, coughing, or any other sounds that would support that conclusion. But the other reason lay with his wife. She had fallen asleep from emotional exhaustion an hour earlier, and even in her sleep she shuddered and cried from time to time.

"No fight with them will be straight up. Not now, anyway."

"So what do you think we should do? Just sit here and take it between the eyes? I've never shied away from a fight, and I ain't about to start now." Elder Anderson had grown up on a farm, and at six foot two, he'd never had to back down from a fight.

"Rash moves will only get us killed. We've got to—"

"Let them do the same thing to us they did to Elder Evans? Is that it?"

Elder Devereux shook his head. "If they had wanted us dead, we wouldn't be having this particular conversation right now. I've been thinking about what happened. I don't think they meant to kill Robert at all. He was supposed to be riding back with us. I think Elder Evan's death was an accident."

"An accident?" The young elder's voice was straining to break free of the whisper. "They killed all of them! That was no accident! Slipping on the ice;

hitting your thumb with a hammer . . . those are accidents! Blowing up a military jeep is not an accident!"

"And what would you do? Unless you're keeping something from me, I suspect your hands are tied tight like mine with a bag over your head. I'd be much obliged if you would share with me your grand plan to break free of the cords that keep us bound and bring down these prison walls around us." He paused to let his words sink in. "Well, go ahead. I'm all ears."

Elder Anderson was silent for a moment, and then he started to cry. Elder Devereux knew he had to be tough to rein in his young companion, but now was the time to show an increase of love needed after sharp reproving.

"Elder," he said softly, "we read that there is a time for everything under the sun. This includes our time to get out of here. I admire your enthusiasm. Fifty years ago I might have led the charge myself, but I have more than my own life to be concerned about. I have to consider Abby. We're both in good shape for our age, but neither of us could run or even walk fast enough to make our escape. I'm not entirely without experience in all this. I spent time in Europe during the last days of World War II. Our best chance of coming out of this thing alive is to survive long enough to be rescued."

"So we just sit here and do nothing?"

"Living long enough for someone to find us is not doing nothing."

Elder Anderson was silent for a long time. "I don't want to die," he finally said, quietly and embarrassed.

"I know you don't, Elder," he said to himself, his sleeping wife still leaning on his shoulder. "I don't want to, either."

ELEVEN

As planned, Saiif's circuitous route bypassed any police interference, but twice they had to dig the truck out of sand. The only roads south of Aswan traced the western shore of Lake Nasser. To the east was nothing but sand and rock hills that stretched all the way to the Red Sea—a tempting route, to be sure, with nothing to pass as roads and thereby not likely to be watched in the slightest by the authorities. But therein lay the danger. He was a master of planning out every detail of an operation, but the deserts were not easily tamed, and a single transport bouncing over the dry river beds, rocky hills, and shifting sands left too much to chance. And while others would petition the blessings of Allah for a successful operation, Saiif did not think God would smile on his choice of profession. No, he would do this himself, and his intended course along the hard-packed roads west of the lake was their best chance to make it to Abu Simbel undetected.

They reached the remote city of antiquity some time after nightfall, a few hours behind schedule but with still nearly ten hours before the mid-morning exchange. Saiif parked the truck down one of the seemingly endless streets and alleys of the poor sector just north of Abu Simbel's airport. Getting out quietly, he walked around back to check on Imad and his American guests. Imad had fallen asleep and was slumped in the back corner of covered bed. Saiif was tired, too, but that was no excuse for endangering them all with this severe lapse of judgment. He pulled himself up into the back of the truck and made his way to the back, kicking Imad with enough strength to express his extreme displeasure.

"Get up!" he said.

Imad jolted out of his slumber, swinging his fists. A moment of disorientation later and he was on his feet, apologizing to his employer and vowing never to let it happen again. Saiif spoke not a word as he set about checking his drugged captives. They were still out cold. The amber liquid he administered in Aswan had not yet run its course, but it would shortly, and that was good, Saiif thought. He touched the woman's face. They were all beginning to show the early stages of dehydration. He needed them alive, for a little while longer at least. Then they were no longer his problem.

"See that they are given water when they wake up," Saiif instructed. "You are not to lay a hand on them, especially the young one. Am I understood?"

Imad nodded.

"I will return when contact has been made. I will send no one in my place." He reached into his jacket and handed Imad a nine-millimeter handgun. "Shoot anyone who says otherwise." Saiif then walked off into the darkness and was gone.

Three streets over, Saiif found the small European automobile he had arranged to be parked there two days ago and fished the keys out from the rear wheel well. The car started quietly and he turned onto the main road past the airport and toward the city proper of Abu Simbel.

In theory, tourism was supposed to provide a city with revenue to increase its quality of life. However, like much of the world where tourism is the primary source of revenue, Abu Simbel and its money usually only benefitted the rich. The city had never been wealthy, but its once-thriving areas were now partially abandoned—the poor being forced to look for work in Aswan. This exodus over the years had left behind modern ruins of its own—ample to conceal a truck loaded with drugged Americans.

Paying for covered parking at the Nefertari Hotel, the terrorist known by many names to many people found a quiet corner, set the alarm on his wristwatch, and settled in for a desperately needed rest. He hadn't seen the back of his eyelids for nearly two days, and his body was starting to show the stress. In a few hours it would all be over, and he would be rid of the Americans. Then the fun would really begin.

TWELVE

CAIRO INTERNATIONAL WAS JUST AS Sam Ryker remembered it. It was funny how all things Egyptian seemed to be timeless and eternal. Situated at the crossroads of the Middle East, Cairo is a business mecca, and the airport plays a vital role transporting pilgrims to its moneyed shrines. There are exotic food kiosks from which unsuspecting visitors were likely to encounter an eventual case of diarrhea, or "Ramses's Revenge" as it was known. Even at this hour, the noise of thousands of hectic travelers echoed off polished stone walls and floors. It is an airport where congestion and confusion reigned: rental car agencies each tried to outdo their competitors; automated conveyor belts spewed forth luggage like molten lava from an erupting volcano; miles of ticket counters represented virtually every known airline in the region; money changers switched out multinational currency for local bills; porters wrested baggage from visitors' hands to gain a gratuity; begging children with runny noses flitted from traveler to traveler; taxi drivers were lined up in their dented vehicles, eager to take passengers on death-defying trips around town or to hotels; and bus drivers waited patiently for those travelers whose funds wouldn't stretch far enough for taxi. *Yes,* thought Ryker, *Cairo airport is one of the insane marvels of the modern world.*

He was met just beyond the arrival gate by two fully armed men in dark military uniforms. Even this early in the morning, they were wearing big aviator sunglasses that covered much of their faces.

"Mr. Ryker?"

He nodded.

"The foreign minister is expecting you. You will come with us." They took positions in front of and behind Ryker and escorted him to the front of the line at the customs desk. Men and women moved out of their way. Ryker kept his eyes down, averting most of the stares, but he did briefly catch the eye of one older gentleman seated across the terminal reading a copy of the most current issue of *Time* before returning his gaze to the tiled floor.

One of the soldiers held out his hand. "Passport." Ryker handed it over and watched as it was scanned quickly and then stamped without question and given back to him. The clerk manning the customs desk was stunned by the show of force and offered no resistance to the expedited manner in which Ryker was rushed into Egypt.

Ryker was led to a black Mercedes sedan, made darker by the tinted windows, where he was ushered into the backseat. The car pulled away and sped quickly under the cover of night. Neither of the soldiers spoke as they drove.

Ryker took in the sights and sounds of Cairo—a city he'd never expected to visit again. The mosques, with their tall minarets reaching toward heaven, were lit up as brightly as if it were day, commanding awe and respect from passersby. They were nestled between the modern skyscrapers, a sharp contrast to the ancient feel of the city. As these sights passed by his window in a blur, he reflected on the city, country, and area of the world he had called home for so long. He and Susan had raised their twin daughters here, surrounded on all sides by the antiquities of the pharaohs and immersed in a culture rich in religious rites and faith. There were few members of the LDS faith living in the city, and most of their Sabbath-day worship took place in their home. Occasionally others would join them, but for the most part, the Ryker family had been a lone Christian vessel sailing on an Islamic sea, following the charts and never losing sight of their eternal goal.

A lump formed in his throat, a dark hole struggling to open deep inside his soul. He closed his eyes to the world around him and leaned back into the cool, leather seats, hoping this wasn't all just a big mistake. Fifteen minutes later, they pulled up to a gated house that lay on a small hill overlooking the Nile as it spread north into the fertile Delta region.

The driver pulled up to the twelve-foot-high fence and swiped a security card across a concealed card reader. A second later, a motor hummed as the gate began to slide out of the way. The car pulled through the open gate and wound its way around the fountains and rock gardens. Nearby, Ryker could hear dogs barking, uncomfortable with the late-night arrival, but he presumed that they had been kenneled ahead of time. They stopped in front of the house, and the soldier in the passenger seat got out of the car almost mechanically and opened Ryker's door. He grabbed the handle of his carry-on bag and made his way up the steps toward the front door.

The opulent home was of Mediterranean architecture, resembling a small Italian villa with a white stucco exterior and a red-tiled roof. The grounds were lit, the lawns and flowerbeds well manicured but not ostentatious. Forty-foot-tall palm trees adorned the front corners of the house, giving it an impression of being situated in an oasis.

Faud himself met him at the door. He liked that. Faud was not pretentious enough to send a servant.

"Do come in, Mr. Ryker. I had been expecting your call." He offered a warm, firm handshake.

"It is indeed a pleasure, Foreign Minister," Ryker replied, stepping into a foyer paved with Italian slate.

"Please, let's go into the living room where we'll be more comfortable."

With a pronounced limp, Faud led the way to a great sunken room furnished in rattan and wicker. The floor was tiled but covered here and there with exquisite Persian rugs of exotic designs and vivid colors. Wall-to-wall carpet, as found in the U.S., was simply not practical in the Middle East. Sand seeped invariably into every home, blown by desert winds or brought in on the shoes of occupants. It was far easier to sweep the sand from the tile, or beat it from rugs, than it would've been to vacuum it from carpet.

"Please be seated." Faud gestured to a rattan sofa with flowered cushions. "My son called and is on his way. He apologizes for not meeting you at the airport in person. I hope my men were cordial."

Ryker smiled. "They certainly were efficient. I'll give them that."

Faud understood and smiled.

Ryker seated himself and saw myriad dotted reflections of light on the Nile through the French patio doors that opened onto an expansive brick veranda.

"My wife will be in shortly. She knows why you are here and is anxious to meet you. She is as distressed by today's events as I."

Ryker nodded.

"You must be hungry. Nayra has provided some pastries and juice. Please, help yourself."

Ryker eyed the platter of delicacies on the coffee table in front of him. He was not at all hungry after his meal with Lubin, but the bakery goods looked as if they'd just come from the oven. He always had a weakness for such delicacies.

Faud seated himself in an opposing chair. Minus the limp, Faud's tall body appeared lean and fit—not only for being in his eighties, but also for *any* age. He was dressed in white linen slacks, a rose-colored silk shirt, and sandals. His full head of snow-white hair and pencil-thin mustache contrasted dramatically with his deeply tanned face.

"Mr. Ryker, how is my brother Jimmy?" Faud asked as Ryker partook of an apple-filled tart. "Still the maverick he fancied himself to be?"

Ryker was taken back by Faud's familiarity but suspected that James Cannon's warm and genuine personality made him a close friend to many.

"I haven't seen him in many years. But he sounded in good health when I spoke with him, Minister."

"Ah, yes, please forgive me. I forget that for you Americans business and personal life are still kept at distance from each other. Every man an island unto himself, isn't that right? And, please, let us dispense with formalities. Call me Faud, and with your approval, I shall call you Sam."

"Thank you and yes, certainly."

"You know, Jimmy and I began our relationship an eternity ago. It was during the war. You were probably no more than an infant when we were trying very hard to stay alive, working to rid North Africa of Hitler's Third Reich. I was an officer in British Intelligence and Jimmy was OSS. We grew as close as brothers. After the war, our careers took us into our respective country's diplomatic corps. Jimmy retired a few years before the Israeli–Egyptian peace accords were signed—he played a big part in seeing that historic moment realized—and I retired after assassins came close to ending my life along with Anwar Sadat's. But enough of this. You are not here to listen to the rambling of an old man. Jimmy told me that you would be coming, and I have pledged the resources of my country to help you."

"I'm not sure where to begin. But when I was told that Hasan had taken a personal interest in this matter, I figured our chances for finding and rescuing these missionaries increased a hundred-fold."

Faud studied Ryker for a minute and then smiled. "I can see why Jimmy called on you to help during this time of crisis."

Ryker washed down another bite of the fresh pastries. "He only called me because he couldn't go himself."

Faud laughed out loud. "He said that?"

"He said he would have come himself if he'd been a few years younger."

"Yes, I believe he would have." Faud smiled. "Go on."

"I have some experience in these matters, but the key to success is to move rapidly, based upon up-to-date information. I have no official status here, so the resources of my government are closed to me. I have friends here in Cairo who might be of some assistance, but the information Hasan has been gathering is critical."

"I concur that without the resources of your CIA, you are very much at a disadvantage."

"*CIA?*" Ryker asked, immediately lapsing into a learned routine of denying any link to his former employer.

"Sam, we cannot fully help each other if we continue to pretend that we are people we are not," Faud said flatly. "Your help to the Egyptian government during your time spent in my country did not go unnoticed, and though your title and position at the embassy said otherwise, it did not take the eyes of a hawk to see who you really were."

Ryker didn't know what to say. "Thank you, sir."

Faud reached for a pastry. "Jimmy speaks highly of you, and I can see why. Your achievements in exposing terrorists bent on disrupting the delicate balance of life in the Middle East have been exemplary. My own government owes you much for your efforts. Perhaps it can partially repay that debt by helping you now. After all, Egypt is embarrassed that this incident has happened. It, too, wants these brigands brought to justice."

"I am just hoping to help Hasan wherever I can." Ryker smiled and relaxed a bit.

"Of course, you understand that this operation will, in all likelihood, be run off the books. There are certainly people at the American embassy, and here close to President Mubarak, who would frown upon such a joint undertaking—especially given your . . . official *status*."

"Agreed. You should know that I have already enlisted the aid of one other asset and I plan to add another before the call to afternoon prayer. Both understand the rules of the game, if you get my meaning."

"Indeed. You are a very determined and resourceful man, Sam Ryker."

"It pays to be so in matters of life and death—don't you agree, sir?"

"From personal experience, I certainly do."

An attractive woman, some years younger than Faud, entered the room and approached. Both men stood.

"Sam, I'd like you to meet my wife, Nayra. Nayra, Samuel Ryker."

They shook hands.

"It is a pleasure, Mr. Ryker." Her English was superb, though not as good as Faud's. "Many men have much faith in you. I pray that Allah will guide your steps and find your missionaries that have done so much to help our people."

Men's voices could be heard from another location in the house. They spoke Arabic, but Ryker couldn't make out the conversation.

"Ah, Hasan is here," Faud announced, getting to his feet and disappearing through an alcove. The other voices undoubtedly had been part of the unseen house security detail.

Ryker watched Faud move with some difficulty across the room. Nayra took notice and leaned over toward him and whispered, "A condition from having his hip shattered by a bullet. It never healed properly. It is frustrating to him; he was always so active."

Ryker nodded his understanding but said nothing, his every nerve beginning to twist and jump in anticipation of meeting his old friend. A few more quick words were spoken in the other room before the two men, father and son, appeared in the doorway. Neither Ryker nor Hasan said a word at first, each taking the sight of a friend they had never thought they would ever see again—alive, that is. A smile broke across Hasan's face, and he reached out and pulled him in tight, hugging his old friend.

"It is good to see you again, Sam!" he said, almost lifting Ryker off the ground with his embrace. "You are alive! I knew it. None of us believed the reports."

Ryker could do little, bear-hugged as he was. "I never thought I'd say it, but I'm glad to be back, too."

Hasan released his American friend, and the men took a seat.

"I am sure you have much to discuss," Nayra said pleasantly. "It has been a pleasure to meet you finally, Mr. Ryker. I wish you luck and Allah's protection."

Ryker was moved to his feet out of respect and bowed slightly. "Thank you."

When she had left the room and closed the double doors behind her, Hasan reached out and rested his hand of Ryker's knee. "In case my father has not yet done so, let me offer you my deepest sympathies on the loss of your family. I assure you that my office did everything possible to find leads to those responsible."

"Thank you," Ryker mustered.

"It is true," Faud added. "My son did not sleep for a week. It was only when he faced administrative leave did he relent in his search. We were all hurt by your loss."

Ryker didn't know what to say. On one hand it was comforting to realize that the attack had affected so many people and that they all shared, to some degree or another, the pain that he had sheltered since then, but with every offer of sympathy came the feelings he wanted desperately to leave behind.

Hasan and his father seemed to sense the discomfort all this talk of his family's death was causing him and returned to the business at hand. "The National Police have been on the case since the beginning," Hasan started, opening a file folder, "but it took time to concentrate our forces there. Had we been in place from the moment of the attack, we might well have men in custody by now. The first hours are the most critical, but we were forced to rely almost solely on the local authorities. And unfortunately they were out of their league. I assume that it is the same in America. Rural police forces simply do not understand urban phenomena, nor do they generally have the resources to respond to it. That is what happened here. Roadblocks were implemented late and not over a large enough geographical area. There should have been air surveillance of the many roads that extend into the desert and a command post established instead of everyone running around like rats in a maze. I learned that much of the early efforts were coordinated over unsecured police radios. There is a long list of should-have-dones, but we cannot change the past. We can only move forward."

Hasan reached for the satchel he had set down when he first entered the room and opened it, handing Ryker a small stack of papers.

"A contingent of my best men are now in Aswan and have control of the investigation and are following up on every lead. Things are just now beginning to surface. I have made arrangements for us to travel there."

"I would like that very much. A fresh set of eyes might discover something new."

"I can only pray that will be case."

Ryker finished scanning the case file. "There is nothing here suggesting the next course of action."

Hasan smiled and shared a glance with his father. "We have them, but I would like to hear your thoughts before contaminating them with our own."

Ryker returned the smile. "Always the professional. Okay, the flight from Paris gave me plenty of time to think about this. First, it's been—what?—almost twenty hours since the attack and abduction, and unless you are withholding some pertinent information, there has been no communication from those responsible, no demands made, no parading them in front of the world to see. Nothing."

Hasan and his father agreed.

Ryker continued. "That's unusual. Terrorists normally want authorities and the public to know their group's identity. Otherwise, how can they promote their cause or grievances?"

"I see where you're going with this," Hasan added. "Whoever orchestrated the kidnapping might only be for hire. Which would mean—"

"That the missionaries haven't reached those who want them. If this is the case, then we can assume that they are en route still."

"But to where?" Faud asked.

"That's just it," Ryker said. "From Aswan there are only a few probable destinations."

"The airport was shut down the moment we knew they were taken," Hasan said. "My men have reviewed all video tape in and out of the airport terminals there. No sign of them."

"Which leaves transport by truck. They wouldn't travel north into more-populated areas, and I guess it's possible that they made a dash due east to the Red Sea, then by boat to who knows where, but I doubt it. First, there are no roads to cross that expanse, and dry wadis will only get a vehicle so far. And even if they did reach the coast, your Division of Antiquities monitors that shoreline so heavily that we would have heard something by now."

"What about the Nile?" Faud inquired.

"Unlikely, father," Hasan said. "Police presence is just too great north along the river and even out into Nasser. Which leaves west or south. Presumably, Libya is too far away to be a destination, and besides, I was told earlier tonight that satellite photos turned up nothing suspicious in the areas west of Aswan."

Ryker continued. "Which leaves south. But they had to suspect that the police would blockade all roads in the vicinity as soon as the incident was reported. There simply wouldn't be enough time to get very far. People make mistakes when they rush into things. The abduction took place far enough away from anywhere that they would need time to recoup and plan their next moves carefully. If it were me, I'd hole up in Aswan somewhere, wait for the search efforts to begin to thin, and make my move. Slipping past the police would then be easier."

"There are only a handful of passable roads from Aswan to Abu Simbel and then even fewer south to Sudan."

Ryker could tell that he had come to the same conclusion that Hasan and his men had, which at least gave them a plan. But something about this hypothesis didn't sit well with him. Frankly, it seemed all too easy. What if they were wrong? What if they were reading too much into it? Or worse, not enough.

"I have a favor to ask," Ryker said.

Hasan was busy scribbling notes on a small notepad. "You have but to ask, Sam."

"I have . . . associates here in Cairo. I need them brought in. To leave them out in the cold at this point would be counterproductive."

Hasan was clearly uncomfortable with this and would have immediately shot down the request if his father hadn't spoken up.

"My son, Allah works in many ways and uses many people from all nations to carry out His will. To refuse God's help when it is presented is never wise."

"And if I refuse?"

Sam was careful with his next words. "I'm hoping you won't."

Hasan took a deep breath. "Sam, you will understand what I say next. I appreciate that you have been asked to carry out a rescue mission, but this is my country, and my neck on the line if anything goes wrong. Do I know your . . . *associates*?"

"You know one of them. The other is a kindred spirit, if you get my meaning. His help with Al-Mina was much appreciated, if I recall correctly."

Ryker could see the conflict battling within his Arab friend. To accept anonymous intelligence that proved helpful in the apprehension of criminals and fugitives was one matter, but it was an entirely new one to actively work side by side someone who was technically considered one of the enemy by his superiors and heads of state.

"And do I assume that this *kindred spirit* is also working outside his official chain of command to help you find your missionaries?"

Ryker didn't answer. He didn't have to.

Hasan looked to his father and then exhaled sharply. "I don't like this, Sam. I can't even begin to imagine the paperwork that will need to be filed explaining *your* presence here—you're supposed to be dead, remember?—let alone working with . . . rogue *kindred spirits*."

"He can help us." Ryker let silence emphasize this point.

Faud cleared his throat after a long pause and then stood. "I believe I have contributed as much to this conversation as I am able. If you will excuse me."

Ryker rose to his feet with Faud and extended his hand. "Thank you, sir, for all you have done."

Faud nodded and then looked to his son. "Find them, Hasan. Use any means Allah has put in your path. It angers God to pray for His help and then refuse it when it comes. Remember, His ways are not our ways."

Ryker remained standing even after Faud had left the room.

"Hasan, I know the position you are in, and to be honest, if the situation were reversed, I would be struggling with the same dilemma you are, but I've already brought him in. We don't have time to waste working on this on two fronts. He's the best there is."

Hasan considered his friend's words carefully. Finally he asked, "How is his Arabic?"

"As good as mine, maybe better."

"Can he pass as just another consultant?"

"He doesn't have Hasidic locks, if that's what you mean."

Hasan ignored the attempt at levity and kept an intense lock on Ryker. "You will all work under my direction. Is that clear? If the missionaries are found and rescued, the ends will justify the means and much will be overlooked. If they are not, I'm not even sure my father will be able to stave off the consequences."

Ryker tried to smile. "Then we'd better find them."

Hasan returned the grin. "Indeed. Will you be accompanying me to headquarters, or do you have other plans until the plane leaves?"

"Now what kind of help would I be if I just tagged along with you all night?"

Hasan gathered up the file folders and replaced them in an over-the-shoulder bag. "My father's driver is at your disposal."

Ryker gathered his things. "That won't be necessary."

"Your kindred spirit?"

Ryker just smiled again and started for the door. "We leave for Aswan in two hours?"

"Military hangar at Cairo International. Do not be late."

"I wouldn't miss it for the world."

Ryker walked to the front gate and was promptly buzzed through. Stepping to the street, he looked up and down the dark road. After a moment, headlights turned on about a hundred meters away, an engine came to life, and an older, late-model Mercedes-Benz pulled up next to him. He threw his bag in the back and took his seat up front. The man driving was the same he had made brief eye contact with at the airport.

"I prayed to God night after night that you had not died that day," Manni Lubin said, looking forward. "And then I receive your call, and it was like hearing the voice of the dead."

Ryker chose to remain silent. He knew their reunion would be uncomfortable at best, but he also knew that contacting him had been the right thing to do. Israeli Mossad agent Emmanuel Lubin was the best field operative he had ever encountered, and there was no one else in the world who he would like to have by his side to find and rescue these missionaries. And for the second time since arriving, he was taken back by the pain that his "death" had caused. He was more than a bit ashamed that he hadn't once considered the loss anyone else had experienced since that fateful day.

Finally a smile crept onto Lubin's face. "It is good to see you, my friend!"

Ryker shrugged off his guilt, but it was replaced by the empty feeling of loss and tears, and he started to cry.

"I still miss her. Not a day goes by I don't wish I had stayed with them. If I had been there, maybe I would have seen the bomb in time . . . or at least been closer to it when it went off."

"You know," Ryker continued, "they say time heals old wounds, but it's a lie. All time does is give you more time to think about what happened. The hurt doesn't go away."

Lubin remained silent for a moment before speaking. "You asked for anything I could find on the missionary kidnapping, and I think I have something that might interest you." He reached to the backseat and tossed Ryker a small file folder.

Ryker looked through the papers.

"Look at the forensic report, third or fourth page in."

Ryker scanned the Egyptian National Police report quickly.

"How did you get this?"

"Come on, Sam. If we went around sharing all our secrets with each other—friends that we are notwithstanding—we'd all be out of a job, now wouldn't we?"

Ryker gave his friend a sidelong glance and continued reading. "What am I looking for?"

"Now look at the next set of papers. For sharing this I could lose my pension."

It felt as if the papers he was holding were suddenly charged with electricity. "This is from Susan's attack. Why would you—"

"Keep reading. Anything strike you as odd?"

Ryker couldn't see what his friend was getting at, and then he saw it, and a sharp sensation raced through his entire body. "Are you sure about this?"

"Embedded just beneath the surface of an embankment fifty yards from the actual impact of the blast, they found a rather large fragment of the incendiary device used in the kidnapping. Cyrillic markings identified it as Soviet Bloc."

Lubin took time to carefully pass a red Chevrolet pickup truck weaving dangerously from one side of the two-lane highway to the other. When they got closer, they could see that the bed of the truck was loaded with two young camels, probably on the way to auction.

"Before I left, I called in some favors and . . . well . . . the fragment was identified as a piece of an anti-tank mine. The markings turned out to be a serial number."

Ryker was still having trouble accepting what he was hearing.

Lubin continued. "After the blast in Jerusalem, metal fragments were dug from the Wailing Wall. They, too, were identified as coming from a Soviet anti-tank device. A piece bearing a partial serial number was also found. The serial number from Jerusalem and that found in Aswan are sequential. Those mines likely came from the same crate."

"This . . ." Ryker started but couldn't finish. It was too outlandish to believe. "You're saying that—"

"Whoever blew up that jeep at Aswan had a direct hand in the attack that took your wife and children."

"*Al-Har'ba.*" The Chameleon! Suddenly a new feeling swept over Ryker. One of purpose. And then a darker one. Revenge.

Lubin nodded in the front seat. He had been the only supporter that Ryker had on his phantom terrorist theory. Lubin had been around long enough to believe that things were not always as they seemed in the world of international terrorism. Lubin had told Ryker in the past that this theory made about as much sense as any other.

"I think we have our first lead," Ryker said.

"What do you mean?"

"Only a few people had our vacation itinerary," he explained. "Someone at the embassy let that information leak. Find that leak and we may be that much closer to finding our attacker."

"Surely your people looked into it."

Ryker scoffed at the idea. "I never even heard of an official investigation. Matheson was all to eager to chalk it up to the wrong place at the wrong time and call it good."

"Do you suspect anyone at the embassy?"

The traffic into town had slowed to a standstill. Ryker took a moment to reflect on Lubin's question as he looked out the side window at the congestion. "Everyone and no one," he finally answered. "I'd like to think I knew my people pretty well, but you can never tell. Agency people have been compromised before. Remember Aldrich Ames? He'd have sold out even his mother if she'd known anything."

"What about non-Agency people?"

"There are career Foreign Service staff and a boatload of foreign nationals who do the grunt work. Could be one of those, I guess."

"Motive?"

"Money. What else? You know as well as I do that most people in our business usually disclose information simply for money—not for any idealistic notion. I wonder how much my family was worth to them?"

"Perhaps whoever sold you out got paid for some kind of information about the American missionaries too. Whoever it is must be getting rich. If he is working for the Chameleon, I wonder if it's directly or through some intermediary?"

"*He?* Don't rule out a woman. Treachery is an equal-opportunity employer."

"Of course, but the point I was going to make was that this guy, or woman, might've been receiving blood money for a long time—from even before Jerusalem. Who else is already dead because of the information being sold? Who else is going to be sold out?"

"Wait a minute, Manni. You're on to something. We suspect that the Chameleon might be tied to both Jerusalem and Aswan. Right? If there's a bloodsucker at the embassy getting a piece of the action, then that's the key. If this person can be identified and squeezed, maybe we can turn a lead."

"But I thought you were here unofficially. You don't have access to your embassy."

"Yeah, that's a problem, but it may not be insurmountable."

"You can tell me after we eat."

"No, there is too much to do."

"Look at yourself. You look thirty pounds lighter than the last time I saw you. When was the last time you had a decent meal?"

Ryker couldn't remember. "Look, we just don't have the time."

"You're acting like you have a plane to catch."

"Actually," Ryker said hesitantly, "we both do."

"Sam . . . ?"

"If you're going to help, I need you with us at every step."

"What did you tell him?"

"I can't have you worrying about staying in the shadows with the lives of these missionaries at stake."

"What did you tell him?"

"Hasan wants to keep our involvement as quiet as possible. Believe me; he wasn't thrilled with the idea, either."

Lubin thought about all this for a moment as he navigated the dark streets. "We could all get in a lot of trouble over this."

"Yeah, but think of all the fun."

"We're not exactly young men anymore."

"But I'm not exactly comfortable with 'old,' either."

Lubin held a straight face for as long as he could but finally broke into a smile and chuckled. "You never were comfortable being a bystander, were you?"

Ryker squeezed his friends shoulder. "It's more fun down on the field."

"Esther was right; you *are* going to be the death of me one of these days."

Ryker laughed out loud, for the first time in nine months. And it felt good.

"So, Mr. ex-CIA-man, what's the plan?"

Ryker opened his cell. "I need you to make a call."

THIRTEEN

DEBORAH REID STOOD AT THE shredder, and with every document destined for office oblivion, her frustration level continued to rise. One American had been killed earlier that day, three more were still missing, and already the office was back to business as usual. The office had been working overtime the past week processing the influx of additional paperwork that came with the season. Easter Sunday was just a week away, and while Israel was the primary destination for the religious holiday, tourists couldn't fly all the way from the States to this corner of the world and not spend a few days to see the pyramids of Giza, or the temples at Luxor, or book passage on a riverboat up the Nile.

News of the attack north of Aswan came as a complete surprise. There had been no warning, no rumblings that could have predicted it, and what bothered Deborah was the speed and accuracy of the attack. The security was tight, routes were changed regularly, and every protection afforded by the Egyptian government was theirs. Whoever pulled this off knew the exact place and time when they would be most vulnerable. It had all the markings of a professional hit, but Matheson didn't want to hear it.

"Speculation, nothing more," he had said via secure satellite link from Istanbul where he and his assistant were attending a small conference of Eastern European embassies. It was what she called a "ham and glam" meeting, where pompous government and embassy officials met to pat each other on the back and feed their ever-growing collective ego over expensive food and even more expensive wine, all on the taxpayer's bill. Ambassador Chandler had refused the invitation, but Matheson had begged it off him.

"Sir, the Egyptian National Police report is pretty thorough. I really would suggest you review it before deciding our course of action to—"

"What have I told you about suggesting? Don't. Not when I'm in the office, and certainly not while I'm away on business."

"Dave, we've got a dead boy over here and three more that are missing and in great danger—"

"Don't you dare imply that for one minute I don't have the well-being of these priests—"

"Health missionaries."

"Whatever. I am *very* concerned with their safety and recovery."

"Then shall I book you on the first flight out of Turkey?"

Matheson didn't respond right away. "I'm sure we can handle this remotely. I want reports emailed every half hour updating me on the progress the National Police are making."

When she had asked what their office should be doing, Matheson's response was to focus on protecting existing American assets to ensure that no further losses were incurred.

"Losses." That's what he had called the murder and kidnapping that morning. Calling in at regular intervals, Dave Matheson, CIA station chief in name only, organized a thorough operation to secure and protect further damage or danger to any and all profitable American business interests. Deborah had never been more angry, but on the two occasions that she felt the need to remind her boss about the still-missing missionaries, she was threatened with reassignment. And it was only when the ambassador paid their office a visit demanding to know what efforts were being made to "find our people" did Matheson authorize their agents and operatives all along the Nile to start asking questions that should have been asked within minutes of learning of the attack. Deborah was not a particularly religious woman, but she kept a prayer in her heart that if there was a God, He would help them, because her office sure wasn't. She had even overstepped her authority and called the station heads in Israel, Saudi Arabia, Greece, and Kuwait trying to enlist their help and coordinate any intel they may have uncovered, but to her heartbreaking disappointment, there was none. Whoever had done this had pulled off the perfect crime.

She looked at her watch. She had come in early that morning, somewhere between five and six. It was now almost three AM the next day. The office roar had quieted to a small buzz, much of the enthusiasm dying with the lack of news about the whereabouts of the missionaries.

She rubbed her eyes and continued her task at hand, namely catching up on shredding the reams of paperwork destined for the basement furnace. Occasionally, some document would catch her eye just before being cut to ribbons by the machine—maybe for only a second or two, but that was enough.

As she fed the shredder, a miscellaneous report signed by the former head of station seized her attention. She missed Sam Ryker. In more ways than one she missed having him around. And the fact that his whereabouts had become classified to the highest levels of the Agency hadn't allowed for any sense of real closure. And then there were these missing Mormon missionaries. She knew that Sam was Mormon, and she had never really understood much about it, but she knew that Sam had been the most upright, honest, and faithful man she had ever met. Unlike his replacement, who had quickly passed off the missionaries' abduction to the local and Egyptian National Police.

The industrial-sized shredder was located in the back supply room, and she almost didn't hear the phone ring through.

"Yes?"

"Ms. Reid," the embassy operator said, "you just received a call from your landlord. It would seem that water pipes have broken on the floor above your apartment. He says that the water damage is likely to be great. He apologized for calling you at the office, but his persistent knocking went unanswered."

Deborah breathed in deeply and then sharply exhaled through her nose. *This is just great! The perfect end to a perfect day!*

"Thank you, Louise."

"Ms. Reid? If I may, we all know you folks are doing everything you can up there to bring them back safely. I just wanted to tell you thanks and let you know that we're all praying for you down here."

Deborah bit her tongue and fought back the urge to complain and get all those negative feelings off her chest, to share the weight that had been bearing down on her all day. Instead she lied and said they were doing everything possible, thanked the operator for her support, and promised to let her know the minute they were found.

She replaced the phone and looked at her watch. If she hurried, she could make the 3:12. One of the benefits of working in a city that never slept was that public transportation operated at all hours of the day and night. She looked at the stack of paperwork remaining. She could stay and finish, but that would require her calling a cab home. Not that she had a problem with Cairo cabbies, but it was a sorry fact that the quality—and aroma—of the service was different at this hour.

Three minutes later, Deborah was standing underneath the clear Egyptian skies. The stars were bright in the crisp air, and she paused for a moment, taking in a deep breath laced with the exotic smells of Cairo. Of all her duty stations, Cairo was her favorite. It was a mysterious blend of East and West, of old and new. The city was devoutly religious yet shamefully decadent. It never failed to excite. Even at this unearthly hour.

She walked down the stairs and along the cobblestone path that led to the opening in the twelve-foot-high brick pillar and wrought-iron fence that encircled the immaculately landscaped embassy grounds. A Marine stepped from his guard shack, checked her pictured identification card, gave a curt salute, and wished her a good night. Exiting the compound, she turned left and walked to the corner. After only a three-minute wait, she boarded the graffiti-covered double-decker bus bound for downtown, already filling with the men and women on their way to early-hour employment—bakers, tanners, and the like.

She eyed an empty seat on the second tier in front of the rear window. She didn't always ride the bus, but she enjoyed it when she did. The other passengers were intriguing: darkly clad Muslim women with veiled faces; finely dressed men sporting red fezzes atop their shiny, shaved heads; Islamic holy men with long, gray beards; hook-nosed Bedouins reeking of body odor and the stench of goats and sheep; farmers on their way to the market with cages of live chickens on their laps; sleepy children with runny noses. At any hour of the day or night, there was also the pervasive smell of tobacco. She'd never smoked—never even been tempted, finding the habit repulsive, not to mention expensive—however, the odor from exotic and aromatic blends of tobacco was not at all offensive and even added to the experience. She imagined that riding the rails on the Orient Express from Istanbul to Paris forty years ago couldn't have been any more exciting than taking an ordinary bus into downtown Cairo.

Casually looking out the rear window, she noticed a gray Mercedes-Benz pull into traffic about six car lengths behind. She had spotted it parked a half-block up the street from the bus stop. There'd been two people in the front seat, but with the glare of the overhead light on the tinted windows, she hadn't been able to discern their faces or gender. CIA protocol required her to take precautions if she suspected surveillance or any other actions that could compromise her employment with the Agency. While she had waited for the bus, she had noticed the car parked along the street and had dismissed it.

She wasn't so sure of her assessment now.

She turned and faced forward, surveying the other occupants of the second tier. Each surely had a story to tell if anyone cared to ask. The bus rumbled on, swaying from side to side, desperately in need of a new muffler and shocks. After three or four minutes, she glanced over her shoulder again. The Mercedes was still following at precisely the same interval. She looked to the front as her heart rate stepped up the pace. Her training quickly compensated for her emotional response to the Mercedes, and she reached into her purse for her cell phone. Just in case.

A minute or so passed, and she looked around for the third time. The car was gone. *You see?* she thought with a wave of relief. *It was just your imagination.*

The bus stop was little more than a block from the apartment, necessitating that she walk the rest of the way. As she stepped down onto the sidewalk, she noticed the Mercedes passing the bus and continuing on down the street. Two men were visible in the front seat, though their faces were still masked by the reflection of the sun and tinted windows. She caught the license plate number. She needed to decide quickly. Was the Mercedes a coincidence or part of a conspiracy to abduct her and force her to tell all her secrets?

Deborah let out a little laugh. If only her life were that interesting and colorful. But just to be on the safe side, she would run the plates through the Agency computers tomorrow and see who the car belonged to.

The bus dropped her off a block and a half from her apartment, and as she neared, her exhaustion only added to her dread of what mess would meet her when she stepped through her door. She lived a pretty frugal lifestyle and wasn't worried about the damage to anything she owned, but the cleanup that lay ahead—the carpet, the walls, her bookshelves—she only hoped that her bed was dry. The cleanup would just have to wait.

As she walked on, however, another feeling began to replace her fatigue. She had a strange feeling she was being watched. She stopped for a moment and looked up and down the street. No one ducked behind a corner, or hastily retreated inside. Nothing was out of the ordinary. Quiet streets. She realized just how much she needed to get to sleep. She really had to do something to keep this newfound paranoia in check.

Shrugging off the feeling the best she could, she continued on, but the feeling was just too much for her to ignore anymore. Real or imagined, Deborah thought it best to reach the busy cross street and her apartment building as fast as her feet would take her. She looked over her shoulder, but this time, instead of an empty street, there was the lone figure of a man.

The thought of yelling for help crossed her mind as she fled up the street. But she was breathing so hard that she couldn't coordinate a scream between her brain and her mouth. He was gaining. The street was busy up ahead. She figured she'd be safe if she could only make it.

She looked back, trying to gauge the distance from her attacker. As she turned her head forward, a figure stepped from the shadow of an alleyway and into her path. They collided. She struggled and was within a microsecond of mustering a scream when a hand clamped over her mouth and pulled her inside.

Deborah had not always been an analyst, and her years of agent training took over, and she found herself immediately on autopilot. With one hand clasped over her mouth and the other around her midsection, her legs were free to do some damage. With a sharp step she grated her foot down the shin of her attacker. The hand covering her mouth broke free, and she threw back her head, missing her assailant's nose but connecting with the side of his face. The grip around her waist loosened, and she spun around, breaking entirely free. Her assailant's hands covered much of his injured face, and her confidence grew seeing that he wasn't putting up much of a fight. Her hand flattened out, and she pulled back to deliver a crushing blow to the man's Adam's apple when she caught a glimpse of his face. Restraining herself midattack was nearly impossible, but she pulled her chop and dropped her jaw.

"Sam . . . ?"

Ryker smiled despite the pain.

"Is it really you?" Deborah asked, still unable to believe the sight before her.

"It's good to see you, too," he said, reaching down to rub the pain from the front of his leg. "I should have known you wouldn't go down without a fight."

Before she knew what she was doing, Deborah threw her arms around Ryker. "Is it really you?" she repeated, shocked and in disbelief. She closed her eyes and hugged him tighter as a wave of emotion washed over her. "I can hardly believe it—Sam, look out!"

She pushed Ryker out of the way as the man who had followed her appeared in the alley. Shooting her foot out with a well-placed heel kick to the man's stomach, she knocked him to one knee. She doubled up her fists and raised them over her head, intending to follow up with a hammer strike to the back of his head when she felt a strong hand restrain her.

"Deb, Stop!" Deborah looked back, confused further. "He's with me."

She stepped back and let the man struggle to his feet.

"I told you this was a bad idea," the man said.

"Deb," Ryker said, "I'd like you to meet Manni Lubin."

Lubin held out his shaking hand. Deborah was too stunned to acknowledge it, so he withdrew it. "You didn't mention she was a human weapon."

"She's as good as they come."

"Sam . . . ? I . . . you . . . you're supposed to be dead." She pulled away from him and stepped back.

"Deb, I'm sorry for the cloak and dagger theatrics, but I needed to make sure you were alone. I can't risk anyone knowing I'm back yet."

Deborah's shock was beginning to wear off, but it was being replaced with deep confusion. She must have fallen asleep on the bus, or maybe she had fainted on the way home and this was all some bizarre dream or hallucination. She looked back and forth between the two men standing before her. "Sam? Is it really you?"

"I know this must seem too unreal right now, but yes, it is me. And if you'll let me, I'll explain everything, but not out here in the open. Okay, Deb?"

Like fog burning off the Nile with the morning sun, Deborah's mind began to finally wrap around what was happening, and she prayed it wasn't just a dream. She looked to the other man with Ryker.

"Lubin? Emmanuel Lubin?" Deborah asked. "As in Israeli Mossad?"

Lubin shot a concerned look to Ryker, who just shrugged back.

"Sam had few genuine friends," Deborah said, feeling the need to explain. "He always spoke highly of you and your work."

Lubin looked a bit relieved and tipped her an imaginary hat.

Deborah looked to both men, still nursing their wounds. "Sam, what's going on here?"

She didn't know how to take the last few minutes. Her mind was still trying to process everything and piece it all together. She was happy to see him, thrilled, but it just didn't seem possible.

"I thought you were dead," she said, and threw her arms around him again. This time Ryker returned the embrace. "How? When?"

Ryker gently withdrew from her arms and pulled over a couple of empty wooden crates stacked in the back alley. Lubin took a position at the head of the alley as Ryker shared the events of the past nine months that made up his life. He chose to omit the part about the Glock on the day President Cannon had called him, however.

"I flew to the States to attend your memorial service," Deborah finally said. "They said you were dead."

"I wished I was." Ryker could never lie to her.

Deborah took his hands in hers and just held them for a silent minute. She could feel him shaking and could only imagine the living nightmare he had been put through. It wasn't fair. It shouldn't have happened to Sam Ryker. She let go.

"You're here for the missionaries, aren't you?"

A seriousness returned to Ryker's face, and Manni Lubin left his post and joined them.

"Does Chandler or Matheson know you're here?"

"No, but it's only a matter of time before they do."

"And you're not on official business, are you?"

Ryker and Lubin exchanged looks. "You remember Ambassador Cannon?"

She did, and as soon as Ryker mentioned his name, Deborah made the obvious connections. "He's the leader of your church now. He knows, probably better than most, that action must be swift to get them back in one piece. He sent you to bring them back." It was all beginning to make sense now.

"And I need your help," Ryker said.

"But what can I do?"

"Manni?"

Manni Lubin took a seat next to them and shared the information about the explosive devices' serial numbers and the apparent connection between the attack on Ryker's family and the abduction of the missionaries. Deborah could scarcely believe it. But then again, certain questions she'd had since the attack at the Western Wall were beginning to become clearer now.

"And the minute my passport information makes it to the embassy, my ability to get these missionaries back is weakened. That's why I have to act quickly."

"I'm coming with you," she said.

Ryker shook his head. "I need you here. We believe the missionaries are still in the country, and after meeting with Hasan, we think we have pretty good idea where they might be, but we have to leave right away."

"Hasan?"

"You don't think I'd be fool enough to think I could do this alone, do you?"

"I'm impressed," Deborah said.

"I need you to stay behind and look into this connection. We now believe that those responsible for the attack at Aswan were hired for the job. If that proves to be true, then we're going to need to know everything we can about them." Ryker paused. "And if we can find how my vacation plans made it into hostile hands, we might be closer to finding out who attacked the missionaries and killed my family."

Deborah held his gaze and would not let him look away. "I wish you'd let me go with you."

"I can't put you at risk like that. Besides, our window to look at personnel is a small one, and there's no one else I trust."

"You mean no one else crazy enough to help you."

Ryker smiled. She understood what she was getting herself into.

"The idea of a leak in the office had already occurred to me," she said. "Matheson was bugged that I wouldn't let it die and finally ordered me to stop. Threatened to have me removed to the States if I didn't."

"Doesn't surprise me."

"I have my suspicions, but I can't do much rogue like this."

"Maybe you won't have to," Ryker said. "I'm pretty sure I could get Hasan's office to help you out." He checked his watch. "We gotta go."

Lubin fished keys out of his pants pocket and left to get the car. When they were alone, Deborah had one more thing to say.

"Sam," she started once they were alone again, "I . . ." but then she thought against telling him how she felt about seeing him again. In fact, she wasn't even sure what those feelings were herself. It was better to keep your tongue in these matters, anyway. But she had to say something now.

"Deb? Are you okay?"

"It's just . . . I never thought I would see you again. It's good to see you."

Ryker seemed not to know quite what to say, and he smiled.

"Just don't you ever do that again," she said.

"Do what again?"

"Leave. Promise me you'll be careful with Hasan. If what your friend says is true, coming back to Egypt could give those responsible for the death of your family another shot at you."

She looked away. "I lost you once. I couldn't bear to go through that again."

The Mercedes-Benz pulled up to the alley entrance and honked. Ryker put his hand reassuringly on her shoulder. "I'm not going anywhere. Not this time. I promise."

* * *

Hasan was waiting inside the hangar when the three of them pulled up.

"Miss Reid," he said once they emerged from the Mercedes. "I should have guessed that Sam would contact you for help with this."

"Always a pleasure, Hasan."

Hasan took a deep breath and looked at his officers stationed around them.

"My men are not accustomed to the company of women on assignments."

"I'm honored you would think I was coming with, but my task lies elsewhere."

"In fact, we need some help that only your office can provide," Ryker said, much to Hasan's relief. "There is information about a civilian employee of the American embassy, an Egyptian national, which Miss Reid, here, needs certain . . . access to."

Hasan raised an eyebrow. "And the resources of her office . . ."

"Are unavailable to her."

Hasan looked at Ryker very seriously. "We could all get in a lot of trouble over this."

"This is not a field for the timid or faint of heart, now is it?" Ryker quipped.

A smile crept onto Hasan's somber face. "Indeed." Turning to the other member of Ryker's "team," he said, "And you are . . . ?"

Ryker had spoken highly of both men to each other for years, he being the bridge between them, helping the two ideologically different agencies come together to work for the common good and safety of both countries. Each knew of the other, and while they had each expressed a desire to meet the other someday, neither had expected that it would be so soon.

The Israeli Mossad agent extended his hand. "Manni Lubin." There was no reason to give a false name. It would be an insult to Hasan's professionalism.

Hasan sized him up and then took his hand. "If you are who I think you are, my country owes you a debt of gratitude."

Hasan and Lubin held their firm grasp, each realizing the symbolism this handshake represented. It felt good.

Hasan turned his attention to Deborah. "Now how can my office be of service to you?"

Deborah explained her suspicions concerning a passport clerk by the name of Abdul Badri. She had narrowed her suspicions following the Jerusalem bombing, looking to bank accounts instead of political persuasions. Matheson had shot down her theories and ordered her to stop her line of investigation, but not before she had learned enough about the man's financials to warrant suspicion.

"Badri?" Ryker asked. "A smug little guy with wire-rimmed glasses?"

Deborah nodded. "He's well educated and is always letting everyone know how underappreciated and underpaid he is."

Lubin pressed. "You must have more than that, Miss Reid. There isn't a government worker anywhere in the world that hasn't felt that way at one time or another."

"True enough," Deborah replied, "but then some months after the Jerusalem bombing, I had occasion to speak with Badri on an embassy matter and noticed a lease agreement on his desk for a new apartment. I checked it out: an upscale place and clearly out of his league. About the same time, he made a healthy down payment on a car. Keeps it in an underground garage at the apartment and never drives it to work. I also found credit card purchases for a computer system. Nice stuff."

"Maybe there's something," Lubin was skeptical, "and maybe not. Maybe he's spending an inheritance."

"But I think a talk with Badri is in order," Ryker said.

"Perfect. If this guy is dirty, the quicker we yank him, the better."

"I agree," Hasan said. "Sergeant!"

A sharp-dressed policeman immediately responded to the call. "Yes, sir?"

"Sergeant Heikel, I'd like to you meet Miss Reid. She has some information pertinent to the abduction and possible rescue of the American missionaries. You are to cooperate with her fully and extend to her every courtesy this office has to offer. Do I make myself clear?"

"Sir, yes, sir!" Turning to Deborah, Sergeant Joseph Heikel offered his hand. "I am at your disposal, Miss Reid."

A maintenance worker approached their small huddle. "The plane's ready when you are, sir."

"All right, men," Hasan barked. "We have a plan. Now, let's go get us some missionaries."

FOURTEEN

SAIIF HAD SPENT THE DAY watching, waiting, and then watching again. News of the abduction had spread faster than even he had imagined. He had watched police efforts from the rock hills that lined the Nile just east of the city, and what had started out as a mad panic and scramble quickly became an organized search of roadblocks and checkpoints, and as he had expected, all traffic along the river was halted for a time. The police scanner he had lifted a month earlier had never been more revealing than it had been that day. Within an hour, the National Police were on the scene, taking charge and fine-tuning the recovery efforts. Of course, they would find no clues, no traces of the kidnapped missionaries, because there were none to be found. They were secreted safely away and beyond the first reaches of the authorities. They wouldn't be safe there for long, but for the time being it was a necessity to hold up and wait for their chance to move.

And now, well into the early morning hours, that chance had presented itself.

"Checkpoints are lifted along the dam," Saiif told Imad, switching off the scanner. "Time to move. You and your brother bring the truck around. Give me a few minutes, though. I think I will spend a little time with our guests."

* * *

Elder Jack Devereux must have drifted off into an uneasy sleep. When he heard voices upstairs behind the basement door, his whole body jerked awake, and he let out an audible gasp, and for a moment he was disoriented, having had the most vivid and terrifying dream of his life. Only when his world remained black even after opening his eyes and feeling the snug fit of the blindfold across his eyes did the hope that it was all a dream fade, replaced with the nightmare that was their reality.

"Jack?" said Abby.

"How long have I . . ."

A laugh caught in his wife's throat. "You were snoring."

A nervous silence ensued, and then Elder Anderson chimed in. "The sound reminded me of being on the farm back home," he said, letting out a little laugh. The Devereux joined him.

But as his wife and Elder Anderson released some pent-up tension, he was unable to shake the triage that was taking place in his mind as he reassessed their situation. He was no expert in the field of global terrorism, but he had always been well-read, a student of the domestic and international scene. He first needed to know where they were. The cool, damp air meant that they were still near the river. Aswan, if he had to guess—close enough to hide them before the authorities had time to set up checkpoints, but big enough to easily elude any dragnet spread for their recovery. If their kidnapping was simply a means to an end—and he prayed to God that it was—their captors would keep them alive and in tolerable shape until their demands were met. Besides being a little shaken up from the whole ordeal, they had fared pretty well so far. They had been allowed a bathroom break a few hours before, and although their captors had handled them roughly, they weren't injured or harmed in any way. He was convinced, more than ever, that Elder Evan's death had not been intended.

As for their demands, he knew that United States policy was to never give into the demands of terrorists, but he was not aware of any such policy being adopted by the Church. Once President Cannon was informed, he knew a plan would be formed without pause and the lines of communication opened right away. The influence of the Church was vast and crossed many borders. In fact, Elder Devereux's faith in his prophet was so strong that the thought of not seeing his grandchildren in Augusta had never really crossed his mind.

More noise, this time descending the stairs, put a quick end to their laughter, and the fear returned. The sound of a thick metal bolt being thrown open was followed by the grinding protest of rusted hinges. By the sound of it, only one of them ventured down into their dungeon. Elder Devereux noticed that the door remained open. *Maybe this is it,* he thought. *Maybe we're being moved.*

"You'll have to excuse your accommodations. Our resources in matters such as these are limited at best." The captor laughed softly.

This captor was not one of the two who had ripped them from their jeep and dragged them down the stairs. This man had a near flawless command of English and spoke it with a refined, almost polished British Oxford accent.

"I hope your stay thus far has been tolerable."

As they had agreed earlier, no one spoke to their captor. Engaging him only gave him more strength over the situation.

"Doctors Jack and Abigail Devereux," their captor continued, taking a seat on the ground across the small room from them, "and . . . what should I call you? *Nurse* Anderson? But, no, that sounds much too feminine for such a fine specimen of manhood."

"Elder," Thomas Anderson snapped before he could catch himself.

"Ah, yes," their captor said, "Elder. An odd choice of titles, to be sure."

For a moment no one said anything, then their captor slapped his thighs, and it sounded like he opened a paper sack. "Well, you must be famished."

Elder Devereux heard him shake up a can of some sort and then pull a metal tab back. "Our chef has taken ill this evening, so I'm afraid you will have to settle for this." There was more shuffling in the bag, and then he moved in front of Sister Devereux. "Now, do not be frightened. I am going to untie this from your neck and pull it up over your mouth."

"Jack?" Her plaintiff cry was helpless, unsure whether or not to trust what was happening.

"Hey!" he yelled and struggled at the cords behind his back. "What are you doing to her?" Elder Devereux felt a strong hand hit his chest, pushing him back into the stone wall.

"Do not mistake my pleasant tone and good manners as weakness!" He continued to apply pressure to the point of causing pain. He leaned in close. "Do I make myself clear?"

"Let him go!" Elder Anderson yelled.

Elder Devereux cringed. "Thomas!"

"Oh, no, Thomas, do go on." The captor released his pressure on the doctor's chest. "You were saying I should let Devereux go or . . . what? What could you possibly do to convince me to abandon months of planning, not to mention the money, and let you go?"

Neither man responded. Sister Devereux began to cry softly.

Their captor switched his accent to a southern drawl. "Will you use those big, midwestern, corn-fed, meat-and-potatoes muscles and force me to let you go? Or perhaps you would reason with me, persuade me to see the errors of my ways and see it in my heart to set you free, is that it?" His Oxford accent then returned. "Shall I continue?"

"Please," Sister Devereux pleaded. "This is all some kind of mistake. I don't know who you think we are. We are members of a small medical team—"

"Abby! Don't."

"Invited personally by the Egyptian government. Please, if you let us go, we won't say anything. Please. I beg you."

The room was silent except for the sounds of their breathing. Then he spoke.

"Your young friend's death was unfortunate, to say the least, and I can't expect you to accept my most sincere apologies, but it is true, nonetheless."

"Please," Sister Devereux continued, "in the name of God, please let us go."

"In the name of . . . ?" Their captor scoffed and then erupted in a mirthless laugh. "You people are just too much—has anyone ever told you that?" He reached quickly around the back of Sister Devereux's head and forced something into her mouth. "Drink! I can't have you dying before the big event."

But she refused, crying out for him to stop.

"Stop," Elder Devereux said calmly. "I'll drink it."

"Oh, isn't that heroic? The white knight coming to the rescue of his fair maiden. Or maybe not quite heroic, but certainly *Christian* of you." Again he scoffed. "For yea and behold, this is eternal life to know Jesus and blah, blah, blah, or something like that. You all look like intelligent human beings—well, not right now, but you did earlier. How can you believe this rubbish? Abby! Turn around."

"T-t-turn around?"

"Yes, woman. I have decided not to wait on your friends here. If you want them to eat or drink, rather, then you will do it. Turn around and show me your hands."

"Jack?"

"Do as he says. It'll be all right."

"It will, indeed." And with her blindfold still securely over her eyes, she was handed the aluminum-topped can, felt for the straw, and guided it to her husband's mouth once he untied the canvas bag over his head.

"I'm not sure about you, Elder Anderson. You look like you could skip a few meals and still be as strong as a bull."

"Ox," Elder Anderson corrected. "Strong as an *ox*."

"Of course. Do you know that Christianity is what I call an after-the-fact religion? It's true. Christianity, as you profess it, and its founder, were not accepted or even widely known until years after His death, time enough for the stories to circulate and develop, time for believers to find similarities in Hebrew prophecies and then have them retranslated to fit the current views. There is no individual, outside evidence that Jesus even existed. Well, there is Josephus, but his one passing reference forgets to mention His divinity. How convenient. With no proof, you expect the world to just take it on faith."

Elder Devereux was taken aback and even a little shocked at the turn in the conversation, and he was suddenly struck with new fear that this was no ordinary terrorist. This was no Muslim extremist bent on making his voice heard through the video footage of their capture and condemning the "Great Satan" while demanding Israel withdraw fully from the Gaza Strip. This was an educated man, a man who had given a lot of thought to reproving another's religion, a man with a devious agenda.

"Doctor?" he asked. "Doctor, I know what you and your colleagues are doing. You and I both know I cannot force you to speak with me, but I leave the invitation open, nonetheless."

Still, Elder Devereux led the missionaries in their united front of silence, and he only hoped that the others didn't take the bait and engage their captor in a way that would only further his wicked purposes. Their captor sensed their efforts but continued speaking to them anyway.

"I have some questions about your faith, your religion. Would you mind answering them for me?"

Silence.

"No? Well, that is too bad. One thing I don't understand, truly, is your devotion to hearsay. I mean, your entire religion, your faith, was handed down to you by word of mouth, and with each telling the story gets more fantastic, more miraculous, until the codex you have created doesn't contradict itself and you have a nice little package for your missionaries to use to seek out the heathen and convert them to the 'truth.' And all the world asks for is a little proof. Something we can touch, something we can feel, hold in our hand."

Elder Devereux just listened, not sure what to say, if anything at all.

"Give me some of the water he turned into wine," their captor continued, becoming more agitated as he spoke. "Calm a raging storm; walk on water; bring someone back from the dead."

Their captor stood and stepped toward Elder Anderson. "If I kill your young friend here . . ."

They all heard the distinct sound of a gun hammer being pulled back and locked into firing position.

"Could you bring him back to life?"

Elder Anderson began to breathe heavy, sucking air in erratic gasps. Sister Devereux's plea for mercy was suddenly drowned out by the deafening discharge of the weapon. Elder Devereux's ears split, ringing with the sound of a massive cathedral bell between his ears. A flash of light caused by the gun lit up the dark recesses of his mind as a wave of nausea crashed over him, and he wasn't sure whether or not the pain would force him to black out or not. The pain was excruciating, and he was unable to cover and massage his ears, only making the pain seem even worse than it was.

The ringing in ears lasted for what seemed like forever, and as his hearing started to return, the sound he heard confused and then infuriated him. Their captor was laughing.

"Oh, that was priceless, Doctor," their captor said in between chuckles. "His fear, her pleas, and your inability to do anything about it. Where was your faith then? Faith, it would seem, is a fair-weather friend." He laughed again. "Relax, everyone is fine. Did you really think I would kill one of you just like that? I told you that I never meant any of you harm. It seems you have neither faith in me nor your God."

"You're sick," Elder Devereux struggled to say.

"Is that your professional diagnosis?"

"Elder?"

"I'm . . . I'm okay . . ."

"Abby?" When she didn't respond, Elder Devereux began to panic. "What have you done to her? She has a bad heart!"

Elder Devereux listened as their captor reached down and checked her vitals.

"She's just fainted."

"You don't know that for sure!"

"And you have no choice but to trust me."

Elder Devereux abandoned all reserves. He just didn't care anymore. "The deepest depths of hell are reserved for men like you."

"Hell? Ah, yes, all your talk of sin. Original or cheap imitation, you guys have quite a racket going. In fact, your entire belief is not based on Jesus, as you profess, but on sin. You don't believe me? Consider this: there can be no Savior, no Messiah, if there is nothing to save them from. No sin, no hell; no hell, no need for heaven. And all this emphasis on the dos and don'ts—more, you'll have to admit, on the don'ts. That's because the don'ts are so much more fun."

Elder Devereux's hands were shaking. He had never before been this angry or so filled with hate.

"In fact, can you even name your own ten commandments? Well, can you?"

The sound of a knife blade locking into place sounded just above the ringing in Elder Devereux's ears. Even in the dark, he could tell that their captor had moved close to his wife. If he laid a hand on her . . .

"Do I have your attention, Doctor? Name all ten commandments and your lovely bride here keeps her fingers. Miss one and . . . I think you get the picture. And, hey, I'll even be merciful and start with the small fingers on each hand—no one really uses them anyway."

It felt like Elder Devereux's tongue had swelled up and his mouth dried out in one arid blast. It was a real effort to speak.

"You want me to . . ."

"List your precious ten commandments. Members of other faiths can recite entire passages of their teachings, page after page. Surely you can tell me the ten big ones, and I'll give you a hint, an eye for an eye isn't one of them. Now go."

Elder Devereux's mind went blank. "Th-thou shalt not kill. Lying. Stealing—"

"I don't want chapter headings, Doctor. I want the full commandment, if you please."

"Thou shalt not steal. Thou shalt not commit adultery. Thou shalt not lie—"

"Wrong!"

"No, wait! Wait! Thou shalt not bear false witness."

"Against . . . ?"

"Against? Uh, against thy neighbor."

"It's good to be specific. That's three. Only seven more to go."

Elder Devereux paused a moment to gather his thoughts. If he ever needed the words of God brought to his remembrance in this, his hour of need, it was now.

"Honor thy father and thy mother . . . th-that thy days may be . . . long . . ."

"Yes, yes, that's enough of that one. We all get the point. That's five."

"Remember the Sabbath day and keep it holy."

"Six."

"Thou shalt have no other gods before me."

"Seven."

"Thou shalt . . ." In his anxiety, his mind just would not produce any more. He tried to visualize the passages in Exodus, but all he saw were jumbled words, letters, and numbers. "Thou shalt . . ." he tried again.

"Are we having trouble with the last three? I could give you one, get you started, but Abby, here, loses a finger."

"You monster!" Elder Anderson yelled.

"Would you like a shot? Make this a *team effort*? Well?"

"Leave him alone!" Elder Devereux said, his confidence returned. "This is between you and me. Thou shalt not take the name of the Lord thy God in vain."

"Two more."

"Thou shalt not make unto thee any graven image—"

"Nine—"

"Or any likeness of any thing that is in heaven above," he continued with force, "or that is in the *earth* beneath, or that is in the *water* under the earth."

"One left, and your time is running out."

"You said nothing of time!"

"Details, details. Give me the tenth one or Abby will only be able to count to nine with the grandchildren."

Elder Devereux reflected inwardly in prayer. Then he remembered. "Thou shalt not covet thy neighbor's house, nor his wife, nor his servants, nor his ox, nor his ass, nor anything that is thy neighbor's. Now let her go!"

Their captor did not respond right away. Finally he said, "You were lucky. It seems I may have underestimated you. Congratulations are in order. But still, so many commandments, so many chances to fall and fail. And this just proves my point. If there were no sin, then there would be no need for your precious Savior, crown of thorns and bleeding hands and all."

Elder Devereux heard him close the knife blade. "And how does this sound? What if there was no sin? What if everyone—you, me, the pope, even the godless aborigine living the middle of who-knows-where—what if our actions were just that: actions. Some wiser than others, some smarter than others, but neither good nor bad—devoid of any moral judgments. What a simple and uncomplicated life that would be. But if that were true, you'd all be out of job. You'd have to start working for a living, like the rest of us."

Elder Devereux's heart and mind had slowly been filling with righteous reproach for his captor, and the time to speak had finally come.

"So you believe that I, my wife, Elder Anderson, and Christian leaders the world over know better and deceive their followers to get gain? Is that it?"

"That about sums it up."

"Do you believe in God?"

"The Christian god or the Muslim god? Or the Buddhist god? Or maybe the many gods of Hinduism? Be specific, Doctor."

"It's a simple question. *Do you* or *don't you* believe in God?"

There was a brief pause. "No."

"Well, I do. We all do." Elder Devereux's words were very precise and deliberate, and he felt a strange calm come over his body. "How do you know there isn't one? I have the words and stories and testimonies of thousands— no, millions—of believers since time began, and you have the gall to think so highly of yourself and your self-deluded audacity to think that you can step in and discount it all? Greater men than you have tried over the centuries, and still faith continues, be it Christian, Muslim, Jewish, Buddhist, or Hindu. We may call Him different names, but he is one God, and I don't need the Bible or the Torah or the Koran to convince me. My belief and faith in God comes from personal experience and quiet revelation."

"Then prove it!" their captor yelled. "Show me a sign! Give me a miracle and I'll believe you! You will baptize me in the Nile this very night, and I will shout praises to your God and be a changed man."

"Nothing will convince you. You have obviously studied Christianity and even read some of the scriptures. If they did not touch your heart—if you even have one—then parting the Red Sea will not do it. Underneath your tough exterior you are a frightened little man. Cold and alone; that's how you live, and that is how you will die."

Those last words had scarcely crossed his lips when Elder Devereux felt a hard fist pummel the side of his head, and he fell over with the blow.

"It is your own deaths that should concern you," their captor said with a chilling edge to his voice.

Elder Devereux was suddenly aware of others waiting at the door, only a second before one of them tackled him and pinned him to the ground. He struggled violently against his attackers as he felt a pinprick in the back of his thigh. A few moments later, he lost feeling in his leg, which spread to his hip and other limbs and finally smothered his consciousness in a blanket of darkness.

FIFTEEN

THE SKIES WERE BEGINNING TO give way to the new day, chasing away the overhead slate and replacing it with hues of orange and red. The flight to Aswan seemed long and uncomfortable and made coach on any other airline seem like first class. There were two rows of seats, one on each side of the narrow aisle. The passengers couldn't stand upright and had to find a seat while hunched over. The Piper Navaho touched down and taxied toward the hangar reserved for government aircraft. It stopped just short of the partially open massive double doors. The copilot emerged from the cockpit, opened the exit door, and lowered the metal steps. In single file, Ryker, Lubin, and Hasan made their way down the stairs. They were followed by two of Hasan's men who had volunteered for the assignment. They were the strong, silent type, abstaining from the conversation during the flight from Cairo. Ryker was a good judge of character and he had no reservations about Hasan's choice for backup. One of Hasan's men, who'd been sent down to Aswan with the first wave of investigators, met them on the tarmac. He sported a thick black mustache, and his ample matching beard extended below his open shirt collar. His thick forearms and the backs of his hands were also covered in dark hair. He was a tall, burly man, ill-fitted to even the baggy desert-colored fatigues encasing his gigantic frame. Ryker wondered with a smirk what the women down here fed their children to turn out such giants. This latest officer looked to Ryker as if he would've felt more comfortable wrestling bears in a circus. In fact, in a dark alley he could have been mistaken for a bear.

"Tell me what you know so far," Hasan said, extending his hand to shake that of Bear's.

"Very little," he replied, "but the day is still young."

"We don't have until then," Hasan said, all business and no play.

Bear growled and nodded his head. Hasan led them to a jeep waiting for them, climbed in behind the wheel, and drove them along the same route the missionaries had taken the day before. The attack site was about thirty minutes north of the city of Aswan. The four of them stood on a small hilltop overlooking the blast site.

"It was a blind corner," Hasan said, pointing to the turn in the road. "Not that the security detail was expecting land mines, but something might have given them advanced warning enough to swerve and avoid the blast."

Ryker took in the scene below him. The twisted and melted metal frame of the lead jeep sat overturned and partially embedded in the hillside. The authorities had cleaned the area of fragments, scorched rocks, or anything else that could tell some story—fill in some blank in this investigation—but as Hasan had informed them on the way over, they knew what happened and when it happened, but that was the extent of it.

"Another vehicle was parked here." Hasan pointed to the base of the hill, just on the other side of the small canyon. "The wind has erased the markings now, but it is clear that the missionaries were dragged to this truck and loaded in the back. The tracks were followed for almost half a kilometer until it reached the paved road."

"Did the tracks turn north or south onto the highway?" Ryker asked.

"That's just it. The truck hit the highway strait on, but the tracks didn't exit the other side."

"So whoever was driving—"

"Purposefully covered up which way he turned. Every detail of this attack was planned out to perfection. Except for the missionary that was killed in the blast. We may never know the answer to this, but can you think of any reason he would have been riding up front in the lead jeep instead of back with the others?"

Ryker had his suspicions but chose instead to just shake his head. He had served as a missionary thirty years earlier in Europe and knew of the passion and zeal that accompanied the calling, leading missionaries to interact with everyone they served. Trusting everyone.

For the next half hour, the four men examined the wreckage in close detail, but none of them found anything else of value to the investigation.

Hasan got a call to which he listened for only a moment. "When? . . . Where did it come from? . . . Can border police confirm this? . . . We don't have time to waste chasing down ghosts . . . Get on the radio to everyone; I want him followed but at a distance. I'll have the badge of any officer that spooks him, understood? Call me the minute you have spotted him." He hung up.

"We may have had our first break in this. Our Aswan office just received an anonymous tip that a member of *Al-Jum'ah* will be crossing into Egypt from the Sudan this morning headed for Abu Simbel."

"*Al-Jum'ah?*" Ryker asked.

"A small, radical breakoff of the PLO," Lubin responded. "A low-level organization, but they do have some ties to some larger outfits in Lebanon and further up into Afghanistan and some of the old Soviet states."

Hasan was clearly impressed with Lubin's intelligence and nodded. "Until now they have been mostly talk, publishing articles in a few of the smaller, more radical news publications, hiding in the hills, so to speak. If they are the ones responsible, this would be a giant leap forward in their place in the world of international terrorism."

As Ryker listened, he couldn't shake an uneasy feeling. "This sounds a lot like Al-Mina. I mean, a small, relatively harmless hack operation suddenly going big time."

"I agree," Hasan said, "but they all have to start somewhere."

"And then that part about their connections to some former Soviet states."

Hasan looked puzzled. "I don't understand. They all have ties, one way or another, to that area of the world."

"Manni, tell him."

"Tell me what?"

Lubin hesitated for a moment before sharing what he and the Mossad had learned about the attack and kidnapping the day before, as well as the information concerning the bombing at the Western Wall that killed Ryker's family.

When he finished, Hasan was clearly upset but not at Lubin. "It would seem that my office might have some leaks to stop up when this is all over." And with that confession, Hasan snapped into command mode.

"Radio ahead," he told Bear. "Have the plane fueled and ready to go when we get there."

At the airfield in Aswan, Hasan received the news that his Piper Navaho was down with a faulty fuel line, but that did not stop him. "What about the chopper out front? I want a pilot here in ten minutes to take us to Abu Simbel. Is that understood, Sergeant?"

It was loud and clear, and ten minutes later they were flying fast and low over the desert sands in the Bell Kiowa Warrior scout helicopter, following their first, and perhaps only, lead in this case.

* * *

The tour guide was bored already with the group, tired of repeating the same stories over the course of the day, and was fed up with stupid comments and questions about topics and information he had just covered if they had only been listening. He had graduated from the University of Cairo in antiquities and had always planned on being an archeologist, but there he stood, under the blazing sun, with only a wide-brim hat to offer shade. Most days he found himself frustrated with the course his life was taking, but he was ill-prepared to break out of the rut he was in. Nothing exciting ever happened. Every day was the same: forcing a smile to his sun-dried face and catering to the scores of sweaty, overweight, and rich tourists visiting his country. He would endure another day and keep all his complaints to himself until he could return home and vent to his cat.

"Legend says that the name *Abu Simbel* was the name of a small child who lived near here during the 1800s," he continued as they reached the steps of the Great Temple. "It was this boy who had seen the tops of the monuments you see above you as the sand shifted from time to time. Eventually, the excavated site, and indeed our lovely city, was named after him."

After allowing the standard time for oohs and ahhs, he continued.

"But the magnificent monuments you stand before were not originally in this spot." The uninterested tour guide repeated the scripted information for this group as he had done for hundreds of groups over the years, explaining that the statues were originally located sixty-five meters below the waterline of Lake Nasser. He went on to explain that when the Aswan High Dam was constructed during the 1950s, the Egyptian government, in cooperation with several other countries, moved the entire temple site to higher ground at the cost of over forty million dollars. Cut with a surgeon's precision, each stone was hoisted up and reassembled in what has arguably been called the world's greatest feat of architectural engineering . . . blah, blah, blah.

Everyone in the tour group was fascinated with the story, taking pictures and recording home videos of the experience, except for one gentleman. Though he pretended to listen, nodding at the right time and even expressing his amazement with parts of the story, his mind was preoccupied with more important things. At ten o'clock, the cell phone in his pocket rang. He excused himself quietly and stepped out of earshot of the others to take the call.

"*Na'am?*" Yes?

"Cargo delivery confirmed."

"*Shukran.*" Thank you.

He hung up and dialed another number. He casually turned and looked across the plaza. There he spotted a man who had been nervously loitering at the foot of the Lesser Temple all morning suddenly and clumsily answer his cell phone.

"Delivery confirmed. Front parking lot, white passenger van. Keys are in the ignition. *Al-hamdu I'illah! Praise be to God!*" he said, though he knew full well that if there was a God, he'd have no part of this. *Religion truly was the opiate of the people,* he thought as he hung up on the nervous man. From behind a pair of polarized Bolle sunglasses he scanned the perimeter of the temple grounds and spotted a darkly clad figure ducking behind a tour bus on the far end of the parking lot. In one fluid and nonchalant move, he reached into his windbreaker and discreetly fitted a small radio earpiece into his left ear and turned on the concealed radio.

It was showtime.

* * *

"North post, confirm target."

Ryker sat behind tinted glass in the backseat of an unmarked Range Rover and listened to the stakeout playing out before him on the radio. They had made almost impossible time from Aswan. A helicopter pilot in his younger days, Ryker was impressed with the extent to which their pilot had pushed the small chopper's limits. Their speeds had crossed over into reckless when a stiff gust of wind pushed a small flock of birds in their way, and the small helicopter was nearly thrown off balance. They had set down at the small airfield just north of the city and were taken quickly to the temple site.

Hasan and his small contingency were briefed in the car. Their target— as of yet unidentified—had arrived at the ruins at Abu Simbel nearly an hour earlier, conspicuously hanging around the Lesser Temple site.

Ryker scanned the crowds of tourists, looking for the target's contact, but none of the hundreds of people looked out of place. Hasan agreed with Lubin that the contact hadn't arrived yet and assigned a dozen officers to patrol the roads in and out of the area. But Ryker wasn't convinced. If this was the work of his phantom terrorist, the Chameleon, he would have already been here, watching *them* instead of the other way around.

Finally their target received a phone call and fumbled to answer it.

"All eyes up front!" Hasan barked. "This is it. I want that phone intact. Is that understood?"

"He's on the move."

"Where is he going? Is he returning to his car?"

"Negative. Approaching front parking lot."

"Stay with him, but stay out of sight."

"Roger that."

"He's headed for a white passenger van. Fifty meters."

"Someone run the tags."

A moment later, another officer joined the conversation. "Reported stolen last week."

"That's them!" Hasan ordered. "Move in! Take the target out, but just wing him. We need him alive!"

Hasan took off with his men, leading the charge. A silenced sniper bullet hit the *Al-Jum'ah* member in the leg, taking him down quickly; there was no need to frighten all those good people visiting the temple grounds with unnecessary gunfire.

"Come on," Lubin said as they got out of the car. "Let's go welcome your missionaries to freedom." He started out after the Egyptian police.

Ryker remained behind, though, convinced that this had been much too easy. He had been on dozens of operations over his rather colorful career and had learned to trust his instincts. And right now his instincts were screaming at him that something wasn't right with this operation. He turned his focus to the crowds of tourists. Word was quickly spreading of the police action in the parking lot, and many were venturing closer with their video cameras to document the whole exciting affair for the folks back home. Then he saw him.

One man watched the assault with neither morbid curiosity nor uneasy fear, and while men, women, and children moved all around him to get a better view or to find a place out of the line of sight, he just stood there, impassionate, watching. Then this man reached into his jacket pocket and produced a small black box. He abruptly turned and looked Ryker's way, and though he was too far away to be sure, it seemed like the man smiled before returning his attention to the police action unfolding beneath the hot desert sun.

It was a trap!

Ryker sprinted after Hasan and his men. "Stop! It's a trap!"

Lubin stopped about halfway to the van and turned around.

"Hasan! Stop—"

The passenger van exploded just at the first teams of policemen reached it. A ball of orange flame erupted, tossing the van high into air. A split second later, the sound and shock waves hit Ryker, knocking him to the ground. A blast of white-hot air washed over him and took his breath away. Forcing himself to his feet, he saw the destruction before him.

He willed himself forward with what was left of his strength toward the smoking van. Ripping open the back doors, he burned his hands on the hot metal, but the pain didn't register. He was delirious from the blast and overcome with intense guilt and pain. The world was spinning around him.

"No, no, no," he kept saying over and over. "Susan! Hang on girls!"

He was only vaguely aware that others had joined his desperate but futile rescue attempt, but as the smoke cleared and the debris pushed aside, he was struck with a sight he could not explain. There were no bodies. Nothing. The back of the van was empty.

Ryker's world spun on its axis one more time as strong hands grabbed the back of his shirt and jerked him over backward. He looked up. It was Manni Lubin, covered with dirt and powder burns. "They're not there!" his friend yelled over the ringing in his ears.

"I saw him, Manni! I saw him. He was setting us up. He was waiting for us!"

His friend continued to speak, but Ryker's world was fading fast.

"Medical is on their way," he thought he heard Lubin say before finally blacking out.

* * *

Saiif dialed another telephone number.

"The deal is off. *Al-Jum'ah* never showed. The Americans are no longer of importance to me. Take them far out into the desert and leave them."

"Alive?"

"They are of no further use to me," he lied.

"But what if they are rescued?"

"You are not being paid to question my orders. Are we clear on this point?"

"Yes."

"Then drive them and dump them. Let us see if their American god hears them in a Muslim desert."

* * *

The airfield firefighting truck and rescue vehicles put the van flames out in no time, and, as Ryker had discovered, there was no evidence that anyone had been inside when the bomb went off. Three police officers died in the blast, but their target somehow survived with first- and second-degree burns to a good part of his body. His life, at least what was left of it until his swift trial, would be filled with excruciating pain.

Hasan had been knocked to the ground in the explosion and had broken his arm in the fall. But other than that, he was all right. Livid, but all right.

"Where are they!" he was yelling at his men as the medic finished wrapping his arm. Ryker had seen glimpses of Hasan's temper over the years, but he had always kept it under control at least until he was alone with his men. This morning, the small assembly of National Police officers was bearing the full brunt of Hasan's aggravation. It wasn't their fault; they had all done their best, which in this case hadn't been enough. They had all been played by a malevolent mastermind—their every move dictated and controlled as if they were puppets on a string.

And then there was the way the terrorist had looked at Ryker. This man who turned and paused before detonating the explosives was a true professional. Amateurs are tense before the moment of execution, so focused on what they are doing and battling their inner voices of right and wrong that they are most often oblivious to their surroundings. But not their enemy today. He was patient, waiting for them, watching, relaxed enough to look over and smile before activating the bomb.

That pause. That smile. It had consumed Ryker's thoughts since first becoming conscious after the blast and the fire. It had angered him—that smug confidence and coolness he imagined this monster possessing. And then to find the van empty! Not that he didn't thank God the missionaries weren't inside, but he knew that every minute the missionaries were in his control, their chances of rescue diminished. Their captor wasn't playing by any rules; he wasn't following any of the patterns. And right then, sitting on the hot pavement, leaning up against the front wheels of Hasan's Range Rover and only partially shaded from the sun, Sam Ryker had the uneasy thought that matters were going to get a lot worse before they got any better.

Ryker was startled briefly as he suddenly became aware of someone standing near him, leaning on the Range Rover's hood. Shielding his eyes, he looked up to see Lubin's smile.

"How long have you been standing there?" Ryker asked. "Didn't hear you."

Lubin smiled. "What kind of an agent would I be if you had?"

Ryker chuckled, but it hurt to laugh.

"You all right?"

Ryker flexed his hands gingerly. "Hands hurt some. Chest feels like it was hit with a baseball bat—not that I would know just how that feels—but all in all, I'm doing fine. You?"

"The blast knocked me off my feet," Lubin said, stepping around and joining his friend on the ground, leaning against the desert-worn SUV. "The medic said the back of my head cushioned the fall, so it could have been worse."

Lubin smiled as Ryker chuckled again at the attempt to lighten the mood. The levity, however, didn't last long.

"We're being set up," Ryker finally said. "Like a deadly game of cat and mouse. I mean, Manni, how could he have known we'd be there? We were in Aswan when we got news of the possible exchange. There is no way he could have known we'd make it in time."

"Maybe he didn't. It's possible it could have been a coincidence."

Ryker shook his head. "If the missionaries had been in that van, then maybe, but he knew there'd be a rescue attempt—he knew we'd be here, even before we knew it, and he deliberately set us up. I don't like this."

A little ways off, Hasan continued to drill his men for answers that none of them had, his voice getting louder and more agitated with every demand. Lubin took a deep breath, reached out, took a hold of Ryker's knee, and pushed himself to his feet. He reached back down and offered Ryker a hand up.

"It looks like Hasan could use every able-bodied man to help," Lubin said, pulling Ryker to his feet.

"Something about all this doesn't sit right with me, though," Ryker said.

"Nothing about terrorism makes much sense to me."

"No, that's not what I mean. At least with Hamas, or the PLO, or even the Muslim Brotherhood, you can see the logic—twisted as it might be—behind the event. To kidnap these health missionaries and then not demand a ransom—"

"But if our terrorist was for hire . . ." Lubin interjected.

"Right, but even if he was paid to abduct them, why go to all that trouble to stage the exchange and then fake their deaths? We're missing something, Manni, and I just can't put my finger on it."

Ryker paused for a moment and stared out over Lake Nasser. The mid-morning sun was reflecting brilliantly off water dotted with the white sails of the traditional feluccas. Further in the distance, he could see a tour boat approaching, most likely from Aswan, with a load of tourists who would no doubt be immensely disappointed when they docked and learned that the entire temple courtyard was off limits and under investigation as a result of the morning's excitement.

Hasan's men had been quick to secure the area, but most of the buses, loaded with frightened tourists, had left before a perimeter could be set up. And those who missed their buses started off on foot toward Abu Simbel and the safety of civilization. Ryker was certain that their antagonist, the Chameleon, had blended in and made his escape with the hundreds of others.

"Sam?" Lubin nudged him. "Are you sure you're all right?"

"No, my friend, I'm not, and won't be until this is all over and our man is stopped, once and for all."

Hasan had every available police, military, and security officer in Abu Simbel gathered at the base of the Great Temple Hill, and Lubin and Ryker found their places near the back and listened to the many reports coming in. The reports, however, fell short of informative and were not helpful in the least.

"Then this has all been for naught." Hasan huffed. "I want tourist itineraries checked, every bus, every boat, every hotel record, *everything!* Am I clear? If you question whether or not to check something, check it!"

A local authority, unfamiliar with Hasan's intensity and temper, dared to raised his hand. "Sir? The Department of Antiquities will not approve of this suspicion and action against foreigners. An operation like this will need their approval and—"

Hasan's men flinched as their chief inspector suddenly pushed through the crowds and grabbed the local policeman by his shirt, pushing him sharply off balance to command his full attention.

"Three of my men are dead," Hasan yelled at the officer, nose to nose, "and you are concerned with the slight discomfort of a few tourists? I would detain a thousand men and women if it meant catching this monster! And until this matter is finished and this terrorist caught or killed, we don't slow down or make anything else a priority! Is that understood?"

The site policeman, whose only real duties included attending to the needs of exhausted or dehydrated tourists or investigating the occasional pickpocket or petty crime, swallowed his pride.

Hasan released his grip on the officer and looked to his captive audience.

"We will find these missionaries," he said softer and with real conviction. "Allah wishes them found, and we have done everything we can except ask His help. Those of you who will, join me." He looked past his men to Ryker and Lubin. "And those of you who will not, I encourage you to pray to your God and petition his intervention."

In what would be considered an unorthodox move, the great and powerful Hasan moved to the front of the crowd, faced east, and fell to his knees, prostrating himself in supplication in the Muslim tradition. Ryker was intimately familiar with this special prayer. Called the *salat al-istikhaarah*, this prayer was used when a Muslim needed special guidance or help. And if they ever needed Allah's help, it was now.

Ryker followed suit and dropped to his knees with this Muslim brothers, and for the first time since losing his wife and girls to the fire of the terrorist bomb, he offered a prayer to that God he had blamed for their deaths, asking for the safe return of the missionaries. He had adopted the belief early on in life that whether one worshipped Allah, God, Jesus, Jehovah, or any other host of names, there was only one God, and He heard and answered all prayers. A lump caught in his throat as he became forcefully aware that it had been nearly a year since his heart had supplicated divine favor. He was surprised to feel at peace as he prayed for the first time in a long time.

But what surprised him even more was the movement to this right as Manni Lubin, faithful Israeli and Jew, joined them in prayer. Though they had never really discussed their religious beliefs over the years, it would appear that Lubin was secure enough in his own faith to believe as he did that there was, in fact, one God. Gone was the ominous feeling he'd had earlier, replaced by a warm feeling that flooded over Ryker's being over the heat of the desert sun, and he knew that God was aware of their efforts and struggles and that somehow things would work out.

As the prayer concluded, Ryker could hear Hasan being called on the Range Rover's radio. Several of the men looked up, distracted by the frantic pleas for the chief inspector's attention. Hasan's lieutenant muttered an apology to Allah for the interruption and quickly made his way to the SUV.

A moment later, Hasan finished the *salah,* and they all returned to their feet. Ryker sensed a renewed energy among the officers, and it struck him that this was perhaps a portion of the logic behind the command to pray always. One could not but help be lifted up drawing close to Deity in word and desire.

"Listen up," Hasan called out. "There is something we are not seeing here. It is no coincidence that we were led here, but it was not to rescue the Americans. Somewhere along the way we have missed something."

And suddenly Ryker knew what it was. "Hasan? May I have a word with you?"

Hasan considered the request, gave some quick instructions to some of his men, and then Ryker, Lubin, and Hasan stepped out of earshot of the others.

"Something has been bothering me since the explosion," Ryker started. "I know now what it is. There was no surprise when he saw me."

"When who saw you?"

"The bomber. *Al-Har'ba,* the Chameleon."

"And why should he have been?" Hasan asked.

"Because," Lubin interjected, seeing where Ryker was going with this, "Sam was declared dead after the bombing in Jerusalem. If we are chasing the same man, then he should have—"

"Paused or stared or been startled in some way when he saw me," Ryker finished. "But he wasn't. He looked right at me, like he *expected* me to be there to warn you."

Hasan was not buying into the story. "Then this was all part of a plan to—what?—bring you out into the open? To finish what he failed to do last year?"

Ryker paced back and forth, looking at the ground and shaking his head. "No, I don't think that was his primary objective, but I can't shake the feeling that that's part of it."

An uncomfortable silence stretched between them.

"Then you're out," Hasan said.

Ryker was shocked. "What?"

"You'll stay and help with the investigation and clean up here, or help my men interview the tourists, if you prefer, but you're not going on."

"Hasan, I don't understand how this affects my ability to—"

"This is not up for debate."

"You can't—"

"Yes, I can. Look, I need every one of my men focused on finding your missionaries. That includes you. I cannot have any member of my field teams thinking that this might be a case of revenge or something other than a search-and-rescue operation." Hasan paused and reached out to Ryker's shoulder. "And if you are correct, and this has all been part of a plan to kill you, then it is my duty as a friend to see that he does not succeed. I will not put your life in danger. I owe you that much."

Ryker was genuinely touched and was unable to respond.

"Besides, Sam, you are the only one who saw our man. There will be video to watch, and pictures to review, and you, better than anyone else, will be able to put a face to this phantom terrorist."

"But—"

Hasan raised his hand. "I have decided. Your friend's help is still welcomed if he wants to remain behind and assist you."

Ryker opened his mouth to protest Hasan's decision, but before he could make a sound, Bear called out to them from the Range Rover.

"Military transport spotted in the desert, headed southwest," Bear reported, winded from the short run. "Commercial jet spotted it and called it in."

"God be praised!" Hasan uttered. "We move! Now!"

Assignments were made quickly. A large part of Hasan's men were to stay behind and begin interviewing the hundred-plus tourists being detained in Abu Simbel. As he had already indicated to Ryker and Lubin, Hasan wanted every picture developed, every video watched, until they had a picture of their man. Another group was to remain at the blast site, scouring the parking lot for any fragment of explosive or detonator that could be traced. Finding the source of the explosives could lead to the purchaser. Weapons dealers were a tight-lipped group, but Ryker knew from his years of counterterrorism experience that everyone has a breaking point. In the end, everyone talks.

Hasan finally turned to his lieutenant. "Take two jeeps and six men, and start out after them across the desert."

"Hasan, you can't do this!" Ryker's anger was beginning to rise. "You have to let me come with you!"

Hasan's pleasant demeanor of a few minutes earlier was all but gone. "And what if this is another trap? What if the missionaries are not on this transport, either? Our man has proven he is not above sacrificing his own men in some twisted game to get to us. I need you to stay behind in case this is another one of his false leads, something to distract us from doing our job and finding every piece of evidence we can to identify this man and stop him. I need you here. I wish you could see that."

Hasan turned to his lieutenant. "Shots are not to be fired at the transport until you are close enough to take out the tires. I will not risk having the missionaries shot in some heroic exchange of gunfire. Am I understood?"

Bear nodded. It was clear to Ryker that Hasan's lieutenant was the kind of man to listen, understand, and obey the first time.

"I'll take two men with me and follow in the air." Hasan scanned the crowds. "Where is my pilot?"

A hand rose up near a medic tent set up at the perimeter of the parking lot. The mass of men parted, like Moses' Red Sea, to reveal the helicopter pilot stretched on a cot, his left leg broken and wrapped tight.

"Is there anyone else qualified to fly a chopper?" Hasan's anger and frustration only increased as he was met with blank stares from his men. "Not one of you can fly?"

Behind him, Ryker spoke up. "I can fly."

Hasan sharply turned around. Ryker had stepped forward. "I flew two years' recon in Vietnam. It's been a while, but I can fly your chopper."

Ryker and Hasan locked stares, both exerting pressure and neither letting up in their battle of wills. Finally Hasan cracked a half smile. "Who am I to stand in the way of Allah's will?"

"Thank you, my friend."

Hasan turned back around to face his men. "All right! You all have a job to do! Do it!"

Hasan secured one of the police jeeps, and the three of them sped back to the airstrip. Ryker walked toward the waiting helicopter. It was true that Ryker had once been an outstanding helicopter pilot in his time, but that had been almost thirty years before. Not including today, he'd only set foot in a helicopter three times since then, and each time as a civilian passenger. *Just like riding a bike*, he hoped. *A big, two-ton bike.*

Climbing into the cockpit, Ryker reached for the communications headset, adjusting the strap to comfortably position the padded earphones. He reached out to the controls and extended his fingers, hoping that the many gauges and indicators would speak to his hands and guide him toward a safe liftoff. But Sam Ryker would have no such luck.

"Sam?" Lubin asked from the passenger cabin, tapping lightly on his shoulder. "You wouldn't lie just to come along, would you?" When Ryker failed to respond to his jest, the Israeli Mossad agent tapped a little harder. "I said, you wouldn't—"

"I heard you the first time."

"Well?"

"Well, what?"

"You know, tell Hasan—"

"Tell me what?" Hasan deftly climbed in next to Lubin and fastened his harness. He was carrying with him a small, locked metal case.

Ryker looked back and shot Lubin a commanding look. "That it's been a while since I've flown. Be certain to buckle up."

Hasan looked to both men and then back to Ryker. "You can do this, right?"

Ryker took a deep breath. "Yes, sir."

But the harder he tried to force himself to remember, the more resistant the knowledge was. He tried one more time, fingers extended, to encourage the Kiowa to tell him what to do, but this time he relaxed and tried to clear his mind. Ryker had always been a big believer in muscle memory, the theory that if you did some act or procedure long enough or did enough times, your body actually remembered what to do next. Ryker was hoping—no, praying—that it would all come back to him. And quick.

He looked up and out of the canopy and checked the main rotor. He then toggled through the throttle: full open, flight idle, and then closed. Finding the starter, he engaged it to check oil pressure and then pushed the throttle up to flight idle. Transmission oil pressure read normal. Fuel at full. Next he pushed gently up and down on the tail rotor pedal. Without being able to see it from the cockpit, he could feel that they were moving to his command. Generator: on. Master avionics: on. The main rotor blades were humming nicely. Caution switch: on. Cage gyro and gyron switch: on. Hydraulic control switch: on.

"How far to the border?" Ryker asked.

Hasan smiled. "There is not exactly a line drawn in the sand, if you know what I mean."

"That's what I was hoping you'd say." Ryker took control of the cyclic-pitch lever. Had he forgotten anything? He didn't know. Maybe, but it felt right to pull back on the stick and take to the skies. "Gentlemen, here goes nothing!"

And with that said, and a choppy first couple of feet into the air as Ryker got the feel of flying again, the three of them were airborne and heading west into the desert.

* * *

In the dark, Elder Jack Devereux could feel a sharp tug on his shoulder. But in his drug-induced state, he imagined the hand belonging to his eldest son, Will. They were at a park just outside of Augusta. Will's youngest, little McKay, two years old and filled with enough energy to power a small city, was calling "G'ampa! G'ampa!" eager to show him a new trick he had just learned. He turned around to see his littlest grandchild jump from the bottom step of the slide onto the cushioned, bark-filled play area. And then in an instant, McKay fell through the bark and disappeared. Will began shouting for help, but as Jack moved, he tripped. His feet were bound and his hands were tied behind his back. As he fell to the ground, another sharp tug on his shoulder pulled him up and out of his nightmare.

But when he opened his eyes, he could only see patterns of light and dark flash across the gunnysack still tied around his head. The journey was tortuous, every pitch and dive the truck took painfully transmitting the force directly to their prone bodies. And then, over the whine of the engine, Elder Devereux thought he heard his name being called.

"Jack? Jack? If you can hear me move your arms."

"Thomas?"

"Shh. Don't talk. Give me your hands."

Elder Devereux pushed his hands away from his body and immediately felt Elder Anderson's hands start to work on the knots holding him bound. It was then that he noticed that his blindfold had slipped from his eyes which allowed for a bit of light to make it through. It was like trying to see through a gauze wrap. By the look of the shadows playing before him, a large mass sat in the front corner of the truck bed, unresponsive and listless. Could their guard be asleep? It seemed too much to hope for. The Lord had saved Alma and his followers by causing a deep sleep to come over their Lamanite captors. So why not them?

Suddenly the big mass in the corner moved, and their captor jumped to his feet, hitting his head on one of the cover's metal ribs. "No, no, no, no!" he bellowed.

Elder Thomas's hands froze, and both of them braced themselves for the beating they knew was coming; but it never did. Instead, their captor stepped over them, grabbed the tailgate, and cursed. Elder Devereux's Arabic was pretty good, but all he could discern from the man's curse was that it involved camels and procreation.

"They're following us!"

"Who?" the other one called back from the cab.

Their big captor remained at the back of the truck bed for a few moments and then stepped back over them. Not one to waste an opportunity, Jack quickly moved his hands back and forth and loosened the rope the rest of the way.

"He has set us up!" the big one said.

"Do not say such things, Nasr," his brother warned. "Even now he may be listening."

Elder Devereux pushed the thoughts of rescue from his mind and concentrated on the work he needed to accomplish *right now*—there would be time later to be rescued. He reached back and took the young elder's hands and began working on the knots, trying to make his movements as small and inconspicuous as possible. If he dared to remove his hood and face his young companion, he could have the knot undone in half the time. But if he was caught, he reasoned, Elder Anderson, and even his sweet wife, Abigail, might never have their hands freed.

As he worked to unravel the ropes at his fingertips, he craned his neck to see, at least peripherally, the movements of their captors. He was pleased to find that as he turned his head, a small hole in the coarse hood aligned itself directly over his right eye.

"Give me the rifle," Imad said.

"Don't touch it!" Nasr yelled.

"Imad! Now! Give it to me!"

As they argued, Elder Devereux kept working on Elder Anderson's wrists, but with each passing minute he had to forcefully fight the urge to give up. Their captors must have been afraid of the boy's size and triple-tied the most unorganized and scrambled knots they could tie. Their captors were no Boy Scouts, that was for sure, and he started in on the next knot, keeping an unblinking eye on the big guy in the back.

Nasr began to complain again about not getting the gun, when his brother shushed him.

"No, no, no! Listen! Do you hear that?"

Elder Devereux paused for a brief moment, too, and strained to hear what was so disconcerting to the driver. He didn't hear anything at first, but then he heard, or rather felt, a low *whump-whump-whump* over the sound of the truck's transmission.

* * *

"There it is!"

Ryker was the first to spot the military transport bouncing along the old Bedouin trail, at times taking flight as it sped through the desert, sending up a plume of fine sand and dust behind it.

"How do you propose we stop it?" Ryker asked.

"The teams on the ground are gaining on them."

"But not fast enough. The longer they run, the more desperate they become. We have to find a way to stop them now!"

"If you can force them off the trail," Lubin suggested, "the desert sands should take care of it."

Ryker chuckled. "You want me to play chicken with a two-ton army transport?"

"What it this, 'playing chicken?'" Hasan asked nervously.

"Or maybe just a couple of close flybys," Lubin said.

"Hang on, guys!" Ryker said as he pushed the lever forward and accelerated to close the distance between them.

* * *

Nasr stepped over the missionaries again, oblivious to their escape efforts, and reached into the truck cab. "You drive! I'll shoot!" After a brief struggle with this brother, Nasr pulled the weathered, Soviet AK-47 from the cab, checked the magazine, and dropped to one knee at the tailgate to steady himself, shooting off a couple rounds. Nasr laughed as he continued firing. The sound was deafening.

Behind him, Elder Anderson finished shedding the cords that bound his hands. Ripping the hood from his head, he started working on his feet. There was no going back now. As soon as they were spotted by either man, the next few seconds would determine who lived and who died.

* * *

All three men flinched as one of the rounds glanced off the helicopter's front canopy and hit the rotor blades. Hasan got on the radio to his men.

"No one returns fire. Is that understood?!" Hasan ordered again. "No one returns fire!"

Both teams acknowledged the command and continued to close the gap between them.

"Hold on to your hats!" Ryker yelled. "Here we go!"

Dropping out of sky, Ryker pulled up and leveled out at about twenty feet off the ground as he passed dangerously close to the front of the speeding transport. Ryker let loose a cowboy "Yeehaw!" as they flew by and climbed up for a second pass.

* * *

Imad swerved sharply to avoid the aircraft and slowed as the truck tires spun to keep the truck moving in the soft sand. He put all his weight on the accelerator and turned the wheel to get back on the hard-packed trail.

"What are you waiting for?" he yelled over his shoulder to his brother. He adjusted the rearview mirror. "Shoot them already—Nasr! Look out!"

Elder Anderson had freed his feet and was now standing, crouched low, with his center of gravity directly beneath him, and was ready for Nasr as he spun around.

Without thinking, Nasr gripped the rifle and jabbed the elder with the butt, trying to push him backward. A varsity wrestler in high school, Elder Anderson was ready for the attack and took hold of the weapon, too, throwing his hip into his captor. Nasr immediately found himself off balance and falling. He let go of the rifle to catch his fall but placed a well-aimed kick at the missionary's knee, collapsing the big American with shooting pain. Nasr grinned and leaped up at the hurt elder. As skilled as he might have once been, Elder Anderson had traded his chin strap and head gear for a stethoscope and cuff, and he took Nasr's assault full on. Both men dropped to the metal truck bed.

Nasr began pelting the young man's midsection with his rock-hard fists, and there was little Elder Anderson could do to defend against it. But he had risked too much to be defeated without a real fight, and summoning strength he didn't know he had, he rolled out from under his captor. Letting his body remember the moves, Elder Anderson wrapped his legs around the big man while running one arm under Nasr's right arm and locked his neck in a half-nelson. Pushing his legs away, Nasr dropped to his stomach, effectively paralyzed, especially when Anderson used his left hand to drive Nasr's face into the truck bed.

An icy-hot sensation pierced Elder Anderson's thigh and hip, and it took him a moment to realize what had happened. As the pain registered, Elder Anderson released his grip, rolling to one side as Nasr got back to his feet.

"You foolish boy!" Nasr spat, holding the knife at the ready, wet with Elder Anderson's blood.

Elder Anderson couldn't move. The knife hadn't cut anything vital, but the cut was deep, and he knew he had to stop the flow of blood. He tried to stand on it, but the pain was too great.

"You will all die," Nasr said. "None of you will make it out of the desert alive."

Elder Anderson just then noticed that the butt of the assault rifle was within reach and scrambled for it. Nasr was quick to respond and grabbed the barrel end a split second before the missionary could reach it, pulling it away.

"You are too slow, boy! You cannot beat me! No one beats me—"

Just then the truck righted itself back onto the Bedouin trail and staggered wildly as all four wheels left the soft sand. Elder Anderson was thrown forward while Nasr lost his balance, dropped the rifle, and reached out for something to hold on to, falling backward over the tailgate. Instinctively, Elder Anderson reached out and tried to grab him before he fell out of the truck, but he was too far away.

Their pursuers had closed the gap and were speeding right behind them. He watched in horror as the driver of the Range Rover tried to swerve out of the way to miss Nasr but couldn't.

Elder Devereux had freed his legs by then and crawled over to the bleeding and shaken elder.

"Are you all right?"

Elder Anderson responded with a blank stare.

"Elder? Thomas?"

Elder Devereux took the young missionary's hand, put his blindfold in it, and directed it to his hip. "Do you think you can keep pressure on this?"

Still no response. Then his arm muscles tightened as he pressed firmly on the cut on his hip.

"Good. Now, I'm going to help Abby. We're not out of the woods just yet."

* * *

"Was that a body?"

The nausea he had felt when he watched as the passenger van exploded and caught fire returned with a quick slice to his heart.

"Was that one of the missionaries?" Hasan barked into the radio.

"Negative," came Bear's deep voice. "He was Arab."

"Can you see them?"

"Affirmative. Visual on two."

"That's them, Manni!" Ryker exclaimed. "I'm coming around again."

Ryker brought the Kiowa Warrior around for another pass and began the swift descent to buzz the transport again when a sudden movement at the furthest edge of his peripheral vision sounded an internal alarm. He abruptly banked left as a hail of white-hot, large-caliber tracer rounds cut through the airspace they had only just occupied. Both passengers were shaken at the sudden movement.

"What is the name of—"

"We have company! Manni, find him for me! Where is he?"

Manni Lubin leaned against his harness as far as he could, straining his neck to see out and behind them. They had the morning sun to their back, and the glare off the white sands and the window made if difficult for him to see anything. Then he spotted a shadow following them.

"Seven o'clock!" Lubin shouted over the headgear.

Immediately, Ryker took the Kiowa Warrior into a sharp dive, turning into the position of their assailant. More white-hot tracer rounds followed them as his evasive action was matched. But still Ryker kept the large-caliber ammunition from seriously damaging their chopper. Ryker leveled out about a hundred feet above the desert sands and opened the throttle as far as it would go. With an abrupt burst of speed, Ryker tried to put some distance between them, weaving back and forth across the old desert trail.

Bracing himself against the rear-hinged door, Hasan reached under his seat and pulled out the metal case he had brought on board earlier. Hefting it to this lap, he opened it and removed a compact, fully automatic submachine gun. Lubin recognized its make immediately and gave Hasan a surprised look.

"You should be familiar with one of these," Hasan said.

"Uzi?" Lubin confirmed. Hasan nodded and handed Lubin the slate weapon, giving him two thirty-two-round clips. "I didn't know Egypt used the Uzi."

Hasan reached in and produced another one. "Not officially." He removed two clips for himself, too, and hit one securely into the pistol grip. "But if you won't tell, I won't."

The Uzi submachine gun was designed and first used during the 1948 Arab–Israeli War. Because of its simple use and economical production, it had been a favorite of the Israeli army, as well as countless military and paramilitary from South America to Southeast Asia and everywhere in between.

Both Lubin and Hasan, guns locked and loaded, scanned the skies for any sign of the other chopper.

"He's coming around again!" Hasan suddenly yelled. "At your four o'clock!"

This time Ryker turned away from the other chopper and pulled up on the pitch lever, catapulting them almost straight up. Lubin had a quick shot at the other chopper and fired a small burst of nine-millimeter rounds out the gun window. Lubin's gunfire was returned by another barrage of phosphorous-tipped rounds that Ryker still largely managed to stay out of the way of.

"I can't do this forever, guys! You gotta shoot him down, 'cause I can't seem to shake him."

"Bring us around again," Hasan said. "Give me a shot at him."

Leveling out again, Ryker hoped his attacker would take the bait and follow after him, giving him another chance to turn the tables and give him a little taste of their own hot lead. Faking left, Ryker slammed the cyclic pitch lever right and pushed the Kiowa Warrior to its structural limits as he brought the other chopper into Hasan's view. Hasan squeezed his trigger and emptied an entire clip in a matter of seconds. If the other chopper was hit, it made no signs of injury.

"I'm coming around again," Ryker shouted. "Hard break left in three, two, one!"

Again the Kiowa Warrior was stressed almost to the point of breaking apart, but she held and gave Lubin another shot at the chopper. Lubin emptied the rest of his first clip and then, with master combat skills, ejected the spent magazine and clipped another in its place in the blink of an eye, continuing to unleash everything the submachine gun had to offer. Again, though, it seemed not to touch the other chopper.

Another shower of enemy rounds burst from the guns mounted on the chopper's landing skids. Ryker weaved erratically trying to avoid them, but several hit them from behind and along the fuselage with sickening thuds. Ryker could tell immediately that at least one round had gotten lucky and had hit where it would do the most damage.

"Tail rotor's been hit!"

"What does that mean?" Hasan yelled out over the noise.

Ryker smiled. "It means you get to see how good I am at crash-landing this thing!"

The Kiowa Warrior began to spin. Without the stabilizing tail rotor blades, the body of the helicopter spun out of control. Ryker tried to compensate for the rotation as he throttled down, keeping the main rotor blades parallel to the ground as best he could. The desert sands rushed up to meet them, and in a matter of a few seconds, the large Warrior-class helicopter hit the ground with bone-jarring force. The fuselage tipped and the rotor blades, still spinning wildly, hit the sands, tossing the body of the helicopter over and around as the rotor blades broke like matchsticks under the force of the sudden stop.

Ryker hit his head sharply on the side of the canopy and was stunned for a moment. Fighting to shake it off, he quickly unbuckled his harness and checked on his friends in the back. Faring in similar fashion, Hasan and

Lubin were struggling to free themselves from their restrictive harnesses and get out of the helicopter.

"Hope your flight was a pleasant one," Ryker tried to joke.

"You crashed my helicopter!" Hasan shouted, still unsure on his feet and a bit dazed.

"I prefer to call it landing with style."

"I call it a nightmare trying to explain how the department's helicopter came to be crashed in the middle of the west desert by a pilot who is supposed to be dead!"

Ryker cracked another smile. "The paperwork's going to be tricky on that one, that's for sure."

"Still glad you insisted on coming along?"

"You know me; I wouldn't miss it for the world."

Hasan just shook his head, whether out of frustration with Ryker's hardheadedness or to shake off the rest of the jarring stop, it was hard to really say.

As the ringing in their ears began to subside, Lubin was the first to hear the approaching danger. "I don't wish to interrupt, but I need to point out that we are entirely exposed, and he is making another pass."

Good humor put aside, the three soldiers ran to the nearest ridge in the sand and took up defensive positions. The other chopper came about and pitched forward, coming in low. The tracer rounds formed an almost continuous line from the large mounted guns into the sand below, throwing up puffs of sand as it sped forward toward them. Hasan and Lubin readied their Uzis.

"Do you still have your Glock?" Ryker asked.

"What?" Hasan answered.

"Your Glock!"

Hasan produced the nine-millimeter handgun and slapped it into Ryker's outstretched hand.

"That's better," Ryker said, standing to his feet, gun braced out in front of him.

"What are you doing!"

Ryker knew they had precious few chances to come out of this exchange alive. They had to take that chopper down. If they couldn't, he was a dead man all over again. Hasan and Lubin began shooting as soon as the chopper was in range. Ryker waited, though. Taking careful aim, he fired off round after round as the chopper buzzed overhead. His first shot hit the front canopy where he saw the same smiling, bloodthirsty face he had seen back at the temple grounds. The other shots all made contact with parts of the fuselage and engine. As it flew past them, the engine began to sputter, black smoke trailing behind it.

"It's burning oil!" Lubin shouted.

Droplets of clear liquid rained down, glistening as they caught the morning sun. "Fuel tank's been hit, too."

"Good shot, cowboy."

The chopper banked right and began heading back toward Abu Simbel, a veritable Goliath fleeing before three small Davids.

*   *   *

Imad had seen the aerial combat play out before him, watching as the first helicopter was shot out of the sky. He was disappointed, though, that there was no big explosion and plume of orange flame when it hit the ground like he'd seen in the movies. Then the second chopper had passed right by him, flying low, not thirty feet off the ground. As it rushed by at twice his speed, Imad glimpsed the pilot—it was their employer. But how did he know they would be followed? Unless . . .

"Nasr was right," he cursed under his breath. They were set up. Betrayed by one of their own. There truly was no honor among thieves. Family were the only people you could trust in this world.

"Crawl back to the cave you came from," Imad exclaimed as the injured chopper flew past him back toward the city. Imad adjusted his side mirror to watch the cowardly retreat when he noticed the police vehicles riding right on his tail. What had happened to Nasr?

In the rearview mirror he could see the old American bent over his wife, freeing her from the ropes. There was no sign of either the big missionary or his brother. Which could only mean one thing.

"No!" Imad swerved sharply across the narrow desert trail, jerking the wheel right, and then left, and then right again, trying to punish the Americans in the back. Off to his right, he could see the wreckage of the police helicopter, and he noted with anger that there was still no fire or smoke. And with that thought, he knew he was not going to live to see the next call to prayer.

Two explosions—a gunshot and blown tire—sounded outside the transport a split second before he lost control of the truck and careened off the road. The big transport bounced a few times as its momentum heaved it across the rolling desert until it hit a ridge and tipped over as it plowed into the shifting sands.

* * *

"Not bad for an old man."

Hasan shot Ryker a disapproving look. "Not bad for a man of *any* age."

"*Touché.*"

Lubin just smiled at the friendly exchange between old friends. Despite the gravity of their situation, experienced combat veterans knew that a bowstring can't be taut all the time or it loses its tension and worth. Hasan had borrowed back his Glock, shooting out the transport's front tire at a distance of what had to be nearly a hundred yards. Ryker was right; it was a pretty good shot, especially for someone who had just survived a helicopter crash. Lubin looked at his own hands. They were still shaking from their fall from the sky and brush with death. Ryker had not exaggerated Hasan's skills and abilities one bit over the years. But now, with the stolen transport disabled and vulnerable, they had to act quickly to make sure their kidnapper didn't have the chance to become a suicide martyr.

Hasan's men had stopped and were holding a position at the side of the road. They, too, knew that desperate men commit desperate acts. Without a radio to coordinate their actions, a delicate rescue operation like this one was only going to be that much more difficult. The chances of avoiding casualties diminished with every passing minute.

"How are we on ammo?" Ryker asked.

Hasan had salvaged what he could from the downed chopper. "Two clean clips. The others were buried in the sand in the crash. We don't have time to clean them, and it's not worth the risk of jamming or worse, blow-back."

Ryker and Lubin agreed. This fine, desert sand was notorious for fouling up the spring and firing mechanisms in automatic weapons. It would be better to make the assault *without* a weapon than to rush in thinking that you had a full clip at your disposal. Ryker had taken back the Glock and checked the magazine.

"I've got two."

Lubin accepted one of the Uzi clips and secured it in the pistol grip. "Then we had better make each shot count, wouldn't you agree?"

Ryker nodded in anxious anticipation. "Let's move while this is still a rescue mission and not just a recovery."

* * *

Imad came to with an intense stinging sensation over his left eye. He reached up and touched his forehead, pulling back a hand smeared with his own blood. He had a large cut over his eye, his forehead having collided with the steering wheel in the transport's sudden stop. He wiped the sticky, gritty mess from his eyes and took a quick inventory. Through the cab window he saw that the Americans had been shaken up pretty badly. The old man was moaning, stirring in pain, while the other two lay still. Maybe Allah had done His dirty work for him. But it was better to be sure.

Imad reached across the cab and opened the glove box, producing a Smith & Wesson, nine-millimeter semiautomatic.

Quick movement over the ridges of sand caught his eye, and he knew that he had to act quickly if he was to faithfully and honorably accomplish the task he had been given. Allah would surely bless him for being a man of his word and seeing his assignment through to the end.

He brought the gun up to his face, almost prayer-like.

"*Al-hamdu l'illah!*" *Praise be to God.* "Nasr, I come to join you in Paradise."

* * *

Elder Jack Devereux, every bone and muscle in his body screaming in pain, opened his eyes just in time to see his captor, the driver, reach through the cab window, arm extended with a small, black handgun aimed toward his still-unconscious wife. Instinctively, he threw himself over her to shield her body with his. Peace cascaded over him as he looked upon the angelic face of his sleeping bride, even if for one last time in this life—

The deafening thunder of gunfire ripped through the truck bed, and Elder Devereux felt his hands and arms relax. He had always wondered how the transition of death would feel—if it would be a startling experience, like the shock of jumping into a cold, mountain lake—but there was no noticeable change. Still, he remained atop his wife, still feeling the same feelings of love and protection for the woman that he had traveled mortality with.

But then Elder Devereux noticed that everything had gone quiet. There was sound, but it was immense and everywhere around him. And then, out of this strange mixture of silence and tonal ringing, he thought he heard his name called.

"Elder Devereux . . ."

He was afraid to turn around. The voice became louder, more commanding.

"Jack!"

But this voice was not the deep, resounding tenor of heaven he had always imagined. In fact, it sounded like—

"Elder Anderson?" He pushed himself up and turned his head and body around to see Elder Anderson, lying prone beneath cab window, hands outstretched and wrestling for the gun with their driver.

He hadn't been shot! He wasn't dead! Not yet, anyway. And the young Elder needed his help. Reaching for the knapsack that had belonged to their other captor, Elder Devereux swung it as hard as he could at the driver's hand and gun. The driver screamed in agony as his wrist snapped against the edge of the window.

* * *

Ryker flinched at the sound of the report.

Hasan yelled to his men, "Go, go, go!"

The faster they sprinted those last few meters, the more the sand gave way beneath their feet, slowing them down to a mere crawl. Ryker found himself on all fours, his hands pushing against the hot sand in an attempt to make it to the transport and the missionaries faster. Finally, he reached the truck, only slightly ahead of the others. Gun at the ready, he threw open the passenger door with enough force to nearly tear it off its hinges, fleeing the other side was the driver. Ryker took a shot in the hope of winging him, but the slug slammed into the side of the door instead. Running around the front of the partially buried truck, he rounded the hood in time to see the driver disappear around the back.

"Does anyone have the shot?" he shouted. Running to the rear, he stole a quick look around and saw the driver drop to his knees, rip open his shirt, and bear his chest in the direction of the truck bed. It was then that he saw the barrel of an AK-47 extended past the tailgate. He followed the barrel inside to see it being held by an elderly woman, her dazed look lending to the already incredulous picture before him. She was being comforted by a man he could only take as her husband.

"Abby, it's OK. Put the gun down. He can do us no more harm."

The assault rifle began to lower. It was then that the driver, their captor, yelled and jumped to his feet.

"No! You must!" and he lunged for the end of the gun.

Without thinking Ryker took aim and fired. The driver spun all the way around once in the air before hitting the ground. It was only then that he noticed both Hasan and Lubin standing opposite him. They had a look of shock and fear.

"Did I forget to say *duck?*"

Hasan just shook his head again and motioned his men to converge on the transport and secure the scene.

Ryker shoved the Glock into his back pocket, and Lubin shouldered the Uzi as they opened the tailgate. Ryker recognized them immediately from the passport photos he had viewed on the flight from Cairo to Aswan. He slowly reached in and took hold of the AK-47. "There we go . . . Nice and easy . . . My name is Sam Ryker. James—er, President Cannon—sent me to rescue you."

At the mention of President Cannon's name, Elder Devereux fell back on his haunches, folded his arms across his knees, and began to sob. Sister Devereux, still in shock, just repeated the name of the prophet over and over. "I knew God would save us. I knew it . . ." she said.

Ryker then noticed that the young elder lying in the back of the bed was hurt and likely needed medical attention. He climbed up and into the back of the truck.

"Are you Elder Anderson?"

The elder tried to offer his hand to shake, but he doubled back in pain. "Yeah, or what's left of him."

Ryker smiled. "You're safe now. We'll get that leg taken care of and get you back to U.S. soil by nightfall."

"Through it all, he never gave up," Elder Anderson said, pointing to Elder Devereux. "He never doubted that God was watching over us and that He would provide us with a rescue."

Ryker was suddenly uncomfortable and shook his head. "You were very lucky, son. You all were."

Elder Anderson shook his head. "No, luck had nothing to do with it. You were on the Lord's errand. You could not have done anything less but find us. It was our duty to stay alive long enough for Him to rescue us."

And there it was again, this sense that Ryker was somehow being used by God, and though he felt an overwhelming sense of relief and gratitude that the missionaries had been found safely and in time, there was still a resentment that God hadn't intervened with his own family—that some hero hadn't saved Susan and the girls.

He shook off the feeling. Now was not the time for these bouts with self-pity and abandon. God, if He did exist, had performed a miracle here in the desert—shouldn't that be enough for now?

Hasan's men were busy taking the driver into custody, paying little attention to the screams of pain from the hole in his shoulder as they secured his hands behind his back. It was only then that one of the officers broke out the first-aid kit and loosely bandaged the gunshot wound. Hasan was busy on the radio, calling in the rest of the cavalry, including an ambulance and medical transport while also alerting them to a damaged chopper. His lieutenant, meanwhile, kept a watchful eye and firm hold on their captive, more worried that he would try to take his own life than try to escape. The other vehicle started back to pick up the body of the other one.

Manni Lubin, Ryker suddenly realized, was nowhere to be found.

"Brother Ryker?" He turned around. It was Elder Devereux. "What day is it?"

Ryker had to think for a minute. He couldn't be sure, himself, but he said, "Saturday, I think."

Elder Devereux looked surprised. "One day? This has all happened in one day? Is that all?"

"Doctor, you've been through a lot. Once we're back at the U.S. embassy—"

"Do you know he was going to cut off her fingers?" Elder Devereux was speaking to Ryker and to no one in particular, his gaze fixed at a time in the past. "He said she would lose one with every commandment I couldn't name. Can you name the commandments? I don't just mean the big ones, but all of them?" His breath became short and erratic. "I couldn't think straight, I . . . I couldn't concentrate. I would have never forgiven myself if . . ." He trailed off and started shivering, starting to show the signs of shock.

Ryker found an army blanket tucked under one of the benches in the back and covered the doctor with it. Sister Devereux was up and attending best she could to Elder Anderson's wound, and from what he could hear, it seemed that the young man would make a full recovery with only a scar and stories to attend to his harrowing fight for his life in the deserts of Egypt. He waited with them in the back of the transport until Hasan's backup arrived with food, water, and proper medical attention.

When he looked for him, Ryker found Manni Lubin resting in the shade around the front of the truck. Neither said anything for a long while. Then Ryker spoke up.

"Quite a day." Lubin just stared out over the desert sands. "Hey, Manni? You all right? About that back there, I didn't even notice you and Hasan until after—"

"Do you believe in God?" Lubin blurted out. "I mean, really believe?"

"What? What brought this on?"

Lubin didn't answer right away. "Do you?"

"I'm not sure what I believe anymore—"

"Before then. Did you believe before?"

Ryker stepped out to get a better look at his friend. "Are you feeling all right?"

Lubin continued his distant stare and smiled. "Yes, Sam. I think I am."

"Well, you had me worried there for a minute. It felt like I was in confession, and I'm not even Catholic." He reached down and offered a hand up.

"There you are!" Hasan called. "The day is not over yet, my friends. Our chopper just went down south of the ruins. Men are en route. They should be there in a matter of a few minutes. I have a jeep waiting."

"Let's go," Lubin said, falling in behind Hasan. He stopped when he realized Ryker wasn't following. "We can't let him get away, not after all this."

Ryker looked over at the missionaries being attended to. "I need to stay with them until I know they are safe."

"They will be fine."

"I just can't risk anymore surprises. I made a promise to bring them back safe and sound, and that's just what I need to do."

"But Hasan's men will—"

"No, Manni. I know what you're trying to do, but with all that's happened today, I feel I need to see this through."

"But Sam . . ."

"Don't think every part of me isn't screaming to go with you and get this murderous—"

"Then let the National Police bring them in. What else could happen?"

"That's just it—I don't know what else could happen. Nothing about the kidnapping, and even their rescue, makes much sense. There are too many questions about it all, and I can't risk loosing them again, or worse, because I set out on a personal matter of revenge. It doesn't feel right. Is any of this making sense? I don't know, Manni. I want to go, but I can't. Not yet."

The seasoned Israeli Mossad agent sized up his American friend. "Ambassador Cannon was right to choose you for this operation."

Ryker smiled. "Thanks."

Hasan hollered for them. "Sam! Manni! Let's go!"

"Manni, you go. I'll catch up with you at the airfield. Oh, and don't kill him if you don't have to. Leave a little for me."

Lubin smiled and nodded and then ran for the waiting jeep. Ryker was torn as he watched them spin out in the sand, turning around and speeding away, but he knew he had made the right decision.

"Godspeed, brethren," he prayed under his breath. "Godspeed."

SIXTEEN

ABDUL BADRI ARRIVED AT THE American embassy in the morning and reluctantly assumed his duties as chief clerk of the passport section. He had never liked weekend shifts. The halls and offices were usually largely deserted. The only ones working Saturday shifts were the cipher clerk, monitoring embassy communications two floors beneath him, and his immediate supervisor. One day he'd have enough put away to quit working here, but until that day came, he'd have to put up with the mindless stretch of paperwork.

Badri was a graduate of Cairo University but hadn't distinguished himself academically in any way. However, during the interview for the embassy job, Badri had impressed the personnel department with his fluency in English and his grasp of computer technology. By American standards, the job equated to little more than minimum wage, but for an Egyptian, employment at the embassy was a coveted plum.

He had debated even coming in this particular morning, with the American missionaries' kidnapping and all, but he figured that his absence would attract more attention than his reluctant appearance. Best to go about his work, offer his concern and condolences, and go on with his unrewarding and unappreciated life working at the embassy.

He drank a steaming cup of freshly brewed coffee as he sorted through photocopies of American passports routinely taken by Egyptian customs at points of entry. Sending copies to embassies was done as a courtesy, alerting embassy authorities to the presence of their citizens in Egypt. The lag time for receiving these photocopies from outlying areas could be as much as a week or two, depending upon the diligence of customs officers. He checked his watch. For whatever reason, this batch from the Cairo airport had reached his desk in record time. Some of the identified travelers had arrived in Egypt as early as overnight and earlier that morning.

Midway through the stack, he choked, nearly spitting his coffee all over his desk. SAMUEL RYKER. He rubbed his eyes and held the photocopy up to better light. This wasn't possible. He'd heard he was dead. Could it be a mistake? Impossible. The stamp was from this morning, and a copy doesn't lie. And with this new information, his dreams of early retirement seemed to finally be within his grasp. But he would have to act quickly—news of this type traveled fast, and information like this was only valuable when it was in short supply and high demand. Badri folded the photocopy of Ryker's passport and picked up the phone. Feigning a touch of the stomach flu to his supervisor, he hurried past the Marines standing guard and ran the seven blocks to his small flat.

Inside the second-floor apartment, he booted up his computer. While the outdated machine loaded its operating system, Badri reached into his desk drawer, all the way in the back, and produced a small Post-it note he had stuck to the underside of his small desk. He shouldn't even have had the email scribbled on the small sheet of yellow paper, but he was not as dumb as his mysterious benefactor believed him to be.

He removed the folded copy of the passport from his back pocket and spread it out on the small desk before him. It had to be a mistake, he reasoned again, but if it was him, his benefactor would want to know, and would likely pay handsomely for it.

His computer finally ready, he clicked the icon for his Internet connection and logged in. It was an encrypted program, and he alone had the password. His fingers froze, though, as he started to enter the special email address. He had never initiated contact with his benefactor—messages and directions had always shown up on his computer, and any attempt to simply reply to the message was returned undeliverable. And though he had no real reason to pursue the email further, he had never felt comfortable being only on the receiving end of their arrangement. What if he ever had to reach *him*? What if he had news that no one else had? Like today.

For all his faults, none of which he would ever really admit, Abdul Badri was a likeable character and had made many friends at the embassy. One such friend worked for the CIA in their information technology department. The kid was a wizard with computers. One day, over lunch, Badri had told him about his dilemma of trying to track down a return email, lying that it was offensive in nature and that he wanted to report it to the authorities, but that no one, not even the police, had been able to track it. Not one to pass up a computer-related challenge, the young kid walked him through the complex process of retracing the electronic transmissions and bypassing the firewalls and other barriers set up to protect the identity of the sender. In the end, Badri had an email address that might net him a rather large sum of money.

Badri swallowed his fear, rubbed his hands together quickly, and then typed in the address and message. He kept it brief—he suspected that his benefactor would appreciate just the facts. When it came time to propose his fee, he paused and leaned back in his chair. He had to be careful with this one. He didn't like just giving away information like this without payment up front, as all his other deals had been, but he knew that his benefactor was a smart man and would find out soon enough—this way, though, he stood a chance of making some money on the information end. Also, he thought with a little feeling in his chest that he could only call pride, with this preemptive offer of valuable information he had the chance to prove his loyalty.

He entered the amount, double what his last fee was, proofed it quickly, and then hit ENTER.

He stood up, stretched, grabbed himself an imported German beer from the icebox, and made himself comfortable on the sofa. He had never set out to kill anyone, and technically speaking, he hadn't. If it was Allah's will that they die, who was he to try to stop it? He was simply an instrument in His hands. He didn't really believe it, but the story helped him sleep at night.

As he flipped through the channels on his small black-and-white television, he recalled the first time he had been contacted by his mysterious benefactor. At first he had thought the unsolicited email was a joke, maybe one of his former college roommates mocking him, that one of the them had somehow learned how desperate he was for cash. A quick call to his bank would put an end to this farce once and for all, but when the teller verified that five thousand American dollars had actually been deposited, he abandoned his curiosity and any reserve he may have had and was only too happy to comply with the request. Besides, the email only asked for basic passport and itinerary information for a few American tourists. Where was the harm in that? It wasn't like he was being asked to acquire and give up state secrets.

Badri had received a few more emails over the next little while, one or two a year, the fee steadily increasing, and with each deposit he was able to more fully live the life he had always believed that he should. He was entitled to peace and happiness and some of the finer things in life, wasn't he? The news of the American missionaries had been mildly concerning to him, but they really shouldn't even have been here in the first place. He didn't voice his opinions to many, for obvious reasons, but if he had his wish, all foreigners would pack up and leave Egypt forever, taking their governments, their ideals, and their influence back to wherever they came from. He reflected how odd it was that he harbored these feelings and worked at the American embassy, biting the very hand that fed him, but a man had to eat, didn't he?

But Badri was not without a conscience. The first time he had felt any guilt or remorse for his actions had been almost a year earlier. He had known Sam Ryker. He seemed a decent fellow and had always expressed his thanks when his office had placed requests to his department. He seemed to really care about not only his own office, but also the entire embassy staff. When he first heard of the attack in Jerusalem and learned that Sam and his family had been victims of a terrorist bombing, the thought crossed his mind that he should go to authorities and tell them of his possible, albeit periphery, involvement. But that would mean losing his job, being arrested, and worse. He knew Egypt had adopted a "no mercy" policy when it came to terrorists and that if he came forward with information, he would likely be charged, convicted, and maybe even executed. And Ryker was already dead. It wasn't like he could save his life by confessing. It was during this time that he figured he would have to leave matters of life and death to Allah. It helped, too, that double his normal payment had been deposited after news of Ryker's death was reported. It was like his mysterious bene-factor could read his thoughts, knew his doubts.

And if this information was correct, and Sam Ryker was *alive,* the infor-mation would surely be worth a small fortune.

And with the sure promise of profit and prosperity, Abdul Badri settled into the cushions of his living room couch and started flipping through the channels until he found an American black-and-white western. As the *William Tell* Overture blared through the small speaker, he dreamed about how fortune would soon be knocking on his door. He only hoped he didn't have to wait too long.

* * *

Deborah and Sergeant Heikel of the Egyptian National Police left the airport the minute the others were in the air, and made their way first to Hasan's office to make some calls and to begin the warrant process, and then to the banking district of Cairo.

It was early Saturday, and the bank was not normally open for business, but a few phone calls from Sergeant Heikel, and the bank manager was waiting for them when they arrived. They parked the unmarked car in the no-parking zone that fronted the building and entered through the revolving door. A young assistant met them at the door.

"The manager, please," Sergeant Heikel said.

"Certainly, sir." The young man indicated an office suite at the rear.

Their shoes clicked on the polished stone floor, echoing into the vastness of the opulently decorated lobby. This wasn't a bank in any traditional sense of the word. There was neither counter nor tellers' cages, only a maze of cubicles housing account executives. People with a few pounds to squirrel away in savings could find another bank to handle their affairs. This one catered more to those with sizeable sums to invest, amounts that Abdul Badri couldn't be earning as a clerk at the American embassy.

The manager was waiting for them outside his office, hastily dressed for the meeting. He fidgeted with his hands as they approached, clearly worried about the demand to meet them after hours. Sergeant Heikel barely acknowledged him as he strode past him and into the manager's office.

"What brings the National Police to our humble establishment?" the bank manager asked, fear and reserve shaking his voice.

The detective reached inside his coat and produced the order signed by the magistrate.

"This should adequately explain our presence." He handed over the document.

The manager took a minute to read every word before speaking.

"I see. This is most unusual," he said, his concern for his own interest replaced with the bank's interest to protect their clients.

"These are unusual times," Heikel replied evenly.

"Yes, certainly," the manager responded. "It is just that I do not believe we have ever received a request like this before."

"It is not a request but an order," Heikel said flatly.

"Oh, I *am* sorry. I did not mean to imply . . . It is just that we pride ourselves on our choice of clients. I cannot imagine that any of them should be of interest to the police."

"We will find out soon enough. Now, if you will just produce the records of the man in question, we will not take much more of your time."

"It should just take a few minutes to pull up his file." He stood and walked to the door. "I will be back shortly. Would you care for anything to drink? Coffee? Juice?"

"Not for me, thanks," Heikel replied.

He then turned toward Deborah, who shook her head.

"I should only be a moment."

The manager disappeared into the maze. He reappeared half an hour later.

"So sorry about the delay," he said, closing the door behind him. He was perspiring even in the air-conditioned building. "The system crashed, and we had to boot it up again." He shook his head as if in disgust. "Anyway, this is what we have on Abdul Badri."

He spread the printout on his desk as Deborah and Heikel stood and approached.

Bingo! she thought. *I knew I was right about him.*

His account showed two five-thousand-dollar deposits just before and again just after the Jerusalem bombing where the Rykers were killed. There was also a smaller one earlier this week. There were more modest deposits, as well, that went back several years, but she and Heikel were only interested today in the most prominent ones: those that Badri would have to explain to their satisfaction.

"You have been very helpful," Sergeant Heikel said, folding the printout and putting it in his coat pocket. "We will take this with us, and you can be sure that the official record will note your cooperation."

When they got back into the car, Deborah asked, "So what now?"

"We take him into custody for questioning," Heikel replied.

"He should be at the embassy," Deborah said. "I noticed he was working the weekend schedule. I'll go and talk to him, try to get him to come with me for coffee or something. It would be less complicated if you picked him up after he's left the embassy grounds."

"Agreed," Heikel said, knowing very clearly the limits of his authority when dealing with foreign embassies.

"Do you have a way to let Hasan and Sam know what we found?" Deborah asked.

"We could radio the tower and pass along a message, but I think we should wait until we have a little more to tell him. I would like to speak to this Abdul Badri myself before we jump to any conclusions."

Deborah was in no position to tell the man how to do his job. "Whatever you think is best," she responded.

Heikel parked down the street from the embassy and waited while Deborah entered through the front gate. She was back a few minutes later, alone. She slid into the front seat.

"Well?" Heikel asked.

"He came into work today but went home sick."

"Sick, huh? I don't like it," Heikel said. "We start looking into his financials and he takes the day off."

"Maybe, but I don't think that's it," she said. "The log shows he left twenty minutes or so after he clocked in. The Marine on duty said that he *did* look pale as he hurried past."

"Well if he *is* sick, I hope he is home in bed. It would make things a lot easier for everyone. But if he is involved, I doubt that we will be so lucky."

* * *

Later that morning, Heikel and Deborah rendezvoused with the other team, positioned down the street from Badri's apartment, waiting for them to arrive. He pulled in behind their vehicle and let the car idle as they exited and went to the driver's side window. She stood behind Heikel.

"Anything?" Heikel asked.

"Only been here a few minutes. A young couple just left, but the man did not resemble *this* guy," the other detective replied, holding up a picture of Badri that had been on file with the government since the beginning of his employment with the embassy. "You sure about him being in there?"

"No, but my new *partner* says that he left work just after six. Claimed to be sick."

The remark about a "new partner" turned heads in her direction. It was plain from their expressions that they disapproved of a woman intruding in the Middle Eastern man's world of police work.

Sergeant Heikel stepped up and defended her presence and honor before his peers. "Her months of investigation landed us this lead, and if she's right—and I believe she is—we may just be able to crack the biggest international terrorism ring any of us has ever seen. So look past the fact that she's a woman and shape up. Do I make myself clear?"

The young officer sat up straight and apologized.

"Miss Reid and I will park up the street in the other direction. You go around to the back of the building. We will go in the front. I do not want him skipping out by the fire escape. He's a middleman, an informant, and is not to be harmed while being taken into custody."

* * *

Heikel led the way with Deborah two steps behind. Badri's apartment was at the end of the hall.

"Are you sure I should be here?" Deborah asked as they neared the apartment.

"Nervous?"

"No. I've had training in these types of matters."

"Training is one thing, but have you ever knocked on a suspect's door, announcing yourself through the door, ordering them to comply or force an escalation?"

Deborah was silent. She hadn't. Maybe the sergeant was right. Maybe that feeling she had in the pit of her stomach was just nerves. Or maybe it was the underlying fear of having to explain her actions to Matheson when he returned from his overseas assignment. But she had made that decision when she insisted on coming with Ryker. She had no regrets—she knew she was doing the right thing—but she still dreaded that meeting.

"And you're certain that my being here is legal?"

"Hasan has deemed you a special consultant. Under Egyptian law, your presence is deemed legal in every way. Besides, I don't think I would know the right questions to ask him. No, Miss Reid, I don't just think it is a good idea—your presence here is necessary."

"Do you think it's safe?"

"Mr. Badri has no prior record, no evidence of past violence or problems, and based on your description of the man, I think he's just an opportunist and one who will break down once he knows that the authorities are on to him. Criminals like him are more common than you might think."

As they reached Badri's apartment number, Sergeant Heikel motioned for Deborah to remain quiet. Standing on either side of the door, they both listened intently. The television was on, evident by the static voiceover and commercial jingles. Heikel took his pistol from its holster, holding it in the ready position and mouthed the words, "Are you ready?" Deborah nodded, her back to the wall on the other side of the door. Heikel reached over and knocked loudly.

* * *

Badri had fallen asleep and woke with a start. He listened and could hear people approaching from down the hall. The apartment building had strict policies when it came to solicitations, and he had chosen an apartment at the end of a hall to ensure himself the most seclusion. It wasn't like he was paranoid, but he had few friends and liked to be left alone.

He sprang to his feet and went to the window, looking carefully out onto the street below. He spotted the police car just up the street, and the blood in his veins felt like they had ice water running through them. He suddenly felt sick to his stomach.

They know! He had been a fool to think he could get away with it for this long.

He heard footsteps on the hardwood floors outside his door. They would not take him alive, he suddenly determined. He was an educated man. He wouldn't survive prison. He had to get out of there! Running to his bedroom, he dropped to his knees and reached under his bed, pulling out a small shoebox. Inside was a small .38 revolver. He had bought it on the streets years ago after another tenant in his building, two floors up, had been beaten and robbed. He had hoped to never use it and had even considered throwing it away a dozen times over the years, but today he was glad he had kept it.

Badri's kitchen, small as it was, did have a large walk-in pantry. Maybe he could hide there and make a quick dash for the door. If he could get outside, he was sure he could lose them. He had grown up around here and knew every street and back alley from here to the river.

How could he have been so stupid! And all of a sudden the money didn't mean as much as his freedom. In fact, he would trade it all for a way out of here.

A loud knock on the door made him feel like he was going to be sick, and he stepped into the pantry and tried to quietly close the door behind him.

"Abdul Badri! This is the police!" a voice called. "Open the door! We have a few questions we need to ask you."

When he didn't respond, he listened in horror as his front door was muscled open. A policeman yelled for him to get down as he burst in, gun out and at the ready. He watched through the angled wood slats in his pantry door as the police officer swept the front room and kitchen then quickly stepped into the bedroom, shouting for Badri to show himself and to keep his hands where he could see them. Of course, the rooms were empty, but the officer didn't know that. Badri repositioned the gun in his hands and checked his grip. His palms were sweaty, and he could actually *hear* his heart beating. Oh, if he could only get out of this, he prayed silently, he would forsake this evil and live a clean life.

"Miss Reid," the police officer called back toward the hall, "the place is clear. Looks like our suspect already left."

"And in a hurry," a woman said, stepping into his apartment. "Television left on, computer still booted up."

Miss Reid? He thought he recognized the name, and now that he saw her, he knew her. Deborah Reid. She worked in the CIA office. This was worse than before! If the Americans had found out and were looking for him, he was as good as dead. He would have to go into hiding, disappear. Maybe his benefactor would help him, reward him for his years of loyal service.

The police officer took out his radio. "This is Heikel," he said into the receiver. "We missed him, but not by much. I need you to fan out, search the exits. Call in backup. We may need to search the building flat by flat."

"Roger that."

Deborah began walking around the apartment, taking in every detail with her incredible gift of memory. She looked through a small stack of mail that he had let pile up over the weeks, moving to a few scattered luxury and travel magazines. Sergeant Heikel noticed them, too.

"Looks like our man has a taste for the high life."

Deborah nodded.

Abdul Badri watched in fear as the Deborah and the police sergeant moved through his small apartment, but that fear turned to panic as she stopped at his computer and began clicking through some of his programs. If she found the email he had sent . . .

"Sergeant? Look at this," Deborah said. "It looks like Badri sent an email at almost seven o'clock. Given the time he signed out of work, he would have had to have almost run to reach his apartment to send this email by this time."

"Are you sure it's not an incoming one?"

"I'm sure. Look at this address. Have you ever seen one like it?"

Sergeant Heikel just shook his head. "But I'm a policeman, Miss Reid, not a computer scientist."

"It looks almost encrypted. Whatever it was, it must have been pretty important to lie about being sick and then rush home at a dead run—"

Badri suddenly dropped the gun, his hands numb from the dread of what he was watching. He caught it before it hit the ground, but it did bump the pantry door. He froze and held his breath. Maybe they didn't hear him. Maybe . . .

Sergeant Heikel put a finger to his lips and motioned for Deborah to move away and closer to the front door, his every sense turned toward the direction of the sound.

He moved toward the door, leaning in, trying to see movement behind the slats. "Mr. Badri? We just want to ask you a few quest—"

Badri pulled the trigger. The muzzle flash lit up the small closet, and the noise from the small handgun was deafening. He had never heard such a loud sound before in his life. His ears hurt, and he shut his eyes tight, trying to push out the sudden pain in his head. When he opened them, the detective lay dead on his kitchen floor. The woman let out a scream. He would have to stop her, too.

The weak door easily gave way under the force of Badri's shoulder, and he rushed out into the apartment. He rounded the corner in time to see Deborah disappear across the apartment hallway and into the utility closet. The thought briefly entered his mind that this was the break he was looking for. He could run right past her, down the back stairs, and disappear. But she knew too much. She had seen his computer screen. She knew about the email. She was a loose end that needed tying up. Back inside his apartment, the sergeant's radio came to life, asking about the gunshot they had heard. It didn't take a genius to know that when the call went unanswered, more police would show up. He needed to do this quickly.

He walked to the utility door and pushed hard against it. Deborah was blocking the other side of the door, screaming for help in English and Arabic even though the room muffled her cries.

He paused and stepped back away from the door. The sounds of her frantic breathing were drowned out by two gunshots through the door. The ringing in his ears deafened him.

Badri needed to be sure she was dead. He couldn't believe he was thinking this. How had it gotten so far out of hand? Today was supposed to be a good day, a prosperous and profitable day. In his darkest imaginations he had never thought he would have done what he had. He was not a killer. They had forced him to. If they had just gone away or simply come back later with their questions, he would have been gone when they returned, and they would still be alive. It was their fault, not his. This was all their fault.

He pushed open the door, sliding the figure slumped behind it as he did. The woman fell over, still alive, her eyes struggling to stay open.

"D . . . don't do this, B . . . B . . . Badri."

He pointed his gun down at her. "You shouldn't have come here! This is all your fault! You're making me do this! I have to now. I have to! I'm sorry . . ."

He took careful aim. "I'm sorry."

The gunshot startled him and pushed him forward. His first thought was that he had lost his balance, but then it struck him that he didn't think he had pulled the trigger yet. Then he lost feeling in his hands and arms, dropping the gun to the ground. His legs gave way next, and he fell over backward, unable to catch himself. His sight was fading to dark, while at the same time bright flashes peppered his failing vision. In one of his last conscious thoughts, he looked back into his apartment and saw that the police officer had moved from the last place he had seen him—still on the floor, but with his arms out in front of him, taking aim with his last bit of strength.

So this is what it is like to die, he thought. Pain registered briefly in his back and chest, and he suddenly found it impossible to breathe.

His world went black around him.

SEVENTEEN

RYKER ALLOWED HIMSELF THE SMALL privilege of closing his eyes and relaxing somewhat once they were on the road back to Abu Simbel. They were under heavy guard, traveling as fast as their medical transport would carry them along the old Bedouin trail without jostling the injured missionaries too much. He tried to calculate how long he had been awake, trying to remember the last time he slept, but the fatigue was too great. He had not been sleeping well for weeks, and his reserves were spent. He was not the man he once was, and age—he was hard-pressed to admit—had little to do with it.

The driver of the stolen military transport was guarded closely, and Ryker heard that he was going to be interrogated briefly in Abu Simbel before being flown via military prison transport to the National Police headquarters in Cairo.

Ryker and the missionaries, on the other hand, were driven directly to the small airfield just north of Abu Simbel and were taken inside a section that had been cleared and secured. Ryker was looked on with suspicion and distrust, and if it weren't for Bear, he would have likely been separated from the missionaries and held pending interrogation.

The missionaries were escorted to a VIP lounge—probably the nicest accommodations in the entire city—with a large picture window overlooking the airstrip and beyond to the blue waters of Lake Nasser. Today, though, its plush sectionals and lavish furniture served to comfort three selfless servants upon their return from a harrowing experience that no one should ever be forced to endure. At the lounge bar, bottled water was given to them. With Ryker's help, the officers also acquired juice, fresh fruit, and pastries from elsewhere in the airport. It was a small operation and not like the larger, international terminals with food courts and a wide assortment and selection of dining.

The missionaries had been markedly quiet since their rescue just over an hour ago. Ryker knew that this was common with victims of terrible crimes and was relieved when Hasan's men let them remain in their silent and contemplative state, not pushing them to tell their story. The time for that would come, but for now their silence was healing.

Twenty minutes later, Hasan and Lubin arrived and were escorted in to see them.

"My name is Hasan al-Mohammed of the Egyptian National Police." He bowed at the waist as he introduced himself. "On behalf of the Egyptian government, I would like to apologize for your ordeal and to commit to you my government's full cooperation and efforts to return you quickly to American soil. President Mubarak is sending one of his personal aircraft to pick us up and take us to Cairo. In a few short hours, you will be safely back on American soil and under the full protection of both of our governments."

Hasan moved and dropped to one knee before Elder Devereux and his wife. "But, more importantly, I want to offer my personal and sincere apologies for what you had to endure, and I assure you that I will not rest until those behind your attack are found and dealt with swiftly and harshly."

Elder Devereux reached out with a shaky hand and put it atop Hasan's. "We do not seek revenge for what has happened. Nor would any of us gain any satisfaction to know that more lives have been lost on our account. But the man who orchestrated this, the one who spoke to us—who tortured us—needs to be stopped. Men like him are dangerous and will hurt others again unless they are stopped. So for that reason, and that reason alone, we say don't stop until he is found. Do not let him do this to anyone else again." He returned his hand to his wife's back, which he continued to rub gently.

Hasan returned to his feet, and Ryker thought he looked like he was standing just a little taller than he had when he had entered the room. He motioned toward the door, and they were joined by a little man with glasses, dressed in a white shirt and tie. "This is Mahmoud. He is a member of my team and is here to listen. I know you have all been through a lot, and I assure you that I am fully aware that now is neither the time nor the place to begin asking you questions about the events of the last day, but it is standard practice, and I would like to ask you if you would share with Mahmoud what you recall, what you remember, while everything is still fresh on your minds. Like I said, his job is to listen. You will be fully debriefed later, once you have been returned to your embassy and have had time to rest. Would you do this for me?"

The missionaries all nodded their agreement. As Mahmoud pulled up a seat across from them, Hasan spoke up again. "Sam, may I speak with you?"

Sister Devereux looked frightened at the thought of Ryker leaving them. "It's all right, Sister. I'll just be outside. You are safe with these men. Don't worry, I'm not leaving you until I know for certain you are safe and back in Cairo." She visibly relaxed, thanked him for his kindness, and then snuggled close to her husband.

Out in the terminal, Hasan led Ryker and Lubin to a quiet corner. "We were too late."

"What do you mean 'too late?'"

"My men were on the crash site mere minutes after it happened, but when they reached it, the pilot was gone. There was blood smeared on the seat, but—"

"He couldn't have gotten far," Ryker interrupted. "Are your men combing the area?"

Hasan raised his hand. "Let me finish. When they arrived, they found the body of a local fisherman and tire tracks leading away toward the city. We followed the tracks until they met up with the paved road, but there the trail runs cold. We are trying to identify the man we found in the hopes that we can then determine the make and model of automobile he had."

Ryker considered what he was being told. "So, the chopper goes down, local fisherman sees this happen and drives over to see if can help—"

Lubin finished his story. "And is killed for his good Samaritan efforts, unwittingly aiding in his killer's escape."

"So, he may still be here, in Abu Simbel."

"Likely. We have pulled in everyone to search the city, but until we know what type of car we are looking for, there is not much hope of discovering anything useful. Abu Simbel is a poor city, and there are abandoned automobiles down every alleyway and parked along every street. This is what you would call looking for a pin in a bale of straw." He tried to smile.

"It's a needle in a haystack."

"Excuse me?"

"The phrase," Ryker said, staring off in thought, "it's *needle* in a *haystack*."

"There are no hospitals in Abu Simbel, and all local clinics and tourist stations have been alerted to report any injuries resembling the one we think our man received either before or as a result of the crash."

"And what of the tourists? Surely someone caught something on camera?"

Hasan sighed. "We have several photos and even some video footage of a man that matches your description, but he is only seen from behind. Sam, it is like this man knew where every camera was, every videotape, and turned at the exact moment to avoid his picture being taken. He is a magician, the Chameleon. With the hundreds of cameras shooting the Great Temple, Lake Nasser, and who-knows-what-else, we don't have one picture of this man."

Ryker closed his eyes tightly. "And what of this man, this member of *Al-Jum'ah*, who was supposed to pick up the missionaries?"

"His interrogation revealed precious little. With the right amount of pressure, he did disclose the location of his comrades in Wadi Hafa, but he was little more than an errand boy, sent to pick them up and drive them over the border. He mentioned a trade and that our kidnapper had verified a delivery of some kind before telling him where he could pick up the missionaries." Hasan paused and lowered his voice. "An operation is already underway to hit their base of operations. It is a delicate thing crossing into a hostile sovereign nation to exact justice. We should know more tomorrow."

From further down the terminal, an officer hurried toward them. "Chief inspector?"

"Yes?"

"A small pickup truck was just found abandoned one street over from the airfield. It matched the description of the one belonging to our murder victim. Also, there was fresh blood found on the seat and armrest."

Hasan jumped to his feet. "He's here! He knew we'd bring them here and—"

Ryker reached out. "Hasan, we can't jump to that conclusion. Not yet, anyway. While I agree we should double security around the missionaries, I have another thought. When was the last plane to depart?"

"All aircraft have been grounded until further notice. Tourists are being cleared and taken to Aswan by bus."

"Are you sure? A private jet, perhaps?"

Hasan's face twisted with frustration. Turning to the young officer, he barked, "Get me airport security, and inform the director I want to speak with him now!"

Two minutes later, all five of them were crammed into the security room at the small airfield. Ryker's intuition had been correct. Although all commercial flights had been grounded since the morning's bombing, a small, twelve-passenger SD3-60 commuter aircraft had been granted clearance by airport security as well as the National Police and had taken off not fifteen minutes before Hasan's men had arrived and set up a command post in the airport terminal.

"The passengers had all been investors and on a guided tour of lands north of the city," the chief of security explained as he sat at a small television and VCR. "None of them had even been near the attack that morning. In fact, they had all been surprised to hear the news when they returned. They had a tight schedule to keep. They all appeared to know each other, and their passports checked out. We decided they were innocent of any wrongdoing and allowed them to leave."

Hasan was getting visibly more and more upset with every word of excuse that fell over the airport security chief's lips. "You will be reassigned to sweeping sand from the streets if this proves you let our man escape."

The security chief stopped rewinding and pressed play. "Here we are."

On the small black-and-white screen, gritty security footage played out before them. The crowd of wealthy men and women were clearly upset with the news of their delay, pacing back and forth, mouthing words that Ryker suspected were curses and threats of lawsuits. Like most security tapes, there was no sound to accompany the visual footage. Ryker leaned forward and watched closer, scanning each grainy face for some sense of recognition.

"Anything?" Lubin asked.

Ryker just shook his head. "I only caught a glimpse of him, but none of these people—wait! There!"

On the screen a new gentlemen walked briefly into view. He had a light-colored jacket draped over his left shoulder. "See how he's holding his left arm?" He was walking with a small group of Caucasian men, speaking with them with animated motions, appearing to be their best friend. He looked around, and then, by chance, he looked briefly at the corner security camera.

"Freeze frame!"

Looking directly at them was the man who had kidnapped the American missionaries, killed three police officers and wounded several others in a car bombing, and had opened fire on them from a helicopter in the desert. The picture was grainy, but there was no mistaking the man.

"That's him," Ryker said, almost reverently but coldly, and without the expected passion. "That's our phantom." He remained fixed on the small black-and-white face looking up at him, and despite the miraculous events of the past day, those feelings of peace and respite were blotted out with images of his family, of Susan looking relieved to find him in the crowds, and then the bright lights, the heat, and then the darkness—the darkness that had refused to give way to the light since that day.

Hasan got on the radio. He was beginning to make the order to call that commuter plane back when Lubin stopped him.

"If that plane turns around, he will know that we have found him. And what you will have then is an air-jacking and hostage situation all over again."

"But we cannot just let him get away."

"Manni would never let a terrorist just get away. What do you have in mind?" Ryker asked.

"Can we get the flight plan for the commuter?" Lubin asked.

The airport director got on the phone and made a call. "Nonstop to Cairo."

"When is it scheduled to arrive there?" he continued.

"Just under three hours."

The Israeli Mossad officer made a quick calculation. "Its cruising speed is just under three hundred kilometers an hour." He turned to Hasan. "What type of aircraft was coming to pick us up?"

Hasan shrugged. "I don't know. Aircraft is not my specialty."

"Sir," the airport director interjected, "I handled the arrangements myself. It is a Falcon 20. Very nice. Very fast."

"How fast?"

"Over nine hundred kilometers per hour. Like I said, it is a very fast aircraft."

Ryker smiled as Lubin's plan began to take shape. "If we could overtake it in the air—"

"And land in Cairo before the commuter did—" Hasan added.

"We would be waiting for him when he lands."

Hasan leaned down on the small security desk and commanded both airport officials with a hard glare. "I want that plane tracked with updates to my men every fifteen minutes. If it reports engine trouble, if it decides to deviate from its flight plan for any reason, if it loses contact with the ground and air traffic control cannot reach them, I want to know about it. Do I make myself clear?"

Both men cowered before Hasan and nodded, the security chief trying to salute him, but he pulled his hand back, embarrassed at the gesture. The intensity of Hasan's presence was broken suddenly by the shrill ring of the telephone on the desk. The airport director jumped and uttered a gasp.

The security chief answered the phone before the second ring, listened briefly, and then handed the phone to Hasan. "It's for you."

Hasan ripped it out of the man's hand. "Yes?"

His eyes widened, and he looked briefly at Ryker before looking away. "When did this happen?"

Hasan checked his watch. "And the woman? I see. You will contact me the moment she regains consciousness." He gently returned the receiver to the cradle. All eyes were on him as he processed this new information and gathered his thoughts.

"Hasan? What is it?" Ryker asked.

"I'm afraid there's been an incident. Miss Reid—"

"What about her?" A new sensation of dread flooded over Ryker. What had he done? He never should have brought her into this.

"I'm afraid she has been shot."

* * *

Ryker was beside himself the entire flight back to Cairo, worried sick about Deborah. The details were sketchy. She and Sergeant Heikel had verified large deposits made to Badri's bank account in close proximity to several terrorist attacks, including the death of Ryker's family and the kidnapping of the Mormon health missionaries. They had obtained the Egyptian equivalent of a search warrant and had paid a visit to Abdul Badri. A backup team was sent to check the exits and to start reconnaissance around the apartment building. When they heard gunshots and were unable to reach the sergeant, they rushed up to Badri's apartment and found both Heikel and Deborah shot and unconscious. Badri was dead in the hall. It didn't take much imagination to put the pieces together and know what had likely happened, but police work is not built upon speculation and supposition. Until either of them regained consciousness and could give an account of what happened, much remained unanswered.

About an hour into their flight, Ryker's attention turned to President Cannon.

"Can you patch us into a land line from here?" he asked Hasan.

Ryker fished a scrap of paper from his pocket and gave Hasan a telephone number to the States, which the pilot repeated over the radio. A minute later, the cabin phone rang and Ryker heard the voice of the police switchboard operator. "I have former Ambassador Cannon on the line, sir. Go ahead."

"Hello?" The line was scratchy and distorted, but over the static, Ryker could hear the voice of his old friend just fine.

"President Cannon, this is Sam."

"Is everything all right? Faud called me a few hours ago and said that you and Hasan were headed for Abu Simbel. What news of the missionaries? Have you been able to generate any leads yet?" he asked anxiously.

"It's all over."

Before Ryker could elaborate, Cannon cut in, "What do you mean *over*?"

He sounded to Ryker as though he were on the verge of an emotional crisis. "No, sir. We were extremely lucky. They're safe and here with me now. A little the worse for wear, maybe, but basically okay. We're en route to Cairo. They'll be able to make contact with their families then. In the meantime, I thought you might want to alert those families yourself and put their minds at ease."

"Yes, I certainly will, Sam," President Cannon assured him. "This is wonderful news. I *knew* you could do it."

"Let's say it was a group effort, sir."

"Now, what about *you*? Are *you* okay?"

"I'm fine. I think this desert air is clearing my mind."

"I'll make arrangements with the embassy to have the missionaries flown home as soon as possible. There'll be a ticket for you as well."

"I'm sorry, sir. I can't go home just yet," Ryker confided. "I believe that the man responsible for this missionary incident is tied to my own family's murder. I'll be staying awhile, working with Hasan to bring this man to account. Please understand that I *have* to see this through."

"Yes . . . of course. I understand. The Lord has guided and protected you this far," Cannon reminded him, "and He'll continue to be your strength, Sam, if you'll open your heart and mind to Him."

"I'll be sure to remember that," Ryker replied. "I'll be in touch. Goodbye, sir." The operator disconnected the line.

On the plane, the missionaries continued to open up, remembering more and more about their ordeal, building upon each other's narratives. The entire time, Mahmoud stood ready with his voice recorder, notepad, and pen. The stories Ryker was hearing were unreal. Although they were not physically mistreated, the psychological abuse the Chameleon inflicted upon them was enormous, pitting them against one another, threatening to hurt one if the other did not comply with requests or answer questions correctly. And one thing that struck Ryker again as they approached Cairo was that their ordeal, as horrific as it was, sounded like scenes from some twisted game. And again Ryker had the thought that somehow he had played, or would play, a central part in all this. One thing he knew for certain was that even with the missionaries home safely, the journey he had begun by answering that phone call in his little Paris apartment was far from being over.

When they landed at the Almaza airstrip, Hasan instructed that the missionaries were to be taken to a secure wing of the terminal and were to wait until they returned. He was told that the American authorities had been notified and were awaiting Hasan's orders to release them into their custody.

"Fine," he said, not really wanting to deal with the request at this particular moment. He checked his watch. The commuter plane should be on approach. "Release them with an armed escort to take them to the embassy. We cannot afford any more surprises when it comes to these missionaries."

The officer saluted and left, but not before Hasan, his lieutenant, Ryker, and Lubin made a mad dash for the other side of the airport. Winded, they arrived in time and set up their positions across the terminal where the private jet passengers would disembark. Ryker and Hasan were almost directly across from the gate, while the Bear and Lubin were about thirty feet on either side of the gate and would provide assistance if the Chameleon spotted them and tried to run. Their man was boxed in and had nowhere to run. They had him!

"Remember," Hasan had said as they took up their positions, "no gunfire. We couldn't clear out the terminal and risk telegraphing our intentions, so be mindful of civilians. If this works out, we should be able to take him with little incident."

The gate door opened. Ryker's pulse quickened. Men and woman began walking up the ramp from the parked commuter. They each had a printout of the grainy photo from Abu Simbel to reference, but Ryker knew he wouldn't need it. He would recognize him without question and would be quick to act.

Single file and in small groups, the dozen or so foreign investors filed into the airport terminal. A large group of disembarking passengers swarmed past them as several other flights had disembarked further up the concourse, making it more difficult for Ryker and Hasan to keep focused. But they never lost sight of a single person as he or she stepped from the ramp. But so far none of them resembled their man. When the last group emerged and started toward luggage pickup, Ryker's pulse raced.

"Where is he?"

Hasan covered the gun at his waist and sprinted across the way, into the gate and down the ramp to the commuter plane. His lieutenant followed close behind, moving for his gun as soon as he was out of sight of the main thoroughfare. Ryker stepped out and began looking up and down the terminal. Ryker started off after some of the commuter passengers, reaching them at a dead run, grabbing their shoulders and spinning them around. Upset words were said and threats made to "unhand them," but none of them were who they were looking for. He caught Lubin's eye, and they exchanged frustrated looks. Where had he gone? How had they missed him? It wasn't possible!

A few minutes later, Hasan emerged from the gate, shaking his head. A small contingent of policemen ran past and into the plane.

"Plane's empty."

"We saw him get on board!" Ryker protested. "Where did he go!?"

"Flight attendant remembers him," Hasan reported. "He was quiet and kept to himself during most of the flight. She noticed his shoulder and got him the first-aid kit on board. She says he told her he hurt it falling down a rocky embankment just before returning to the airport. He said it with such conviction that she never doubted it for a minute."

"But where did he go? We were waiting for him right here. It's not like he could have just walked right by us."

"Apparently," Hasan said, "that's exactly what he did. I have security tapes being pulled as we speak, but I doubt they will help us any."

Lubin put his arm around Ryker's shoulders. "It looks like you named him well, Sam. A human chameleon he is."

As they were planning their next course of action, two American Marines approached.

"Are you Samuel Ryker?" one of them asked.

Ryker nodded.

"You are to come with us to the American embassy. Ambassador Chandler wishes a word with you."

EIGHTEEN

SAIIF ENTERED HIS LAVISH HOME through the underground parking entrance and slammed the door behind him, yelling and cursing at the top of his tired lungs. It had all been so simple! Every detail attended to and backup plans to ensure Ryker's death, only to watch as his mortal enemy survived every attack. *If there was a god, he must be Mormon*, he mused angrily.

He lived in a spacious flat adjacent to this office and place of business in the financial district of downtown Cairo. Penthouses such as this one were rare in the older sections of the city, but Saiif's home exuded wealth and old-world luxuries and indulgences. It was decorated not only with Egyptian artifacts and décor, but also with period pieces of ancient Arabic and Persian history. The rugs were plush and massaged his bare feet as he drew himself a hot shower. He studied the gash in his shoulder as the mirrors fogged with the hot steam. He would have to get that looked at. And soon. He had bandaged it as best as he could, but it was deep enough that it needed stitches. *Ryker will pay for this,* he thought. But what else did he have besides his life that he could take? He had nothing else, and Saiif took some pleasure in reminding himself of that stark fact.

Cleaned and dressed in a loose-fitting *bisht,* he retired to his home office. Whirling the leather swivel chair around, he fell into its soft padding and swung himself back around to face a computer keyboard and monitor. He continued to mumble ill will and curses to the great Sam Ryker as his fingers moved quickly across the keys. Ryker may have won the battle, but the world would soon witness that the war was far from over.

He always worked well under pressure, but the events of the past forty-eight hours had succeeded in agitating him. His world had been one of order. It's what had kept him alive and had propelled him to the top of his craft. Now there were signs of fraying around the edges of that world. He sat back in his chair, regaining some composure before continuing. He needed to focus.

A tone alerted him that he had an email waiting in his inbox. This caught his attention since he had logged into his personal account. No one had access to this account. It had been encrypted by the best and brightest IT minds the world had to offer. He had never received an incoming message here. With fear and trepidation stalling his next move, Saiif finally hit ENTER and viewed the message.

His hands began to shake with anger. He reached out for the first object he could grab hold of, which happened to be a desk lamp, pulled it free from the wall outlet, and sent it flying across his small office, shattering it. He had no one to talk to, no one to express his anger with, so he bottled it up, cursing that fool Badri. Did he know how much was in jeopardy because of his little email? He should have arranged an accident for the embassy clerk once Ryker and his family had been hit. He would have to take care of the weasel sooner rather than later.

Forcing the ill news from his mind, Saiif returned to the business at hand, taking some comfort in the reports and numbers that flashed across his screen. Between his directional currency trades, hedged funds, and land deals that went through while he was gone, he had made a cool $7.5 million dollars since yesterday morning. *Not a bad day's work,* he thought with a smile. Not bad at all, but mere pennies when he thought of what the next few years held for him. Assuming he could rid himself of Ryker once and for all.

Returning to his encrypted address book, he scrolled down the list until he found the number he was looking for. He dialed the Israeli international code on his cell. He would've preferred to make contact from a pay phone, but he was pressed for time and a cell was the next best choice.

Someone picked up on the fourth ring. Saiif lowered his voice and spoke a five-number code in Hebrew. If his plans were in place and moving ahead by design, the person who answered on the other end would reply with a similar prearranged code.

The response was correct. Saiif's Haifa network had been established years earlier and was very active in underwriting Middle Eastern terrorism. Switching to Arabic, he ascertained that the goods he had ordered some weeks earlier had been delivered and were being stored until he arrived and gave further instructions.

He smiled in anticipation as he terminated the connection. Picking up a yellow notepad from his desk, he began to scrawl: first an itinerary with times and cities; then, in the center of the page, he proceeded to sketch circles, lines, and curves until the sheet of paper looked like a child's scribbling.

Ripping the page from the pad, he held it in one hand as the other searched for a match in the top desk drawer. He struck a flame and set fire to the page, letting it fall into an empty metal wastebasket. Swiveling his chair, he pulled open another drawer and extracted a small black address book. This one held common, public numbers that he referenced regularly. He found the listing for a local travel agency and dialed the local number. Arrangements made, he closed the book and replaced it. The next number he had memorized. Dialing the international code for Tel Aviv, he entered the short string of numbers and waited. A pleasant female voice answered in English after the first ring, "Cable News Network. How may I direct your call?"

NINETEEN

Ambassador Joseph "Joe" M. Chandler warmly greeted the three missionaries as they entered the large foyer of the American embassy. He was a career diplomat from the "Great State of Texas," as he was fond of bragging to everyone. He was good at what he did but looked like he would've been more comfortable on the back of a horse rounding up strays for branding. Even in a tuxedo at evening soirees, he wore western boots and a belt buckle that would've been the pride of any rodeo rider.

"Welcome back to the United States," he announced before shaking each of their hands. American embassy grounds, in any country, are considered territorial possessions, and he no doubt assumed the missionaries would be comforted by that. "I'm sure I can't even begin to understand what y'all have been through. Please don't think this trite, but I am *truly* sorry for the death of your friend and colleague, Mr. Evans. His death is a terrible and senseless loss."

He could see that the missionaries were too tired and emotionally haggard to do anything more than nod politely at his remarks.

He continued. "You've got to be exhausted. We've prepared rooms for you here in the embassy. Please get some rest. Now, I reckon y'all are anxious to get back home as soon as possible, but we want to make sure you're all right and fit to travel. This is no small ordeal you've been put through. Arrangements have been made to fly you to Rome and then back to the States the day after tomorrow. In the meantime, Egyptian government officials and certain people here at the embassy will be talking to you—a debriefing, if you will—about the last couple of days. Any information you can provide will, no doubt, be of inestimable value in rooting out those responsible for your abduction. But all this can wait until y'all have had some sleep."

He summoned a member of his staff who ushered the three workers to guest rooms on the ground floor in the rear of the building. When the missionaries were out of earshot, he turned to Ryker, the smile on his lips fading slightly. He took him by the arm, walking slowly in the direction of his office. Even though he'd been as good a friend as Ryker had had during his stint as station chief, the pleasantness of his voice had lowered a notch.

"Don't take this wrong, Sam," Chandler started, "but I never hoped to see you again. You're supposed to be—"

"Dead? They did a pretty good job at it, too."

"It was for your own good," he said. "You know that. Given what happened and the fact that the attack did seem personal, we concluded your life was in jeopardy and did the best we could to protect it. You've got a lot of brass showing up like this, not to mention going rogue with the Egyptian police—" He raised his hands as Ryker tried to interrupt. "No, let me finish. But I must say we had it comin'. We should have been all over the missionaries' recovery. The bureaucratic wheel just turns too slow in this line of work." Chandler smiled. "Good job. Without your insight and help, those missionaries of yours wouldn't have stood a chance out there. Those families owe you a debt of gratitude they'll not soon be able to repay. Ambassador Cannon has been on me like a tick since this all went down. He hinted that he was working on it, but I had no idea the ace up his sleeve was you."

Ambassador Chandler offered his hand. "You done good, son. I and the United States of America owe you our thanks."

The two entered Chandler's office and seated themselves—the ambassador behind his inlaid walnut desk and Ryker in an adjacent chair upholstered in navy blue and peach. It was the first time that Ryker had relaxed in a long time. Chandler buzzed his intercom and instructed the stenographer to come in. Her machine set up, Ryker began the story, starting with the phone call from former Ambassador Cannon and ending with his and the ambassador's current conversation. Lubin was referred to only as a friend who'd volunteered to help. It was simpler that way. Other than that, nothing was left out. Chandler listened with rapt attention, interrupting only to get clarification on some aspect or another. Ryker's testimony recorded, Chandler excused the reporter and closed the door after her.

"And you say Badri was a common thread to your family's death and the missionary incident?" Chandler asked.

"It looks that way, Joe. Of course, it would've been nice to question Badri. Squeeze him for everything he knew."

"You should know that Dave Matheson is livid about all this. He's fixin' to lodge a formal complaint against you and is threatening to have Deborah Reid brought up on criminal charges. And he's only been back from Istanbul a few hours. Who knows what he's likely to do when he really gets cranked up."

"Yeah, I figured he wouldn't be a happy camper even if Deborah *hadn't* gotten hurt," Ryker confided.

"You can say *that* again. He wanted you 'clapped in irons' when you arrived back with the missionaries. I had to banish him to his office. I was afraid he'd make a scene in front of everyone."

"I appreciate that."

"But I had to promise to invite him in here after you and I talked. Sorry, but it's only fair. You won't have to go over your entire story with him, though. I'll fill him in on everything pertinent that you've told me. But bringing him in here and letting him vent might not be such a bad idea. Might mellow him out a bit. Besides, my office is kind of neutral territory. I don't think that he'd dare 'terminate' you in front of a witness. It wouldn't be good for the carpet, either." Chandler chuckled.

"Let's get this over with," Ryker said. "Send in the lion." He resigned himself to being verbally torn apart by his former subordinate—a man whom he felt had held great promise as station head but who'd allowed himself to take the low road in Agency matters.

The ambassador reached over to his intercom and held down a button.

"Tell Dave I'm ready to see him now."

"Yes, sir," Chandler's duty officer intoned.

In less than a minute, the door to Chandler's office opened, and Matheson marched in. He was out of breath from bounding down the stairs from the second floor and was puffing fire and smoke. Chandler remained seated, but Ryker got to his feet and offered his hand.

"Dave, nice to see you again."

"Don't 'Dave' me. I'll have you prosecuted for meddling in this. And you know I can do it, too. I can think of at least seven violations that you could be jailed for. And as for Deborah, I'm going to make an *example* out of her. She may not go to prison, but she'll never work another day for the Agency. Her office belongings are being boxed up even as we speak."

"Now, just *wait* a minute. Deborah was only—"

"How did you talk her into all this? Or maybe you didn't have to. I always thought there was more than business between you two."

Ryker grabbed him by the lapels of his Armani suit, their noses nearly touching. Chandler sprang from his chair and started to come around the desk to act as referee.

"If we were anywhere else and you'd said something like that, you'd be on your back by now. How *dare* you defame Susan's memory with a lie!" Ryker shoved him away as if being that close would be contagious.

"Take the gloves off, you two; this won't get us anywhere," Chandler said as he positioned himself between the clashing titans.

Matheson straightened his suit between rounds. He had to suspect that Ryker *could* have vacuumed the carpet with him. Ryker was older and out of shape, but he was still a formidable figure to reckon with. The rescue in the desert had been proof of that, if any proof was needed. Nonetheless, his taking charge of this affair had made Matheson look ineffectual. And that wouldn't say much for the station head's administrative abilities.

"I'm sorry, Joe," Ryker said. It's just that—"

"I know, I know. You don't have to explain," Chandler interrupted. He looked in Matheson's direction. "Dave, those remarks were uncalled for. Slandering Sam isn't going to get us anywhere productive. Now let's just sit down and discuss this in a professional manner."

Ryker returned to his seat, and Matheson pulled up a chair next to Chandler's desk, but not too close to his former boss, who was still seething but seemed resigned to play Chandler's game for a while.

Chandler turned to Matheson. "First of all, Dave, how *is* Deborah doing? What's her condition? Have you seen her yet?"

"No, I haven't seen her. I just flew in and was briefed on the way from the airport. And it wouldn't have done any good, anyway. She was still under the effects of surgery. Doctors say that she should be strong enough to talk by morning."

"She was pretty lucky," Ryker added. "Hasan said she had lost a lot of blood by the time the ambulance got there. His men on the scene kept her alive until medical showed up."

Matheson's contempt at being upstaged by Ryker in front of the ambassador was clear for everyone to see. The hate in the man's eyes was tangible.

"Well, keep me informed," Chandler said, ending it.

"Yes, sir, but what was she doing at Badri's apartment with the Egyptian police in the first place?" Matheson asked the ambassador while looking at Ryker.

Ryker jumped in, seeing that Matheson was attempting an end run. "I think you *know*, Dave. Deborah suspected Badri of passing information to the terrorists who took the missionaries and who killed my family. She said that she'd talked to you about it and that you'd shut her down without giving it the attention it deserved. Isn't that so?"

Matheson looked sheepish but didn't respond.

"Dave, is Sam right? Did your people suspect a mole in this embassy?" Chandler's voice was tinged with incredulity.

"Whether we did or didn't is *classified* information," Matheson responded, hiding behind the time-honored—though transparent—ploy of intelligence gatherers.

Chandler pursued his quarry. "I can't believe that you considered the possibility of a link to terrorists working in this very building too sensitive to discuss with *me*. It's inexcusable!"

"Maybe, maybe not, but I want to know Deborah's role with Ryker," Matheson said with a sneer.

"It's simple." Ryker explained how he'd facilitated a police contact when Deborah's investigation had reached a point where a look at Badri's financial records became necessary. "That done, it appeared likely that Badri was tied not only to the Jerusalem bombing, but was also somehow connected to the abduction of the missionaries. Deborah had been requested to witness Badri's interrogation. So you see, she was only doing her job. She was attempting to get information that would lead to the rescue of the missionaries."

"But without proper authority," Matheson said. "She acted on her own, using confidential and highly sensitive information from this office and sharing that information with another intelligence gathering agency. What she did was treasonous any way you look at it."

"You'd be way out of line to try to discipline her for *that*," Ryker countered. "As a matter of fact, if you *do* try, someone at those hearings might want to know why you chose to be out of the country when an international incident involving your office was taking place. I don't even think *Daddy* could help you out there. Rather than trying to ruin her career, you might give a thought to saving your own."

Matheson stirred in his seat, his eyes narrowing as he considered the threat levied against him. Problem was, it wasn't an idle one. He had known about the missionaries and had chosen not to act on it. How could he have known that the fate of three health workers would invoke so much attention? Clearly, he knew he was far from being the station head that Ryker had been, but being given a lecture by his former boss was definitely not going down well.

"I'll have general counsel look into it, for Deborah's sake, but what gave you the right to interfere in this case? You have no official standing," Matheson said smugly. "In fact, you're not even supposed to exist anymore."

Ryker smiled. He expected this accusation. "As a private citizen and consultant to the chief inspector of the National Police, I was well within my rights to aid and assist. Further, I can assure you, and get testimony to support it, that I shared no intel nor did I use my former position and influence to jeopardize national security. Run that by general counsel while you're at it."

Chandler smiled as he watched Ryker get the best of Matheson. The current station head was too much glitz to be a good intelligence administrator—more concerned about his imported Italian loafers and embroidered silk shirts than about paying attention to business. He'd been upstaged, and that was that.

Matheson took a few breaths to compose himself. "So now that the missionaries have been rescued, I guess you'll be leaving with them." He appeared anxious to be rid of Ryker as soon as possible. "We can follow up on any leads that come from the terrorist that the Egyptian authorities brought back."

"No, I'm afraid not. Now that I'm here, I'm going to stick around for a while and see if anything turns up about my family's murder. There's reason to believe that the Chameleon was behind all this."

"Not again! The Chameleon? You can't be *serious!* We've been over this before. He's nothing more than an unsubstantiated rumor. No intelligence agency in the world gives his existence any credence. Every time the source of a terrorist act couldn't be ascertained, you always blamed the Chameleon. While you're at it, why not tie him to the Tehran hostage crisis and Sadat's assassination. It's all rubbish!"

"It's all there. Hasan is as convinced as I am that the man who kidnapped the missionaries is directly linked to the bombing in Jerusalem among other crimes."

"Oh, that's just great! Hasan spends one day with you, and now he's chasing a ghost, too. Both of you are lunatics. Face the facts. The man *doesn't* exist!"

Ryker turned to Ambassador Chandler. "Joe, it should be clear why I have to remain. It doesn't look as if I'm going to get any Agency help in bringing my family's killer to justice. Hasan and I believe the Chameleon may even be here in Cairo, and we intend to track him down before he kills again."

Matheson asked condescendingly, "How, may I ask, are you going to proceed to find this *elusive* Chameleon?"

Ryker looked at his wristwatch then back to Matheson.

"Deborah saw the man who we suspect carried out the kidnapping. When she is able, she's going to be interviewed by National Police detectives. Thanks to her photographic memory, she may be able to provide some information hidden to most of our think tank operatives. I understand that the computer files in Badri's apartment are already being accessed. Maybe there's something in them that will help identify his contacts. But if you were on the job, you'd know that already, now wouldn't you? Anyway, that's how it's done—by working at it step by step. Are you sure you don't want to help? Can you admit that you're *wrong* about the Chameleon?" Ryker stared right through Matheson.

Ryker got up from his chair. "I'm going to get cleaned up and rest a little before Hasan and I have a crack at the guy we brought back." He turned to Chandler. "Will you be needing me for anything else, Joe?"

"Not for now, but I suspect you'll want to be present when the National Police debrief the missionaries. They're speaking to their families and should be getting to bed soon. I know I sure would after something like this. Should be first thing in the morning. I'll see that one of the guest rooms is made available."

"Thanks, but that's not necessary. After all, I'm just here on holiday." He couldn't help but look at Matheson to rub it in. "I'll call your office with a number you can reach me at. I can't remember the last time I saw the back of my eyelids."

"And again, thanks," Chandler said to Ryker. "It's good to see you again. Glad you're safe."

Matheson had stood and was following Ryker out the door when Chandler called him back. Ryker went out, closing the door behind him. He paused long enough to hear the ambassador barking at the station head.

"I ought to skin you alive for this! And don't give me any of that *classified* bull. How could you not tell *me* about Deborah's suspicions? Of all the irresponsible . . ."

Ryker couldn't help buy smile as he walked past the Marines and off American soil. He flagged a passing taxi and made his way to the Cairo Marriott & Omar Khayyam Casino on El Gezira. He and Manni had much to discuss still, and they both had figured that the Marriott offered them as much security and privacy as anywhere else. Besides, Ryker had said, Omar's Café had the best Thai food this side of Bangkok.

* * *

Manni Lubin had been whisked from the airport by one of Hasan's men and had already showered and fallen asleep by the time Ryker finally checked in. Seeing the condition of his own clothes, Ryker had his and Lubin's clothes picked up for dry cleaning and asked that they be brought up first thing in the morning. Watching his friend sleep, he recalled the first time the two of them had met. Fate had drawn them together in the months preceding the finalization of the 1979 Israeli–Egyptian Peace Treaty. At the urging of the United States, a special task force had been formed to mount a full-court press to keep the Islamic Terror Syndicate—as the British would eventually come to call it—from literally blowing the diplomatic processes sky high. But beyond the Islamic Jihad, Hamas, PLO, and other extremist Muslim groups, there was also the fear that hard-line Israeli factions would attempt to sabotage negotiations.

Sam Ryker, the CIA's point man on the task force, had immediately recognized Manni Lubin, the Mossad's counterpart, as a kindred spirit. Both preferred action over rhetoric, though their respective agencies were often at odds with the risks they took to bring stability to an otherwise unstable environment. From that first association had sprung a bond of friendship that had lasted far longer than most. They had kept in contact since those days, sharing in their triumphs, and comforting each other in their defeats.

Ten minutes later, Ryker crashed on the other double bed. They slept until five-thirty the next morning. Lubin ordered room service and they both devoured the fresh fruit and warm pastries from the bakery while Ryker recapped his meeting with Matheson and the ambassador. Lubin didn't appear surprised by the station head's attitude. If and when it got back to Mossad that Lubin had been freelancing, Ryker figured that his friend would have to beg for mercy to keep his job. He was sorry for that. He knew that intelligence agencies simply took a dim view of unsanctioned operations.

They finished off the rest of the fruit and juice and took the rented Mercedes to the hospital to see Deborah. Uniformed police blocked every access to her floor. It was a precaution that Ryker had suggested to Hasan when they first heard of her condition.

Trying to talk their way past the security details would have been futile, so Ryker used the pay phone in the hospital lobby to contact Hasan's office. Hasan was already at his desk when the call came in. He'd been going over the data retrieved from Badri's computer files—nothing of any consequence yet, but it looked promising.

Hasan had exchanged his desert fatigues for a brown, pinstriped suit by the time he reached the hospital. His eyes were bloodshot, and Ryker wondered if he'd gotten any sleep since the plane had landed.

The men conferred briefly and then proceeded to Deborah's fourth-floor room.

"She had an incredible memory. Every move, every word, every detail of yesterday morning was relayed to my office," Hasan said. "She also gave us what she claims was an email address on Badri's computer, but I'm ashamed to say that my office is stumped on how to trace it."

"I'm pretty sure Dave isn't going to be much help, but I know the ambassador would force the issue and get you the help you need."

"Thanks, Sam."

As they neared the hospital room, Hasan paused and pulled Ryker and Lubin aside. "Sergeant Heikel didn't make it. He was shot in the stomach. The surgeons did all they could, but the damage was just too great."

"I'm sorry to hear that."

"Well, one of the nurses here thought she was doing the right thing and told Miss Reid this earlier this morning. She is taking it pretty hard."

Ryker just nodded. "I appreciate knowing this."

Those standing guard along the way stepped aside for Hasan and his guests.

Deborah started when the door to the room opened, but she smiled when she saw Ryker.

"Sam, I guess I made a mess of this. I'm sorry," she said as the men approached her bed. Her voice was hoarse from having oxygen tubes down her throat during surgery.

"You've got nothing to be sorry about, Deb. We're only glad that you're alive."

"If I had acted quicker . . ." she said, looking out the window at nothing in particular, "if I had thought to arm myself before we went in, I might've been there to help instead of running away. It's *my* fault he's dead."

"Nonsense, Miss Reid," Hasan interjected. "If you hadn't fled, you would be dead, too. There was nothing you could have done."

"But—"

"I will hear no more of this nonsense. You have enough to worry about without blaming yourself with the death of one of my men. My men are the bravest, most professional men on any police force in the world, as far as I am concerned. He lived and died doing what he loved. With his last breath he rose and stopped Badri before he could finish you off, too. To insist that you are somehow responsible for his death is to diminish his valor and his memory. *If* you had been armed . . . *if* you had been someplace else . . . It is a dangerous game to play, this *if* game."

Deborah's eyes teared up. "Thank you, Hasan. He was a brave man, and I will forever be grateful for his heroic actions to save my life."

Hasan reached out and took her hand. "I will convey those words to his wife when I meet with her later today."

After a moment of silence, Ryker asked for an update.

"Ah, yes," Hasan responded. "Just as I was leaving, my people retrieved from the hard drive the last thing that Badri entered. It will come as no surprise that it concerned you. The text of the email reads, *Samuel Ryker not dead. Back in Egypt. Have info. Double fee. Awaiting instructions and payment. Badri.*"

"Pretty sloppy using my name and his in the clear like that," Ryker commented.

"I don't know that much about computers, but amateur or not, why didn't he delete the message after sending it?" Lubin asked.

"My people indicate that the message *had* been deleted, but there are ways to retrieve it, nonetheless." Hasan looked over the report. "The message was sent to an unregistered server via an encrypted address. My men can only track it so far."

"We have kids at the embassy who could break it," Deborah offered.

"Whoever set this up knows how to avoid detection."

The room fell silent for a moment.

"Okay, that leaves us with the man we brought up from Abu Simbel," Ryker continued.

"Right," Hasan said. "Maybe *he* can shed some light on the whereabouts of our phantom terrorist," referring to the grainy photo in his hand. "But I am not getting my hopes up."

They readied themselves to go. Ryker took Deborah's hand in his and squeezed lightly.

"Now you just get plenty of rest, Deb. Don't try to rush your recuperation. When you're strong enough to leave here, we'll have dinner at that little restaurant we both like and talk about old times."

"Sure, Sam," she responded weakly, still a long way from being herself. And in her voice there carried a bit more than the usual amount of concern. She couldn't help herself. She cared for him more than she cared for anything else in the world. She couldn't bear to lose him again.

* * *

Sam Ryker had never seen his Egyptian friend so upset. He and Manni Lubin had followed Hasan back to his office at National Police headquarters. They had scarcely walked through the front doors when they were met by one of Hasan's young lieutenants.

"He's gone, sir!"

"Slow down, kid. Who's gone?"

"The prisoner we picked up in Abu Simbel," he explained, fearful of the inspector's wrath. "They took him. I just found out from booking."

The young lieutenant had Hasan's full attention.

"Sir, we heard you were on your way and went to check on the prisoner, and he was gone. Taken by those neanderthals from military intelligence. Apparently, they had the necessary paperwork to remove him. Signed personally by Mubarak. They have been in the fifth-floor interrogation room with him for an hour or more. When we found out, we went up there but could get nowhere near. You know how they are, sir."

Hasan listened impatiently. "I certainly do," he said. "Those butchers have a history of going too far. Get Rakiim up here, and pick up a few more men and meet us by the elevator on the fifth floor. This is *our* prisoner and *our* building, and *we* are going to take charge!"

Within five minutes, Hasan's small assault force had assembled and was marching down the fifth-floor corridor in the direction of the interrogation room. Rakiim, Bear, as Ryker still called him, flexed his neck and rolled his shoulders in anticipation of a confrontation. Ryker began to wonder if he was in over his head on this one.

Two soldiers stood outside the door to the room. They looked startled and a bit inquisitive as the group approached.

"Take these men's sidearms, and escort them downstairs to a holding cell," Hasan ordered.

Lead by Rakiim, three of Hasan's men stepped forward swiftly as Hasan had directed, amid the unruly objections of the soldiers.

Hasan burst into the interrogation room, Rakiim at his side and followed by the remainder of his contingent. Ryker knew Hasan had done the right thing when he saw the condition of the prisoner. The animals from military intelligence had stripped the prisoner, his face so battered and swollen as to be nearly unrecognizable. Electrodes hooked to a car battery had been used to deliver current to various parts of his body. The prisoner had received medical attention for the shot in his leg in Aswan, but the wound was now unbandaged, the stitches torn loose.

"What is the meaning of this?" the senior of the two officers yelled in protest. "You have no business here. This is a military matter. *Get out!*"

"I think not," Hasan replied evenly, with a tone of absolute command. "Relieve these two *gentlemen* of their weapons, and take them downstairs to join their colleagues."

"You have no right to interfere!" the soldier protested. "Our orders come directly from the office of the president, and if you think—"

"Get medical personnel up here right away," Hasan ordered Rakiim. "And I want what these criminals have done here documented for their court martial. Take them away, and don't be too gentle about it."

"Our pleasure, sir." Rakiim and his other men stepped forward and roughly grabbed the stunned military men by the shoulders and dragged them from the room.

"We will have you *shot* for this!" one of them screamed from down the hallway, but Ryker recognized idle talk when he heard it. The soldiers had crossed over the lines of propriety with the prisoner, and they knew it. Two additional detectives closed the door and stood guard outside. Only Hasan, Ryker, and Lubin stayed inside with the prisoner and surveyed the damage. The man was barely conscious and near death. His ribs had been broken, and by the color of the blood coming from the corners of the man's mouth, Ryker guessed a lung had been punctured. Other internal injuries were undoubtedly severe as well.

Hasan cut the bonds that held the prisoner to the chair, and he and Ryker eased him to the floor. If the man—at that instant—had been in a hospital emergency room, it would've been unlikely that he could've been saved. The trauma was just too extensive. Hasan called for medical support.

"What kind of *people* could do this?" Ryker asked.

Hasan responded, "Very *determined* men, but from the old school. Terrorism often brings out the worst in those who must confront it."

"So what do we do now?" Ryker asked. "It's obvious that the man's condition renders him useless to us."

"I would have liked to ask him if he had ever seen *this* man before." Hasan pulled out the photo of their suspect.

"Yes, that might've been helpful," Ryker replied. "But I think his eyes are swollen permanently shut. He might as well be blind. Whatever he *might* have told us is lost."

"What about whatever he told the military interrogators?" Lubin asked. "He might have given up something we could use."

"I think not," Hasan said, thumbing through a spiraled notebook left behind. "If he had talked, he would not look like this now. This says the only thing they got from him that we didn't already know was his name: Imad."

Ryker had seen the results of torture, or "coerced interrogation," as it had been more euphemistically named, but what they had done to this man was barbaric and criminal. No one deserved this. Not even this man.

"These buffoons didn't know about our investigation into the death of Sergeant Heikel and the attack on Miss Reid, so we can assume that their questioning did not address our mastermind." Hasan indicated the picture again. "Not that there would have been any answers forthcoming. Likewise, they would have been more interested in information about the terrorist group *behind* the missionary incident and would not have been privy to our suspicions about the involvement of *Al-Har'ba*."

Beaten to the verge of death, Imad stirred as the two of them talked. He tried to speak, but his words were distorted by the gurgle of blood seeping into his lungs. Ryker fell to his knees and propped the dying man's head off the floor.

"What did you say? Tell me," Ryker asked evenly in Arabic.

Imad coughed and spit up a mouthful of blood.

Ryker was more forceful this time. "What do you know about *Al-Har'ba? Tell me!*"

"Sai . . . Saiif." Imad coughed again, spraying the air with his blood. Ryker turned his head in time to avoid the hack.

Ryker could barely make out what he was saying.

"Saiif? Is that *Al-Har'ba*? Is that his name?"

Imad's head fell forward, and his body went limp in Ryker's arms. He was still breathing, but it was becoming even more irregular. The man was at death's door.

Help arrived moments later, but it was too late. The man died without uttering another sound, his bruised and swollen eyes closed forever. Whatever else he may have known about the Chameleon was lost with him. Outside, the three men discussed what the man had revealed. Ryker was animated.

"Sam," Hasan said, "before you get too excited, take a step back and look at what little information, if any, he gave us. We have what *might* be a name. Saiif. It could be any number of things. But I do agree with you—it is more than we had before, and I am hopeful that the information will bring us closer to this murderer. That name—if it is a name—could mean anything, though."

"No, I don't think so," Ryker insisted. "He must have recognized us from the rescue. I've been thinking of this. At some point he must have realized that he had been abandoned by his leader. And when the other chopper turned and fled, my money is on this man's loyalty deserting with it."

"Possible," Hasan said, sighing. "Assuming that you are correct, where would we start looking? Here in Egypt? Lebanon? Syria? As uncommon as it might be, finding and interrogating everyone with that name would be an impossible undertaking. There is not enough manpower in all the Middle East to launch such an investigation. And why would we think that our man used his real name? *Saiif. Sword.* Make it *al-Saiif* and you have *The Sword of God.* Sounds like a terrorist name if I've ever heard one."

"No, listen to me. What you're saying is true, but whoever the Chameleon is, he wasn't always the invisible terrorist he is now. He has a past. And I'm betting that at some point in his life, he was nothing more than a common criminal. If so, he may have a record somewhere."

"But what—" Hasan and Lubin said simultaneously.

Ryker cut them off. "I know what you're going to say: What solid proof do we have that *Saiif* is his name now or was his name before he became the Chameleon? We don't have any. But still . . . Hasan, Egypt has friendly ties with most countries of the Middle East. What would it take to contact the national police agencies of your Arab neighbors and ask them to do a name search?"

Hasan thought before he answered. "I want this man, too, but what you are suggesting is a long shot at best. I have a few strings I can pull, maybe even a few favors to call in, but it may take time. I just do not want you to expect a miracle when the age of miracles has passed."

Ryker smiled. "A miracle is *just* what I'm counting on, my friend."

TWENTY

IT WAS JUST AFTER LUNCH when the missionaries were escorted to Ambassador Chandler's office. Several more chairs had been brought in to accommodate the gathering. Dave Matheson had opted not to be present during the debriefing and had sent one of his deputies, Donald Taylor, to stand in for him. Even with hours of rest, the missionaries still seemed psychologically, if not physically, drained from their ordeal, but their interviews just couldn't be delayed any longer. In fact, the questioning should've been conducted immediately after their rescue—probably before even leaving Aswan—while events were still vivid in their minds. Obviously recognizing their deteriorated condition, Chandler apologized for dragging them from their rooms but indicated that the debriefing session was vital.

Ryker had introduced Hasan to Chandler and Taylor before the missionaries entered the room. The ambassador knew the man only by reputation; Taylor not really at all. Lubin was there, as well, but stood unobtrusively in Hasan's shadow. Hasan laid out the ground rules. The murder of one missionary, and the abduction of the remaining three, though an international incident, was an Egyptian problem to be resolved by Egyptian authorities. Therefore, he would be the spokesman, but others in the room would be free to ask relevant follow-up questions.

For the next three hours, the missionaries were interviewed singly and collectively. They gave a detailed account of the attack on their two-vehicle convoy. The fate of Elder Evans brought an emotional response from all three, necessitating interludes in the process. Nothing was left out as they recounted their harrowing story. Because they'd been almost immediately hooded, the missionaries couldn't give much information on the three men who had initially abducted them. Hasan shared with them the fate of the two accomplices that had driven them out into the desert, which elicited genuine concern and mourning for their deaths. This show of compassion surprised the ambassador and the chief inspector but not Ryker so much. He had once known firsthand what it felt like to be in a spiritual state capable of such forgiveness. He wondered if he would ever be there again.

When the questioning was finally complete, the missionaries were informed that Aswan police had packed up their apartment and were sending their belongings to the embassy.

"But I don't want to leave," Sister Devereux said. "Our mission is not over. There is still so much to do." She looked around the room for support but found little. She took her husband's hand. "Can't we stay?"

Ambassador Chandler was floored by the request. "After what you've been through, you want to stay and continue your work? Aren't you afraid?"

Sister Devereux stared the big Texan square in the eyes. "If good men and women gave up when things got a little rough, the evil of the world would triumph. I know there are probably rules you have to follow in a situation like ours, but couldn't you at least see what you can do? I love the people of Egypt. I want to help. I want to stay." She looked at her companions. "We all do."

Ambassador Chandler leaned back in his chair and exhaled loudly. "Well I'll be. In all my years I haven't ever seen anything like you folks. Y'all are the most Christian people I have ever had the good fortune to meet."

He leaned in close to Sister Devereux. "Understand that there are rules, like you said, that we have to follow in cases like this. But if the Egyptian government is willing to consider it, I will work hard to get you back here real soon. Fair enough?"

Sister Devereux smiled. "You're a good man, Ambassador."

"Thank you. Now, if you will excuse us."

And with that, the missionaries were escorted back to their rooms. When the door was closed, Ambassador Chandler turned to Ryker. "You Mormons are a different bunch, aren't you? They want to stay."

"It could be early stages of Stockholm Syndrome," Hasan offered. "Showing an allegiance to their captor, or in their case, the land and people she associates with being responsible."

"Perhaps," Chandler agreed. "I'll have the embassy psychologist visit them one more time before they fly out."

Ryker just shook his head. "They're fine. It's not Stockholm, and they aren't suffering from any shock. It's called faith. And it's something they have in abundance."

"Faith, huh? I heard tell of that once when I was a church-goin' man."
He smiled and chuckled. "No one is *that* faithful."

Ryker smiled back. "Mormons are."

Ambassador Chandler and Deputy Taylor seemed eager to change the
subject and get down to business. With a nod, Taylor was given the floor.

"I have information on that email address you gave us earlier today. The
boys at IT had never seen anything like it before. All attempts to trace it
back to its source seemed to fail. The messages went through, but the
address was bounced between servers so fast and across such distances that
even they couldn't follow it. So I called in a favor with an old college buddy
that now works for the NSA."

Taylor looked around confidently. "It didn't take him long. We got
him."

Taylor distributed manila folders to Ryker, Hasan, and the ambassador.

"It seems that the address belongs to a small, exclusive investment firm
located right here in Cairo. Salahdin Investments. Salahdin, or Salahdin
Ayyubi, was the sultan of Egypt and what is now Syria during the twelfth
century. He opposed the European Crusades and led Muslim forces to
victory over the invaders, recapturing Palestine and Jerusalem."

Hasan nodded. "He is a hero. When you were children, you played
cowboys and Indians. When we were young, we acted out these battles. We
would all fight to be Salahdin. It was a very noble time in our history."

"Anyway," Taylor continued, "we have only been able to discover a few
facts concerning this Salahdin Investments. One, they only cater to the
extremely wealthy. Minimum deposits are in the neighborhood of a
hundred million dollars, and they diversify their investments across the
globe, focusing heavily in land acquisition and spot market speculation,
where large sums of money are made and lost in a matter of minutes. It's a
very volatile and risky form of investment, but apparently Salahdin has done
quite well. We were only able to identify one source of income for the
company, but its assets far exceed fifty billion."

Ryker leaned over to Hasan. "Look on page two."

Taylor followed Ryker's lead. "Yes, on page two is the logo and letter-
head for Salahdin."

"Notice anything familiar?" Ryker asked.

Hasan recognized it right away. "There's our sword. *Saiif.*"

Beneath the Arabic calligraphy that spelled out the name of the business
was a sword, alight in heaven's flame superimposed over a representation of
the world.

"This is our man."

"What can you tell us about the owner of Salahdin?" Ryker asked Taylor.

"Well, without crossing too many lines in the sand, so to speak, I figured that our friend here, the chief inspector, could follow up and finish completing this puzzle."

"Consider it done." Hasan rose to his feet. "Your help in this investigation is appreciated beyond that which I can express. I thank you. We will not let you down."

"Chief inspector?" Ambassador Chandler said. "I needn't remind you that the United States has a stake in what this man has done."

"Egypt's laws are clear when it comes to terrorists, and justice is swift and severe. I will do what I can, but once he is apprehended, his fate will likely be out of our hands."

Ambassador Chandler considered his words and nodded. "Thank you. I know you will do what you can."

"Sam? It would be a shame not to continue to employ your services in this, our hour of victory."

Ryker was on his feet, too. "You couldn't keep me away if you tried."

"Then it's settled," Hasan said. "Mr. Ambassador, again, please accept my thanks, and offer my deepest gratitude to your men. Great good was done today."

But there was much good to be done.

* * *

Not far from the American embassy, deep within the heart of Cairo's older banking district, Saiif had watched as email after email was received via his encrypted Internet connection. He suspected the Americans were behind this latest round of "fishing" for this email server ID, and he knew that it was only a matter of time before they succeeded in identifying everything they would need to know to move in for the kill. He breathed in deep, switched computer screens, and went about his work.

It was time to go. But not before taking care of some unfinished business.

TWENTY-ONE

IT WAS LATE AFTERNOON WHEN the tactical strike unit positioned itself outside the building that housed Salahdin Investments. At Hasan's order, every street and alley within the neighborhood was barricaded.

"Sergeant?" Hasan whispered into his radio.

"Sharpshooters in position, sir."

"Lieutenant?"

"Gas team ready."

"Copy that. On my order."

Bear worked the slide on his Uzi. He didn't care much for Israeli goods, but in this case, he recognized a quality product when he saw one.

"If you do not mind my saying so," he confided to Hasan, "I hope we are correct on this one. We have short-circuited every standard procedure, to say nothing of the use of manpower."

"Trust me. The Americans tracked the email address to this location. They have equipment that the technicians in our lab never even knew existed. Besides," Hasan looked up at Bear, "my gut says this is who we are after."

Ryker and Lubin stood on the other side of Hasan. They wore flak jackets and toted automatic weapons. With tactical exactness, they stormed the epicurean high-rise alongside ten of Hasan's most experienced and capable counterterrorist agents. They stopped and fanned out on the sixth floor. Hasan took up a position across from the single-locked door. The National Police had identified the registered agent and owner of the exclusive investment firm, but it wasn't the offices that interested them right now. It was the penthouse suite that was owned by a man of the same name. Hasan lifted the bullhorn and spoke firmly.

"Saiif Khalil! This is the National Police. You are surrounded. Surrender yourself peacefully, and you will not be harmed."

Silence screamed from behind the large, ornate wooden door.

"Mr. Khalil, this is your only chance to avoid injury. Come out with your hands clasped behind your head."

Nothing.

Hasan exchanged the bullhorn for his radio.

"Lieutenant. Four rounds."

As soon as he spoke the words, two tear gas grenades were launched from his men on the ground, crashing through the plate glass in the front and two more through a bank of high windows at the rear. Legions of police drew a bead on the sixth-floor windows and waited anxiously for any sign of movement. The man inside was a cop-killer, having taken the lives of three officers in the explosion in Abu Simbel, so to the officers outside, this confrontation had become personal. Hasan wanted the man taken alive, but he knew that any resistance would result in his death. He would likely be powerless to restrain the men under his command. He stepped aside and motioned for his team to take action.

Moving with synchronous precision, four men wearing body armor and gas masks gained entrance with the help of a sledge hammer and stormed the smoking suite. Hasan kept a strict watch on the door as the small team rapidly searched the premises, flinching ever so slightly as he heard them kicking in doors. Minutes later the lieutenant passed the word to him: empty.

As soon as the tear gas dissipated, Hasan, Ryker, and Lubin entered through the splintered front door, followed by Bear and reinforcement officers. Inside, they split up. Almost immediately, an officer approached Hasan.

"Sir, you had better take a look at this."

Hasan followed the young man to a room in the back. "Sam? Manni? Get over here."

Manni Lubin, a man of few words, let loose a whistle when he saw what Hasan's men had discovered. "A bomb-maker's workshop. There's enough material back there to fashion every type of detonating device that you could imagine." Lining the walls were spools of wire of every gauge, soldering equipment, tools of every size and shape, and well-used wooden workbenches. Acetylene tanks occupied one corner, while rows and rows of computer and cell phone motherboards and other pieces were lined up and catalogued. The back room had been converted into an electronics and small-arms workshop.

Ryker joined in, "It's the perfect cover. No one would expect it, here, amid the wealth and lavish living arrangements. Everything he needs is here at his fingertips. If it wasn't so horrifying, I'd say I was impressed by his genius."

Startling them, a commotion erupted outside the terrorist penthouse.

"What's wrong?" Hasan bellowed.

His lieutenant appeared at the door of the workshop. "Motion sensor alarm. We tripped it on our way inside. There's a transmitter at the window, and we haven't been able to shut it down."

"Bomb?"

"It would make sense, given all this," he swept his arm over the work-shop.

Hasan agreed. "Everyone out!" he yelled.

Just then a telephone blared throughout the penthouse. Hasan motioned for the lieutenant and his men to exit the building. The telephone was on the counter, but no one dared answer it for fear of a booby trap. On the fourth ring, the phone's recorder activated, putting the caller on speaker.

"Good afternoon, Chief Inspector." The caller spoke in Arabic. "I am truly sorry to disappoint you, but I have no time to entertain house guests. You'll have to forgive my lack of manners. Perhaps if you had phoned ahead, you could have saved yourself the trip."

The three detectives looked at each other, confused.

"How, you might ask," Saiif said through the speaker on the recorder, "did I know you would be leading the charge, Mr. Son-of-the-Foreign-Minister? It would seem your every movement is at my fingertips."

They all looked one another in disgust. Was there no end to this monster's network of informants?

"And to your guest of honor." He continued. "The great Sam Ryker. Do you mind if I call you Sam? Though we have never formally met, I feel as if I know you like a brother. I do regret not being there in person. We have much to catch up on, wouldn't you say? Oh, and before we venture too far down this path, let me congratulate you on rescuing the Americans. The National Police account of your actions was extraordinary. I was, however, disappointed in your own CIA report. It would seem that not everyone in your office is pleased to see you again. Your Mormon missionaries must have found favor with their God. He must have smiled on you to find them so quickly and save them. Too bad that favor did not extend to your own family."

Enraged, Ryker grabbed the receiver from the console as the tape machine kept recording.

"You're a dead man!" he screamed.

"Not even so much as a *hello*?" The voice was cold. "I'm hurt. Really, I am. And yes, figuratively speaking, you are correct: I am dead. You have finally succeeded in compromising this identity. But this is not the end. You can no more stop me than you can stop the sun from setting or the rain from falling. It is fruitless to try."

Ryker's anger was boiling over. "I will find you, and when I do—"

"You'll what? You are a helpless old man. You were helpless to save your family, just as you are powerless to stop me now."

"Don't you ever speak of them! Ever!"

"Still sore, are we? Did I ever tell you that I almost didn't go through with it? No, of course not. When I looked upon your daughters—what were their names again? Oh, well—when I first saw them, I was moved by their beauty and thought to myself that killing them would be like destroying a great work of art, like Michelangelo's *David,* or the *Venus de Milo.* But then I got control of my hormones again and did what I do best."

Ryker couldn't speak for the anger built up inside him. "I will stop you," he finally said.

"You think you've stopped me, but you haven't. You can't. And when I'm done here, there will be nowhere you can hide. I'm not just going to kill you, but everyone you care about. That pretty little assistant of yours, your Jew friend, your Egyptian policeman. Everyone."

Ryker's fingers had turned white around the phone. "I will kill you! You'll never be rid of me! You took everything I held dear—"

"Oh, please! Spare me. Before I forget, do allow me to thank you for all your help. For the name, I mean. I fear I have taken your assistance for granted all these years. All the money in the world could not have purchased a reputation like the one you gave me. What greater gift could you give me during this festive season?" Saiif paused. "Good-bye, Mr. Ryker."

Click. The line went dead.

Lubin was the first to speak. "I heard something in the background when he was speaking. Near the beginning and then again at the end. It was garbled. Rewind the tape, and play it once more."

Hasan moved to replay the recorded phone conversation when Ryker stopped him.

"Do you hear that?"

"Hear what?"

"Shhh. That."

Manni Lubin was the first to hear it, too. "A hissing sound."

All three of them looked around quickly. Hasan was the first to smell it. "Gas!"

"Incendiary!" Ryker yelled. "Everyone out!"

But before he did, he had the presence of mind to grab the answering machine before sprinting out of the abandoned suite. All three had just cleared the hallway and dove into stairwell when the entire floor erupted in a blast of yellow and orange. The force knocked all of them to the ground as shards of glass and metal exploded throughout the large apartment. The heat was so intense that it singed Hasan's pants and melted the soles of Ryker's shoes. Two more explosions from deeper inside Saiif's lair shattered any hope they had of recovering forensic evidence connecting Saiif Khalil to the phantom terrorist *Al-Har'ba*.

Hasan was not one to regret events he could no longer control. "How's that tape?" he asked Ryker.

"A little scratched up but intact."

"Rakiim, bag that tape," Hasan ordered. "And I want our people in there the minute fire control says its safe. I want anything and everything not charred through tagged and taken in. Everyone leaves a trace, and I will not lose this monster now."

Hasan brushed the debris from his clothes. "Sam, Manni, you're with me."

Thirty minutes later they were back at Hasan's office. Police technicians began analyzing the tape right away, isolating every sound, voice pattern, background noise, etc. At one point Lubin spoke up.

"There, did you hear that?"

Hasan had the tape rewound, and played it over and over. "Announcements, sounds like departure times. Airport?"

Lubin shook his head. "Trains. Sounds like a train station."

Hasan snapped his fingers. Several officers jerked to attention. "I want schedules for every train station in Cairo, Alexandria, and Port Said in my hand in five minutes!"

Three minutes later, one of the young lieutenants handed Hasan computer printouts and summarized the details. "Three trains left Cairo within half an hour of his call. One went south with a final destination of Khartoum. Another is headed for Libya via a coastal route through Alexandria. The third is on its way to Port Said. All have multiple stops and connections along the way. Each could eventually transport him out of the country."

"Yes, but which one would he choose?" Hasan asked, almost to himself.

"What did he tell us?" Ryker asked. "He said something about a gift for the holidays. Think about it. That can only have reference to Israel. This year, the celebrations of Passover and Easter fall within a day of one another. That has to be it. Jerusalem will be packed. That's *exactly* where he's headed. No matter what train he's on, he'll find a way to get into Israel."

"Maybe we could intercept him." Rakiim looked at his watch. "Those trains cannot have gotten far. They could be searched at their next scheduled stop."

"It's worth a chance, I guess," Ryker said hesitantly, "but I doubt it'll do any good. He knew we were coming, which means he might also assume we'd be coming after him. With all of his contacts and working around the world, no one has ever described the same man. He's a master of disguise. He's the human chameleon. The picture we have won't do us any good. Even if everyone could be pulled off those trains and questioned, I think he could still be overlooked. He hasn't survived this long by making it easy. He even evaded all four of us, and we were looking right at him."

Rakiim looked dismayed as he turned to Hasan and said, "But once he crosses into Israel, we will have lost him. We have to try, sir."

"All right, alert the various police jurisdictions, and have the trains delayed at their next stop. Have the identification papers of every passenger checked. Make sure that the photo we took from the airport security tapes is faxed to every departure point. Any passenger who even remotely resembles that picture is to be pulled from the train and taken into custody until things are sorted out."

"Yes, sir," Rakiim responded as he raced from the room.

Hasan turned to Ryker. "What else can I do? Once *Al-Har'ba* crosses into Israel, my jurisdiction ceases." He was disheartened by the prospect of being close, but not close enough, to the human wisp of smoke.

"We're not going to let him get away, Hasan," Lubin said. "Your jurisdiction may stop at the border, but mine does not. Sam and I will continue the hunt. I am not without resources in Israel. Besides, if it comes to a confrontation, your dislocated shoulder would only get in the way. Can you arrange a flight to Jerusalem for Sam and me?"

"Certainly. When do you wish to leave?"

"As quickly as you can take us to the airport," Lubin replied.

"Also, get in touch with Taylor at the embassy," Ryker directed. "Tell him to fax a picture of the Chameleon to the American embassy in Israel and to have an official request made of the Israeli government for surveillance of all major ports of entry and border crossings, just in case."

Lubin said to Ryker, "If you're right about Passover or Easter celebrations being the targets, we've got less than a week to stop him."

Lubin then made the call to Mossad headquarters in Tel Aviv, refusing to offer much background information but indicating he'd explain everything when he returned.

On the other line, Hasan spoke to Donald Taylor, who was only too happy to comply with his request for help in stopping another international incident. Hasan then called the airport to arrange use of the Piper Navaho. There were a few questions on the other end that he didn't have time for.

"Perhaps you would like to speak with President Mubarak, himself?" Hasan bluffed. "I am certain he could find time in his schedule to personally authorize this flight. Yes . . . Yes, I knew you would see it my way."

* * *

With lights pulsating and siren blaring, they arrived at the secondary airstrip in record time. The squad car screeched to a stop beside the waiting plane. Lubin had been sitting next to Hasan up front.

"We'll do our best, my friend," Lubin assured him. "I look forward to meeting again in better times." He shook Hasan's hand

Hasan nodded.

"Take this," Lubin said, extracting a business card from his jacket pocket and handing it to Hasan. It was one of Hasan's own cards that Lubin had taken from a stack atop his desk. "There's a phone number on the back. If anything else turns up here, dial the number and identify yourself. The people on the other end will know how to contact us."

Hasan turned the card over, confirmed the number, and put it in his shirt pocket.

Lubin exited and began to ascend the metal stairs from the plane's cabin. Ryker remained momentarily in the front seat. He reached over and offered his hand.

"Thank you for all you've done, Hasan. The missionaries couldn't have been rescued without you. I promise that we'll try to end the Chameleon's reign, once and for all. Tell Deborah what's happened and that I'll contact her when this is over."

"Yes, certainly," Hasan replied as he reached into the left outside pocket of his suit coat and brought out the Glock and two extra magazines of ammunition. "I have a feeling you might be needing these. If you find him . . . I mean *when* you do, he will not be taken alive. Be careful, my friend. May Allah guide your footsteps."

* * *

A police search of the three trains caused substantial chaos and consternation among passengers and railway officials alike. Authorities knew that under normal circumstances it would've been a long shot, but when the man being sought is known for his invisibility, the odds were even greater.

However, as conscientious as the police were in their massive manhunt, no one seemed to take notice of the man who exited the train at the Port Said station, dissolved into the crowd, and made his way in darkness through a brief thunderstorm to the wharf.

TWENTY-TWO

RYKER HAD BEEN RACING AGAINST THE clock since he first received that fateful phone call from President Cannon, and psychological fatigue was setting in. The Chameleon had evaded their grasp and had pledged to strike again. How many innocent people would die this time if he couldn't be stopped? How many wives would be widowed? How many children would grow up parentless? How many parents would be deprived of the joy of watching their children mature?

He and Lubin had spent their adult lives as warriors. Their uniforms may have been different, the true objectives of the battles they fought not always clear, but they'd been good soldiers. He'd opted for retirement, and Lubin was well beyond the apex of his career, but nothing had *really* changed. They were still soldiers in pursuit of an enemy. One man. It was their destiny, and they'd need all their faculties if the enemy was to be vanquished. The clock was ticking. Less than a week remained until Passover celebrations were scheduled throughout Israel—the largest in Jerusalem. Only a few hours later, Easter sunrise services would commence. In either event, thousands would be flocking to places of worship, among them the rich and influential. Targets of opportunity for the Chameleon wouldn't be in short supply.

It was unlikely that every religious gathering could be put under surveillance, even with the combined resources of the Israeli army and intelligence services. If the Chameleon remained true to form, he would use explosives. Satchel devices planted throughout the city? Rockets fired from hand-held launchers? Car bombs like those used to destroy the U.S. Marine garrison in Beirut? And what about chemical weapons? Certainly there were enough in circulation since the Gulf War with Iraq. Use of nerve gas would be a different *modus operandi* for the Chameleon, but deception and doing the unexpected was expected of him.

Was the Chameleon working under the same time constraints as those trying to find and stop him? Did *he* have less than seventy-two hours to concoct and carry out a plan, or did he have a network in Israel that had been conspiring for weeks or months? The variables boggled the mind and contributed to the exhaustion of the two intelligence operatives as the plane droned toward its destination.

In addition to the mission at hand, Ryker's thoughts strayed to the last time he'd flown to Jerusalem. What was to have been a joyous family reunion filled with wonderful memories had turned into tragedy. The events of that day were indelibly etched in his mind. Every time he closed his eyes, he saw his family's slaughter by a terrorist's bomb—the Chameleon's bomb.

He'd spent enough time in hostile environments—first in Vietnam and later in the Middle East—to know that unfathomable things happen all the time to the innocent. But they were only supposed to happen to *other* people. As a student of world history, he'd read of the six million death camp casualties of Hitler's Third Reich; of the tens of millions who fell victim to Stalin's paranoid egomania; of the ethnic cleansing in the former Yugoslavia which had left entire city populations decimated. Death in the millions, however, was so abstract that his mind had difficulty grasping the enormity of it. But he wasn't wrestling with the deaths of millions—only three.

Nearly nine months earlier, the bell had tolled for him and his family, and he'd come face-to-face with the stark realities of the world's dark side. It had left him an emotional cripple, and the thought of that day was now *almost* more than he could bear. Last week, before Cannon's phone call, with his finger curled around the trigger of his Glock, it *was* more than he could bear. He smiled at the thought that he was making progress.

Eyes fixed straight ahead, he sat silent, sensing that his present and past were about to converge. Why had Cannon been prompted to contact *him* after so many years? Surely there were others he could have called. And why had he agreed to come on this errand of mercy in the first place when common sense should've restrained him? But here he was, racing again in a desperate attempt to stop a man few even believed to exist. His faith was weak, but Ryker couldn't shake the feeling that perhaps God was using him for some other purpose. After all, the missionaries had been rescued. That was the bargain he'd made with Cannon. Mission accomplished. But it wasn't accomplished, and he wasn't sure he fully wanted to know how it was all going to end.

Ryker realized that he couldn't think straight. Everything was moving all too fast, and he and Lubin were *so* tired. Tired enough to make the kind of mistakes that could get one or both of them killed.

* * *

The flight from Cairo to Jerusalem was over before either man could relax enough to sleep. At just before eleven PM, airport control directed the Piper Navaho to a remote section of runway where a cadre of Israeli intelligence officers waited. It had been raining heavily earlier that night, but now only a light mist hung in the air.

The plane rolled to a stop, and the twin engines were shut down. Lubin and Ryker were framed in the doorway as the copilot lowered the metal stairs. Before they could descend, one of the men on the ground sprinted up the steps and entered the cabin. He bypassed the only two passengers and spoke to the pilots. They weren't to leave the plane. A refueling truck would arrive in a few minutes and ready the aircraft for a return flight within the hour. There'd be no charge for the service—a *professional courtesy.* The man conversing in Arabic with the pilots was polite enough, but there was no doubt about who was calling the shots.

Lubin's boss, Levi Goldman, met them on the tarmac. A uniformed officer in desert fatigues stepped forward and quickly but thoroughly frisked Ryker, relieving him of the Glock and ammunition clips. They were handed to Goldman, who put them into the outside pockets of his overcoat. No one spoke.

Lubin wasn't looking forward to what was about to happen. Goldman had been his superior, off and on, for almost twenty years, and the last thing in the world Lubin wanted to do was disappoint the man standing before them. Goldman, a German Jew, had lost most of his family to the Nazi Holocaust. He was five years old when he stood naked, shivering in line, to receive his tattooed Auschwitz identification number by the butchers who ran the infamous extermination camp. Miraculously, he'd survived and had immigrated to Israel after the war. He seldom wore long-sleeved shirts, as he wanted people to see the fading mark on his forearm and *remember.* Lubin knew Goldman was a hard man who'd dedicated his life to the defense of the Jewish state.

"Get in," were the only two words directed toward the weary intelligence officers as Goldman gestured to the black limousine, its rear door open.

Lubin and Ryker crossed in front of Goldman and climbed in, positioning themselves on one of the two facing backseats. Goldman and two others, younger men who Lubin recognized as Goldman's fawning assistants, followed suit and took the opposing seat. The driver, who'd been standing by the open door, closed it and resumed his place behind the wheel. He put the idling car into gear and sped off in the direction of an alternate, and seldom-used, airport exit. The two other vehicles trailed behind.

It was Goldman who broke the silence. "So . . . I trust your *vacation* was pleasurable." His words to Lubin were harshly spoken and intended to convey that he already knew everything of consequence about Lubin's recent sojourn. Goldman's lieutenants were taking malicious pleasure in watching a senior agent squirm, especially one with such envious credentials. Lubin sensed that it wasn't meant for him to respond to Goldman—at least not yet.

"Sir, Manni was only coming to the aid of a friend. He—" Ryker never finished the sentence. Goldman's glare was sufficient to stop him.

"We'll get to you soon enough, Mr. Ryker," Goldman said. "Right now I'm trying to ascertain where this little adventure is taking us." His voice was gravelly, and his English was tainted with what Lubin had thought to be a New York accent—the kind of accent attributed to East Coast Mafia dons. It was a voice that compelled people to listen. Lubin had always found humor in the different English accents and dialects spoken in Israel by people who'd never lived anywhere else. The rabbi who'd taught English to Goldman must've emigrated from the Bronx.

"Did you *really* think that your foray into Egypt would go unnoticed, Manni? Unsanctioned mission . . . unauthorized use of assets . . . cavorting with Egyptian police authorities . . ."

Lubin didn't know what to say.

"Yes, we had you under surveillance most of the time. When your leave application was processed, and it was found that your wife wasn't traveling with you, I smelled something not kosher. We had a team on you from the moment you left Tel Aviv. I didn't give the order to reel you in because I wanted to see just how much rope you'd require to hang yourself. What could you have been *thinking*? Did you figure that I'd gone completely senile? Our friendship goes back decades, and I covered for you in '83, but I'm not sure that even *I* can save you this time."

Lubin was unsure if the rhetoric was as severe as it sounded or if Goldman was simply ramping him up for effect.

The Mossad chief continued. "And in both instances Mr. Ryker has been involved."

Lubin looked at Ryker and saw confusion spelled out on his face. Ryker was astute enough not to ask about it now, but he was sure to ask as soon as they were alone.

There was a lengthy pause, and Lubin figured that it was time to come to his own defense, though *defense* was probably not the right word. The established rules of the game declared what he'd done as "indefensible." If he hoped to live the rest of his life on this side of prison barbed wire, he would have to offer a pretty convincing explanation.

"I don't know what your *surveillance* team has told you, Levi, but for what little good it'll do me, let me try to put all this into perspective."

Goldman was stoic but gave the impression that Lubin should proceed.

"Approximately nine months ago, three Americans—Sam's wife and children to be exact—and seven Israelis were killed as a result of a terrorist bombing at the Wailing Wall. Metal fragments identified the explosive device as a Soviet anti-tank mine. There's plenty of that kind of stuff on the black market since the breakup of the Soviet Bloc. Then, last week, four American health workers, missionaries for the Mormon Church, were attacked on a road just south of Aswan. One was killed outright in a bomb blast. The other three were to be turned over to a Sudanese terrorist group that has since been identified as *Al-Jum'ah.*"

It appeared as if Lubin wasn't telling Goldman anything he didn't already know. He continued. "One of our people in the area retrieved bomb fragments from the explosion, and our lab ascertained that not only did the fragments from both incidents come from the same *type* of mine, but also that remnants of the serial numbers found on the fragments were sequential. That tied the two incidents together and gave our agency more than a passing interest." Lubin stopped long enough to take stock of Goldman's reaction. There was nothing overt, but he sensed that his boss may not have been aware of the degree of connection.

"All right. Go on," Goldman commanded.

"Within a few hours of the abduction, Sam was contacted outside official channels and asked to go to Egypt to see if he could lend a hand in facilitating a rescue."

"Who initiated this action?"

"Former Ambassador James Cannon. He is now the leader of the Mormon Church."

"And why would they call on Mr. Ryker?" Goldman asked. "Weren't they satisfied with the efforts of the Egyptian authorities or the American embassy?"

"Would you sit back and leave the fate of members of your faith in hands that were more concerned with how a rescue operation might look to the press and in the opinion polls of the world, or would you act and deal with the consequences later?" Ryker asked.

"That's a loaded question, and you know it."

"It's true, those missionaries were of my faith, but I would have gone if they had been Catholic, Protestant, Muslim, or Jew. It was the right thing to do, and you know it." Ryker forgot who he was speaking to for a minute and followed up with an apologetic, "sir," after he had finished.

When Goldman refused to respond, Ryker proceeded to explain further, this time with more control and respect for the situation he was currently in. "I guess Cannon figured that not enough was being done to find the missionaries and feared the worst if efforts weren't stepped up. Anyway, he enlisted my support and sent me to confer with Egyptian authorities, specifically with the chief inspector of the Egyptian police, the son of Egypt's former foreign minister. Cannon and Faud have been friends going back to World War II, and Faud arranged a contact for me."

Goldman turned to Lubin. "So where do you fit into all this?"

"Once Sam knew that he'd be going to Egypt but without any legitimate standing—he is retired, after all—he contacted me for anything that would help him know where to begin once he arrived. Our friendship goes back almost as far as yours and mine, Levi, so I decided to *personally* lend a hand. As I indicated, Israel has a stake in this."

"Don't give me *that!*" Goldman roared. "Even if there *is* a strong connection, as you say, you still had no right to freelance an operation. Why didn't you come to me with the facts? I'd have likely given a green light to some *official* involvement on our part."

"I'm sure you would have, but by the time you'd have run it up the chain of command and waited for it to come back down, the missionaries would have been in their graves. And you know I'm right."

The traffic was unusually heavy for that time of night, due primarily to the crowds of visitors who didn't want to waste time sleeping during their once-in-a-lifetime trip to the Holy City. It would've been almost quicker to walk to their destination since the vehicles persevered at a snail's pace.

"All right . . . maybe that's true. Continue," Goldman ordered.

"Sam and I hooked up with Hasan, the chief inspector and a decent human being, I might add."

"Forget the testimonial; just tell me what happened," Goldman snapped.

"The Egyptian authorities were tipped off that a member of *Al-Jum'ah* had crossed the southern border. They had been loud in their protest of American missionaries since they had arrived, and it was believed that they were somehow connected to their abduction. It turned out he was double-crossed and survived an attack directed toward us, but only gave up minimal information we could use. *Al-Jum'ah* was involved, but we don't think they were necessarily behind it. It's complicated, and I will make sure to detail our thoughts and consensus in my report, but to make a long story somewhat shorter, we intercepted them in the desert between Abu Simbel and the Sudan border and effected a rescue."

Lubin hesitated in telling him the next part. "Levi, it appears that the abduction was planned and executed by the phantom terrorist, *Al-Har'ba.*"

Goldman bowed his head and rubbed his temples. "Who?"

"For the past few years Sam has been formulating a theory concerning a rogue, nearly undetectable terrorist he's dubbed 'the Chameleon.' The Chameleon, he claims, was behind several of the world's most heinous acts of terror, but he's had little evidence to support it."

"My family was killed because I got too close," Ryker added.

"But with what has happened over the past couple of days, I am convinced that the Chameleon is not only real, but that he has entered Israel and plans to strike again. However, by the time we discovered this, we were too late to apprehend him. I'll put it all in a report—in minute detail."

"You *bet* you will! In *triplicate!* Now what about *Al-Har'ba*? This spirit has taken on a shape, has he?"

"As dark as night," Lubin said.

"What's *his* stake in this? I mean besides the money he was probably paid." The tenor of Goldman's voice was a notch mellower.

Ryker jumped in. "I don't think he was paid *anything* for the Wailing Wall bombing. That was personal. It was his sole intention to kill me *and* my family in that explosion. The fact that other people were killed as well helped turn the incident into just another terrorist attack, which he hoped would cover his tracks. I think he knew that I was amassing too much information on him, and he wanted me silenced before that information led to his identity. The Aswan incident was something entirely different. He was the brains behind it, all right, but the motivation was what it has generally always been for him: money."

"Are you suggesting it's only coincidental that Mormons were involved in both incidents? First you and your family, then the missionaries?" Goldman asked.

"I'm not much for coincidences, either, but this time I think that the incidents are only connected by the perpetrator—not by the victims," Ryker responded.

"Maybe so. Still, in our profession, one must consider all angles. Please continue," Goldman said.

Ryker and Lubin took the next few minutes recounting the events of the past two days, beginning with the rescue, the disappearance of Saiif in Cairo, the investigation of Abdul Badri and the attack on Heikel and Deborah. Little was left out as they detailed the findings of the American National Security Agency and the subsequent raid on Salahdin Investments and Saiif Khalil. Ryker produced a mini-cassette tape and handed it to Goldman.

"This is a copy of the phone call we received just before the place went up in smoke. He's real, sir, and I am sure you will agree once you listen to it that he plans to strike, and soon, in Israel."

Lubin watched Goldman's expression as Ryker delivered the tape Hasan had made for them and recapped the day's activities and their conclusions. It was obvious to him that Goldman already knew about the *Al-Har'ba* investigation and its results. Of course, the Mossad was likely to have assets within the Egyptian National Police or at least close enough to obtain reports and gather information.

"Any idea how he plans to enter the country?" Goldman asked. "The Egyptian and American embassies here, within the last couple of hours, have made official requests to help find this man. As a result, we've increased surveillance at airports, docks, and highways entering the country, but something tells me that he won't look anything like the composite picture that was provided."

Ryker confirmed. "I think you're right. He's likely to get past entry surveillance, no matter what."

"So where does that leave us?" asked Goldman.

"I think the American expression is 'up a creek without a paddle,'" Lubin replied. "But he couldn't have brought much with him on the train, and our points of entry would have sniffed out anything suspicious, which means he has help on this side of the line. Ryker's file assumes that he has networks all over the Middle East. He's bound to have one in Israel, given the Palestinian and Syrian problems. We've got to lean on our informants, Levi. All of them. Somebody knows *something*, even if they don't think they do."

"Obviously," Goldman said, a hint of annoyance and frustration in his voice. "But where do we concentrate our efforts? Israel is a small enough country, but with the influx of Christian tourists to celebrate Easter and even larger numbers involved with Passover, where do we start? Is blowing up a crowded bus going to satisfy him, or is Mr. Ryker correct: has he set his sights on something higher? And where? Jerusalem? Haifa? Tel Aviv? Or *all* of the above?"

One of Goldman's aides looked out the heavily tinted side windows. They were the variety that allowed passengers to see outside while remaining invisible to passersby.

"We're here, sir," the aide informed Goldman.

Goldman looked over and nodded. The vehicle slowed and turned off the street into a parking area beneath a five-story apartment building. A second vehicle turned in and took a position just in front of Goldman's limousine. The remaining car stopped near the entrance to the parking structure. A man in each emerged and stood at the ready with a shoulder-slung Uzi.

"You two get some rest . . . apartment 1-B," Goldman said, extracting a key from his inside coat pocket. He flipped it to Lubin. "A car will be sent for you tomorrow morning at six. And, Manni, don't think that you're out of the woods on your recent exploits. As for you, Mr. Ryker, I haven't decided what your status, *if any*, is going to be in all this. In the meantime, I'll hold on to your hardware." Goldman patted the coat pocket containing the Glock.

The chauffeur came around to the rear door, opened it, and stood silently as the two men exited. Lubin looked back inside as if to say something but thought better of it.

"Remember . . . six o'clock," Goldman said. "Oh, and by the way, Manni, I spoke to your wife. She thinks you're still on assignment in Gaza and that you won't be home for a while longer. Esther's a very gracious and understanding woman. I've always wondered what she saw in you." Goldman smiled for the first time that evening.

The chauffeur closed the door and resumed his position up front. All three vehicles disappeared into the damp night, leaving the duo to ponder the future.

The first-floor apartment was one of several throughout Jerusalem designated as a safe house by Mossad. Used primarily as locations to interview informants or as temporary residences for agents in transit, their accommodations were adequate but spartan. 1-B was a little better than most. It contained two bedrooms with a shared bath wedged between and a larger room comprising the kitchen, dining, and living areas. The refrigerator was stocked with a variety of fresh foods, and the freezer section offered a selection of microwave meals. An assortment of clothing in various sizes hung in the closets.

It was close to midnight by the time the men emerged from lingering hot showers and fixed a snack. Their bodies screamed for bed, but their minds were still racing. They sat at the two-stool breakfast bar and ate their hastily prepared sandwiches.

"You know, Sam, Levi is right. Finding the Chameleon before he attacks is a million to one. He's eluded capture for what . . . at least twenty years? Now it all comes down to a couple of days. Sure, we're going to go through the motions, but what chance do we *really* have of snagging him before he strikes again? Remember, he's not someone who makes mistakes."

"That's just it," Ryker countered. "He *is* making mistakes. He planned the missionary abduction but was careless about the plan's execution, and one of them was inadvertently killed. He led us to Abu Simbel and then twice missed us. He got hurt and narrowly escaped our snare at the airport. And then there was that phone call. He didn't have to make it. He could have just detonated the charge and killed us once and for all. But his pride wouldn't let him. It's like he *wants* us to find him. We now have a face to go with this name. No. Manni, he's been making one mistake after another."

"Perhaps, but it just doesn't make sense. After all these years of executing flawless crimes, why would he start making mistakes? Why now?"

"That's just it. There is no perfect crime. I'd be willing to bet that he's made these kinds of mistakes before, but no one has been on his tail until now. He's had the element of mystery to protect him. But now that we have a clear picture of him, it's only a matter of time before he's finished. And maybe there's more to it. Maybe after all these years of living in the shadows, he's coming apart psychologically. As strange as it may sound, subconsciously, maybe he wants to be stopped."

"I don't know. I guess it's possible. It wouldn't be the first time that a killer has gone over the edge. Still . . . we'd be foolish to think that he's just going to walk in off the street and give himself up."

"Oh, I agree. He has every intention of going through with whatever he has planned. And who knows how long he's been working on it? Maybe it's an operation he put together when he was thinking much clearer. But right now I know that *I'm* not thinking too clearly. My head's pounding. I'm going to take a couple of aspirin and get some sleep. Who knows? Maybe things will look a little brighter tomorrow." Ryker slid off his seat and walked to the bathroom medicine cabinet.

"Oh, I almost forgot," he said returning to his stool. "Back in Goldman's car, he mentioned that you'd been called on the carpet, so to speak, about an incident involving me, something in 1983. What was he talking about?"

"Oh, that . . . well . . . I broke one of the cardinal rules of Mossad. I let myself get *personally* involved in a matter after my superiors had ordered me not to."

"And it concerned me?"

"Actually, yes. The terrorist bombing of the American embassy in Beirut. The one that killed nearly everyone attending—ironically—an anti-terrorism seminar."

"But I wasn't there."

"I know, but you *would* have been if I hadn't pulled strings to get you detained at airport customs."

"You did *what*?"

"I had information about a possible embassy attack. At the time, my people didn't think that the information was substantial enough to merit alerting American authorities. I was told that my responsibility ended with telling my superiors and that under no circumstances was I to pass the information to any American contacts I might have."

"I see," Ryker said.

"So I didn't tell anyone, as I was instructed, but I knew that you were scheduled to attend that seminar. I just couldn't take the chance that my information was correct, so I bribed a Lebanese customs official to have you detained. As it turned out, my information was good. I'm not sure how my people found out about what I'd done, but they did. They took me out of action for a long time. Said I was a security risk. Eventually, through Levi's intercession, all was forgiven, and I was reinstated as a field agent."

"All those people dead because the Mossad wouldn't act on your information?" Ryker was incredulous. The incident at the American embassy in Beirut had been one of the worst in Agency history.

"Hindsight is twenty-twenty, Sam. I don't think my people would've purposely let that happen, but it *did* happen. If I *had* contacted the embassy, maybe they wouldn't have believed me, either. Anyway, I've lived with those deaths on my conscience ever since."

"It's a rough business we're in, my friend," Ryker said, reaching over and touching Lubin's arm. "A *very* rough business."

TWENTY-THREE

THE MORNING CAME AWFULLY EARLY. Ryker and Lubin showered, shaved, and chose a fresh wardrobe—something identifying them as more than tourists but less than corporate executives. The texture of the microwave waffles was reminiscent of cardboard, but with ample maple syrup and washed down with a glass of orange juice, they were palatable. Lubin set the dishes in the sink along with the remnant plates and utensils from the previous night. He indicated that Mossad's "maid service" would take care of household duties while they were away.

A little after six, there was a knock at the door. Lubin tiptoed to the Judas hole and saw the face of an agent he recognized. Levi was smart to send someone whom Lubin would know. The stakes of the game were risky enough without deliberately adding suspense. Lubin opened the door.

"Ready?" the agent asked without stepping into the room.

"Yeah, just let us get our coats," Lubin replied as he walked to the back of the couch and retrieved two zippered jackets. As Ryker made his way to the door, Lubin tossed him one. He flipped off the light switch and closed the door behind them. They followed the agent to the parking structure where an unmarked car was idling, a woman sitting behind the steering wheel. The escort slid into the front passenger seat, and they climbed in back. The car emerged slowly from the parking area and turned toward the center of town.

There was normal banter among the passengers but nothing directly related to the issue at hand. Compartmentalization was so ingrained within the intelligence community that neither Lubin nor Ryker could be certain whether the two agents in the front seat knew anything about the Chameleon or his plans. So they just sat back and endured the ride. Traffic was heavy.

Mossad headquarters is in Tel Aviv along with other agencies of the Israeli government. *Officially,* Mossad doesn't exist, like America's largest intelligence gathering organization, the National Security Agency, but knowledge of Israel's elite force has been the subject of reports, books, and even movies since its inception during the early days of statehood. It is the smallest—though most savvy—intelligence agency in the world, thanks to its dedicated employees and its extraordinary use of *unofficial* resources. Goldman had elected to set up camp at the branch office in Jerusalem. The drab, concrete, single-story building didn't particularly draw attention to itself other than the fact that anything of recent design in a city millennia old tends to look a trifle out of place. It was also closest to the majority of the religious sites in Israel.

The car was driven around back, reclaiming its appointed stall amid the covered parking area. It was while exiting the backseat that Ryker noticed the extensive camera surveillance of the building. He suspected that the cameras were backup to an unobtrusive human element. His time at Langley had been spent having his security badge scrutinized at virtually every opportunity by men and women whose sole functions had been to ensure that access to anything of consequence was severely limited. Had this been the CIA compound in Virginia, driving up and parking next to a building without a load of security checks would've been unthinkable. Yet in a country where terrorism was commonplace, the level of security appeared very low. He'd once been told that Israel simply refused to be intimidated by those whose political grievances culminated in violence. Responding otherwise would've thrown the citizenry into perpetual panic.

They were ushered into the building and taken to an executive office suite nicely appointed in exotic wood. No one was seated behind the huge desk when they entered. The young agent who'd picked them up at the apartment didn't linger after opening the door for them.

Levi Goldman, dressed in a short-sleeved, military-cut khaki shirt and trousers, was seated at a small grouping of casual furniture and rose to shake hands. The tattooed forearm spoke volumes to Ryker and put Goldman's life instantly into perspective. The Mossad chief bade the men to take seats around the coffee table. Facing him, a manila file was spread open on a coffee table. From their angle, neither he nor Lubin could ascertain the contents.

Goldman spoke. "I've just been going over your file, Mr. Ryker."

"*My* file?" Ryker asked somewhat incredulously.

"Yes, certainly. There are gentlemen's agreements about not spying on one's allies, but nothing precludes either side from getting to know their friends better. In case you're thinking that your friend, here," he nodded toward Lubin, "contributed information to this file, I can assure you that he did *not*. I never asked him to and he, undoubtedly, would've refused. I am envious of whatever bond exists between you two."

Ryker looked over to Lubin, who sat expressionless, trying to divine where the conversation was headed.

"Your credentials are impressive," Goldman continued, "though it's been a long time since you were active in field work. That was obvious when you were nearly killed trying to rescue those missionaries. You were a lucky man, Mr. Ryker. Had the man's aim been an inch in either direction, we wouldn't be having this chat now."

Lubin nodded, almost imperceptibly, but Goldman caught it.

"And *you* didn't fare much better. From what I understand, if the American woman hadn't fired when she did, your bones would be bleaching in the Egyptian desert."

Lubin sat without speaking but wondered where Goldman had gotten his information, since he hadn't filed any reports detailing the events leading to the missionaries' rescue.

"Both of you are out of shape and out of practice for this kind of work. Field operations are games for young men to play. The minds of old men make commitments that their bodies can't keep. *I*, however, understand that. You don't see *me* running around the desert with an Uzi slung over my shoulder, trying to single-handedly bring justice to the world. You two apparently don't admit to those limitations."

The two aging intelligence officers wanted to defend themselves against Goldman's barbs but figured that discretion was *indeed* the better part of valor.

Goldman continued. "I can't afford to get good men killed because they're having to look over their shoulders to see if you two are keeping up. Therefore, you won't be teamed with younger agents. You'll be your own team."

"You mean we're *in*, Levi?" Lubin asked.

"Yes. Against my better judgment, I'm going to let you try to finish what you've started. But don't get me wrong, Manni, all is not forgiven. You were way out of line on this thing. However, stopping the Chameleon before he strikes again may substantially mitigate the consequences."

"Thank you, sir. You won't be sorry," Lubin offered.

"I already *am*," Goldman replied with a half grin. His attention turned to Ryker. "As for you, Mr. Ryker, I have other reasons for letting you continue in this case. As a younger man, I went to the ends of the earth to find the Nazis responsible for the extermination of my family in the furnaces of Auschwitz. History bears out that I was reasonably successful in that endeavor. I've tried to convince myself since that I was acting for the common good, but I suspect that I was driven primarily by hatred and revenge—emotions which never ennoble the human spirit." He paused a moment, then said, "I'm starting to sound like a rabbi, and I don't mean to, but learn from my own experience. It is possible that this one man is responsible for killing your wife and children and that you want him dead in return. I understand this." He touched the faded numbers tattooed on his wrist and forearm. "This won't bring them back, but it sometimes helps ease the pain a little. But even if you do find him and mete out the justice he deserves, don't expect closure. It will still hurt. Only directing your life onward will do that."

Ryker didn't know what to say but felt as though Goldman were talking to his soul rather than directly to *him*.

"Israel became a state in 1948. Since then, thousands of Israelis have died as a result of terrorist violence. It has angered us to the point of exhaustion, yet Israel has no death penalty for these crimes. Our national conscience has progressed that far. Only Nazi war criminals are subject to capital punishment, and I'm not sure, more than fifty years later, if even *that* carries the meaning it's supposed to."

"Sir, I don't follow," Ryker finally said.

"What I'm saying is apprehend the Chameleon if you can. Bring him to justice. But you're *not* to be his judge, jury, and executioner. I want us to be clear on this before we proceed further. *Are* we clear?"

"Yes, sir."

"Good," Goldman said as he rose and walked to the desk. He opened the top left-hand drawer and extracted the Glock and clips of ammunition. "Nevertheless, you'll more than likely need these." He handed them to Ryker, who put the pistol in his waistband and extra ammunition into the pocket of his jacket.

Goldman then looked at Lubin.

"Take what you need from the armory down the hall, and make sure they give you a cell phone. Mr. Ryker's name and reason for accompanying you is need-to-know only. There is no *official* story as he was listed killed in action last July, but when an explanation is required, you will convey that he's a consultant and on contract. Understood? Be back here in twenty minutes for a complete briefing, and come with some ideas. By my count, we've got a little less than three days to discover and put a halt to the plans of *Al-Har'ba*."

They stood. Lubin moved toward the door to leave. Ryker offered his hand to Goldman.

"Thank you, sir," he said. He wanted to say more but sensed that Goldman already understood the effects of their conversation.

Goldman nodded, released his grasp, bent to pick up the file, and walked back to the desk. Lubin held the door open for Ryker as both of them exited.

* * *

Michael Rodriguez stepped from the small Egyptian steamer. His genuine rattlesnake-skin cowboy boots made a pronounced clip-thump, clip-thump on the wooden walkway joining the luxury passenger ship to the docks of Haifa, announcing to other passengers standing in customs lines that the overweight Southern Baptist, Texas Ranger from the Lone Star State had finally arrived in the Holy Land. Holding his head proudly, like his mama had taught him to, he surveyed the area. The anticipatory smile so common among tourists, and half-hidden beneath his bushy mustache, faded as he saw the long, slow-moving lines already formed behind several customs tables. Behind them, three customs officers or Israeli police—he couldn't be certain which—periodically glanced nonchalantly from a sheet of paper and then to the forming lines. Only a trained eye would know that they were searching the crowd for someone. In this instance, trying desperately to match a face to the computerized photo clutched in their hands.

He chose what looked to be the shortest line, one he hoped would file through the quickest. Being thoroughly checked and inconvenienced by customs was a recent phenomenon that had come about as a result of an escalation of tension between Israel and the Palestinian Authority.

He found himself sandwiched between a harried mother trying to control two cranky children and a young couple honeymooning on the Mediterranean. Not five minutes into his wait, the older of the mother's two children, named James Patrick, apparently—his mother emphasizing the middle name Patrick as she yelled at him to stand still and behave—spun around in a frantic attempt to distance himself from his annoying little sister. In doing so, the boy jostled him, causing him to drop his small suitcase and garment bag. The boy was thrown off balance and would've fallen had he not reached out and steadied him.

"Whoa, partner!"

"James *Patrick!* You get over here and away from the nice man. *Now,* mister!"

Michael released his grip and sent the boy to his mother.

"Sorry, sir." Holding the boy's sister in one arm, the mother made a motion to pick up the fallen luggage, but the Texan objected.

"No, ma'am. I'll get my own cases. Wouldn't dream of havin' a young thing with her arms full of such a beautiful child bendin' over to pick these up."

"Thank you. You really don't have to do that. And I do apologize for Jimmy's behavior. He never behaves this way when his father's around."

"No harm done. The boy was just playin'."

"You're too kind, sir."

"Mike."

"Pardon?"

"Mike. Mike Rodriguez, and I'm pleased to make your acquaintance, Missus . . . ?"

"Hanks. Audrey Hanks."

And a promising friendship began. They talked for the forty-five minutes they were in line together. It turned out that the woman's grandfather had been born and raised in Fort Worth, about fifty miles south of where Rodriguez said he was from. She'd spent summers growing up there and was so excited reliving old memories that she thought nothing of the fact that he seemed to be unfamiliar with the local landmarks of the area. She indicated that she was visiting her husband who was working construction, building a new high-rise along the coast in Haifa. She hadn't seen her husband in almost a year and couldn't wait to spend the week with him, seeing the sights and traveling to Jerusalem to attend sunrise services on Easter morning.

"Well, I'll be!" he exclaimed. "That's where I'm goin', too. Been plannin' this trip for a good long while."

The woman, with children in tow, said good-bye to her new friend as she passed through customs and was gone. It was finally his turn.

"Passport, please," the overworked customs officer requested.

The document was in order, and the exit stamp from Egypt appeared valid though a bit smudged.

"The purpose for your visit to Israel?"

"Whacha mean? Why I'm here? Well, all my life I've wanted to see the Holy—"

"No, Mr. Rodriguez. Is your purpose for business or for pleasure?" He rubbed his temples as if to massage away a headache, muttering under his breath in Hebrew that difficult people always chose his line to stand in.

"Oh! Excuse me. How silly to think you'd want to hear my life story. Pleasure. Purely pleasure."

The officer asked the series of rote questions while another clerk took the man's passport and scanned it over a photocopying machine, making a few notes in the upper right-hand corner of the copy. Afterward, the passport was stamped and returned to the loud Texan.

"Enjoy your stay, Mr. Rodriguez. *Shalom.*"

"*Sha*-what? Well, same to you. See y'all later."

Rodriguez picked up his belongings. He'd cleared the customs desk with only a cursory glance from the men surveying the crowd. It was now time to *really* turn on the Southern charm.

He swaggered over to a group of three men obviously standing watch by the rental car desk. One man was taller than the others and overweight; another had longish hair and a five-o'clock shadow—even at seven in the morning. The third had a military air with a cropped haircut but was dressed in a civilian suit. A mustache and a few pounds were the only physical differences between the faxed composite picture they held and the man approaching them, but the threesome weren't looking for an arrogant Texan, his head held high, and his stride making the unmistakable sound only boot heels could; they were looking for a disguised Arab. The man walking toward them portrayed himself to be a cocky Mexican-American, a Southerner, and that was exactly what these men saw. But merely walking by them was too easy and scarcely made his pulse quicken. Besides, he wanted to have a little fun.

"Pardon me, gentlemen. I was wonderin' if any of you could point me in the direction of the Hertz Rent-a-Car place? I have reservations for the biggest American car y'all have in this tiny country."

One of them looked away and then shot a glance back to the American and simply threw his thumb over his shoulder toward the terminal behind them.

"Much obliged, and thank you."

The other two muttered something and chuckled, watching the American stroll over to the rental counter and speak in the same polite but overbearing voice to the cute little brunette who unconsciously used her computer monitor as a buffer zone.

He casually looked back at the policemen still searching for a man who had not only sneaked past them but had also engaged them in conversation. He was good. No, he was the best.

The lady handed him the keys to his rented Lincoln Continental, relieved almost to tears to have him on his way and far from the counter.

That was at eight-thirty in the morning, and by nine-forty, Rodriguez, alias Saiif Khalil, alias *Al-Har'ba*, was leisurely driving down the coast from Haifa to Tel Aviv, enjoying the rich blue of the Mediterranean, the rear suspension of the Lincoln easily supporting the heavy cargo just loaded into the trunk.

* * *

There was no doubt about who was in charge at the standing-room-only briefing that was anything but brief. Those in attendance included representatives from all Israeli intelligence services as well as selected military officials. They gave the distinct impression that they'd been here and done this before. Goldman gave a masterful performance as conductor of the group, though at times, there was an air of raucousness to the proceedings.

Though it was not an official joint operation, Ryker had hoped that Goldman would have solicited help from other experts in the local intelligence community. CIA representation at the meeting was conspicuous by its absence as was that of any Egyptian authorities from their embassy. It was clear that tracking the Chameleon and subverting any plans he might have was going to be primarily an Israeli operation despite the fact that the initial alert had come from the Americans and Egyptians. They weren't totally out of the picture, but any involvement of embassy personnel was being limited to aiding Israeli authorities in screening aircraft and ship arrivals and checking main thoroughfares into the country. Goldman indicated that this surveillance had been going on since the previous night, but as of yet, this phase of the operation had drawn a blank. No one matching the Chameleon's description had been confronted.

Ryker was shocked with what was presented next. All these years he had thought he was alone in his belief in a terrorist mastermind. Mossad's file on the illusive *Al-Har'ba* was summoned from a computer and projected onto a large screen in the semi-darkened room. It was even more complete than what Ryker had been able to develop in Cairo. Considering that the rest of the world intelligence community scoffed at the existence of *Al-Har'ba*, Mossad showed once again that it was way ahead of the competition.

Ryker leaned over to Lubin and whispered, "Where did they get all this?"

"You mentioned your theory a few years ago, and I noted it in my report. I knew they had started following up on your claims, but I had no idea it had grown this big."

The information was dissected and scrutinized. The thoroughness shown by Israeli authorities in gathering bits of seemingly unrelated information and collating them into something useful was impressive. Mossad's processes of analysis appeared significantly more advanced than those employed by Langley. Maybe that was another reason why the Agency hadn't been invited to this party, Ryker surmised. Professional jealousy always reigned supreme in the intelligence game.

The gathering was much more disciplined than similar groups encountered within the CIA. Ryker chalked up the difference to the fact that the Israelis had had more practice in confronting terrorism. Nevertheless, there was still a tendency for those present to ride off in all directions; thus, Goldman's role was crucial to bring forth order from potential chaos.

Amid heated discussion, certain considerations, assumptions, and directions emerged. Goldman made it clear that the primary focus of the operation was to stop a terrorist incident from occurring. If the Chameleon could be apprehended in the process, well and good, but common sense dictated that public safety outweighed the capture of one individual. However, if he remained at large, regardless of how the current incident turned out, he'd be the subsequent focus of attention by all Israeli intelligence and military services until he was *permanently* eliminated as a threat.

Identifying possible locations that the Chameleon might strike was next on the agenda. If he was planning to inflict massive damage in conjunction with upcoming religious events, as Lubin and Ryker strenuously argued, then Tel Aviv and Jerusalem would offer the most appeal. If Jews were being targeted, virtually every synagogue would be holding services in commemoration of Passover. There would also be religious gatherings at selected Jewish historical locations. Easter celebrations would be confined primarily to the New Testament environs of Jerusalem, especially the Garden of Gethsemane and the location generally accepted by Christians as the site of the crucifixion. It was agreed that these would have to receive priority attention. Military officials were directed to confer with customs authorities and to have as many explosive-sniffing dogs as possible brought to Tel Aviv and Jerusalem. The dogs and their handlers would be working overtime.

Goldman pressed that the Chameleon wasn't going to be thinking in terms of anti-tank mines like he'd used at the Wailing Wall and in Aswan. True, a well-placed explosive device of any size, triggered at the appropriate time, would inflict substantial damage, but he agreed with Ryker that the Chameleon wouldn't be satisfied with just another terrorist incident. He was planning something to cap his infamous career. Therefore, he would use large quantities of explosives. Somehow, Saiif would have to transport and hide them until ready for use. Additionally, these explosives had to come from somewhere. There were quantities of demolition ordnance—like the Semtex made in the former Czechoslovakia or even C-4 stolen from NATO forces—on the black market, but the amount in question had to leave a trail. If that trail could be found, maybe the means of fabricating a bomb could be derived.

The senior military officer in the room, a tall, hard-looking man of maybe forty-five, who gave the impression that he took no prisoners, asserted his recommendation.

"If you're accurate about the quantities of explosive material, then I suggest we blockade all highways entering and exiting the cities in question. Every means of conveyance should be searched."

This idea was seconded by several others but overruled by Goldman.

"I'm sorry, but the ranking members of the Knesset have already vetoed that approach. An emergency session was called late last night where I made that suggestion myself."

"What was their reasoning?" the general persisted.

"They recognized the seriousness of the situation but feared the disruption caused by widespread roadblocks."

"*Disruption*? What do they think is going to happen if *Al-Har'ba* is successful? *Disruption*? I can't believe it! Couldn't the prime minister sway them?" asked the animated officer.

"The prime minister sided with them, reasoning that he didn't want to give the impression that Israel was being held hostage by one man and was having to resort to a lockdown of the country to deal with the situation."

"This is *insane*! The man was elected on promises of taking tougher stances on terrorism than Shimon Peres. What are we to conclude? Politics as usual? Perhaps he would like us to fight with our hands tied behind our backs."

Others were vocal in siding with the general. To quell the outbursts, Goldman raised his voice a few decibels and called the group back to order.

"I believe we've had this discussion before, General. Your position is that Israel will never be safe as long as even one of its enemies is left alive." Goldman smiled, giving note to those in the room that he was embarking on logic designed to bring the group back together.

The general replied, "That's a little strong, maybe, but the gist of it."

"Would that apply only to Arabs or would our detractors from the Western world be included? Maybe we should throw in all Israeli dissidents, too, as long as we're going to do it right."

"Now that's not fair," the senior officer protested.

"*What's* not fair? You think that we should have the right to walk the streets unmolested by criminal intentions. So do I. It's just that I'm not willing to promote a police state to achieve it. It was relatively safe for the general citizenry to walk the streets of Moscow for seventy years. Nazi Berlin must have been a shining example to the world of what could be done to establish *order.*"

"Levi, that's *really* unfair. All I'm suggesting is that we redraw some of the lines. The average Israeli wouldn't object to a little more structure."

"That's what worries me, General. We'd been under bondage to Pharaoh for four hundred years when Moses led us to freedom. But when being free became difficult, there were those who petitioned Moses to return to Egypt's *structure.*"

"But—"

"No, let me finish," Goldman interrupted. "Granted, a democracy may not be the most efficient form of government, but it's probably better than any alternative. We can't redraw the lines. It's probably bad enough that we color outside them as often as we do."

"You win, Levi," the general relented, "but Netanyahu—"

"Look . . . trashing the prime minister isn't going to solve the problem at hand. Let's refocus. While blockades are out, he did authorize a liberal use of *administrative detention.*"

World public opinion, and especially the United Nations Security Council, had consistently condemned Israel for routinely invoking this practice where individuals' rights to due process could be suspended indefinitely. There wasn't any question that the practice had been abused, but given the circumstances, the idea of "rounding up the usual suspects" didn't seem like such a bad idea. Besides, there was always the chance that a nationwide dragnet would turn up someone with viable information. This announcement seemed to appease the gathering, and the noise level diminished.

One point they all agreed upon was that the Chameleon couldn't undertake this operation alone. He was going to need help. Maybe only two or three trusted accomplices. Maybe a whole network. The more people involved, the better the chances that someone, somewhere, might let something slip. In

conjunction with administrative detention, Goldman stressed, every informant of record was to be leaned on and leaned on *hard*. Known leaders of
dissent were also to be shadowed as a precaution. They might not be actively
involved with the Chameleon, but their sympathies were clear.

After a short break in the proceedings, Goldman announced that Mossad's
psychological unit had developed a profile of *Al-Har'ba* and would make a brief
presentation. A bearded young man with wire-rimmed glasses took center
stage. He was casually dressed in blue jeans and a polo shirt. Growing perspira-
tion stains were evident under each arm. The noise died down.

"Let me preface my remarks by stating that the file information we've
been working from has been sketchy, at best, but it's our opinion that the
psychological profile of *Al-Har'ba* falls into a general category that has
surfaced time and again in other terrorists who have been captured and
interrogated extensively. We suspect that somewhere in his past is an
unhappy—probably abusive—childhood. He was raised most likely in
poverty by a single parent and was never fully accepted by his peers. He
always found himself on the outside looking in and lashed out at his plight.
He sidestepped any responsibility for his own behavior, always blaming
others. He has evolved a distorted view of the world."

"Wait a minute!" the general blurted. "Tell us something I can use. Half
the people in the neighborhood I grew up in fit the profile you're giving.
Come on! You've got to do better than this."

The young psychologist straightened and didn't retreat.

"General, there is a misconception about terrorists that needs to be
corrected. We do ourselves a disservice when we attempt to dehumanize
them. Your point that a lot of people fit this profile is well taken. Terrorists
aren't alien life-forms implanted from some distant world. Not only are they
indistinguishable from us; they *are* us. Prime Minister Rabin's assassin wasn't
one of *them*; he was one of *us*."

The general remained still as anger crept into his expression. "You've
made your point, but is there anything in *Al-Har'ba's* past or present that
will help us apprehend him?"

"On the contrary. This is a man who has lived in the shadows for his
entire adult life. I doubt that he's developed any real friends and certainly
none that know his true identity. He's probably a mystery even to his
networks. Reason demands that we assume his power and respect is based
on fear. He's a loner who only uses extremist groups to his advantage. He
may have had some political philosophy early in his career, but that has
likely evolved into a business, if you will, of orchestrating these acts for his

own purpose or gain. His deluded self-importance is driving him in this particular instance. We could be wrong, of course, but it's our opinion that whatever he's currently planning to do is of his own accord; that he's not in the employ of anyone. It's some personal gratification that he hopes to achieve. And that gratification is heightened by giving his pursuers a subtle advanced warning, as he did in Cairo."

"Could he have a death wish?" someone called out.

The psychologist thought for a moment. "If by that you mean that he may be purposely putting himself in harm's way to effect his own demise, I'd have to say no. The man has every intention of getting away with this. He wants to make a statement about *who* he is. Dying as a result puts a definite crimp in his logic."

"So what are you saying? That he's going to succeed in blowing up a city no matter what efforts we expend?" the general asked.

"If we were having this discussion even last year, I'd have said yes. But our team agrees with the assessment voiced by Mr. Ryker. For whatever reason, *Al-Har'ba* has shown poor judgment over the past week. Considering his alleged previous accomplishments—if they can be described as such—he just isn't using common sense. That *may* give you an opportunity, but my opinion is that if you do find him before he acts, it'll be by accident. Psychologically impaired or not, the man has tremendous survival instincts. The file is very clear about *that*."

The psychologist's conclusions weren't applauded, but they were universally understood.

The give-and-take dialogue continued.

The most offensive consideration was saved until last and would have been bypassed altogether had protocol not demanded it. Only vestiges of strained goodwill existed between the Israeli government and the Palestinian Authority, but it was reluctantly agreed that even they would condemn the prospective act of violence as detrimental to Middle Eastern stability.

When the discussion concluded, Goldman divided the labor. The drill was familiar, and protests were few. The briefing room was designated as the command center, and the various factions were instructed to report any information immediately. Telephones, radios, and computer terminals would be monitored around the clock.

As a parting comment to the group, Goldman said, "And remember . . . if we don't find him in time, it may be your friends or family who pay the consequences. Time is of the essence." It sounded trite, but it was true nonetheless.

In addition to utilizing Lubin's and Ryker's general expertise, the two were also assigned as liaisons to the Egyptian National Police. Goldman seemed to know that the Egyptian investigation into the recent activities of the Chameleon was continuing at breakneck speed and that the development of relevant information was likely. Ryker strongly suspected that Mossad had assets within the National Police but kept the thought to himself.

The meeting broke up shortly after two o'clock in the afternoon. Lubin drew a set of keys from the motor pool dispatcher, and he and Ryker drove around Jerusalem identifying possible targets and trying to get into the Chameleon's convoluted mind. One thing was obvious: there were crowds everywhere. If he were looking to run up a body count, he couldn't go wrong exploding a device anywhere in the Holy City, and Tel Aviv was only slightly less congested.

* * *

Before checking into the Palestinian hotel in downtown Tel Aviv, Saiif detoured to a site of rented storage units. They were flaked with white paint that had yellowed over the years. He pulled up in front of a faded aluminum overhead door, opened the padlock, and drove the luxury car inside. He locked the door from the inside and flipped on the double light switch for the windowless garage. It was swept clean, and his fancy boots echoed as he walked on the cement floor. A workbench and wooden stool stood along the east wall, and an old chest freezer topped with oily and soiled rags was tucked away in the back corner. A ceiling fan whirred to life, circulating the stale air. He walked to the workbench and sat down, the work space looking just as he'd left it over a year ago: mechanic and jeweler tools were organized next to spools of wire and duct tape; every type and size of battery lay next to voltage/amp measuring equipment; and a soldering gun sat upright next to coils of solder. Everything one could conceivably need to fashion a bomb was there—except for the explosives and detonators currently in the trunk of his rental car.

It took him nearly an hour to unload and stack the eighty blocks of C-4, stolen from NATO reserves in Germany. They were all stamped with United States Army Corps of Engineers, as were the special electric blasting caps. It was fitting that so many Americans were going to be killed by devices of their own making.

Before leaving the garage, he plugged the freezer into a wall socket. The motor ground for a moment, then started to hum. It wouldn't be long before the interior dropped to the required temperature. He drove the couple of blocks to his hotel in south Tel Aviv, showered, and rested for a few hours. He rose by an internal clock just as the sun touched the horizon in a splash of color.

He changed into loose-fitting, contemporary Arab clothing and drove southeast to a celebrated Palestinian restaurant adjacent to the Hassan Bek mosque in north Jaffa. The beautifully ornate clock tower standing defiantly in the middle of the intersection chimed as he parked his car behind the restaurant and entered through the back.

He'd reserved a table in the back and had asked that the surrounding tables be left empty that night. He also requested that the lights be dimmed so that this particular table was partially obscured by shadow. The amiable restaurant owner was paid in advance for any loss of income as a result of this arrangement and was simply told that someone important would be visiting that evening and wished to be relatively alone.

Saiif arrived and took his place at the back table and ordered an iced tea. He surveyed the establishment. It was decorated in dark green and cedar, and the atmosphere was very Middle Eastern, very serene. He'd just settled back to enjoy his drink when a drunken disagreement between two men escalated from an argument into a brawl. Like desert scavengers surrounding a dying animal, nearby patrons encircled them and cheered on the fight.

Saiif slammed his glass down and sprang from his chair to quell the disturbance. The last thing he needed tonight was a response by the police. But before he could clear the shadows, the little brass bell atop the entrance door jingled ever so softly, and two men in finely tailored suits stepped inside and intently scanned the room. Their gaze fell on the two combatants, and within seconds a hushed whisper spread through the crowd, the drunks freezing midswing. An uneasy silence, thick with fear and religious respect, captivated the room as the two men escorted a frail old man dressed in traditional Arab robes to Saiif's table.

The old man steadied himself on the arm of one of the men escorting him, and with a whisper, the two bodyguards excused themselves and took seats two tables away, ever alert. The man's aura of power impressed Saiif.

"Farouq, my friend," Saiif said, reaching out and gently holding the elder's hand. "It is good to see you after all these years. Allah be praised for keeping you in good health."

The old man returned Saiif's grip with a surprising show of strength.

"Allah smiles from His courts on high at our reunion." The old man smiled, showing black gaps where teeth had once been, but the smile was

warm and genuine. "I have taken pride in your work since you left my tute-
lage in Libya and Syria. Your actions have spoken loudly. You were, and are,
the kind of student every teacher wishes to instruct."

"A student is only as good as his master."

But they both knew that to be false in this case. Saiif had surpassed
Farouq's expertise shortly after leaving his company in the mid-eighties. Saiif
had sought out Farouq and had learned all he could from him, just as he'd
done a few years earlier with another old man in *Hezbollah*. In time, Farouq
had risen to lead a splinter of the Muslim Brotherhood known throughout
the world by its acronym, HAMAS, the *Harakat al-Muqawama al-Islamiyya*,
or "Islamic Resistance Movement." His religious fervor and articulate
condemnation of Israel quickly made him a man not to be questioned or
reckoned with. His authority and influence put him in a position to aid
Saiif over the years with supplies of arms and explosives when they were
needed on short notice. Sheikh Farouq Abdallah was not a man to be
slighted.

"My esteemed and blessed friend," Saiif said, "word has reached
throughout the world of the power you wield as a Holy Man, but to stop a
heated argument with a glance . . . The reports fail to give you the credit
you deserve."

"I speak the word of Allah and of the Prophet. To praise me is to praise
the Almighty. If I am His mouthpiece, Allah be praised, I am indeed a lucky
old man." The old man wheezed as he chuckled. "But this is not why you
have summoned me this evening, to talk about old times. Your message was
clear, and everything you require shall be provided."

With a nod of his head, one of the Sheikh's escorts approached the table
and placed a medium-sized leather gun case before Saiif.

The sheikh continued. "There is a garage behind the Cedars of
Lebanon Cafe in the Muslim Quarter. Do you know this place?"

Saiif nodded that he did.

"What you asked for is waiting for you in ample supply. The proprietor
will assist you in loading the material. He is a good and loyal man and will
serve you without question."

Saiif cracked open the case and smiled at the contents: a Makarov nine-
millimeter, his pistol of choice, and a Scorpion submachine gun with extra
magazines of ammunition.

"As promised," Saiif said, "funds have been wired to your Lebanese bank
account."

The old man raised his hand and summoned his bodyguards.

"With that, my enigmatic friend, I bid you farewell." He struggled to his feet. "But what you have requested forces me to question your motives. Is this the will of Allah or the inspiration of the Evil One? In any event, do not contact us again." He turned without uttering another word.

The Evil One? Saiif had never been condemned before, and it was to this that he attributed the eruption of rage that filled him. He felt cold and his stomach knotted.

Farouq and his men moved slowly through the restaurant and exited. Saiif grabbed the case and stormed out the back door, slamming it closed in the process.

He got behind the wheel of the Lincoln and was suddenly repulsed by what it stood for: American decadence. And then a revelation struck him. It was no longer safe to drive this car. Ryker had tracked him down in Cairo, and, he admitted to himself, it might only be hours before Saiif Khalil would be linked to Michael Rodriguez. Ryker had been lucky so far but, in truth, wasn't a worthy opponent. *Why not taunt him a little?* From his pocket he produced a ballpoint pen and the forged American passport and scribbled a short note on one of the blank pages. He'd gotten all the use out of the car and the identity that he could've hoped for. It was time to abandon them both. Leaving the passport in the glove box, he locked the car and walked two blocks to where he hailed a taxi.

* * *

The afternoon and evening had been thoroughly unproductive. In fact, Ryker would've called it a failure. Though everyone at the briefing now had some idea of who they were looking for and the extensive damage he was capable of, it didn't change the fact that they had absolutely no leads to follow up on. Several teams were sent to "inquire" of Palestinian and other Arab fundamentalist groups known for instilling and inspiring terror, while others, like he and Lubin, combed the streets in hopes of unearthing some clue, some lead from which to start.

But nothing was uncovered. Usually reliable informants for the Mossad swore that they knew nothing of any impending terrorist attack, and Ryker believed them.

The day had been proof to Ryker that the Chameleon was working alone on whatever he was planning. He was freelancing, and whatever the motivation was, it was personal, just as the young psychologist had suggested.

A lot of people were going to die if they couldn't come up with something. And in a hurry.

TWENTY-FOUR

THE COMMAND CENTER WAS ALREADY very much alive when Lubin and Ryker arrived the following morning. Phones were ringing nonstop, and those assigned to respond to the calls were having difficulty keeping up. Information, or lack thereof, was entered directly into the database for subsequent analysis. An inherent problem in intelligence gathering is rooted in the policy that not *everyone* needs to know *everything*. There are sound and obvious reasons to treat sensitive data in this manner, but the downside is that someone will find a crucial piece of a puzzle desperately needing to be solved yet not realize the piece's value—or worse, that there's even a puzzle. Consequently, the information isn't given the necessary attention it deserves, and the overall success of the specific intelligence mission is thwarted.

Mossad wasn't about to let that happen as this operation unfolded. A team of analysts reviewed every scrap of information entered and was in constant contact with Levi Goldman, who dispatched personnel and material based upon incoming data.

Goldman was on the phone, deep in conversation, when he spotted Ryker and Lubin and waved them over. He hung up the phone just as they made their way through a labyrinth of bodies rushing here and there. He addressed them both, but his words were directed more to Ryker.

"Just spoke to one of my people up north. Seems like a contact with a low-level informant in Cyprus may have given us our first break. The guy's a dockworker. Sees a lot of stuff being loaded and unloaded: weapons and ammunition being of particular interest. I'm sure you know that for the last ten years or so, Cyprus has been the hub for the weapons trade in the Middle East. Cyprus took the trade over from Lebanon when Beirut became so unpredictable. Sometimes it's legal . . . sometimes it isn't. Either way, it pays us to have a pair of eyes out there. We don't want our *good neighbors* throwing any surprise parties for us."

Goldman continued. "Last week, the informant reported that three crates had been loaded onto a Greek trawler . . . middle-of-the-night stuff. Suspicious. The ship was bound for an unknown destination, but our guy says that since its return, he's talked to some of the crew. They say the crates were off-loaded onto a smaller boat just outside the harbor at Haifa to avoid customs."

Lubin broke in. "There could have been *anything* in those crates, Levi. No doubt there was something suspicious about it, but—"

"But what? Are you going soft on me? We have to follow *every* lead."

"I know, but it would be nice to have something more to tie the Chameleon to Haifa than a few mysterious boxes of who knows what. So have we got someone nosing around up there? Do we have an approximate date that the Greek trawler was supposed to be there?"

"Yes and yes. We've got a couple of teams making inquiries. They'll get back to me one way or another. Now go make yourself useful, Manni. You're giving the wrong impression of our all-knowing infallibility to Mr. Ryker." He smiled and turned away from the two, taking another phone call.

Ryker checked the message board. Nothing yet from Hasan. They were about to leave the room when an attractive woman of about twenty-five, in a khaki uniform, called out to Lubin.

"Sir, telephone call for you. Cairo. National Police. Shall I put the call through?" She motioned to a phone station just inside the door.

"Yes," Lubin said. It was only a second or two before the phone rang and he picked it up. Both he and Ryker could feel a tightness of anticipation rise in their chests. "Hello? . . . Yes . . ." It was Hasan. "Yes, he's here with me now . . . Wait, I'll put the call on speaker so he can hear, too." Lubin punched the appropriate button on the phone console and replaced the receiver. "Go ahead, Hasan."

"Sam, it looks like the miracle you were counting on just materialized. Your people and mine have been working around the clock on tracking the names of Saiif Khalil, and we have found something of interest. It seems that a very old Salahdin investment account, one of the oldest we could find, was originally set up under the name Haleh Abd al-Rahman. It looks like Saiif Khalil is a cover for his . . . other activities. I had every friendly country and police agency I could contact running this name, and it turned out you were right. There are hundreds of Abd al-Rahmans who have been in trouble with the authorities over the years. And then the authorities in

Turkey ran the name and downloaded sixteen criminal files of people with the last name of Abd al-Rahman. Technologically speaking, Turkey is further along than most other Middle Eastern countries, and we were able to download pictures. That is when we found him."

Ryker could hear papers being shuffled in the background.

Hasan continued. "It seems that back in 1979 a certain Haleh Abd al-Rahman, then attending the University of Tehran, was wanted for questioning in connection with the murder of an Iranian government functionary. We have a college picture of him. It is grainy and thirty years old, but it matches the surveillance footage we have. Saiif Khalil and Haleh Abd al-Rahman *are* the same person. But that is only the beginning. Listen to this: Reports from those who knew him said that he was leading the charge when the group of Iranian students stormed the American embassy in Tehran in that same year. I dug a little deeper and called someone I know working in Iran's civil service. I was able to find out, unofficially, that Haleh Abd al-Rahman was orphaned at fourteen when his mother shot herself in front of him. His father had been executed in the fifties by the Savak, Iran's secret police. The mother blamed the Shah and the West for his death.

"I am not a criminal psychologist, but it looks like we may be dealing with someone who has been committing acts of terror for thirty years out of revenge and hatred, probably passed on to him by a fanatical mother. Anyone who may have thought that he was a holy warrior can put that theory to bed."

Listening on the speakerphone, the entire command center was hushed. Not only did the Chameleon have a face, but he was also flesh and blood. The psychologist in the briefing the previous day had been pretty close to describing what they'd just heard from Hasan. The Chameleon was human and vulnerable after all.

"Sam? Are you there?"

"Yes, I'm still here."

Hasan continued. "Now, back to the task we have of stopping this psychopath. If he was on any of the trains leaving Cairo, he gave us the slip. It was a long shot, but we tried. Just in case he was never on the train or got off without being detected, highway border crossings, airports, and docks received extra surveillance. Again nothing. If he left here Monday night as we think, it is likely he is already in Israel. Let us just admit that the man is *awfully* thorough at disguising himself."

"Undoubtedly. Anything else?" Ryker asked.

"We did not know if this would help, but at all major points of exit, especially airports and docks, we had customs officers photocopy all passports.

The hope was that he would be traveling on foreign documents. We have been forwarding those photocopies back to various embassies to see if they can be cross-referenced in any way. Maybe knowing how he is disguised or what name he is traveling under is too late in the game to be of any value, but we will play it out to see where it goes. Miss Reid was released from the hospital last night. She is staying at the embassy as a security precaution. She indicated to me that she planned to lend a hand in going over any American passports."

"Do you think that she's really up to that? I mean it hasn't been that long since her run-in with Badri."

"My thinking exactly, Sam, but you know Miss Reid better than I. The only way to stop her from helping would be to physically restrain her, and I do not think that Ambassador Chandler is man enough." He chuckled. "Anyway, he needs all the help he can get in bringing further resolution to the missionary incident."

"What about Talib?" Ryker asked. "Has he given up anything more that might help?"

"We transferred him up from Aswan, and my men have been questioning him, but I think we can assume that he has told us everything he knows. We do know a little more about *Al-Jum'ah* and its workings but nothing related to the Chameleon or what he might have planned for Israel. Military intelligence wants to talk to him, too, but it will only be under National Police supervision. I want Talib alive to stand trial."

"Anything else pulled out of the shop and apartment?"

"Nothing. We found pieces of a personal computer, and there was hope for a while that something might be pulled from it, but it had not only been erased, but also destroyed before the bomb went off. Even your men at the embassy said they hadn't seen anything quite like it."

"This guy thinks of everything," Lubin commented to Hasan. "So far, I'd categorize what you've said as interesting but not very encouraging. Don't you have anything *useful* to tell us?"

"I think we have something that will brighten your day, my friend. We ran a check of Khalil's phone records. Nothing out of the ordinary. In fact, he only makes a handful of calls during any given month."

"Which means he has another phone. Any cell phone records? Personal? Business?"

"We've looked into it. Nothing official."

"I would have been surprised if he had been that careless."

"Let me finish. We contacted the company that handles most cellular traffic in the area and found that there were no billings to the address of the investment firm or penthouse apartment, and none to Saiif Khalil or Haleh Abd al-Rahman at any address. We thought we had drawn another blank. Then they ran a computer check on the names of those who initially signed contracts for cellular service, and there he was. He had made a mistake. He had used identification under the name of Khalil to establish service but had the billings going to a post office box under a different name. We asked the company to produce a list of cellular calls to and from that number."

"C'mon, Hasan, cut to the info we can use," Ryker pressed impatiently.

"The list went back a couple of years, but there are not many calls. He apparently used the service very infrequently. He never *received* any calls, and the calls he made were sometimes several weeks apart. But then he made five calls within two days: two calls Saturday morning, one of which was to our friend Talib and the other to a number we're still trying to track down; two calls Sunday morning, one to a local travel agency and the other one to directory assistance in Tel Aviv. The last one was to his residence. We all remember that one, don't we?"

"Did you say Tel Aviv?" Lubin asked. "But there was no follow-up call?"

"Perhaps they simply transferred him to whatever number he was looking for."

"How long was the call?"

"No, you're right, Manni. The call only lasted forty-five seconds."

"Can you tell me the exact time of the call to directory assistance? I think I can pick up the trail from there. Telephone utilities have a special relationship with the government. I'm sure we can track down who he wanted to call."

Goldman jotted down the time the call was placed. "Also, give me that number you were trying to track down. I'll have my men start working on it." Hasan did, and Goldman had one of his assistants start making calls. He had the directory assistance information he was looking for in no time at all. He passed his findings to Goldman.

"It seems that he called looking for the number to the CNN Bureau in Tel Aviv."

"CNN?" Ryker said. "To alert the press?"

Lubin shook his head. "They are required to immediately report any information they may have that might affect national security."

"Still, it's an odd call to make."

Goldman shot him a hurry-it-up glance.

"And what of the missionaries?" Ryker asked, aware that they were the real reason that he was even in this part of the world—the reason he was even still alive. "Did they get off all right?"

"Yes, yesterday morning. There was a police escort right to the door of the plane. We were not taking any chances that *Al-Jum'ah* would somehow try again to harm them. My father insisted on being present and speaking to them prior to their departure. He asked them to convey his best regards to Ambassador Cannon inasmuch as he was sure that he would be meeting with them on their return. You know my father. This missionary incident has taken a toll on him. He feels partially responsible for what happened."

Goldman glared at Lubin and gave him the signal to wind up the call. There'd be time for casual conversation later after this emergency had passed.

As the conversation was nearing an end, Hasan was interrupted by someone who whispered to him in the background, "Call for you, sir, on line two. The American woman."

"Hold on for a moment, Sam," Hasan announced. "Miss Reid is on the other line for me." Hasan cut out. A few moments later he was back.

"Miss Reid may have something of value. It seems that an individual holding an American passport boarded a ship bound for Israel out of Port Said. The passport bore an Egyptian entry stamp dated a week earlier. She has searched the embassy records for such an individual. No one by that name can be found. The passport picture is substantially different from the original composite she gave us, but she is certain it is the same man."

"What name is he using now?" Ryker asked.

"Michael Rodriguez. And I will wager that name can be confirmed with the travel agency here in Cairo."

"And where in Israel was the ship headed?" Lubin questioned.

"Haifa. I have not had time to check it out, of course, but I would assume that the ship would have docked sometime yesterday morning."

"That may fit with something else we discovered here, Hasan. Good work," Lubin said.

"It is not *my* doing. It is Miss Reid who deserves the credit. Also, she said that the passport photo has been faxed to the American embassy there. You can get it from them. Of course, he may have already assumed a different identity."

"Probably," Ryker confirmed.

"Oh, and Sam, Miss Reid says that you are to be careful. She does not have a good feeling about all this and wants you to get through it in one piece. She said that she already has dinner reservations. She said you would know what that means."

"Yes, I do. Thank you, Hasan. You've given us something concrete to go on. We'll be in touch. So good-bye for now." Ryker hung up the phone and looked at Lubin and Goldman.

Goldman turned to another worker bee buzzing around the cramped quarters. "You heard the inspector. Contact the American embassy and get us a copy of the passport photo of Michael Rodriguez. Tell them to send a runner with it. I don't want a fax of a fax. And while you're at it, ask them why you even have to make the call. Tell them that picture should already be over here."

"Right away," was the answer.

"Sir, I have confirmation on that phone number you gave me . . ." a young agent said, hesitant to interrupt the boss.

"Well, just don't stand there, son. Tell me," Goldman spat.

"It's assigned to an address in the warehouse district at Haifa."

"Haifa?" Lubin blurted. "Levi, that's the third time this morning that Haifa has figured into this."

"Oh, so now you think that there *might* be a connection, huh?" Goldman asked sarcastically. "You think those mystery boxes might have had something in them that the Chameleon needed?"

"It looks that way now. Too coincidental for it to be otherwise." Lubin ignored Goldman's tone.

"CNN?" Ryker asked again, unable to shake an underlying feeling. "What could he have wanted with them?"

Goldman replied, "I don't know. I've got personnel in Tel Aviv who could check it out, but I think you two should go. We've got the time of the call. Maybe you can find out who received it. The station manager is an American. Maybe he'd be more comfortable talking to a fellow countryman. Anyway, get over there and find out something."

"We're on our way, Levi," Lubin said as he and Ryker made for the door.

They stopped as Goldman said, "I'll get our people in Haifa some reinforcements, and they can check out that warehouse. We could get lucky. The prospect of three crates of explosives—if that's what's in them—detonating anywhere in Israel is *highly* unacceptable."

Goldman looked at them wide-eyed.

"Well, what are you two waiting for? There's a deranged psycho out there, and he means to strike again in my country. Get out of here and call me from Tel Aviv when you've got something. No one dies by this man's hand, not on *my* watch. Now go! *Go!*"

TWENTY-FIVE

THE SHORT DRIVE DUE WEST on the express route from Jerusalem to Tel Aviv wasn't particularly picturesque under normal driving conditions, but at the speeds Lubin attained, everything hurtling by was transformed into a blur. Had the journey been the last leg of the Grand Prix de Monaco, he would've earned the checkered flag.

A long-time resident of Tel Aviv, Lubin didn't have any difficulty driving directly to the offices of CNN. The building that housed the media giant was not likely to be featured anytime soon in *Architectural Digest* unless the magazine planned to run an article entitled, "Design Disasters of the Modern World." It was a three-story, nondescript structure surrounded by a chain-link fence that protected a fleet of news vans toting satellite dishes.

They parked in the section of asphalt identified for visitors and entered the air-conditioned lobby through the sensor-controlled double doors. A uniformed guard rose from behind his granite workstation to greet them.

"*Shalom.* May I help you?" he asked.

Lubin flashed his credentials, and the guard, duly impressed, stood a trifle more erect.

"We'd like to talk to whoever's in charge," Lubin said.

"That would be Mr. Sanders; he's the bureau chief. If you'd like, I'll ring his office for you." The man picked up the phone receiver and punched a single button. "There are two gentlemen here to see Mr. Sanders . . . No, I'm sure they *don't* have an appointment . . . Yes, I understand he's a busy man, but . . ." The guard continued listening but looked at Lubin, whose eyes had narrowed to mere slits in disapproval. "Yes, I'm well aware of my duties, ma'am, but I think Mr. Sanders is going to be obliged to speak with these gentlemen no matter what his morning schedule is . . . Who? They're from the government . . . Intelligence officers . . . No, I think it would be best if Mr. Sanders spoke to them personally . . . Yes, I'll tell them . . . Thank you." The guard put down the receiver and smiled at the visitors.

"Well?" asked Lubin, his eyebrows raised.

"Mr. Sanders will be down presently."

Ryker wondered why they hadn't just been directed to Sanders's office but then figured that it must have something to do with executive posturing. They'd come unannounced, and now they could wait at the pleasure of the king. During his career with the CIA, he'd been equally unimpressed when he'd seen government bureaucracies play the same game. No matter what kind of guy Sanders turned out to be, this interview was getting off on the wrong foot.

It was a full five minutes before the adjacent elevator doors opened and a young man in his early thirties emerged. He was tall and blond with gold wire-rimmed glasses. He wore starched tan chinos, a striped shirt and tie, and suspenders. If there were a dress code for journalists, Ryker figured this would be it, though the utility of suspenders had always eluded him. *Didn't they become obsolete with the invention of belt loops?* he thought.

The man strode purposefully to the security station, but there was something effeminate about his gait. He ignored the guard and shook hands with the two men. His sleeves were rolled up to mid-forearm, exposing a gold bracelet on one wrist and a Rolex on the other, suitable accoutrements for giving the impression that they were about to address someone important.

"I'm Keith Sanders, the bureau chief. Now what's this all about?"

Lubin tendered his identification and watched as Sanders scrutinized it.

"Is there someplace we could speak in private?" Lubin delivered the question as though it were a statement that disallowed a negative reply.

"Yes, certainly," Sanders said, returning the identification. "If you'll follow me, we'll go up to my office." He turned and escorted the men into the elevator and up to the third floor. The doors opened onto a suite of offices in lieu of a corridor. They marched through the waiting room and past a secretary next to Sanders's door.

"No calls, Rita," Sanders ordered as he stood to the side of his open office door and gestured for the men to enter. He followed them in and closed the door. He motioned to a grouping of leather furniture, and all three sat down.

During the drive from Jerusalem, they'd given some thought as to how they should proceed with interviewing CNN personnel. If they just laid the cards on the table, a media blitz would follow which might both hamper efforts to stop a potential tragedy and to possibly capture the elusive terrorist. They'd elected to give up as little information as necessary.

Sanders looked from one to the other. "So?" He gave the distinct impression that he was in a hurry and wanted to move the conversation along.

Since Lubin was the one with official identification, it had been agreed that he'd initiate the interview. Ryker would hold back and involve himself only if things started to go stale. At this point, Sanders didn't appear to be balking, so Ryker just sat and listened.

"We'd like to enlist your cooperation," Lubin began, "in a routine matter of inquiry. We have reason to believe that someone working at CNN received a telephone call from an individual in Cairo on Monday. We're trying to ascertain just who that person is."

"You've got to be kidding. Most of us who work here receive countless calls a day. Hundreds go through my secretary alone, and there's a receptionist on every floor. You'll have to be more specific. For instance, the *name* of the individual who called?" Sanders had to sense that an open answer wouldn't be forthcoming.

"I'm afraid we're not at liberty to discuss that, but the call would have come in sometime around four in the afternoon. Are incoming calls logged in any fashion? Perhaps we could start there," Lubin suggested.

"I'd like to help you. Really I would, but there are ethical concerns here. We get leads on a good portion of stories through sources that must be kept anonymous. Surely you understand that. There must be similar issues with the Israeli media."

"Who's said anything about revealing sources?" The tenor of Lubin's voice was noticeably different from the moment before. "We already know *who* called. We want to know who he talked *to*."

"So you say, but I have to take the worst-case scenario . . . that you really *don't* know. You must understand. What if this individual called with information, thinking that his identity was safe with us and then we double-crossed him? It would get around that CNN couldn't be trusted. Then where would we be?"

"I can tell you where you *will* be if certain events unfold, and it's determined that your cooperation could have prevented them." Lubin regained his composure and continued. "I can assure you that the person who called was not a news source, Mr. Sanders. There would be no ethical issues at stake by helping us to determine whom on your staff he spoke with."

"I think that I can make a similar case for protecting the identity of our reporters," Sanders postulated. "You know . . . Bill of Rights and all that."

Lubin had had enough and was on the way to his feet when Ryker touched his shoulder and motioned for him to remain seated.

"Mr. Sanders," Ryker began slowly, calmly, "this is not some university debating competition. This is a most serious matter, and any arguments in defense of free speech are irrelevant. Besides, this is *not* America." Ryker's tone was firm and cold.

"You know, your English is *very* good. And I don't recall seeing your ID earlier," Sanders commented in a condescending manner, detaching himself from what Ryker had just said.

Ryker didn't have time to either verbally beat him into submission or play the official game with him and figured that honesty might just be the best policy in this situation. "You didn't see my ID because I don't have any. I'm an American . . . consultant, and I'm here helping the Israeli authorities try to find the man responsible for murdering three Americans nine months ago at the Wailing Wall. No doubt CNN covered the story." Essentially, Ryker had told the truth, just not the *whole* truth.

Sanders was caught off guard. "Y . . . yes, I remember the incident quite clearly. Wrote some of the follow-up pieces myself. And your name would be?"

"Samuel Ryker."

Sanders's eyes widened in surprise.

"Yes, of course. It was your wife and children who were killed in the explosion. No one ever came forward to claim responsibility for the incident, either, if I recall correctly."

"That's right. But now some leads have surfaced that we're attempting to follow. We're trying to bring a murderer to justice."

Anyone else might have gone for it, but Sanders was still hesitant to throw in his lot—CNN's lot. The rules were still the rules. Confidentiality policies precluded one from being a good Samaritan.

Ryker turned up the flame. "Let me put it another way. A total news blackout wouldn't be in your best interest, would it? I mean . . . with all that you must have scheduled over the next few days. You'd be surprised how innovative the Israeli government can be in alleging certain media improprieties. Of course, CNN could maybe *buy* footage from the other networks, but I'm sure that it wouldn't be of the same quality."

Sanders jumped to his feet. "How dare you! I'm not going to be blackmailed by you *or* the Israeli government. Maybe it's time you two *gentlemen* left my office!"

"*Sit down*, Mr. Sanders!" Ryker ordered.

Sanders eased back into his seat.

"This situation is just too desperate for us to walk away. Look, you seem like a decent person, so we're going to make you a deal. Something that'll earn you the Pulitzer Prize and get you an appointment at one of the plum bureaus: Paris. London. New York."

"I'm listening," was all Sanders said, but Ryker knew that he finally had his attention.

"What I've told you thus far is true: I *am* Sam Ryker, my family *was* killed at the Wailing Wall, and we *are* pursuing the man responsible. But there's more—lots more."

"And most of it affects Israel's national security," Lubin interjected. "If you attempt to disseminate any of the information we give you, you'll be taken into custody and not released for a long time. I assume you'd be set free eventually, but you won't like the inside of an Israeli jail; I *guarantee* it. A lot of people never even survive the experience."

A certain curiosity, mingled with contempt, showed on Sanders's face.

"On the other hand," Ryker said, "if after you hear what we've got to tell you, you decide to help us, you'll be given exclusive rights to break the story. A story that goes back at least twenty years, and one that's never been told. How about it, Mr. Sanders? Are you interested?"

Sanders must've figured that he had little to lose and a lot to gain. A journalist of his talents deserved a better assignment than Israel. Greed won the day.

"All right, I'm in. Let's hear it."

And hear it he did—from Tehran to the assassination of Anwar Sadat to the current crisis with a dozen stops in between.

"Wow!" Sanders said when the story concluded. "Pulitzer Prize, huh? You've got that right, and I've heard that the Chateaubriand at the George V Hotel in Paris is something to *die* for." He was almost salivating. "What do you want me to do?"

Ryker and Lubin knew that they really hadn't given away much. If whatever the Chameleon had in mind materialized, the story would be thrust to the surface anyway. Sanders was just being given a preview of coming attractions. Then there was always a chance that the Chameleon's telephone call to CNN was nothing of consequence. Maybe he only wanted to know which sites of religious celebration were going to receive coverage so that his heinous act would be sure to be captured on film. But maybe, just maybe, he had an accomplice working at CNN. The call simply couldn't be discounted. It was a lead that had to be followed even if it guaranteed Sanders—an egotistical opportunist—a promotion in the process.

Lubin answered Sanders's question with two of his own: "Is there any way to tell who that call came into? As I asked before, is there a log of some sort?"

"I think we can do you one better than that. The switchboard operators initially tape all incoming calls. The time that the call came in is also noted automatically. American police departments use the same concept for 911 calls. In our business, it's important that our callers don't get lost, either."

Lubin could hardly believe their good fortune. Sanders was going to offer up the needed information on a silver platter. It was almost *too* good to be true.

"Do you mean that all we have to do is to pull the tapes for that particular day, find the right time of the call, and we can listen to our guy speak to the receptionist and ask for the staff member if, in fact, that was his reason for calling?"

"You got it," Sanders responded, smiling.

"What about a tape of the subsequent conversation, if any? Would it have been recorded as well?" pursued Lubin.

"No, I'm afraid not. The call would be forwarded to the person or office asked for. If no one answered, the call would go automatically to voice mail, but there'd be no record of that. A voice mail message, however, would remain until deleted."

"Still, this is better than we could have hoped for," Lubin said. "Where are the tapes kept?"

"At the switchboard downstairs. Come on—we'll have a look and listen." Sanders stood, walked across the office, and opened the door. Lubin and Ryker followed behind. "I'll be out of the office for a while, Rita. Just take messages."

As Ryker passed, it looked to him as though the secretary's morning disposition hadn't improved, but he smiled again at her anyway. They made their way down the elevator to the lobby and turned right, through a set of oak double doors.

Three women sat in front of the busy switchboard. Incoming calls were accompanied by annoying buzzes, and the board was a mass of flashing lights. Neither Ryker nor Lubin had ever seen just how busy a media center was and were overwhelmed by the activity.

There wasn't a break of more than a few seconds between calls, but Sanders managed to get an operator's attention.

"Yes, Mr. Sanders, may I help you?" The woman was a young Israeli with a very soothing voice—the kind that could put irate callers to ease the moment they heard it. In fact, it was obvious from listening to the others that they'd completed the same course in telephone etiquette. From calls that came in while the men were standing there, it was also evident that the women were multilingual.

"When you get a moment, I'd like the tapes from Saturday."

She nodded, routed one more incoming call, and disconnected her headset. She swiveled her chair, stood, and walked to one of six gray metal file cabinets behind the console.

"Saturday, you said?"

"Sometime after four, to be exact," Sanders answered.

The woman rummaged through a file drawer, closed it, and opened another. She was frowning.

"This is strange, but there don't appear to be any tapes from Saturday." She consulted a sheet of paper attached to a clipboard lying on top of the cabinet. "And no one has checked them out, either."

"What do you mean there aren't any? Where could they be?" Sanders snapped, as though upon hearing his voice the woman would come to her senses.

"You can see that they're not exactly kept in a vault. They're not *really* a controlled item, though we do try to keep track of them through a signout sheet," the woman responded in a calming manner that seemed to defuse Sanders.

"Could they be misfiled?" Sanders asked hopefully.

"I'll look again, but I don't think so." She turned back to the first file drawer that she'd opened. "The tapes from Friday are here, as well as those from Sunday. There's just a blank space where Saturday's should be." She looked dismayed as the three men exited the switchboard room.

"Well," Ryker said, "what are the odds that the only relevant tapes are the ones missing? I'd say that whoever our man talked to wasn't taking any chances that someone might put two and two together."

"All right, how about this?" Lubin offered, addressing Ryker. "We look at the personnel records of everyone working Saturday. Maybe we'll find something that would make one person more suspect than another."

"Maybe, and let's not even rule out one of the switchboard operators as a possible suspect. No one would have had more opportunity to make those tapes disappear."

"True enough," Sanders said.

Ryker continued. "Which means that to be on the safe side, we're going to have to look at *everyone's* personnel file, but those who worked on Saturday are priority. I'd have to agree with you, Manni."

"Gentlemen, normally a news bureau in a country this size wouldn't be very large, but Tel Aviv is a hub for the Middle East." He paused as if counting the number of reporters, cameramen, producers, editors, and assistants who would have been working Saturday. The report of the world's news knew no Monday-through-Friday schedule. Sanders's frown meant that there were a lot. "I guess I can have the files pulled for you, but what are you going to be looking for?"

"Your guess is as good as ours," Ryker responded, "but we better get started. There's a lot at stake here."

"All right, this way to the personnel office," Sanders said, leading out.

Before he and Ryker started going through the files, Lubin called Goldman and explained the events of the day so far. Goldman temporarily went into orbit when told of the exclusive rights of the affair being given to CNN.

"You *what*? And who authorized *that*?" Goldman blared.

Lubin replied, "Come on, Levi. We gave up practically nothing. Plus, we have Sanders's undivided attention, and we've turned up another lead."

"Okay . . . okay, but if Sanders goes public with any of this before being given a green light, I'll arrest him *personally*." Goldman calmed down almost immediately, letting Lubin know that he was doing what he enjoyed most—keeping his staff off balance. "So what are your chances of identifying the person who this guy called?"

"We don't know yet. There's a lot of staff who work here. I'm hoping we'll get lucky."

Goldman sighed.

"What about the Haifa lead?" Lubin asked. "Have our people reported back?"

"Just minutes ago. The phone number is to a small warehouse not far from the wharf. The three crates are still there, minus the *real* cargo."

"The crates are empty?" Lubin asked.

"No. They contain pottery clay, but the explosive sniffing dogs went into a frenzy just the same. Looks like the ordnance—plastique of some sort—was hidden inside the clay just in case customs stumbled onto the crates."

"How much do you suppose there was?"

"The shipping manifests were still attached to the sides of the crates. Assuming they're correct, and allowing for the weight of the clay left behind, our people say there must have been about two hundred pounds."

"Two hundred pounds of plastic explosive? That's enough to level a city block. The Chameleon has gone beyond being a terrorist, Levi. He's a madman. If he's successful at exploding that much stuff anywhere, there'll be wholesale reprisals against all Arabs by every Israeli right-wing group, no matter how innocent those Arabs might be. Whatever peace negotiations we may have with our neighbors will go up in smoke. Generations would pass before anyone could be coaxed back to the negotiating table again."

"I don't need a political science lecture from *you*, Manni. All I want is for you and Ryker to *find* and *stop* him. Now get to work!"

* * *

Only a few kilometers away from where Ryker and Lubin were plying their trade, Saiif walked from his hotel to the central market for breakfast. He found a table at an Arab-run cafe across the street from the stands and wagons that made up the fresh fruit and vegetable bazaar. It was crowded with an influx of tourists, both Jewish and Christian, visiting the Holy Land for upcoming religious holidays, and he found it difficult to concentrate. He ate breakfast quickly then made his way to a pay phone attached to the back wall near the restrooms. It was nine o'clock.

"Good morning. CNN. How may I direct your call?"

"Ah, yes, good morning. Mr. Henri Collette, please."

"One moment, sir, while I connect y—" The operator cut herself off in the switchboard transfer.

The phone didn't even complete its first ring before it was snatched off its cradle.

"Collette." The accented voice sounded strained and forced.

"Good morning. This is your uncle. I arrived in Israel yesterday and cannot wait to see you again. Are you free for lunch this afternoon?"

Henri Collette dropped all pretenses. "Listen!" he whispered just below a scream. "They're here! Asking questions!"

Saiif's stomach dropped, and his heart jumped to his throat. It took every ounce of self-control to remain calm, but he had to ask, "*Who* is there, Henri? *Who* is asking questions?"

"Israeli authorities. They're not wearing uniforms. I think they might be Mossad. They have found us out!"

Collette was coming unhinged. Saiif just hoped that the Frenchman would hold it together long enough to see his plan through to the end.

"No, no. No one has found out anything. Listen to me. Did you destroy the tape as I directed?"

Henri was frantic. "*Oui.* The tape no longer exists, and no one saw me take it."

"Then we have nothing to worry about. They may know I called CNN, but they can't trace it to you." But he knew that with enough time they would. "They are fishing for clues. Do not give them any. Relax. Go about your morning business as you normally would. If they ask you questions, answer them. They do not suspect you. Talk to them as little as possible, and do not try to mislead them. You are a busy man and have an enormous amount of work to do before tomorrow's shoot. Excuse yourself on that basis if you have to. We will talk over lunch at the designated place. Do you understand?"

"*Oui. Je comprends.*"

"Then be there by twelve-thirty, and remember: relax. The plan is perfect. This changes nothing. They got lucky, and now they are hoping for another lead." Saiif took a deep breath. "Are you all right?"

"*Oui.*"

"Then I will see you at twelve-thirty. Actually . . . make it one o'clock."

"Yes . . . yes. One o'clock," the Frenchman said.

"Just think, Henri. This time on Saturday you will be a new man—a rich man."

Saiif slammed down the receiver, nearly breaking the plastic grip. Perhaps he had underestimated his American nemesis. He had clearly followed the invitation to follow him, and he had been smart enough to track him to Israel, but this was too close for Saiif's comfort. Too much was riding on this for him to just let Ryker get lucky and be in a position to stop him. He now realized that taunting Ryker was foolish; it only strengthened his resolve. There was only one thing to do with Ryker, and he had to do it soon. But how? And as soon as his question formulated, the answer became clear. If Ryker had somehow been able to convince Mossad to get involved, then he had him right where he wanted him. But for this plan he'd need a vehicle, because he'd abandoned his own car the night before.

It was as if a shadow descended, as he once again became *Al-Har'ba.* His eyes narrowed, and he cocked his head toward the busy dining area. It took him only a few seconds to pick out the sound he was listening for.

Near the window, a lone American tourist was struggling with simple Arabic words from a useless pocket phrase book. The waiter was growing impatient as the man massacred the language. Saiif intervened just as the waiter was about to move on to other patrons.

"What seems to be the trouble?" he asked the frustrated diner in English.

"Huh? Oh, I'm having a dickens of a time trying to order breakfast. Seems my Arabic is worse than I thought."

Saiif turned to the waiter and told him in fluent Arabic to remain for a moment.

Returning to the man seated at the table, he said, "I picked up a little during my business travels over the years. Name's Hill. Franklin Hill. Here on holiday this time."

"Mark Simon." He offered his hand to the stranger. "Would you care to join me? I'd enjoy the company."

Saiif ordered breakfast for the man and coffee for himself. For an hour they talked about home and their impressions of the Middle East. By ten o'clock they were well on their way to becoming fast friends. Simons, alone on vacation, was more that happy to give Franklin a ride anywhere he needed to go this morning. His rental car was parked up the alley, around in back. They exited the cafe and made their way to the rear of the building. Saiif quickly surveyed the area. Confident that they were alone and unobserved, he reached around Simon's neck and snapped it effortlessly. He found the man's keys in his pants pocket and then hefted the body into the cafe's metal garbage dumpster.

He now had a car.

On his way to the rented storage unit, he stopped by a corner market and purchased a cheap digital watch, a small box of plastic garbage bags, and a roll of duct tape. Ten minutes later he sat at the wooden workbench, cast in a diffused bluish light from the bare florescent tube above, busily fashioning a simple but deadly device. He looked at his own chronograph, calculated the hours in his head, and set the timer on the now-dissected watch that was attached to an array of wires embedded in a half block of C-4. Within thirty minutes he was on the road, a small, watertight package concealed carefully under the passenger seat.

TWENTY-SIX

BENJAMIN ROSEN ROLLED OVER AND fumbled for the ringing alarm clock on the nightstand, accidentally knocking it to the floor. Struggling to open his eyes even a sliver, he squinted at the bedroom window. Narrow beams of late morning sun shot through the blinds of his small Tel Aviv apartment like lasers in a low-budget science fiction movie. He propped himself up on his elbow and tentatively kissed the cheek of the woman still sleeping next to him. She recoiled from his affection, cringed as if in pain, and tried to burrow further into the sheets, mumbling something about her aching head.

As he swung his legs over the edge of the double bed, he was overcome by a wave of nausea, his head feeling as though it had been split with an axe. He pushed off the bed and stumbled twice on his way to the bathroom. It was almost eleven-thirty. Time to shower for work.

Rosen's full name was Benjamin Parker Rosen, and although he would've preferred that his friends call him Benny, none of them did. He hated being called Benjamin. It sounded so proper, so respectable, so much like his dead older brother. And Rosen, by his own admission, was anything but. Even his wife, now sleeping off a hangover in the other room, chose to call him by his given name. And, in a way, he resented her for it. They'd been married for two years but didn't love each other. Theirs had been a marriage of convenience from the beginning. She was a cocktail waitress, and he worked for a small cleaning firm that serviced certain government buildings and satellite offices and apartments. Rents in the Tel Aviv and Jerusalem were steep, and neither of them commanded much of a salary. But by splitting the cost—as husband and wife—each still had enough money to party. They only occasionally showed each other affection afforded husband and wife, and then only if they had too much to drink—like last night.

He brushed his teeth as he let the water run in the shower. He stepped in just as the steam began fogging the top of the mirror that hung over the sink. The hot water felt good as it soothed his pounding head. He was leaning back to rinse the soap from his hair when he heard the bathroom door open.

"Sorry, honey. I didn't mean to wake you," he hollered over the splash of the water.

No response. There seldom was. She was a quiet woman and didn't feel obligated to speak just to fill silence—much like himself. He liked that.

He was running a few minutes late and was about to ask her to brew some coffee when a line of soap trailed over his brow and into his eyes. Turning around, he put his face into the stream of water to wash it out when the lights suddenly went out.

The shower door was ripped open, slamming into the wall with a thick bang. His clouded mind was trying to register what was happening when a gloved hand grabbed the back of his neck and yanked him out. His heel slammed into the lip of the shower floor on his way out, and he let out a whimper. With what little courage he possessed, he reached behind his head in a feeble attempt to pry loose the vise grip that held him. It was no use. He ceased to struggle and surrendered to whatever was in store. His face slammed against the wall.

As the fear of his situation settled in, he lost bladder control, too scared to be embarrassed. The hand at the base of his neck moved up to the back of his head and gripped his wet hair.

"*Shalom*, Benny."

Only one man ever called him Benny.

He'd secretly hoped never to hear that voice again. In fact, he'd hoped that the man with that voice would've forgotten him or, better still, would have died a painful death somewhere far away. "Remember *me*?" And as if reading Rosen's mind, he added, "I certainly remember *you*."

Between sobs Rosen relived that night four years earlier: the drinking, the deceptive surge of courage, and the enormous wager made without the funds to back it. If it hadn't been for the man now driving his face through the bathroom wall, he would've paid that debt with his life. That night, Benjamin Parker Rosen had been broken, and his life had continued to deteriorate ever since.

"It's been a long time, my friend, and the deal you made with the devil has finally come due. Are you listening?"

Rosen nodded as best he could.

"Before I begin, understand that this isn't a request; you cannot refuse. The task is simple and far from being worth the price I paid for your miserable life. Consider this your lucky day." The grip tightened. "If you fail to do exactly as I say, or if you go to your employer or tell *anyone* about our little conversation, I will not only kill you but everyone you hold dear. Are we clear on this?"

Rosen grunted an acknowledgment, tears streaming down his cheeks.

"Good boy. Now listen closely."

* * *

Henri Collette's blond hair blew in the gentle sea breeze as he sat at an open-air table at the Dolphinarium. Situated on the coast halfway between Tel Aviv and Jaffa, the Dolphinarium was a world-renowned center for the study of dolphins and other aquatic mammals. He'd arrived a few minutes early and had ordered a stiff drink while he waited for the man who'd very soon make him a millionaire twice over. Henri was selfish and greedy; it was as simple as that. He'd abandoned his ailing father to a French nursing home when he had taken a news assignment abroad. He'd seldom managed to send even a greeting card on holidays, and when the old man finally died from heart failure, Collette was too busy to attend the funeral. But he found time to collect his inheritance. A graduate of the Sorbonne in journalism, his credentials were impeccable and his work first rate, but he had convinced himself that he was underappreciated.

Just then, the man joined him.

"You're late," Collette said boldly.

"I was unavoidably detained," Saiif said flatly. "I had to see an old friend for a favor."

Collette was suddenly afraid and regretted accusing him of being tardy. The man's eyes were sinister and cold. Collette cringed, blinked, and shifted his gaze out toward the Mediterranean.

"I'll keep this meeting brief."

Saiif spoke quickly, never pausing long enough for Collette to interrupt or interject a question. Though he wouldn't have posed a question even if he'd been given the chance. He listened intently as the simple details unfolded before him. It was perfect. No angle had been overlooked; every scenario had been well thought out. And the best part was the bottom line: two million American dollars.

But one thing continued to bother him.

"What of the two men I spoke to you about this morning? Should we—"

"Forget about them," Saiif cut in. "They are of no importance to us."

"But—" A look from the man stopped Collette short and let him know that speaking further on the matter would be dangerous.

He said nothing more, and they parted company.

* * *

Saiif watched Collette look around nervously as he got up and made his way through the throngs of tourists to his car. He grinned. Collette really had no idea what kind of man he was dealing with, and the more he thought about it, the more he looked forward to killing him when his usefulness ran out.

Collette had been recruited like so many others. He'd been a freelance reporter for the American networks, CNN, and the BBC, covering the atrocities of war during the days of Desert Storm. Saiif had chosen him out of many. He had talent—that was obvious to anyone who'd seen his work— but he was an unknown and was greedy and self-centered enough to do anything to break into fortune and fame.

In the summer of 1992, Saiif approached and offered him twenty thousand dollars for just a moment of his time. Collette cautiously accepted. In return for some yet undisclosed assistance in the future, Collette was promised special, advance notice of what were certain to be international headline stories. As a gesture of good faith, and in addition to the up-front cash, he was told to be in New York in the vicinity of the World Trade Center on a certain February day in 1993. His camera was rolling, and his firsthand account of the bombing sent his career spiraling upward. His pictures were featured on the front page and cover of every major newspaper and magazine. He was suddenly famous, and the royalty checks quickly introduced and sustained a lavish lifestyle. A few years later he was in Israel and in the crowd at the very moment a young angry lawyer walked up behind the Israeli prime minister and fired at point blank range. Once again, his pictures were used worldwide, and once again, his career was boosted. Money kept rolling in. But his love of fast cars, and even faster women, eventually depleted his savings and ruined any line of credit he'd established. That was when Saiif called him again. Collette was eager to meet and only hesitated briefly when he heard the request that his mysterious benefactor was putting to him. It would necessitate that he forever leave the identity of Henri Collette behind, but, to recompense his loss, he was offered two million dollars. Collette accepted, and with that acceptance, almost a year ago, he started down the path that would shorten his life by forty years.

Saiif had confided in Collette only that which he needed to know. Collette, no doubt, felt that they were, somehow, partners in this whole thing. Saiif prided himself on being a convincing liar and able to charm the venom from a snake, and while his knowledge and expertise extended to many fields, Collette's occupation and position afforded him access to otherwise restricted areas. And now, thanks to Ryker, those areas would undoubtedly become nearly impenetrable. Saiif needed an expert, someone on the inside, someone who could improvise. He'd spent too much time and too much of his own money to have his little surprise upset at the last moment. This attack was just too important. Too much was at stake, and he wouldn't have another chance at this in his lifetime. And while only a handful would die at this, their deaths would just be the beginning. Hundreds more would die, and given time, thousand more would join them.

* * *

Ryker was already going through a stack of files when Lubin returned to the room and informed him of the conversation with Goldman. Sanders had retired to his office but had given orders to the personnel director to help the two men with anything they needed.

"Three crates?" Ryker asked in astonishment. "There are tactical nuclear weapons that wouldn't deliver that much punch. There isn't any way he could isolate a target with that amount of ordnance. Christian, Jew, or Muslim. American, Israeli, or Arab. It won't make any difference. Anyone within a reasonable radius of that explosion is going to die." With that, the attention of the two men was redirected to the pile of folders in front of them.

By two in the afternoon, the only things they had to show for their effort were tired eyes and two yellow notepads containing scribbled thoughts. They'd found nothing conclusive. If they'd had more time—if they could've done some in-depth background checks—maybe something would have surfaced. Lubin was prone to focus on Arabs in the employ of CNN—some common bond with the Chameleon. Ryker reminded his colleague that it hadn't been an Arab who'd killed Prime Minister Rabin. They just couldn't count on nationality playing a role.

They were just finishing the sandwiches and soft drinks that Sanders had arranged to be brought in from a delicatessen down the street. Ryker suggested that Lubin give Goldman a call with the bad news.

Lubin said, "I'm glad we're calling from here. I'd hate to be telling him in person."

He started to get up from his chair, but Ryker grabbed his arm and pulled him back down.

"Wait a minute! Maybe we've been going at all this from the wrong angle. We've been focused on finding the Chameleon's contact here. Maybe we should go beyond looking for the who and start looking for the why. We should be asking ourselves what kind of service this person is providing, or going to provide, and if it actually involves CNN."

"Okay, keep going," Lubin said.

"We suspect that the Chameleon is planning to use large quantities of explosives. Right? That much would probably need to be transported, probably by vehicle. Right? Now, we know that the police and the army plan to cordon off traffic at likely sites. So how is he going to get those explosives near enough to do the damage he plans?"

"Good question, Sam," Lubin finally replied.

"What did we notice when we first pulled up in front of this building? Vans . . . mobile units, that's what. The police can stop routine traffic, but they're going to have to let the media cover the religious commemorations, and to do that, media personnel need close access to the equipment found in those vehicles. That could explain the call to CNN."

"So what do you suggest we do about it? Since we flew in from Cairo, we've seen these news vans and others all over the place, covering one event after another. Just the Christian aspects are keeping the networks busy. Palm Sunday . . . Holy Thursday . . . Good Friday . . . and finally Easter Sunday. All significant in the life of Jesus. Throw in the start of the Jewish Sabbath and the subsequent Passover the following day, and those vans will be doing double and triple duty. Sure, we could have them all checked at one time or another, but what if the Chameleon plans to hijack one or more of them?"

"I thought about that, too. Wherever those news vans stop, they're just going to have to be shaken down. I don't see any other option."

"And what do we give as a reason that won't *create* a news story and possibly cause a panic? We could request to have dogs at all major sites to sniff those vehicles to their heart's content, but I doubt that we've got that many qualified dogs."

"Okay. How about this? There's no use checking those vans for anything now. They'd be clean. But we monitor their movement. The aerials on the vans indicate that they have radio communication. We get an itinerary from Sanders and have them check in at prearranged times. That way, if there's an attempt to hijack a vehicle, we'll know approximately when and where."

"Not if the crew is in on it," Lubin cautioned.

"So why don't we start with the crews. How many vans could there be? Twelve? Fifteen at the most? If you figure that there'll be two to three people manning each van, we've narrowed our list of suspects to something manageable."

"And if we narrow it further by focusing on the crews that'll be in or around Jerusalem and the other large celebration sites, that should cut it down even more," Lubin suggested.

"Agreed."

Sanders delivered his news crews' itineraries; the list was lengthy. For the next two hours, they scrutinized the files of those who'd be filming at sites that could logically be targets. Then they interviewed as many as were there that day. They were about to widen their search to include *everyone* connected to a news van when Lubin's cell phone buzzed.

Lubin punched the talk button. *"Shalom,"* he said. It was Goldman. Lubin listened for a while before speaking. "I see . . . In Jaffa and right here in Tel Aviv, huh? Give me the addresses. We'll check them out. Yes . . . I'm sure the police have, but maybe we'll stumble onto something they missed. Sure . . . sure . . . I understand. That would be helpful." He turned to Ryker. "Find out what the fax number is for this place." Ryker returned in a minute and gave the number to Lubin, who relayed it to Goldman.

The conversation went on for several more minutes with Lubin exploring the news van theory. Goldman was initially skeptical but warmed to the idea. He'd even order direct surveillance of the CNN motor pool area during the night for any suspicious movement. Lubin terminated the call.

"What was all that stuff at the beginning?" Ryker asked.

"An abandoned rental car turned up not far from here in Jaffa. The rental agreement in the glove box was made out to a Michael Rodriguez."

"So he's right here under our noses."

"That's not all. He knows *you're* on his trail."

"What makes you say that?"

"The phony passport was in the glove box. There was a message written in it. Translated, it said, 'Better luck next time, Ryker.'"

Ryker could feel his blood pressure rising and a throbbing at his temples.

"This has become a game of cat and mouse for him, Manni. He's toying with us and laughing all the while. Where was the car found?"

"Behind a Palestinian restaurant. It's not far from here. I told Levi that we'd have a go at the owner of that establishment."

"Anything else?"

"Yeah, it was determined that he'd had explosives in the trunk. At least the dogs apparently thought so. Clean now, though. Also, a body was found in a dumpster south of here. Neck had been snapped. American by the name of Mark Simon. Tourist. Just entered the country yesterday."

"Does Goldman think there's a connection?" Ryker asked.

"Wouldn't you? The guy still had a wallet full of money and a passport in his pockets. There was documentation that he'd rented a car when he arrived. No sign of it now. All of Israel has been alerted to the make and license number. I'd say the Chameleon needed a vehicle after abandoning his own. Coincidental? I think *not,* and neither does Levi. I told him we'd drive over there, too, and have a look around. He's faxing us that photo of 'Michael Rodriguez.' Might come in handy. It's proving to be a long night."

"Yeah, looks that way."

Ryker reviewed the list of CNN's scheduled activities comprising the rest of the day and those projected through Easter. Coverage of religious events over the next couple of days was limited to no less than a dozen throughout the larger Jerusalem area, and background footage was scheduled to be filmed at several other locations within Israel. Sanders had balked when they suggested that his remote crews check in regularly but had consented in the end.

Neither Ryker nor Lubin mentioned the phone call from Goldman as Sanders accompanied them down the elevator, across the foyer, and out the front door. The Mossad chief had ordered a media blackout on the abandoned car and the dead American. Sanders would just have to wait to begin the quest for his Pulitzer.

"Don't forget, now. A deal's a deal," Sanders reminded them.

"We'll keep our end of the bargain," Lubin replied. "Just make sure you keep yours. We'll be in touch. Probably tomorrow. Keeping track of your mobile units may be integral to this investigation."

They walked to their car and exited the parking lot. In the rearview mirror, Sanders could be seen standing in front of the building, presumably contemplating his good fortune and his next bureau assignment. Life was good.

Futile would be the best word to describe the next several hours. It was as though the owner and staff of the Palestinian restaurant were deaf and blind. It was also apparent that their attitudes toward even minimal cooperation with Israeli authorities needed substantial adjustment. It didn't make any difference how hard Lubin leaned; the staff leaned right back and sneered as they did. Brief recognition registered on the owner's face when shown the picture of the man claiming to be Michael Rodriguez, but he denied ever having seen him.

They were only marginally more successful when questioning the staff at the cafe behind which the American's body had been discovered. When shown the dead man's passport picture, they admitted that he'd eaten breakfast there. They remembered, because the man had trouble ordering from the menu. He spoke no Arabic, and only halting Hebrew, and none of the staff spoke English. They also indicated that another man joined him.

"Did he appear to know this individual?" Ryker asked in Arabic, surprising the restaurant staff with his fluency and lack of foreign accent.

"It is hard to say. Maybe, maybe not. But they seemed friendly enough toward one another."

"Can you describe the other man?" Ryker persisted.

"No, he sat with his back toward where I was standing at the cash register. And when they got up to leave, he was shielded by the American and out the door before I could see him. The American paid for them both."

Ryker tried one more time. "Might the other man have looked anything like this?" He showed Rodriguez's picture.

"Like I said, I did not get a good look."

That was it. Nothing more. The dead man's car rental agreement gave the name of the hotel where he'd been staying, but there was no sense going there. The police already had and achieved nothing for their efforts. No, the man had just been at the wrong place at the wrong time, and it had cost him his life. Another pawn in a deadly game of chess, just as Ryker's wife and children had been. Undoubtedly, the stolen car would turn up *only* after it had served its purpose, but an alert had been issued as a matter of routine. Bone-weary, they first returned to the command center, ran a copy of Sanders's mobile crew itinerary for Goldman, then drove back to the safe house. Though not deserted, the roads were relatively free of congestion, and they made good time. They arrived shortly after midnight, made themselves a quick sandwich, and headed for bed. Both dreaded the prospects of the next day.

* * *

At eleven-twenty PM, the remote control was complete. Operating on an ultra-low frequency, the detonator could be activated from a distance of just under a quarter mile. Everything had gone as planned today and *inshallah*, God willing, his luck would continue. There was only one thing left to do before returning to the hotel. Closing the garage door behind him, Saiif walked into the night. The moon was rising over the jagged horizon, casting a soft, peaceful glow on the streets below, but he hardly took notice. He was searching for the final element to complete his plan and hadn't walked ten minutes before finding it. A bundle of rags and crumpled cardboard in a back alley hid a beggar beneath. He appeared to be roughly the same size as Saiif, though his fetal position made it difficult to know for sure. Waking him, Saiif helped the man to his feet. Perfect.

"If you'd permit me, I'd like to buy you a meal," Saiif said in Hebrew.

"A meal?" The man seemed disoriented and surprised that anyone would take time to speak with him let alone offer food.

"Yes . . . a meal. Consider it my Passover gift to you."

The beggar's stench was nearly overpowering, and Saiif took short, shallow breaths as they walked down the alley.

"My friend," Saiif said, "God has something very great in store for you."

They never made it to a restaurant. Under the pretext of wanting to provide the man with a warmer coat, Saiif led him back to the garage. Positioning himself behind the man in rags, he broke his neck, much like the American that morning. He dragged the body to the freezer and dumped it in.

TWENTY-SEVEN

THE LIGHTED DISPLAY ON THE bedside alarm clock indicated 2:44 as Lubin rolled over and took a peek. He'd fallen asleep immediately, but now his bladder was under pressure. He lamented both draining that can of soda prior to crawling in between the sheets *and* his enlarged prostate. He tried rolling over and going back to sleep but didn't find that to be a comfortable option. Certain urges just couldn't be ignored.

Throwing the bed covers off to one side, he sat on the edge of the bed for a moment and scratched an itch. He then stood and trudged off to the bathroom.

A minute later, he was back in bed and looking forward to a few more hours of sleep before beginning another day, the conclusion of which didn't look too promising. He could hear the water replenishing the toilet tank, but, rather than shutting itself off, it continued to run.

He told himself that he was too tired to get up again and adjust the float mechanism or whatever the problem was. It happened all the time at his house. Or maybe the chain inside the tank had come loose from the handle and fallen, disturbing the seal at the bottom of the tank. The noise of running water was vaguely annoying, but there was no danger of anything overflowing. He pulled the second pillow over his head. After a moment, it was obvious that approach wasn't going to work. He was going to have to make the trek once more, this time to play plumber.

He turned on the bathroom light and walked to the toilet. The water was still running through the bowl. He jiggled the handle, and it was obvious from the lack of tension that the chain had detached. He lifted the tank lid and reached down to retrieve the hook on the end of the chain and affix it to the handle. He saw something then that pumped enough adrenaline into his system to bring him wide awake, though he was unsure exactly what he was looking at.

It appeared to be dark plastic bound into a small package with duct tape. It was wedged between the overflow tube and the back of the tank. He fought the instinct to remove it.

"*Sam!*" Lubin could hear him snoring in the other room. "Sam! Get in here!"

"What?" Ryker asked hesitantly, apparently unsure if he'd been dreaming or if someone had actually called his name.

"We've got a problem." Lubin could hear the bed creak as Ryker hung his feet over the side and stood up.

"Do you have any idea what *time* it is?" Ryker asked as he walked from his room to the open door of the bathroom. "What's the matter?" He rubbed the sleep from his eyes.

"Have a look first. Then we'll figure out what to *do* about it."

Ryker crossed the room to where Lubin stood and looked in the direction his friend was gesturing with his head.

"Holy—" He looked back at Lubin for confirmation.

"My sentiments exactly."

"It's a long shot, I know," Ryker said, "but maybe it's just something that belonged to former occupants? You know . . . something they forgot to take with them."

"Something that needed to be stored in a toilet tank at a Mossad safe house? Come on, Sam. You can do better than that, even at *this* hour. You know what it is as well as me."

"This is supposed to be a safe house, isn't it? Who'd plant a bomb? Only *your* people even know we're here."

"The good fairy didn't put it in there, Sam. I've got a feeling that the Chameleon has penetrated my agency, too. He knows we've been on to him since Cairo. We were only a few hours behind him today. He's trying to take us out of the game before we get any closer. Maybe we know more than we *think* we do."

"So what do you suggest? Evacuate the building?"

"For starters, yes." Lubin raced out through the front door into the hallway, and pulled on the fire alarm. Nothing happened. He tried again. Still nothing. "We got another problem!" he called back inside.

"Where's that alarm?"

"That's the problem."

"You mean . . . ?" Ryker ventured, standing at the bathroom door.

"We have to deactivate it," Lubin said. "Or everyone in this building dies a quick death."

"I was afraid you were going to say that. Listen, I don't know about you, but everything *I* know about dismantling a bomb could be put in a thimble with room to spare."

"Yeah, but if we're lucky, we'll save lives, because if we run, too, it may blow before everyone's out of the complex."

"What makes you think that?"

"Simple. I figure it's a timed device and not tied to the toilet being flushed. Otherwise, we wouldn't be having this conversation."

"Okay. Makes sense," Ryker admitted.

"It's got to be set to explode when we'd most likely be here. An early morning hour is my guess."

"Like about *now?*"

"Yeah, like about *now,*" Lubin repeated. "You start to peel away some of that covering so we can get a good look at it. I'll call the command center and alert the bomb disposal unit. I have no idea what their response time could be, but maybe they can give us some technical advice in the meantime." Lubin left the bathroom and headed for the cell phone on his bedside nightstand. He called back over his shoulder, "But be careful not to jiggle it."

"Yeah, sure thing," Ryker replied sarcastically, his hands shaking as though he were suffering from an alcohol tremor.

Ryker reached for a disposable razor on the sink and smashed the head with the bottom of a heavy bathroom glass. He extracted the blade and began to cut through the strips of duct tape, careful not to cut any deeper than necessary and careful not to jostle the package.

Lubin dialed the number for the command center. The call was answered before the first ring.

"Yeah . . . Manni Lubin here. I've got a problem. Connect me with the head of our bomb squad . . . Yeah, that's him . . . No, he *can't* call me back!"

"We're going to feel awfully foolish if we open this thing up and it turns out to be a toilet bowl disinfectant of some kind," Ryker commented loudly, the sound echoing slightly in the tiled room.

"Wouldn't bother *me,*" Lubin responded as he returned to the bathroom doorway, still waiting to be patched through.

"I'm slicing the plastic bag now."

"What do you see?"

"You're right! Definitely a bomb. About a pound of C-4 from the looks of it," Ryker said. "Timing mechanism is a digital watch. Numbers are counting backward, leaving less than three minutes before blastoff."

Ryker sat backward on the toilet seat, looking into the tank and taking stock of the device but nothing more.

Lubin turned his attention back to the phone and spoke rapidly in Hebrew. "Moshe? Manni Lubin."

A brief wave of relief washed over Lubin. Moshe Rabinowitz was as good as they came, despite the fact that he had lost two fingers on his left hand several years earlier while attempting to dismantle an explosive device found in a suitcase outside the chambers of the Knesset. By all rights, the blast should've killed him, but his protective clothing, in conjunction with a shatterproof polycarbonate shield, had saved his life. Rather than quit that line of work, he'd simply vowed to be more careful the next time. Still, there was no one else Manni Lubin wanted on the other end of the phone.

The exchange of crucial information happened quickly, but there was one question pressing on Lubin's mind.

"How quickly can your people get here?"

"Ten minutes," came the answer.

"They'll be able to sift through the rubble with the fire department in about two, but send them anyway. Apartment 1-B. Ben-Gurion Complex."

It was a three-way conference call, and the command center was already dispatching a disposal unit to the address. Fire engines were en route.

"Manni," Ryker shouted, "time's running out . . . *fast.*"

"Okay!" Lubin yelled back. He then resumed his conversation with Moshe. "I know it'll be hard—you not being here—but talk us through this. I'll relay your instructions, because your English *stinks.*" He couldn't help but introduce some levity into the perilous situation.

"Describe the device," Lubin said to Ryker.

"A digital watch body—an Armitron, if that makes any difference— embedded in a block of C-4 and counting backward toward three AM. Can't see any detonator, but there are wires, lots of them—red, black, and green— protruding from the watch and leading to what appears to be the contacts of a nine-volt battery, also embedded. Wires then disappear below the surface. That's all I can see . . . All wrapped in plastic and sealed with duct tape."

"Feel around the sides of it," Lubin relayed to Ryker. "Are there any other protrusions?"

There were none.

"He says the device can be removed from the tank. The odds of it being triggered by a mercury switch concealed inside are remote. Too hard to transport."

Ryker removed the rectangular mass and placed it on the tile floor, where he had better access. He looked in Lubin's direction.

"Do I cut one or more of the wires . . . or what? And if I do, what am I going to cut them with?"

Lubin relayed the questions and answers.

"Leave the wires alone! The colors may have no significance, and besides, without x-raying the device, you can't tell where they're attached beneath the surface. The nine-volt battery is there to send an electrical impulse to the detonator or detonators. It's fashionable these days to use more than one. The watch is there only for its timer and alarm capabilities."

Ryker sat back on his haunches. Lubin listened intently for a moment.

"This may sound almost too simple, Sam, but Moshe says all that may be needed is to stop the watch from completing its backward count. After all, we weren't meant to find the device. There'd be no reason for elaborate procedures to deactivate it. Look on the face. Is there a notation indicating which button on the edge of the watch should be depressed to stop or clear the numbers being displayed?"

Ryker bent closely over the device. "There's a symbol indicating stop, but there's no button," he replied. "All of the function buttons have been removed. The wires are protruding from where the buttons would be. Can we get into the back, extract the battery, and stop it that way?"

Lubin relayed the information.

A long pause ensued, then Lubin said, "By dislodging the watch body you're apt to disturb whatever wire contacts have been made. That could be *disastrous.*"

Ryker was getting desperate, the tremor in his hands becoming more pronounced. "Look, we've only got slightly less than a minute. Your friend better think of *something*. What about submersing it in water? The watch *was* waterproof, but the protruding wires have voided that feature. Wouldn't that short out the battery and stop it?"

"He says it's hard to tell . . . might send a premature surge of current. That's probably why it was wrapped in plastic in the first place." A pause. "Says he's out of ideas and to leave it and get out of the building."

"Wait a minute!" Ryker said. "Water's the answer. There was a bomb expert at Langley when I was a rookie—a former OSS agent. He said back during World War II, he immersed an explosive device in water . . . no . . . salt water . . . something about draining the power from a battery source. It's worth a shot. See if there's any salt in the kitchen. Hurry!"

Lubin sprinted away, tore through the cupboards until he found a nearly full box of salt, and raced back to the bathroom. He tossed it to Ryker.

"I'm sure there's some ideal ratio, but here goes," Ryker said, dumping the salt into the toilet bowl, and swirling it around with his hand. "If that old guy was right, this should do it . . ."

There were nine seconds remaining on the digital display when Ryker, on his knees, picked up the bomb and placed it in the salty water. Lubin watched on from the doorway.

Eight . . . seven . . . six . . .

The watch was still running.

". . . or maybe *not*!" Ryker jumped to his feet and raced from the room, grabbing Lubin as he passed and flinging both of them to the floor on the far side of the living room, their heads buried in their arms.

. . . four . . . three . . . two . . .

It was a second that seemed like an eternity, but nothing happened. No explosion. No fire. No body parts torn asunder. No tortuous screams from maimed survivors. Lubin looked over at Ryker, who was just lifting his head.

"Looks like we're still among the living," Ryker declared as he and Lubin got to their feet and walked slowly across the living room and into the bathroom. They looked down into the toilet bowl. The watch's display was blank. "There must've been a delay as the water found its way to the battery."

Lubin picked up his phone from the floor. "You still there, Moshe? It's all clear, but you better get over here just the same." He hung up.

They walked to the living room sofa and flopped down in their sweat-soaked pajamas, emotionally drained. Lubin got up briefly and retrieved a blanket from his bed to drape over them.

Outside, fire trucks wailed to a stop, flashing lights illuminating empty streets and sirens signaling to evacuate. Their crews went to work immediately alerting the tenants and getting everyone out safely.

A few minutes passed before four heavily clad members of Mossad's elite bomb disposal unit entered and went to work removing the device from the premises. Moshe Rabinowitz arrived some minutes later and spoke to members of his team who were just finishing up a further check of the apartment. He approached Lubin.

"You immersed it in *salt water*?" Rabinowitz asked incredulously.

Lubin nodded. "Sam's idea." He gestured toward Ryker. "Old World War II trick. I'm surprised you didn't think of it yourself, Moshe."

"I *did* think of it, but without the proper saline concentration, the odds favored triggering an explosion. It was a gutsy thing to do, my friend. I'd say you two were lucky, but even luck wouldn't quite cover it. It was a miracle you survived. The unsuspecting tenants of this place owe you their lives. I'll leave three of my men here until you're gone. Obviously someone knows your every move. I've also given orders for them to check out your parked car before you leave." He shook Lubin's hand, warmly nodded to Ryker, exited the room into the corridor, and was gone.

They dressed hastily and accompanied their escorts to the parking structure. The car passed inspection, and they headed for the command center.

Goldman greeted them as they entered. He looked tired, dark circles accenting his bloodshot eyes.

"A man my age could have used a couple more hours of sleep, but I guess it wasn't meant to be. I don't think anyone will be sleeping now until this thing's over." He'd already been briefed by Rabinowitz concerning the early-morning activity, but he wanted to hear it from his subordinate's lips. "So talk to me, Manni."

Lubin did.

"Only you two and maintenance have been inside that apartment since you arrived," Goldman commented when Lubin had finished the story.

"How can you be sure, Levi?" Lubin asked.

"Camera surveillance. That means there's a penetration. A moonlighting job."

"You're talking about someone who's passed an extensive background check and possesses security clearance."

"So?" Goldman said. "It wouldn't be the first time. We do it to others; why not have others do it to us? I've already given direction to have this man brought in for questioning. We'll know what he knows before breakfast."

Lubin didn't doubt Goldman's resolve for a second. This may have started out as just another terrorist incident in a series of hundreds, but now it had become personal. The Chameleon had penetrated their ranks—albeit at a low level—and there'd be hell to pay.

TWENTY-EIGHT

Tel Aviv

HENRI COLLETTE MOTIONED FOR HIS camera man, Bob Green, to climb into the passenger seat of CNN mobile unit 12. The camera man almost spilled his Styrofoam cup of coffee down his shirt. It was just after five AM, and he was still fuzzy. He regretted having stayed late at his wife's company Easter party, and even though he'd volunteered to be the designated driver and had remained sober, his four-thirty alarm had come too early.

Henri Collette got in behind the wheel and started the van. They were getting an early start as they had the farthest to travel to get the required film footage for tonight's broadcast. It seemed odd to Green that Collette had chosen a van with no satellite communication capabilities, but who was he to question the actions of the bureau's number one correspondent?

Traffic was expected to be light this early in the morning on the way north from Tel Aviv to Nazareth and the Sea of Galilee. The bureau was producing a two-part special on the life and ministry of Jesus and had been sending teams on shoots for the past week. Green was excited that he'd be working with Collette. If he was as good as everyone said, they were sure to be the highlight of the segment.

Collette pulled out of the motor pool area and headed north.

Green said rather timidly, "It's a real honor to accompany you on this assignment."

Collette seemed preoccupied and didn't appear to hear him.

"Sir?"

Collette snapped to. "Huh? *Oui. Oui.* I'm happy you're happy. Uh, Bob, is it? I need to stop briefly to pick up some special lenses and equipment. That okay with you? It will only take a moment."

Green thought Collette looked anxious but assumed it was all part of the artistic flair.

"Sure. It all pays the same."

Fifteen minutes later, the van approached a row of storage units and stopped. Collette exited and lifted the overhead door, exposing a darkened interior. Then he got behind the wheel, drove in, and parked. Green was just getting out, coffee cup in hand, when the door closed behind them. A fluorescent light flickered on, and the last thing he saw was a glint of metal under his chin. He dropped like a marionette with its strings cut.

* * *

Saiif wiped the bloody blade on his overalls.

"Put him in the corner," he ordered. "Over by the freezer."

Collette remained stationary, momentarily in shock by what he'd just witnessed. Saiif recognized the signs and knew that if he didn't act quickly and blunt his conscience, Collette would be emotionally paralyzed and become more of a liability to this operation than he already was. He grabbed the Frenchman and shook him.

"I said move him!" he barked.

"I . . . don't know . . ."

"What did you think this was going to be?" Saiif snarled. "A pleasant stroll down the *Champs-Elysees*? No, my friend." He forced Collette to look at him. "This is a rough game whose players are very serious. Now move him out of the way and be done with it."

Dazed, Collette dragged the corpse into the far corner.

Saiif said, "Your hands are now stained with his blood, but take comfort. By tomorrow your two million dollars will have cleansed your hands as well as your mind."

Collette looked down at his hands and wiped them with a crumpled rag he found on the floor.

"*Oui* . . . two million." And with that acknowledgment, Collette's humanity slipped from him like sand through an hourglass. He turned and peered into Saiif's dark eyes and smiled. "Let's get to it."

* * *

Benjamin Rosen crumbled like an overbaked piecrust even before any questions could be put to him. When he answered the knocking on his door at

about four-thirty in the morning, he didn't even wait for the two men to identify themselves. He knew immediately who they were and what they wanted.
He made no desperate attempts to conceal his actions of the previous day,
though his near-psychological breakdown made it apparent to the agents that
he'd performed under substantial duress. Whether that mitigating circumstance would make any difference to an Israeli court was unknown but
unlikely. What was certain was that Rosen would be going to prison for a long
time and that someone of his sensitive nature would have a rough go of it.

Agents picked up Rosen's colleagues, but it was determined after
rigorous questioning that Rosen had acted alone. The others were released,
wiser for the experience.

Apart from Rosen's confession of complicity, and a recounting of the
events in his life that had contributed to his current predicament, he
couldn't offer any significant information about the man who'd accosted
him in his apartment. The passport photo of Michael Rodriguez and the
composite picture developed in Cairo had been shown to him. He
confirmed the obvious.

Reluctantly, Lubin and Ryker admitted that the Chameleon still
appeared to be one or two moves ahead in this chess game of terror, but that
was understandable. He already knew where he was headed.

It was still early in the morning, and though activity was brisk, the
atmosphere of the command center was as somber as a funeral home.
Everyone was performing at exceptional levels, following through with
assignments to the nth degree. The combatants in this war against terrorism
were as sharp and as keen as their specialized training had prepared them;
nonetheless, there was a pervasive feeling of helplessness.

Ryker shared a thought with Goldman and Lubin as they stood near
one of several computer terminals, hastily eating stale bagels and washing
them down with tepid orange juice.

"Manni, you said something earlier this morning that's been nagging
me ever since."

"What was that?" Lubin asked as he gulped a mouthful of juice.

"Something to the effect that maybe we're closer than we know, and
that's why the Chameleon attempted to kill us."

"Yeah?"

"So what is it that we know?"

"That's just it, we don't *know* anything."

"CNN is our only lead, and that hasn't turned up much. I just don't
know what we have done that would spook him like this. Trying to blast us
out of that apartment was an act of desperation."

"Maybe his intent was merely to disrupt ongoing efforts; making us temporarily redirect our focus," Goldman offered.

"If that was his intention, why not have Rosen plant that bomb in *this* building? That *definitely* would've been a disruption," Ryker countered. "No, he specifically wanted *us* out of the way."

Goldman nodded his concurrence while tearing off a piece of hardened bagel with his fingers rather than subject his partial dentures to the task.

"So what's your thought, Sam?" Lubin asked. "What have we done to rattle him? By most accounts, every door we've opened has been slammed in our faces."

"Again, the key has to be CNN," Ryker began. "We know he talked to someone there days before he left Cairo. The missing tapes confirm that it wasn't an innocent call. Then at the same time that we were questioning CNN staff, and getting nowhere, he kills an American tourist and steals the guy's car, presumably because he'd already abandoned his own. He hastily fabricates a device from his stash of C-4. He drives to Rosen's apartment, coerces our likely whereabouts out of him, and *persuades* him to cooperate. All of this has to be a detour from his original plan, triggered by our presence at CNN."

"I think Sam's right, Levi. Somehow he didn't plan on us turning up at CNN, and, when we did, the danger alarm rang in his head. He didn't care about us knowing that he was, or had been, in Jaffa. Otherwise he wouldn't have abandoned his rental car there and certainly wouldn't have left that message for Sam. He was taunting us, knowing that we'd find only another dead end. I say we go back to CNN this morning, Levi, and nose around. Sanders is being cooperative. Something might come to us while we're there . . . unless you've got a better idea."

"What makes you two think that the Chameleon won't have another go at it—still try to take you out somehow?" Goldman asked.

"I don't think he has that luxury. Time's running for him the same as for us. Passover celebrations will begin at sundown, and Easter will commence only hours later. Whatever he has planned won't be some random act of violence. It's going to be well orchestrated, and it's going to require his personal and undivided attention. He can't afford another deviation."

"You may be right, but after this morning's events, I'm taking you out of the action. You're just too hot right now. I can't afford to lose you two like this. Not when there was opportunity for me to save you."

This was the last thing they expected to hear from Goldman.

"You can't do that!" Lubin protested. "*He's* coming after *us*. You take us out, and he wins. He thinks we know something. If anyone has a chance to flush this guy out, it's us."

"That's just it. The hunter has become the hunted. It's too dangerous. I refuse having to explain to Esther why her husband didn't come home. You might be right about CNN, but you won't be the ones to follow up. I'll have someone else check it out."

"But Levi—"

"There's nothing to discuss, Manni. You two are grounded. Your wings are clipped. Call it what you want, but you're staying put for now. That's that."

* * *

Collette carefully tore apart the interior of the van while Saiif set the explosives in relay and tested the connections for current. Somewhere around two in the afternoon, they took a ten-minute break for lunch. As planned, Collette called Keith Sanders and reported that they had experienced mechanical trouble and would be unable to make it back in time for the editors to use what they'd filmed. They were sure, however, that it would be repaired in plenty of time for them to proceed to their assignment the following day.

"Oh, and by the way, Keith, call Bob's wife and tell her it's not likely that he'll be home tonight. He doesn't want her to worry."

They worked well into the night to make sure that the van appeared perfect in every way in the likely event that they'd be stopped at one roadblock or another. By the time they were done, nearly two hundred pounds of C-4 explosive had been concealed and rigged for detonation. Saiif wouldn't set the remote frequency until they were in position. It was unlikely that an ultra-low band would be broadcasting anywhere near the van on its way to Jerusalem, but Saiif wasn't about to take any chances. Dying by his own hand was *definitely* not part of the plan.

Collette stepped back when they were done and sipped the last of his warm beer. "'Behold,'" he said reverently, quoting from the New Testament, "'a pale horse: and his name that sat on him was Death.'"

He looked to Saiif for a response but found to his surprise that he'd disappeared from his side. Struck with a sense of fear that Green's fate might be his own, he spun around, not wishing to be taken by surprise. Movement in the back corner caught his attention.

"Collette, come here. Help me with this."

"Help you with what?" But when he walked to the freezer and saw its contents, he instinctively turned away and thought that he'd be sick.

"Who is he?"

"Help me put him in the back of the van."

"Of the *van?* What's this all about?"

In a move almost too fast to be seen, Saiif grabbed Collette by the shoulders and pushed him up against the wall.

"Let's get something straight, shall we? I am the one that asks the questions. I am the one that tells you what to do and when to do it. You do not need to *know* everything. You don't *want* to know everything. You have a job to do, and up to this point you have done it well. But unless you want to change places with him, I suggest you keep your eyes open and your mouth shut. Do I make myself clear?"

Collette cowered against the wall, turning his face so as to not see the devil he had made the deal with and closed his eyes and nodded nervously. "Yes."

"Yes, what?"

"Yes, you make yourself clear."

Saiif let him go. "Now help me put him in the back."

Task completed, Saiif stepped out of his mechanic's overalls, wearing a pair of faded blue jeans, an Oxford shirt, and a field jacket similar to the one Collette was wearing. He bent down and snatched Green's CNN press pass from his chest and clipped it to his own jacket. He bore a passing resemblance to the dead man if one didn't overly scrutinize the photo.

"We should get moving," Saiif said. "The streets are going to be packed, and we still have one last stop to make."

Collette nodded his obedience, but new doubts crept into his mind, and for the first time he realized that he was disposable, like that poor sap they loaded in the back. He would have to be careful to make it out with his life, let alone the money.

Collette backed the vehicle out. Saiif then closed the overhead door and climbed in the passenger side. He put the leather case containing the nine-millimeter Makarov and the compact Scorpion submachine gun on the floor between his legs. The camera concealing the remote control device was placed next to him on the seat. Neither of them spoke as the van headed east.

* * *

Lubin was right, and Goldman knew it. Pride took its course, and Goldman finally relented late in the day and assigned them to stakeout duties. They were to undertake surveillance of Jewish activities scheduled for Jerusalem's Great Synagogue. Their fallback position in the morning, should it be necessary, would be the Garden of Gethsemane at the base of the Mount of Olives. There'd already been a gathering at the garden earlier in the week to commemorate Jesus' transfiguration and suffering prior to His arrest, trial, and crucifixion, but visiting Christians seemed mesmerized by the peacefulness of the area, and a large Easter sunrise service was scheduled there for dawn. The combined locations of Jesus' crucifixion and the supposed tomb where He lay for three days before His resurrection would also gather enormous crowds as would church services at Saint James Cathedral. These latter two sites were being given particular attention by the men and women under Goldman's command.

Once leaving the expressway, pedestrians, cars, carts, and animals clogged the streets and contributed to the men's frustration. If a lot of things had gone differently, Ryker surmised, maybe the Chameleon would have already been in custody. But he *wasn't* in custody, and he'd strike again with a vengeance in a matter of hours. He thought about his wife and children, victims of a madman who'd taken their lives as easily as one might turn down a bedspread—almost no thought given to the act. Last week it had been Robert Evans, someone who'd only wanted to heal the sick and afflicted. Then there was Deborah, narrowly escaping the death that Badri's bullets nearly achieved. Several policemen in Cairo were already in their graves because of the Chameleon. How many other men, women, and children had been touched by this devil over his long career? How many would yet be touched? How many lives of survivors would be seriously altered? Certainly his own had been. He'd have thought himself a religious man whose faith had prepared him to confront and conquer adversity, but when the hour came, he'd succumbed to depression and despair. Had it not been for President Cannon's phone call, he, too, would've passed into another existence—one hopefully better than this one, as the congregation at his family's memorial service had been assured. There was no question but that his life had been spared, but for what purpose? To rescue three missionaries? Okay, that had been accomplished. Maybe he should've returned home. Now, other people were likely to die because he fell short of the field officer he once had been. How many more deaths were to be etched on his conscience? Weren't his family's enough? They had died because of what he *was*. Now others would die because of what he *wasn't*. And what about Deborah? Yes, there were feelings between them, but what did he have to offer her? He was close to being a basket case. No, she deserved better than anything he could give. It just wouldn't work out. Still . . . he wanted to see her again.

The buzz of the cell phone made them jump. Lubin reached for the receiver with his right hand while swerving the car to miss a young boy leading a donkey across the road.

"*Shalom* . . . Yes . . . yes . . . I see. You're sure the conversation didn't sound forced? Yes . . . yes . . . between here and Nazareth, huh? Well, thank you for letting us know, but it doesn't sound as if there's anything to worry about. Yes . . . yes . . . You can rest assured that we'll keep our end of the bargain. Good-bye, Mr. Sanders."

Ryker looked over at his friend. "What did Sanders have to say?"

"Mobile unit twelve just called in. They broke down on the way back to the bureau. Just outside of Nazareth. Wanted Sanders to know that he'd have to do without the film they'd shot this morning."

"Really? Wouldn't they be able to transmit that stuff via satellite? Most of those vans have the equipment on the roof."

"Yeah, I know, but Sanders said that particular unit is brand-new, and that the electronics hadn't been installed yet." Lubin steered the car around a cart loaded with tourist trinkets. A street vendor, attired as he would've been at the first Passover, was pushing it.

Ryker consulted Sanders's list. "Number twelve is manned by Henri Collette and his cameraman, Robert Green. We didn't interview either one of them yesterday, did we?"

"No," Lubin replied. "I think they were about next on our list when Levi called and pulled us away."

"Then why does Collette's name sound familiar?"

"He's CNN's ace reporter according to Sanders, remember?"

"Right. So did Sanders think everything sounded on the up-and-up when he called in?"

"Yeah. Said breakdowns are common enough."

"I don't like it, though." Ryker shrugged off the doubts. "Besides, nothing is scheduled in Nazareth."

"True, but I'd better make Levi aware just the same."

Lubin dialed the command center and talked to Goldman.

Goldman had heard of Henri Collette and knew of his professional credentials and even admired his work, but he wasn't taking any chances at this stage of the game. There were only a couple of main roads coming out of Nazareth. He already had a team in the area, so he'd have it take a look. If the van were broken down, it would be easy enough to spot.

Lubin broke the connection and relayed the conversation to Ryker, who grunted approval. They fell silent as the car continued its journey, dodging whatever obstacles lay in its path.

* * *

The official presence of the Israeli government was obvious as Lubin and Ryker entered the old city. While there may not have been widespread use of roadblocks or pedestrian checkpoints, the strategic placement of armed personnel among the crowds was evident. Most notable were those dressed in military fatigues with Uzis slung over their shoulders. They strolled the streets in teams of two but appeared not to be intimidating to those who milled about. The sight of patrolling soldiers was common; it was simply a fact of life in that region. Visitors quickly acclimated themselves and even felt safer as a result of the visible military presence.

In addition to roving soldiers, Lubin noted to himself several other faces in the crowd as the car wound its way along. They belonged to fellow Mossad personnel who undoubtedly carried concealed weapons under their civilian attire.

The sun was just setting when they arrived at Jerusalem's Great Synagogue located in the west of the city. Erected in 1983 in memory of the six million Jews of the Holocaust, as well as in commemoration of Israel's fallen soldiers, the marble and stained-glass edifice stood opposite the Sheraton Hotel. As the largest of Jerusalem's synagogues, it could accommodate seventeen hundred worshippers, and tonight it would be full.

Ryker felt a tightening in his throat when he saw the hotel. Being seated with his family around a breakfast table in the opulent dining room was one of his fondest memories. Everyone had been so excited to be together again. Then . . .

As their car approached a checkpoint a block from their destination, a young soldier came forward to inform the driver that no vehicular traffic was allowed beyond this point. Lubin let the boy finish his spiel and then offered his credentials. The soldier took a step backward and straightened momentarily to attention. He then consulted a clipboard containing the vehicle license plate numbers and intended passengers cleared to enter the area. Confirming the vehicle and passengers in question, he motioned for colleagues to move the barrier aside.

A CNN van and one belonging to the British Broadcasting Corporation could be seen parked off to the left, undoubtedly setting up for stories and reports about the upcoming celebrations. A German shepherd on a long leash lifted his hind leg, urinated on a tire, and leisurely continued to walk between the two vehicles. The explosive-sniffing dog was nonplussed.

Ryker glanced again at the list that Sanders had given them. Unit number nine was scheduled to cover this event, and the number printed on the rear of the van in question confirmed it to be the right van. Apparently, everything was as it should be. The BBC van had passed muster.

Lubin parked the car, and they exited and found the ranking military officer in charge of securing the area. Lubin recognized the man as an old acquaintance, and they shook hands warmly. The colonel indicated that the area had been thoroughly searched throughout the day, that nothing suspicious had been found, the only vehicles within the immediate area being officially cleared. The officer was quite confident that nothing was going to mar this, the largest of Passover services.

"I'm sure you're right, Saul," Lubin said, "but we'll just have a look around ourselves. No one can afford to be too cautious in a circumstance like this."

"I agree. If you need anything, I should be over there." He pointed to a jeep parked twenty-five yards away. "If not, my troops will know where to find me." He offered his hand to Lubin once again and then walked toward the jeep.

"Well?" Ryker asked.

"Saul's a good man—a *thorough* man. No stranger to this kind of operation. If he says the place is clean, then you can pretty well count on it. But like I told him, we'll wander around a bit ourselves."

Lubin and Ryker particularly scrutinized the crowds of faithful who had come to experience Passover in the Holy City. They suspected that if the Chameleon was in this throng, he would've surely altered his appearance, yet they made eye contact with as many passersby as possible in the hope that some flicker of recognition would manifest itself. Nothing.

They returned to their vehicle after encircling the area and sat with both front doors open. The evening was cool but not unpleasant. Occasionally, Lubin would start the engine and listen to the radio traffic. If the Chameleon struck anywhere, radio communications would be frantic. Only surveillance posts checking in and reporting an all clear could be heard. Lubin turned off the engine, and the radio fell silent. He looked over at Ryker.

"Sam, these gatherings will be breaking up soon. Maybe the Chameleon caught wind of the increased security and abandoned his scheme. I'm sure that Levi has ensured that every other location is as tight as this one. Levi hasn't risen to the top of Mossad by being timid. If he's made up his mind not to let the Chameleon get close enough to exact the death and pain he intends, then you can take it to the bank. Forewarned is forearmed. Up till now, the Chameleon's greatest asset has been surprise. He never should've hinted that he'd be coming to Israel."

"Change his plans? Spare Jerusalem his hatred? I'd like that to be true, but my feeling is that his arrogance will propel him forward. He's still planning to pull this off right under our noses. How? I don't know, but he's not going to back off. I think Deborah is right about that. Saiif is relentless.

In another ten minutes, the crowd started to dissipate, looking for parked cars, returning to awaiting buses, hailing taxis, or simply walking into the beautiful spring night. Lubin idled the car again. There were no reports of carnage. No calls for ambulances or fire trucks. Nothing.

"Twenty more minutes or so, and we'll know that Passover commemorations weren't the target," Ryker commented.

"Yeah, looks that way. The next hurdle to overcome will be Easter services." He looked around one more time to assure himself that everything was, in fact, all right. He closed the door and started the car.

"Come on, Sam. There's another place I think we should stop tonight."

TWENTY-NINE

MANNI LUBIN TOOK BACK ROADS to Temple Mount. Traffic barriers had been set up at several intersections, posts manned by armed, uniformed personnel. It was still two days until Easter morning, but security was already tight at the holy site. Goldman had seen to that. At each one Manni identified himself, presented his identification, and was subjected to close scrutiny. He wouldn't have had it any other way and would've been upset if security had been any less tight. Lubin knew that this trip was for the best and hoped that his friend would understand.

He pulled the car into a small parking lot and extinguished the headlights. The area at the base of the Wailing Wall was well lighted though deserted.

"What are we doing here?" Ryker asked.

Lubin put his hand on his friend's shoulder. "Since the minute you called me from Paris I have been thinking about this. I don't need to be a rabbi to see you're still in pain. We might not get another chance."

Ryker regained some composure. "Look, I know you mean well, but I'm really messed up. I don't know if this is the time. Maybe after this is all over. Maybe then I'll—"

"It would be easy for me to say, 'Sure, whatever you think is best,' but then I wouldn't be true to our friendship. There's no good reason for delay. All's quiet here, and there's no time like the present. Sam, you've got to get on with it. You need to heal yourself; you need to confront the past head-on."

Ryker just sat there, staring over at the Wall like it was some unconquerable foe, and then he opened his door. Lubin got out of the car with him.

"Sam, I'm going to check in with the team parked near the entrance. I'll be along shortly, okay?"

"All right," Ryker replied.

Lubin watched his friend start toward the site of the nightmare that had been haunting not only his sleep, but also his waking hours.

Lubin walked over to meet his colleagues and spoke through the car window.

"So, David, did Levi assign you two to guard *this* place?"

David Epstein was the newest, and certainly the most polite, member of Lubin's Mossad unit. Epstein represented a new breed of agent for the twenty-first century. A scholar from Hebrew University, he was fluent in seven languages and possessed a burning desire to serve Israel. Lubin wasn't one to be easily impressed but felt that the Mossad would be in good hands as Epstein progressed through its ranks.

"Yes, sir, after a manner of speaking," Epstein replied. "He needed a surveillance team here just in case your man decided that he'd be content blowing up antiquities instead of civilians. Goldman also thought that you two would be around at some time and wanted someone here who knew you, so you wouldn't have any difficulty gaining access to the Wall."

"Levi actually *predicted* that Sam and I would show up here?" He laughed softly.

"Well, you know Goldman a lot better than I. It's that sixth sense everyone says he has."

Lubin knew exactly what Epstein was referring to. Goldman *did* have an uncanny way of processing information and projecting it into the future. Apparently he'd looked into Ryker's soul in the command center and had seen what drove him—what haunted him.

The young agent continued. "So that's him, huh?" gesturing with his head toward the figure walking away. "I heard he's retired CIA."

Lubin just shook his head. There was no way to keep information away from the best intelligence gathering agency in the world.

"I remember that attack. His family were the three Americans killed in the blast?"

Lubin just nodded.

"And now he's back to avenge his family's death?"

"Maybe that was motivating him a few days ago, but I don't think that's what's driving him now. I think he now only wants to resolve the confusion he feels inside."

"If he doesn't want to hunt the Chameleon down and kill him, then he's a better man than me, because that's exactly what I'd want to do under the circumstances."

"Yes . . . well . . . he *is* a better man than you *or* me. I've known Sam Ryker for more years than I care to remember, and I can tell you that you'll never meet a finer, more decent human being. He wouldn't agree, of course, because he's too modest and unassuming, but it's true nonetheless."

"That's awfully high praise. You're right; I haven't been around long, but I know enough to respect your judgment. If you feel that way about him, then I'm sorry I never had the privilege of working with him."

Lubin looked out toward the Wall.

"Keep an eye out, David. I think I'll head over there with Sam for a while. He hasn't been back here since it happened. Maybe I can lend a little support." With that, Lubin turned and walked off in the same direction that Ryker had.

* * *

Ryker walked the length of the cobblestone plaza that lay at the base of the Wailing Wall. He halted when he reached the spot where he'd last seen Susan and the girls. He knew it was the exact location. Some of the paving stones had been replaced with newer ones, and others showed the scars of scorching from the intense heat generated by the explosion.

Upright metal folding chairs dotted the plaza. They were there for use by supplicants who came in throngs each day to pour out their hearts to God. He drew one close and sat down, never taking his eyes off the blackened stones. Now that he was here, he was unsure what to do. He briefly looked over his right shoulder to see Lubin standing at the driver's door of the other vehicle.

He had never imagined himself setting foot at the base of the Wall again, and he was unprepared for the overwhelming feelings that seized his heart and mind. So many questions, so many fears, so much pain. Knowing that people came to this location from around the world to speak with God, he reasoned that he could do no less. He bowed his head.

"Father in heaven . . ." he began but couldn't finish anymore. The words stuck in his throat. He hadn't prayed vocally since Susan had died, and it felt awkward. He was unsure how receptive God would be to someone who'd turned his back on Him when life had gotten hard. His religion had taught him to meet opposition head on, and he'd thought it to be a good principle. In practice, however, he hadn't been strong enough to endure the pain, and his beliefs had suffered. Inwardly, he felt hypocritical asking God to intervene in his life and to restore the sense of peace that he'd once known, especially being aware that he'd often cursed God since his family's death.

But his prayer persisted and, had it been heard by a passerby, would have sounded as though he were simply talking to a friend sitting on a park bench. There was no pretense, no stilted language, just words from his heart—plain words spoken in humility.

He sat there, emotionally drained, tears streaming down his face, though his eyes remained closed. He'd never felt like this before and had certainly never before prayed in this manner—as though he'd been face-to-face with the Creator. He'd come as far as he was capable. It was now up to the Lord to meet him somewhere on the path if, indeed, He was so inclined.

The cool night breeze ceased, and he could feel a presence behind him. It was still, and he felt a warmth grow within him. He was afraid to turn around for fear there would, in fact, be no one there. So he kept his eyes closed and his head bowed.

Sam, darling.

His whole being began to shake, and he started to cry. Oh, if only this were real. But it was. He was sure of it. More than anything he was sure Susan was there with him.

We love you, Sam. We will always love you, and we'll be together again.

He couldn't be sure whether the words were spoken aloud or not, but it didn't matter. It was Susan's voice, and she sounded even more lovely than he remembered.

"I'm so sorry . . . so sorry that I failed you and—" He couldn't finish the words. But unlike before, he wasn't restrained from finishing his words out of shame or guilt, but by a stern reprimand from his loving wife. And then he felt it. A reassurance that he had never failed them. He had been a loving husband and father, his faults and shortcomings far outweighed by his love and faith. He tried to fight the feeling but it was just too powerful. His heart felt as if it would burst with joy and beauty, and the tears continued to flow.

"But I miss you so much," Ryker cried.

And then he felt the presence merge with him as he partook of that peace and joy that was the spirit of his wife. He breathed in deep, the floral scents wafting down from the ancient gardens that dotted the hillsides reminding him of the perfume Susan used to wear. He was taken away, leaving his doubt and pain behind as he glimpsed, if only for the briefest of moments, the image of Susan, standing tall and more beautiful than she had ever been. And she was not alone. Standing on either side of her were images of his daughters, Natalie and Niccole, smiles on their faces and hugging their mother around the waist.

The vision began to fade.

"Wait . . . no, please. I—" He felt a hand on his shoulder. He looked up quickly, fully expecting to see Susan standing there. It was Lubin.

Ryker looked around and then wiped the tears from his eyes. "How long have you been there?"

"Only a few moments. I didn't want to disturb you."

"Did you . . . I mean, could you hear . . . ?"

Manni Lubin's eyes began to water. "I have heard of many miracles taking place on this ground. Our people believe that God dwells here, and that the gate of heaven is located just above it. Did you know that?"

Sam Ryker smiled and nodded, unable to find the words to express what just happened to him. And with that smile so much of the pain and anger and guilt was washed away.

Lubin put his hand on his friend's shoulder. "You look like you could use a drink. There's an artesian well not far from here. Legend holds that King Solomon used it—that it was the mineral content of the water that made him so wise. It's kind of a tourist attraction. During the day, there'd be a line of people waiting to sip water from it, but at this time of night, the place will be empty."

"Wisdom, huh?" Ryker said with a half laugh.

"That's what they say. As you can see, it's worked for me." Lubin grinned.

"Yeah . . . sure. What could it hurt?"

Just then Ryker's cell phone rang. He looked at Lubin with some surprise. Who would be calling him at this hour? He looked at the display. "It's Deborah. Why would she—? Hello?"

"Sam, it's me."

"What's wrong? You're supposed to be taking it easy."

"Sam, I know why he's there."

"Deb, what are you talking about?"

"It's not just for the two holidays. Sam, he's going to hit the peace summit."

"Peace summit?" he said, partially out of surprise, but also to let Lubin in on the conversation. "What peace summit?"

"It's not on any of the radars yet," she said, her voice excited and almost out of breath. "It's been kept a complete secret to prevent anyone from doing this very thing. It's going to be held at the Dome of the Rock in the morning." Deborah quickly shared what she knew, and Lubin leaned in and listened in with Ryker. Disgusted by their respective governments and political agendas toward each other, three religious leaders from Christianity, Judaism, and Islam were taking the initiative and doing something to promote peace. This weekend, she explained, not only held the religious holidays of Passover and Easter, but it was also the first of the Islamic month Dhul-Hijjah, the time most loved by Allah as the faithful prepared to make the pilgrimage to Mecca. Initiating this call to peace was the Greek Orthodox Arch Bishop of Lviv, a senior rabbi of Jerusalem's Liberal synagogue, and the Mullah of Mecca, and they planned to address the world from the one place sacred and holy to all three faiths: the Dome of the Rock.

"The three holidays have never shared the same timeframe before," Deborah continued. "This is truly a once-in-a-lifetime event. Think about it, Sam. Three of the world's religious leaders coming together to plead for peace. It would be wonderful, wouldn't it?"

The Chameleon's plans suddenly became clear. "Not only would the peace summit put a dent in his business, but if something were to happen to any one of them—"

"Or all three," Lubin added.

"The backlash would catastrophic," Ryker agreed. "The death toll on all sides would be devastating. Deb, you should get a medal for this."

"I'll settle for you coming back in one piece."

"Who have you shared this with?"

"Just Taylor. I have a message in for Chandler."

"Deb, we gotta go. Good work, and let me know if you learn anything else." He ended the call.

"Manni?"

He was already on his phone. "I'm on it."

Ryker began scanning the darkness just beyond the lights of the Western Wall. He was out there, and now they knew what he was up to. The advantage was now theirs. One way or the other, tonight the chase would end.

THIRTY

"STOP THE VAN!" SAIIF SUDDENLY ordered. They were on the roads criss-crossing the hills overlooking the Jewish Temple Mount on their way to the Muslim Quarter and the Cedars of Lebanon. "Stop! Now!"

Henri Collette stomped on the brakes and jerked the wheel, pulling over in a skid of dirt and rocks. "What?" he nervously asked.

Saiif was looking out the passenger window at the lit square below. "Allah be praised," he muttered and then got out of his seat and stepped into the back of the van. Collette looked out across the news van and saw two figures lit by the lights at the Western Wall. The van's side door slid open, startling Collette. Looking back, he saw Saiif lining up the men in the sights mounted atop a very large rifle.

"This is too poetic," Saiif muttered again. "It is all too perfect."

In a rare display of courage, Henri Collette was suddenly urged to do the right thing. Over the years he had reported on countless deaths and murders, sometimes being close enough to reach right out and touch the lifeless bodies. But there was always that professional distance he had been able to create. They weren't people, they were stories. But when he watched Bob Green fall to the ground, and then felt the blood on his hands, something had snapped inside of him, and he realized that there was a good chance that he would not live long enough to see any of the money. And to make the change of heart complete, no amount of money was worth this killing. He did not know who the men were at the Western Wall, but he wanted no part in their deaths.

"So much for your God's favor," Saiif said softly as he lined up one of the men in his sights.

Collette shut his eyes tightly for a moment and then threw himself at Saiif, knocking into him the instant he pulled the trigger.

* * *

"Goldman just found out about the summit, too," Lubin said excitedly. "It seems Deborah and he have the same source. He's moving teams into area but needs us to keep an eye out—"

Sam Ryker heard the bullet strike the wall behind him before the sound of the gunshot reached him. Both he and Lubin ducked and dropped to one knee. Manni Lubin was in the middle of explaining Deborah's news when the shot rang out and he dropped the phone to the stone plaza. Pieces of it scattered.

"What was that?"

Lubin scanned the hills but couldn't see anything. "Are you hurt?"

"I'm all right."

* * *

Saiif had been taken completely by surprise by Collette's action. He was knocked out of the van but recovered fast enough to land on his feet. Collette was not so agile and fell to the ground. Turning quickly, Saiif struck Collette with a solid blow to the side of his head. The French reporter collapsed and rolled a short way down the embankment. Saiif quickly grabbed the rifle and took aim for another shot.

* * *

Another gunshot rang out. This time missing Ryker by mere inches, kicking up a small chunk of the stone ground. But this time he got a fix on where the shot had come from.

"There," he pointed. "That van. See it?"

Lubin did, and he grabbed Ryker by the arm and pulled him up and across the courtyard toward their car. Ryker moved to get in behind the wheel.

"What do you think you're doing?" Lubin asked.

"I'm driving."

"Not a chance. This is my city, in case you'd forgotten, and we don't have time for me to give you directions at every turn. Move over."

Ryker did as he was told and smiled, grateful for his friend's ability to keep a cool head even when they found themselves at the receiving end of a sniper's rifle.

* * *

Saiif threw the rifle into the back of the van and sped off down he hill. He didn't think for a minute that Ryker and his Israeli friend were running away. They would be coming for him. But he wasn't ready for them. How could this be happening? It was not supposed to end like this! He reached over and pulled the nine-millimeter out of the glove box. If it was a fight Ryker wanted, Saiif was only too happy to oblige him.

* * *

Lubin had the pedal to the metal as he maneuvered their big Ford Victoria through the maze of streets that twined through the city, pushing the eight cylinders to give up their full potential. A minute later they found the van. Ryker was on the radio, informing Goldman that they had found their man and were in pursuit. A quick flash from the van up ahead and their front headlight shattered.

"Try for the tires," Lubin said.

"What if I hit the C-4 instead?"

"Bullets won't set it off. We have to stop him."

Ryker leaned out the window and fired a short burst just as the van veered left then right. It would've been a tough shot even in the daylight.

Another flash came from the driver's window of the van, a round hitting the top corner of their windshield. It didn't shatter, but the bullet tore a large hole through it. The van continued without slowing, but Lubin pulled the vehicle abruptly to the left, out of the line of fire.

"I think Goldman was right: we are *definitely* too old for this line of work," Ryker commented dryly.

"Yeah . . . but it does give purpose to the day; you have to admit *that*," Lubin responded. Ryker leaned out of the passenger window, waiting for a clear shot.

"I'm done playing with this guy," Lubin said. "Are you ready? Take him out."

As the Ford approached, Ryker let loose a round of shots. The van braked and swerved left, making Lubin pull behind and back toward the right. The car was met with another burst of semiautomatic weapon fire, striking the hood and then taking out the rest of the windshield. A slug pierced the engine compartment firewall and struck Ryker's right thigh.

Involuntarily, he dropped his gun and retreated back into the car, his hands tightly grabbing the widening red stain seeping through his pants.

"How bad is it?"

Ryker didn't respond but grabbed his friend's automatic Uzi and pulled back the bolt. "Don't slow down," he said, letting loose a barrage of nine-millimeter Parabellum rounds. In the one headlight they could see bullet holes riddle the back and side of the van. The back tire suddenly blew out and the van swerved off the road and up the hill, coming to a stop about a hundred meters into the small grove of trees. Lubin slammed the brakes and pulled over, throwing Ryker into the dashboard.

"Where are you going?" Ryker asked.

"Tell Goldman we're at Gethsemane."

"Wait, you can't go after him alone."

"I'd invite you go come along, but the crutches are in the other car," Lubin joked. "Don't worry, I won't be long." He took the Uzi back and then he was gone.

Ryker yelled in frustration, slammed his fist into the driver's seat, and then started looking for something to cinch over the hole in his leg. There was no way Lubin was going to take down the Chameleon all by himself. It just didn't feel right. He would need someone to watch his back. *Al-Har'ba* was just too good for Lubin to take down by himself. Ryker heard shots fired. He couldn't wait any longer. He didn't care about the pain.

Ryker started out after his friend, limping and then dragging his wounded leg behind him. As he rounded the first giant olive tree, he heard another shot and watched Lubin jerk backward and fall to the ground.

Manni!

Ryker kept pushing himself forward. He could feel the warm blood oozing down his leg, but it didn't deter him from reaching his fallen comrade. He dropped to one knee once he reached Lubin and felt for a pulse. At first he couldn't find it, but then he detected one. Weak, but steady. In the dim moonlight he could see a dark stain growing across his shoulder. He could hear the sounds of approaching sirens.

Ryker picked up the Uzi and checked the magazine. There were only a handful of rounds left. They would have to be enough. He moved the firing selector to allow the release of one round at a time. All he needed was one.

"Saiif!" Ryker called out toward the stalled van. "You have the right to remain silent, and all that. But I wish you wouldn't." A minute later he saw movement inside the cab and took his shot. The dark figure was thrown backward into the back of the van. Ryker waited a minute before approaching, automatic weapon at the ready.

It took him almost half a minute to cover the ten meters or so. There was no sign of Saiif at the van. Dread flooded over him at the sight of what was inside. There must have been a hundred bricks of C-4 explosive. There was enough plastique here, he thought, to level a small city. And with the proximity the news van would have afforded him, there would have been little, if anything, left of the Dome of the Rock or its peace summit. He moved on. The passenger door was open and he could hear shuffling and scratching on the far side of it. Wary of a trick, Ryker stepped around the back and cautiously toward the sounds.

"When I'm done with you, you'll beg for the sweet release of death," he ventured out into the darkness. "How many people have died by your hand? A hundred? A thousand? More? I don't think there is a hell deep enough for a man like you."

Ryker kept moving forward, his every sense on high alert. A deep, wet cough focused his attention like a whip, and he had to restrain himself from pulling the trigger. There on the ground, crawling away from him on his belly, was the man he had fantasized about killing for nearly nine months. Two hundred and seventy one days. But now that he had the chance, he couldn't pull the trigger. Not yet.

"You think you know me," Saiif struggled to say, coughing into the ground face down. "But where would you be without me? You need me. But I—" Another fit of coughing and he turned his head, stretching to meet Ryker's stare. "I don't need you."

Saiif pulled his right hand up toward his chest. Ryker tightened on the Uzi and just watched as he pushed himself over on to his back. "Am I everything you hoped I would be?" Saiif tried to smile but coughed up blood instead.

Ryker couldn't take his eyes off of him. There before him, helpless, shot, and probably dying, was the monster that had stolen his life, his reasons for living, and for what? To protect an identity? To remain safe in the shadows? But he didn't look like a phantom terrorist or criminal mastermind now. Tonight he was just a man. Pathetic. Common. Little. No different than anyone else. How could this man have commanded his life for so long? He felt almost ashamed for allowing this murderer to control his every thought for so long.

"Ah," Saiif said, smiling, "there you are." The sirens were getting closer. "They're coming for me, aren't they?"

"If I don't kill you first." Ryker's hand began shaking with the internal struggle racking his spirit. Here Saiif was, the killer of hundreds, perhaps thousands, and with the simple squeeze of the trigger he could be stopped, once and for all. Never again to hurt another human being. Never again to make widows or the fatherless. And then there was the prospect of a trial. A fiasco of media coverage and then what? Life in prison? Lethal injection? It was too compassionate for a killer like him. His finger twitched as if it had a mind of his own, and then pulled on the curved piece of metal and fired the Uzi.

The round buried itself into the ground just to the side of Saiif's head.

Saiif started to laugh but couldn't continue because of the fluid filling up his lungs. "You won't kill me. You can't. That's the difference between you and me. You think I'm a monster. But you're a coward, deep down. And . . . and between the two, I'd rather be a monster."

Just then Ryker noticed Saiif's other hand. It was holding something. A small brick. But not just a brick—a block of C-4 explosive.

"Until we meet on the other side," Saiif said just before flicking a switch on an electronic timer connected to the small bomb. The display read 0:10:00 before beginning to countdown quickly. Ten seconds!

"Coward," Saiif said, starting to laugh. "Coward!"

Ryker didn't hesitate and turned to run. His leg slowed him down some, but the adrenaline pumping through his body propelled him forward. Without missing a beat, he reached down and picked up Manni Lubin by the shoulders and started pulling him away from Saiif and the bomb. Finding shelter behind the giant trunk of a nearby olive tree, they were still knocked to the ground by the force of two concurrent explosions. The ancient olive tree acted as a shield and a protection for them as it absorbed a majority of the heat and force from the explosion. He was only dimly aware of what was happening around him.

Glass and torn pieces of metal littered the ground. Ryker tried to get to his feet, but he was disoriented from the shockwave and fell back to the ground. It struck him during this moment of confusion that he was alive. The explosion, large as it was, failed to triggered the van's C-4. The second explosion he felt must have been the exploding gas tank instead. Then a wave of nausea crushed him, and he slipped into unconsciousness. A few moments later, he awoke and was able to get to his knees and reach out to Lubin. There was a ringing in his ears that drowned out everything around him. He put his hand on Lubin's chest and checked to make sure he was still breathing. Ryker's hand felt cold when he couldn't feel it moving. He felt for a pulse, but this time there was nothing to feel.

"No, no, no . . ." The words were muffled in his ears. "Manni, please . . ."

A hand touched his shoulder, and Ryker spun around, his hands flailing in his defense. A woman wearing the insignia of a medical team reached out to him and spoke. He couldn't hear what she was saying, but it was clear to him that she was there to help. He leaned back out of the way, letting her and her associates tend to his friend. They, too, checked his signs and began CPR immediately.

Ryker watched as they tried to bring him back to life. He began to shake and sob. It wasn't fair! It should have been him that died. Not Manni. Please, God, not Manni. Take me instead, he pleaded. Please, take me instead . . .

Manni Lubin was gone. The medical personnel had stopped working on him and turned their attention on Ryker. He couldn't believe it and waived them off, pointing to Lubin. They kept talking to him, insisting that he let them attend to his leg, but Ryker wouldn't allow it. He swept them aside and went to his friend's side. Taking Lubin's hand, Ryker brought it to his forehead, and with all the energy of his soul he pleaded for the return of this man's life. If he could trade places, give his life for Manni's, he would do it. He had a wife and family at home, waiting for his return. It was not right that one more life be lost at the hand of a madman. It wasn't right . . . It wasn't right . . .

Lubin's chest violently heaved, and he started coughing. The medical team rushed over and began administering to him, feeding him oxygen and stabilizing a pulse. Ryker just rocked back and leaned against an olive tree, thanking God for hearing the desperate but sincere prayer of a humbled and faithful servant.

EPILOGUE

SAMUEL RYKER FINISHED READING THE *New York Times* headline article and refolded the main section of the paper, placing it on Ambassador Chandler's oversized desk. A promise was a promise, after all, even if it was made to entice and elicit cooperation. Keith Sanders had handled the interviews with great skill and professionalism, careful not to report anything that could compromise the ongoing investigation. He didn't sensationalize what had happened—Ryker suspected that would happen in Sander's memoir or the novel that he was sure to write. And though Ryker had kept his statements reasonably sterile, he knew that there would be official consequences for talking to a member of the press. *Oh well,* he thought, *let come what may.*

Seated next to him was Deborah, out of the hospital only three days and looking healthy and fit for someone who had nearly lost her life a week earlier.

Chandler's expression left no doubt that he was not happy.

"I'm informed that the office of public affairs is in an uproar over your interview on this. They've been in contact with the Agency's general counsel and inspector general. They're sending out a special task force to look into this embassy and your office."

"It's not my office anymore."

"You know what I mean," Chandler said, his tone lightening up. "Matheson was taken into custody shortly after our last meeting. Miss Reid's actions started the right people talking, sparking an internal investigation. Now, I know that a man's innocent until proven guilty, but it would seem that our Dave Matheson had already abused his position and may have even been compromised due, in part, to some . . . *ungentlemanly* addictions." Chandler leaned back in his leader wingback chair. "Yes, sir, Dave's in a world of hurt. I don't even think his daddy's going to be able to bail him out of this one."

"And my . . . involvement?"

Chandler leaned forward again. "They want you placed under arrest. The deputy director called me personally and wanted you detained pending official charges being drawn up."

Ryker looked around the office. "I don't see the MPs."

"I've had the attorney general look into the law, both of the land, of which we stand upon, and the Agency's, and I'm convinced that you two have done nothing wrong."

"As much as I'd like to believe you, I can't see how that's entirely true. Not that I want to spend my golden years stamping license plates, but we all knew the kind of risks we were taking when we acc—"

Chandler cut him off with a wave of his hand. "Before I let you confess to something I'd rather you didn't, let me tell you the way I see this whole thing. First of all, your official Agency protection was just that—your protection. I can find nothing in Langley's policies or procedures that requires the subject to remain buried. If you choose to come out of hiding, that appears to be your choice and not something the Agency can punish you for."

Ryker was still skeptical. "And what about going behind Dave's back?"

"You said it earlier: this is not your office anymore. If you were still employed with the Agency and Matheson was your superior, you're right . . . you could be in a whole heap of trouble. But again, as far as I see it, and as an American citizen without specific instruction to the contrary, you were under no legal obligation to follow or adhere to any internal workings of that office. As far as I'm concerned, what we have here is a private U.S. citizen visiting old friends on vacation who just happened to be at the right place at the right time to do a couple of good deeds."

Deborah squirmed a little in her seat. "But what about me? I *am* still employed here and Dave *is* my superior."

Chandler smiled, expecting this concern. "Two things will keep you out of the hot seat, Miss Reid. One, nothing you did last week was premeditated or planned in any way. You didn't wake up that Saturday morning knowing you were going to meet your old boss—who you thought was dead—and conspire with the national authorities and go behind this embassy's back. So you got that going for ya."

Deborah smiled and looked down. "When you put it like that . . ."

"And two, there is the matter of your official reports filed over six months ago concerning the very real possibility that this embassy's security had been compromised and that this leak may have cost three American lives. I do have to admit that I agree with the Agency's general counsel in saying that you should have come to me first before going out on your own, but I supported your on-the-spot decision to follow your instincts and get the job done."

Deborah looked up. "Thank you, Ambassador."

Ryker shook his head in disbelief. "Why are you doing this?"

Ambassador Chandler leaned back in his chair again and took a deep breath before speaking. "The way I see it, this office caused too much suffering in at least one too many people's lives. If you hadn't stepped in, and stepped up, three of the world's most influential religious leaders promoting peace between them might have been assassinated, instigating retaliation from every side. It would have been Armageddon. It is high time we started doing the *right things* instead of always worrying about doing *things right*. Does that make sense?"

Both Deborah and Ryker just nodded.

"And speaking of right things, as you know, there is a leadership void left in a certain office on the second floor since Matheson was abruptly removed. After much discussion—and debate, I might add—I have been authorized and instructed to offer the place and position to Miss Reid."

Deborah could not have been more shocked. In fact, the meaning of the ambassador's words took a moment to register with her.

"Sir? Me? Station head?"

"Now, it's only a temporary appointment until Langley can choose from their pool of qualified candidates to fill the post permanently, but rest assured that you have my recommendation and endorsement, Miss Reid."

"But sir . . . thank you, sir . . . but that's not possible. I'm an analyst. Station heads are—"

"Field agents? True enough, and your year and a half in the field back in '84–'86—before you made the career switch to analysis—qualifies you for the job just fine. You know what the job takes, and given your recent . . . initiative, there is no one else I want keeping this embassy's secrets—and our citizens traveling and living abroad—safe."

Deborah struggled with her words. "Ambassador, I . . . I don't quite know what to say."

"Say yes, Miss Reid, and let's start doing those right things."

"What about Sam?" she protested. "If anyone should be offered the job, it should be him. He was the best this office ever had at the helm."

Chandler looked quickly at Ryker to gauge his reaction to Deborah's words and felt confident with his response. "No one disputes that, but for starters, I don't think Sam would take the job even if it were offered at double salary." Ryker smiled and nodded. "And second, there would be too many . . . complications given the past week to ask him to assume any official standing at the embassy."

"Deb," Ryker said. "This is one of those life-changing moments. You know the operations, you know protocol better than anyone else, and you inspire trust in those you work with. And from what I'm hearing, it sounds like you were doing a fair amount of Dave's work since he took over. I have to agree with the ambassador: you *are* the logical choice."

But though he said the words he knew needed to be said, his heart wasn't in it. He had enjoyed the time he had been able to spend with Deborah. Their renewed friendship felt right, and being separated right now made Ryker's heart ache. But he would never stand in the way of Deborah's career opportunities—and this one was unparalleled.

Deborah looked over and caught Ryker's eyes and seemed to know what he was thinking. She smiled.

"Thank you, Ambassador—"

"Then it's done! I'll have my secretary forward the paperwork—"

"No, Ambassador. I meant thank you for the offer and the encouragement, but I think I've given enough in the service of my country. Lying there in that hospital bed gives one plenty of time to think and ponder the things in life that really matter."

She stole another quick glance at Ryker.

"When I realized how close I had come to dying, my priorities seemed to shift. I've been given another chance at life, and it's about time I started doing things for me."

Ryker listened intently, and as he did, his heart started to beat stronger. Like Deborah, he, too, had been given another chance at life, a precious gift that he was only too happy to share with . . .

"Deb?"

"All I'm saying is that I would like to start . . . pursuing other interests."

Deborah and Ryker shared a warm smile.

Although not the most sensitive of men, Ambassador Chandler was not blind, either, and could see what was happening there in his office.

"Is there anyway I could persuade you to reconsider, Miss Reid?"

She just shook her head, her eyes still fixed on Ryker's.

"There will be statements still to be made, and affidavits to sign, but I'm sure my office can handle whatever needs to be done."

Ryker and Deborah both stood up. Chandler extended his hand to both of them.

"This office, and the whole of the United States of America—and the world—owe the two of you a great debt of gratitude. You have served as an inspiration to all us, and I thank you from the bottom of my big Texan heart."

After another round of thank-yous, Ryker stood and helped Deborah with her overcoat.

"If you'll excuse us, Joe, we have dinner reservations," Ryker said, catching Deborah's glance, "and some catching up to do."

ABOUT THE AUTHORS

The story for Shadow Hunter was pieced together from fragments of a dream and fleshed out over a game of pool many years ago. Jeffrey R. Galli spent a distinguished career in law enforcement, beginning as a military policeman in Cold War Germany over forty years ago. He is a former warden of the Utah State Prison. Born overseas and educated in Middle Eastern studies, Guy M. Galli is a professional mediator, negotiator, and technical writer. Guy can be contacted at www.guygalli.com